Praise for the novels of

Curtiss Ann Matlock

"Once again, Matlock delivers a gentle, glowing tale
that is as sweet and sunny as its small town setting.
Readers will be delighted by this deft mix
of romance and...slice-of-life drama."
—*Publishers Weekly* on *At the Corner of Love and Heartache*

"Matlock's down-to-earth characters and
comforting plot will please many."
—*Booklist* on *Recipes for Easy Living*

"This is a delicious read for a lazy summer day.
It's not overly sweet, and it has enough zing to
satisfy readers thirsting for an uplifting read."
—*Publishers Weekly* on *Cold Tea on a Hot Day*

"Ms. Matlock masterfully takes readers into a world
full of quirky characters and small town simplicity
where they will wish they can stay."
—*Romantic Times* on *Cold Tea on a Hot Day*

"With realistic characters and absorbing dialogue,
Matlock crafts a moving story about a
woman's road to self-discovery."
—*Publishers Weekly* on *Driving Lessons*

"This is simply a great read."
—*Romantic Times* on *Driving Lessons*

"This one will warm you."
—*Romantic Times* on *Lost Highways*

Lost Highways

Curtiss Ann Matlock

MIRA®

MIRA®

ISBN 0-7783-2118-5

LOST HIGHWAYS

www.MIRABooks.com

Printed in U.S.A.

ACKNOWLEDGMENTS

My sincere appreciation to the following people:
Kay at the Tri-State Fairgrounds in Amarillo; Holly Stokes
at the University of Oklahoma; Peggy Morse, writer
and true barrel racer; Mark Whitman, horse trainer
and encourager; Robin Kaigh and Leslie Wainger, who
have supported me from the beginning; the "team"
at MIRA Books; and all the booksellers who have
recommended my books through the years and the
kind readers who have told me they enjoyed them.
As always, my thanks to my family and friends, whose
warm love and understanding light my life.

"Life is like an ice cream cone—
either you lick it, or it drips on your shoes."
—Michael Porter

CHAPTER 1

I'll Know When I Get There

A faded red car came up the entry ramp on her right. A little pissant economy job that looked as if it had been through the wringer. The driver door was primer gray. Giving out a puff of black smoke, it pulled right over in front of her.

Highly annoyed, Rainey thought that the driver obviously did not know the foremost rule of the road, which was that the biggest vehicle had the right of way. She would have moved over to make room for the little red car, but there was an eighteen-wheeler coming up on her left that would, she was fairly certain, mow her down without compunction.

Her nerves went to twanging as she came up on the little car that seemed incapable of gaining speed. It had a fluffy pillow in the back window...no, it was a cat, and a tennis shoe. The cat's head came up, its eyes widened, and it fled.

She tapped her brakes, harder and harder, to keep from running over the car, and she imagined her mare, her mother's mare, back in the trailer, trying to suck her hooves on the floor in order to stay on her feet.

The eighteen-wheeler moved on ahead, leaving room for Rainey to pull into the left lane. Looking at the open road ahead with satisfaction, she began to press the accelerator.

The next instant, to her immense surprise and alarm, the little red pissant car pulled to the left, right in front of her again. The only reason she could come up with for this erratic move was that the driver felt the need to try out both lanes before settling on one.

Hands gripping the steering wheel, she again tapped the brake. She pictured running up on the little car's bumper and pushing. If her sister Charlene had been beside her, she would have been saying, "Now, Rainey…now, Rainey."

Charlene accused Rainey of being an aggressive driver. "Road rage. It's the epidemic of the modern age," Charlene said. "I saw all about it on CNN, and you've got it."

"I don't have rage…. Don't blow annoyance at inconsiderate drivers into rage. I am a considerate driver and expect others to be so. That's not too much to ask, if you ask me."

Maneuvering back to the right, she pressed the accelerator more forcefully this time and edged ahead while keeping a sharp eye on the faded red car for further signs of foolish behavior. She was ready to repel the little car if necessary.

Like a big ocean liner, her diesel truck took a bit to pick up speed, but once it got going, it really went down the road. She glanced in the side mirror and saw the little red car fighting the buffeting winds in the wake of her passing. She felt a little guilty. It might have been inconsiderate of her to pass so quickly that she blew him off the road.

Leaving the little car behind, she headed on down the interstate highway out of San Antonio, breezing along with the sedans and semis and Winnebagos in her mother's old dingy-white Ford one-ton pickup truck and the matching gooseneck horse trailer with the name Valentine painted in flowing turquoise across each side.

The truck and trailer were both twelve years old, and for the first years her mother had driven the dog out of them. The truck was on its second engine, and that had nearly a hundred thousand miles on it. The air conditioner worked when it took a notion, which it did not right then, so she had the windows down, allowing the warm, end-of-the-day wind to blow her hair and bat her silver feather earrings. The sun visor no longer stayed in any one place. When not in use, it had to be wedged up with a piece of wood, and when in use, it wobbled so that the sun's rays blinked at her. It was quite disconcerting. Driving into the western sun, as she was doing at that moment, she would sit up straight and dodge and bob, trying to keep the best position behind the visor, which kept rapidly changing, since she was going nearly seventy-five miles an hour down the highway.

She had been driving the rig for over a month, and it was her name on the title now, but she still considered it her mother's truck and trailer. Her mother's ragged brown sweater and faded lavender satin pillow were tucked behind the seat, and she still hadn't brought herself to clean out her mother's classic Jim Reeves and Patsy Cline cassette tapes from the console, nor had she removed the pocket New Testament and wad of napkins—the two things Mama always referred to as her "emergency kit"—from the glove box. They would pop out like a jack-in-the-box every time it was opened, as if to remind her of their presence. *Here, save your soul and wipe your greasy hands at the same time,* sort of like Mama was still watching over her.

Once she cut her finger, and the first thing she grabbed were napkins from that wad. After that she was careful to replenish the wad with two extra each time she stopped for a meal.

She had even returned to her maiden name of Rainey Valentine. It was easier than making the explanations that ended up sounding so tawdry.

Just then, despite her own top rate of speed, a pale pink Cadillac with Mary Kay in pink script on the side window came flying past. Drivers in Texas didn't waste time.

The cotton-candy-haired woman at the wheel of the Cadillac tooted and waved. She had obviously seen the Mary Kay bumper sticker on the back door of the horse trailer.

Rainey returned the wave happily in the camaraderie of the road and Mary Kay users.

How her mother had put so many miles on the truck was by traveling all over Oklahoma, Texas, Kansas and a few points beyond, selling Mary Kay cosmetics and riding barrel races. That could be considered something of an unusual combination, but it didn't seem unusual next to the fact that Mama had raced barrels and sold Mary Kay until the age of seventy-five.

On the back of the horse trailer Mama had stuck a collection of bumper stickers. Along with the one touting Mary Kay, there was one for each state to which she had traveled to barrel race. There was one for the American quarter horse, another for barrel horses and another that said, Cowboy Up. One said Love from Valentine. Below that were the ones that said, Trust in the Lord, and Honk if You Love Jesus. Then there was the one that said, American by Birth, Southern by the Grace of God.

Charlene thought the conglomeration of bumper stickers was tacky, and Rainey had to agree with her.

"Lots of people might start botherin' you for the Mary Kay, and you don't sell it," Charlene pointed out. "And that Southern saying is in poor taste. Somebody might pick a fight with you over it. I always worried about that with Mama, but you couldn't tell her anything. You ought to go ask Freddy to have the boys down in his body shop get them off," Charlene suggested.

Freddy was their older brother; he owned the only Ford dealership for fifty miles.

Rainey didn't care for the idea. "If they're taken off, there will be all these rectangle places all over. I'd need to get the trailer painted, and then the truck would look awful next to it."

She wasn't going to touch those bumper stickers. For one thing, Freddy most likely would make her pay for the job. Freddy was not noted for his generosity, and on top of that, he considered her the spoiled late child who had always been given too much.

Removing the stickers herself would have been a major undertaking and would have ruined her fingernails, about which she was quite particular. And despite their being so tacky, she rather liked those bumper stickers. They seemed a testament to Mama, who had died in the spring, suddenly, of heart stoppage.

Heart failure was what the doctor said, but Rainey rejected that term. Her mother's heart had never in this world failed. When people said that Coweta Valentine's death had come as a surprise, she would think of how her mother would have laughed about that. Her mother had been eighty-two, and she would often say, "When I kick the bucket." When people would try to hush this kind of talk, she would say, "The one sure thing is that a person starts dyin' soon as they're born. Why, dyin' is a part of livin', might as well get used to it."

Her mother had lived more thoroughly than anyone Rainey had ever known. And what Freddy said was true—Rainey *had* been her mother's favorite, her late child, and the one closest to her.

Mama always said that Rainey was her twin soul, and Daddy

said Mama carried on whole conversations with her from the time she was in the womb. She and Mama would finish up each other's sentences, driving Daddy and Freddy wild, and call each other at the same exact moment, so that their phone lines connected without ringing.

She was the one who knew the instant Mama was stricken. She had thumped the bottle of Glyco-Thymoline she had been pricing down on the counter and listened, just as if hearing someone call her name. Then, hollering to Mr. Blaine as she ripped off her white coat, "I think somethin's wrong with Mama," she had dashed out of the drugstore like the wildly alarmed woman that she was, running the entire four blocks to her parents' big home and around back to the little apple orchard, to find her mother lying on the moist ground, holding her chest and whispering desperate, shocking things, until Rainey had said, "Shut up, Mama, and hang on."

She had thought at the time that her mother had been out of her mind with pain and talking crazy. It was later, during her mother's final hours, that she was faced with the profound shock that what her mother said was true fact.

The picture of her mother clinging to life and to one final ordering of everyone else's lives returned to her again and again—her mother lying in the hospital bed, her father holding her mother's hand, Freddy looking from their parents to Rainey, and Charlene sobbing loudly over by the doorway. In this memory she would see her mother's mouth moving, revealing the shameful secret, but Rainey truly did not hear a sound, except for Charlene's sobbing.

Mostly Rainey found any of it too painful to think about.

As original in death as in life, their mother had skipped over their father and left all she owned to her children. Coweta Valentine had been listed as one-eighth Chickasaw on the rolls, although she had argued for years that she was one-fourth. The old Indian way was to trace the blood lineage through the women rather than the men. It was figured that the mother of a child was certain, whereas exactly who was the father was not. This was a practicality that had seemed to escape a number of societies in this world, as well as turning out particularly apt in Coweta Valentine's case, Rainey thought a number of times.

Charlene got the family Bible, dating from the mid-1800s and listing births in Mississippi, before the great Indian hater Andrew Jackson (history books said Indian fighter, but Mama always vehemently corrected the term) forced the family off their land and out west, a pair of earrings said to have come from Georgia gold, and the old house and acreage on Church Street, even though their daddy remained alive and living there. Daddy had his own money, but he really didn't have many belongings. Mama had trusted Charlene and the rest of them to take care of Daddy.

Freddy, the eldest and only son, was pretty upset about Charlene getting the house. Although he had received the bulk of his mother's portfolio, he felt the house, one of the grandest in town, with a cupola and wraparound porch, five acres of lawn, orchard and corral, and a border of lilacs, should have been his. No doubt he thought it fitted his station as owner of the Ford dealership, and his wife Helen thought this even more. Helen was all the time throwing dinner parties, and Rainey imagined Helen saw herself having parties out across the porch, the kind with Chinese lanterns and waiters in black tie, although God knew where she'd get them.

"I am not about to move out of my modern home into that big old museum," Charlene told Freddy in the firm way she had of talking with her hand on her hip. "Joey's spurs would gouge the floors in no time."

Charlene's husband Joey was a professional horse trainer. His spurs never came off his boots, and when his boots went on in the morning, they didn't come off until he went to bed. Charlene worshiped her wool wall-to-wall carpet because of this. She was also a walking advertisement for heat pumps and modern insulation.

"You and Helen can live there when Daddy's done with it," Charlene assured Freddy, then added, "Of course, I'll keep the deed."

Rainey's inheritance had been Mama's truck and horse trailer, her old barrel racing mare Lulu, and her considerable stock of Mary Kay cosmetics. There were probably enough cosmetics to last a lifetime, which was a pretty good thing, because Rainey had always enjoyed makeup. Nature had been good to her, but nature does often require a helping hand.

She guessed her mother had wanted her to have at least some small security for life all the way around, because she also left her oil leases that currently brought in nearly eight hundred dollars a month. This income would go up drastically if those Mideast countries got crazy again.

Oh, Freddy'd had a lot to say about that. "She'll piss it away like she has everything else. Mama should have let me take care of it for her."

Freddy looked at Rainey, and everyone else, with more scorn than usual during the weeks following their mother's death, while Charlene loved everyone more than ever, and their daddy went along in his silent sorrow.

As the days passed, the length and breadth of their loss sunk in. Their beloved wife and mother, who had always been there with a ready ear and wise answers and strong, loving arms, was gone.

For Rainey's daddy, this meant that his wife would never

again warm her cold feet on his thighs or yell at him to take his cigarette out on the porch, put his vitamins in his hand or find his discarded jacket.

For her and her brother and sister, it was a stark reminder that they were no longer children. It meant that they now carried around a permanent empty hole in their hearts, that they had to solve their own problems, and that they had taken their place in line for old age and death.

Her daddy spent a lot of the first month of his widowhood rocking on the front porch. Rainey knew this because she went over to clean for him and to make certain that he got at least one hot meal a day. It seemed as if all life had gone out of him. He looked like a deflated bag of skin rocking there. He didn't say more than five words to her on any one day.

Then one morning barely four weeks after Mama had left them, Rainey went over and found widowed Mildred Covington sitting with her daddy, and words were pouring out of his plumping up body. It was like with every breath he took to speak, his body filled a little more.

Five weeks after Mama died, Freddy broke off with the girlfriend no one was supposed to know about and took up taking Helen to the Main Street Café for breakfast each morning and sitting beside her on the pew of the Southern Baptist Church each Sunday.

Charlene started looking in the mirror and crying because she was turning forty-five, and then she began to pester Joey when he came in from work, dragging him into the bedroom in a desperate attempt to hold the years at bay by trying for a fourth baby.

Rainey looked into the mirror, too, playing with all the Mary Kay, and she saw a woman who was almost thirty-five, twice divorced, had lost the only child she had ever conceived, and was living in a forty-year-old run-down farm cottage behind her sister's house. Gazing back at her from every plate glass store window she passed was a lost woman who did not know who she really was, nor where she belonged.

A few false starts will make you stronger, her mother had told her a number of times.

"How many of those, Mama? How many mistakes and wasted years? What if I never get it right?"

Her mother was not there anymore to give the perfect answers.

Rainey did as much crying as Charlene, but there was only her own pillow to soak up the tears.

After about a week of crying, she got out and washed and waxed her mother's legacy of the truck and trailer. She very carefully waxed a second time around the bumper stickers, and then she loaded up Mama's eighteen-year-old mare and took off to race barrels. It was the only action she could think to take.

She and Mama had raced barrels together the entire time she was in high school and until she'd gone off to college, where she had met and married Robert, who had considered any horse activity other than the Kentucky Derby the preoccupation of the lower classes. From that time on, she never really got into the sport again. She guessed she'd stayed too busy trying to earn a living and deal with her second husband, Monte. Later she guessed she'd just been too busy dealing with regrets.

Thinking back in the despondent manner one always falls into after a loved one dies, Rainey felt so many regrets and questions. Racing barrels gave her something to do in which she could lose her grief and confusion, and at the same time connect to her mother. Also, racing barrels gave her somewhere to drive *to* and *away from* home. Something to make her forget the pain of lost years behind, the confusion of present life, and the fright of the uncertainties in life ahead.

She got so caught up in this endeavor that she finally quit her job at Blaine's Drugstore and took off to travel the rodeo circuit for the remaining weeks of summer.

"Just where are you goin' with this, Little Bit?"

Her daddy always called her "Little Bit." Directly on quitting her job, she had driven over to tell him her intentions. She had found him watering her mother's fragrant old garden roses.

"I don't know, Daddy," she said, her voice coming hoarse and stammering. "I guess I just need to get away...you know, have time to myself to sort things out. And I like racing. I want to do somethin' I like."

Daddy nodded. He never had much of an expression, and he didn't now. Disappointment sent her spirit slipping out her toes.

He asked her to pull more hose for him, and she did that, then she went in to check his refrigerator, thinking that she might need to go grocery shopping for him before she took off. The refrigerator was full of fruit salad and cottage cheese and skim milk and a plate of shredded barbequed roast. She figured it was Mildred Covington's work.

Staring at all the shiny plastic-wrapped dishes, she felt a sad sense of fading away, turning invisible.

Daddy came in and said he had a couple of things for her. He went upstairs and came back with two cardboard boxes.

He said, "Since you're goin' travelin', you can take this one over to your Aunt Lillabel in Ardmore. It's the silver brush and comb from your mama's dresser. She always said Lillabel should have it, and this one is the mystery books your mama had meant to send to your cousin Rowan down in Waco. You get by both those places. Like as not there'll be rodeoin' somewhere around them."

He looked at her for a moment before breaking the gaze. She knew he was trying to give her places to go to be with people she knew. Between them, her mother and father had an enormous family scattered all over Oklahoma and Texas.

As she started to leave, her father cleared his throat and said, "Rainey, don't you worry about not knowin' where you're goin'. I imagine you'll know when you get there."

Greatly surprised, she looked up to see him again averting his gaze and taking out his handkerchief to mop his face.

"Thanks, Daddy," she said. Very hesitantly, she dared kiss his cheek, closing her eyes and sucking in the dear, familiar scent of him, of Old Spice and tobacco and earth.

He grabbed her hard then, about startling her socks off. He crushed her against his chest, smashing the cigarette pack in his pocket and burying her nose into his salty neck. For a moment he held her tight, and she clung to him.

Then he let go and turned away. Her vision blurred and her throat nearly swelled shut, Rainey watched him walk out the back door, stiff and bent, weighed down by such a cloud of sorrow.

"Have you lost your *mind?*" Charlene wailed.

Rainey must have interrupted her sister and Joey when she had called to announce her leaving, because Charlene was clutching around her what appeared to be one of Joey's denim shirts, and it could have been all she had on. This shocked Rainey; Charlene had always been the one to hold tight to decorum.

She said, "I guess I have, but I think that I did it a long time ago," and turned to throw her bags in the back of the truck. She didn't want Charlene to see her tears, or her shock. Keeping her face averted, she slipped in behind the wheel, while Charlene hollered through the window.

"Oh, Rainey, would you just quit bein' so dramatic? What

are you gonna live on? You ain't good enough at barrels to earn any kind of money, and eight hundred dollars a month sure hasn't made you independently wealthy, you know."

"Lulu and I made a hundred dollars last weekend."

She didn't like Charlene having the idea that she and Lulu were the bottom of the barrel, so to speak. Maybe they weren't about to take the finals by storm, but they had begun to place about every other go.

"Oh, that's gonna pay for a day's fuel and meals and motel," Charlene said sarcastically.

"I'm only takin' off for a month or two, and I imagine I won't be stayin' in a lot of motels," she told her sister, gazing out the windshield while she spoke. "The first place I'm goin' is over to Aunt Lillabel's. I have to make a delivery for Daddy. I'll call you every few days. I'll always let you know where I am, in case you need me for anything."

She said that, but she couldn't foresee that anyone would need her. Mildred Covington pretty well had Daddy covered, and Helen was over there a lot now, keeping things up so they would be in prime condition when she got to move in, whether in one year or twenty. Freddy had Helen, and Charlene had Joey and the kids. Rainey was the odd man out, so to speak.

Charlene raked back her hair and said, "Rainey, I know... well, we're all pretty unsettled right now. But it is only the shock. It will straighten out in time."

She supposed that her sister was trying to be Mama for her, but she and Charlene had never been particularly close, and right then was not an opportune time to start.

"I imagine so. I'll call you from Aunt Lillabel's."

As she started away, Charlene surprised her by running alongside the truck, sobbing and yelling at her not to be stupid and that Mama would be upset.

Rainey doubted Mama would have been upset. Mama had left upset behind.

And she didn't know what to do. She saw Charlene's shapely pale legs catch the sunlight and her bare feet step lightly on the grass and gravel. She was a little afraid Charlene was going to fall down, or possibly throw herself in front of the truck. She would have simply outrun her sister, but she didn't think it would be very nice to stir dust in her face.

"Rainey, you can't run away from yourself, you know!"

Rainey thought maybe she could try.

"Where in the world are you goin'?" Charlene finally came to a stop, stamping one bare foot.

"I don't know," Raincy called back to her, "but I'm goin' somewhere, and I guess I'll know when I get there."

As she turned onto the county road, she decided not to even tell Freddy she was going.

With one quick glance in the rearview mirror, she left Valentine behind.

CHAPTER 2

Sudden Gifts of Fate

The sun was about to drop from the sky when she saw the sign for a Texaco Star Mart. She took the exit, pulled through the entry and over to the diesel pump.

Hopping out, she hurried back to the trailer to check Lulu, which was the first thing she did any time she stopped. She suffered this nagging worry that somewhere along the way she might have made a turn or hit a rough bit of road that caused Lulu to fall down and break her leg, and that the mare might be lying there in pain, or maybe even dying, while she drove on along. Mama—everyone, actually—had always said that Rainey had a good imagination. Recalling the incident with the little red car, she was a bit frantic.

When she saw Lulu's nose pressed on the polyester net over the open window, relief washed all over her.

As soon as she released the net, Lulu poked her head out and sniffed for the expected treat—the Twinkie cake. Lulu was a fool for Twinkie cakes, a habit brought on by Mama's policy to take sweets along to entice her horses. While the mare sucked down the cake, Rainey buried her nose against her sleek neck, relishing the warm horse smell.

Then she fastened Lulu back inside and went to pump fuel into the truck. While she was going about this, a black three-quarter ton drove up on the opposite side of the fuel island, a real shiny job with lots of chrome and lights. It had the words No Fear across the top of the windshield.

A cowboy got out of the truck. He wore a sharp black hat, starched blue shirt, and a shiny belt buckle so round that he would have had trouble bending. He looked like the kind who drove one-handed, with a bottle of beer between his thighs, and likely yelled "Hey, baby," to women on street corners.

As he got his nozzle from the pump, he said to her, "Hey, honey…are you one of those fast can chasers?"

She dealt with this by saying, "I'm sorry. You must have me mixed up with someone else. My name isn't Honey," and returned to washing bug spots off her windshield.

She heard him say something about "Excuse me, bitch," and he went about his own pumping.

Inside the store, when she came out of the ladies' room, he was pulling a long-necked bottle of beer from the cooler. He ignored her.

She went to the pay phone at the front corner and dialed Charlene's number. She had to make herself do this, because lately Charlene had been making noises about Rainey coming home. After nearly two months, Rainey thought maybe she should go home, but every time she imagined doing so, she felt great dread. So far, in six weeks of traveling, Rainey had renewed acquaintances with many relatives, begun to hone her barrel-racing skills to the point of placing first in a couple of small rodeos, achieving times below eighteen and a half seconds, learned to navigate back roads all over south Oklahoma and half of Texas, and managed to deliver her parcels. She did not feel, however, that she had gotten anywhere in particular with her own troubled self.

She was relieved when Charlene's answering machine picked up and she didn't have to speak directly with her sister.

"I'm on my way to Uncle Doyle's," she said into the phone. "I'll call you when I get there."

Then she hung up and went to the cooler containing soft drinks, took out a bottle of Pepsi and moved along until she found the Lipton tea, with lemon and sugar. She took two of those and then, continuing on along the aisles, she loaded her arms with Twinkies, Moon Pies, oatmeal cream cakes, fig bars and peanuts. Since she had begun traveling, she had taken to compulsive snacking and had gained five pounds, which she didn't think was so much considering the amount of sugar and fat she was consuming. Also, she figured it could all be counted as muscle from her extremely active days.

At the counter she snatched up a couple of packages of pretzels, which were fat free. It was going to be a long, lonely night.

As she dug the money from her pants pockets, she brought out a tube of lipstick from one pocket and a pocket knife from the other.

"Looks like you're a lady ready for anything," the clerk said. Her voice sounded smart, but her smile was warm.

"I guess—unless I get one confused with the other," she told her, smiling in response as she handed over several bills.

It was funny how the tiniest thread of friendly connection coming out of nowhere could be immensely precious. It made her grateful in that moment to be alive, made her think that life was worth living after all.

She thought this as she carried out her grocery sack of snacks and saw that the setting sun had turned Mama's old truck a pale gold color. The entire world—the fuel pumps, the parking lot rails, the grass bent in the breeze—was washed golden. Like old pictures in an album, all the ugly was softened and made lovely.

The next thing she saw was a long-tailed frisky puppy wriggling and wagging in the bed of her truck, regarding her as if he had just found Jesus.

She swiveled her head around to see the black No Fear truck disappearing down the entry ramp to the interstate. She looked at the empty spot where it had been beside the pump, and then again at the puppy. A dark-gray-and-brown mutt, a sort of German shepherd mixed with something equally big and clumsy.

She threw her sack onto the seat, hoisted the thirty pounds of puppy out of the bed, aided by aggravation, and went back into the store.

"That dang guy in the black truck just dumped this dog on me. Right in my truck." Maybe she didn't have proof of this, but she just knew it was so.

The clerk said, "People have nerve, don't they? People drive up here all the time and leave dogs and cats, and once somebody left fightin' roosters. I imagine they'd leave children, if they thought they could." She shook her head with wonder. "Why don't they just drown them?"

Rainey said maybe they didn't have water. She suggested the clerk call the police or the dog pound, but the clerk said the police didn't handle it, and there wasn't any dog pound to call.

"Just leave him outside. Either someone will take him, or he'll get hungry and go off lookin' for food, or he'll get runned over."

A line was forming behind Rainey. A sweaty man in a faded

T-shirt and Bermuda shorts made impatient sighs at her shoulder. The clerk, who had seemed to be her *compadre* ten minutes earlier, now regarded her in a far less favorable light.

"You need to move your rig," the clerk said. "There's a customer waitin' to use the pump."

As Rainey turned for the door, a mother jerked her son away from her, saying, "No, you can't have that dog." Then she shot Rainey a weak smile.

Outside, Rainey set the puppy down and strode away quickly, picking up the pace until she was fairly running to jump into her truck.

The puppy's head was almost caught in the slammed door.

She looked out the window. He gazed up at her, an expectant, hopeful light in his marble-brown eyes.

Jerking back inside, she started the engine, having the idea that the powerful roar would scare the puppy away. As she shifted into gear, the image of the puppy squashed beneath one of the wheels filled her mind.

Pressing the brake, she peeked out the window again. She didn't see the dog.

A horn honked. In her side mirror, she saw a rusty gold Cadillac Seville nosing the bumper of the horse trailer. Apparently there was a wide lack of knowledge about the unwritten rule of the road.

She strained to catch a glimpse of the puppy, hopefully wagging up to someone else. Not seeing him, except in the horrendous picture continuing in her mind, she jammed the lever into park again and jumped out of the truck. The guy in the Cadillac started yelling at her.

The puppy came wriggling from in front of her rumbling truck, wagging his tail and again looking at her as if she were his beloved savior.

She could not bear to look at him as she lifted him and put him over into the truck bed. She squinted out of one eye.

"Don't jump out, or that'll be the end of you, and it won't be my fault."

He put his paws up on the side, cocking his head to the side.

She was startled to see the guy from the Cadillac striding toward her. A big man with a bulging belly, he yelled, "Look, lady, do you want me to get in and move this truck for you? I ain't got all night."

The puppy barked his young bark fiercely at the man.

"I'm sorry to have failed to see you are the only one with a life," she said, and then hopped into her truck, halfway expecting the guy to grab her by the collar and yank her out, which she believed he could have done with one hand.

Slamming the door, she again shifted into drive and started off slowly, mindful of Lulu and not wanting to give the Cadillac guy the idea he had compelled her into hurrying. Circling toward the road, she checked her mirror to see if the puppy jumped out. She felt certain the Cadillac guy would run him down if possible.

Then she saw the puppy's face in the side-view mirror. He was up on the side of the truck and happily jutting his face in the wind. His paws indicated a really big dog to come.

Looking north, she saw the road sign that listed Abilene as being 152 miles ahead. She pressed the accelerator, and the old truck and trailer rumbled out onto the blacktopped state highway.

The puppy tapped on the back window glass. He wagged his entire rear end at her.

Sighing, she looked ahead. On her left, the sky reflected the last coral rays of the sun, and on her right, a bright half-moon was rising. It seemed as if she were driving in a corridor between them. As if she were going right up a launching ramp. And she had an odd feeling, as if something were pressing between her shoulder blades, urging her onward.

Shrugging the sensation aside, she thought that she would definitely have to get rid of the puppy. Maybe she would drop him in the first town. Or maybe in Abilene, which would likely be big enough for her to get away unnoticed. She would drop him there in the first yard she passed with a house with lights on.

As she stuck a George Strait cassette into the player, she caught a glimpse of herself in the mirror. She thought maybe she should have refreshed her lipstick, but then her eyes strayed to the grocery sack of snacks. Digging inside, she pulled out a package of peanuts.

It was good and dark, and she was on her second George Strait cassette and opening her second Twinkie cake, having polished off the entire package of peanuts, when her headlights flashed on a figure at the edge of the road.

A man, in a dark sport coat and slacks.

It happened so fast. She saw the figure illuminated by the headlights, his pale profile turn to her, and then she glimpsed him blow away like a paper silhouette into the darkness.

Oh, Lord. The awful knowledge that she had not been paying sufficient attention fell all over her.

Oh, God...ohmyGod, don't let me have hit him.

Her headlights beamed on the blacktop ahead, as her mind did an instant replay. She thought that surely she hadn't hit the man. She hadn't been that close. She hadn't felt anything like a whop.

Maybe there hadn't been a man. Maybe it had all been her imagination.

This possibility was as unnerving as thinking she'd run someone down.

All the while her mind was dealing with this, she was pressing the brakes, mindful of Lulu back in the trailer sucking the flooring with her hooves. Coming to a stop, she tried to see the man in the side-view mirror, but even in the moonlight, it was too dark to make out anything.

Of course, if he were dead on the side of the road, she wouldn't see him standing.

A thump made her just about jump out of her skin.

It was the puppy with his big paws on the rear window glass.

She swung the truck and trailer around as quickly as she dared, mindful of Lulu. Texas had really good state and county roads, paid for with all the oil money in the seventies and eighties. They all had wide graveled shoulders. Her tires crunched on the gravel, the right back tires spun slightly, and then she was heading back the way she had come, peering intently out the windshield. She turned off the stereo. She hadn't realized how loud the stereo had been, and the wind, until now.

There was no one.

She peered hard, sticking her head out the window, but there was absolutely no one alongside the road or in it. No one and no car anywhere.

Getting very nervous now about possibly losing her mind, she retraced her route almost a mile, then once more turned around and came back slowly. She had begun to tremble but would not raise the windows for thinking she should get fresh air to clear her brain.

Then there he was. She hadn't been imagining things after all, which came as a flash of relief, quickly surpassed by rising concern as she watched him in the beam of her headlights, bent over, dark sport coat, darker slacks, and loafers, appearing to be getting to his feet.

Coming to a stop much faster than she should have and

probably causing Lulu to scramble for balance, she slammed the truck into park, slipped her daddy's little Colt .25 from its pocket on the side of the seat and hopped out of the pickup, ready to deal with what had every appearance of a crisis.

Rainey had a talent for dealing with crises, a point upon which many agreed. Charlene was one to say that crises just seemed to find Rainey. She was always cautious, but not fearful. Her mother used to tell each one of them, "You are a child of God and not given a spirit of fear," which didn't speak to stupidity at all but had succeeded in instilling a certain amount of confidence for dealing with demanding situations. Rainey had held her own with green colts, wild college boys and rowdy cowboys, so one slender man in a sport coat and slacks on a road in the middle of nowhere did not overly frighten her.

"Are you all right? Did I hit you?" she called to him from a position beside her truck fender.

He lifted his arm against the glare of her headlights. She stepped back to the truck and cut the headlights down to the parking beams, then slowly went forward, the pistol held discreetly, and politely, down at her side.

Her eyes adjusting quickly, she saw he now stood looking off at the land. The thin moonlight shone on the top of his head, but the rest of him was deeply shadowed and colorless. Her impression was of a tall, thin, youngish man.

"Are you okay?" she asked again, finding her voice on the lonely road sounded a little startling.

"I wrecked my car," he said hoarsely. "It's down there."

She stepped forward a few more feet and saw that the land dropped away sharply some feet past the graveled roadside. The roof and rear end of a car, a sporty type, glowed in the thin moonlight. There came a faint hissing and the smell of stirred dust.

"It's not comin' out of there as easy as it went in," she said, which was the first thing that came to her mind.

He said he didn't think she had hit him.

"I was just getting up to the road, and your headlights startled me," he said. "I slipped back down."

"I didn't hit you?"

"I don't think so. I think I slipped on the gravel."

He seemed a little confused, which she thought would be natural, given the situation, although she did not discard the possibility of him being under the influence of something.

Nevertheless, she took it as good news that she had not run him down. She felt redeemed. She had not been a totally irresponsible driver after all. Feeling very expansive, she immediately offered to give him a ride, and he accepted.

The next instant, she wondered if she might have been a little foolhardy, but there really wasn't anything else she could do. She couldn't very well leave him there twenty miles from anywhere and vulnerable to any crazy who might come along, such as drunk cowboys looking for mischief or a carload of illegals looking for a good suit of American clothes. And it could very well be all the way to Abilene before she could find help she could send back.

She also sensed he was no threat, in the way a woman always knows these things. Rather than overcoming her, she felt he was pretty well overcome. She felt responsible to help.

Not wanting him to get the idea that she herself might be dangerous, she took care to keep the little Colt out of sight as they got inside her truck and told him to just scoot her old boots out of the way on the floorboard.

In the low glow of the overhead light, her first impressions of him were immediately confirmed. He was young and thin, and, more, he was very handsome. Inside the confines of the cab, he seemed even taller than she had first judged. He sort of folded himself into the seat and sat gingerly and all compressed, like a person does when they're uncertain of touching the furniture. Or as if not certain what to do with himself.

His face was a pasty color, she saw just before he closed the door and the light went out. As she shifted into gear and started off, she decided not to replace the gun in its pocket but tucked it beside her thigh, near at hand.

Then she experienced a little panic, remembering her recent maneuverings and Lulu in the trailer. Stopping more quickly than she had intended, she threw the lever into park and opened the door at the same time. The stranger looked at her with a startled expression.

"I'll be right back. I have to check my mare."

She had forgotten the puppy, too. He stretched over the side of the truck bed, sniffing eagerly as she passed. She thought that she was picking them up all over the place this night.

She flipped on the interior trailer lights and saw Lulu's form through the screen. Stepping on the running board, she looked inside, making certain the mare was on all four strong legs. Lulu gave her what amounted to an accusing look when she did not receive a Twinkie cake.

Relieved, Rainey returned to the truck, which rumbled softly. She suddenly felt very foolish—*why, he might have jumped behind the wheel and driven off, with her truck and her horse.*

Then, when she opened the driver's door and the overhead light came on, she found herself looking at her daddy's little Colt resting in the man's wide palm.

"I believe this is yours," he said, stretching it toward her.

She stared at it.

He said, "An offhand thought is that you might need to keep your gun out of the hands of the person who is the threat."

"Thank you," she said with inordinate politeness, taking the gun from him as she slipped behind the wheel.

He nodded and sank back, resting his head on the seat back.

She replaced the gun in its pocket and shifted into gear, heading on down the highway.

"Where would you like me to drop you?" she asked.

"Wherever you're headed will be fine," he said.

The very weariness in his voice caused her to look at his face in the shadow, his head back and his shoulders sagging. She herself had felt such weariness. It was more than of the present moment, but went bone deep and encompassed a weariness of all of life.

She said slowly, "I'm goin' up to Childress, but I'm goin' *through* Abilene, if you want to go there. It's probably the first town where anything's goin' to be open."

"Okay," he said.

So there she was, going down the road, with a stranger who appeared to have no better direction than she did. As the big diesel engine wound out and picked up speed, the accelerator suddenly seemed harder to push. The truck acted as if it had taken on an enormous addition of weight and was having a hard time getting going.

The puppy came up on the back window with a pretty good thud, but the stranger didn't so much as twitch. He'd folded his arms and slumped down in the seat, his eyes closed.

She drove on down the highway, peering through the windshield as far ahead as the glow of the headlights cut the dark.

He had fallen fast asleep. Thinking that the wind might be a bit too much on him, she pushed the button, closing his window. He didn't move.

A few seconds later she caught a scent—not alcohol, as she had continued to suspect, but some expensive, alluring men's cologne that made her shift in her seat.

When she drove through a small sleeping town with a single empty main street, she slowed beneath the pole lamps, trying to get a better look at her passenger. His hair was dark and thick, long on the top and combed straight back from his face.

She thought him good-looking, but with his eyes closed, he seemed a little refined for her taste, which had the poor tendency to run toward tough-looking men. Robert had been six foot and thick, with a big crooked nose, and Monte had the sort of wild dangerous look to him that made women lose their good sense.

She judged him to be at least thirty. She made this assumption more from his shoulders, which were those of a man in his prime, than from his face, which could have been as young as twenty-five. It was so hard to tell people's ages these days.

She guessed that whatever this stranger did was indoors; his face was smooth, and she suspected he had the type of careful tan a person would get from a golf course or tennis court. Maybe a week in the Bahamas. His shirt beneath his sport coat was the fashionable no-collar type, silk or some fine cotton, and the watch on his wrist looked most definitely expensive. No wedding band, although that didn't mean he wasn't married. Robert had broken out from every ring she had given him, and Monte had simply removed his most of the time, using the excuse that wearing a ring in the oil fields was too dangerous.

A lawyer or stockbroker, she thought. His car would be either a Mercedes or a BMW. On another look she thought that he might be a scientist of some sort. Where this idea came from she couldn't say, but there was an aura of confused intelligence about him, a professor, perhaps, but since Robert had become a professor, she generally didn't like to think about them.

The truck did not ride like a Mercedes, and while crossing a railroad track, her passenger bounced severely, causing his arm to flop out.

At that point she left off worrying about him being a professor, and her mind sped quickly over how he had seemed spaced out, certainly unsteady, how his face had been pasty, and then he'd fallen almost immediately to sleep.

She became concerned that he had fallen into a coma, or, worse, possibly died right there in her seat. He had, after all, just come out of a car wreck.

Alarmed, she glanced repeatedly at his chest. She thought she spied movement, but that would not rule out a coma. She wondered how far away a hospital might be, and how she would explain coming up with a dying or possibly dead stranger in her truck.

Charlene had often accused her and Mama of being morbid and dwelling far too much on death. They didn't consider themselves morbid so much as down to earth. Death was a part of life. Rainey didn't fear it or find it untouchable, while Charlene could hardly bring herself to go to a funeral.

In fact, her sister had gone to only one funeral in her entire life, and that was Mama's. Even then she'd had to get up in the middle of the graveside part of the service and go down to the limousine, where she stood bawling and shredding Kleenex.

Mama and Rainey, on the other hand, dealt with all sick and dying family members, as well as horses, dogs, cats and once a pet parrot. Any animal that needed to be put down, she or Mama were called in to handle it. Mama'd had her own vet supplies, and she would give the animal a shot, while Rainey held its head.

At twelve, she had helped her mother care for her grandfather, who spent his final six months in bed in their living room. She would sit with him and tell him the color of the sky and the trees, because he'd gone blind by then. The last week of his life, he slipped into a coma, and she sat and told him the color of the sky in detail and the latest report of farm market prices, which had always been his special interest.

Charlene, who'd still been at home then, would run through the living room as long as their grandfather was there. She threw a fit about Rainey being allowed to sit with him, especially when he had gone into a coma. She maintained that Rainey was too young to endure such a thing. She just about came undone when she found out Rainey had been sitting there holding his hand when he died.

"Good God, she will be scarred for life, bein' exposed to all this sickness and death," Charlene said.

Rather than being scarred, what Rainey had discovered early was a gift for taking care of people. Her job at Blaine's Drugstore often required she deliver prescriptions, and along with the bags of medicine she would dispense sympathetic care, too, if needed.

That was how she met Monte. He was laid up with a leg broken in three places from rolling a motorcycle and was all alone in his studio apartment above Mr. Ryder's garage behind the auto parts store. When she delivered his pain prescription, she had to go in, get a glass of water and put the pill right in Monte's hand. He had no one at all to care for him, which was amazing, considering all the women he had after they were married. Maybe she had simply been the first female to walk through the door that afternoon.

She had stayed to get him something to eat and straighten up his place. She had been ripe for Monte. She had begun to think of going back to school to be a nurse, when she married

Monte instead. Mama said being married to Monte worked out to be the same thing as being a nurse. She meant nursemaid.

That was the type of man that she always seemed to find.

She looked over at her passenger. He was slumped down more than ever.

Reaching out, she gave him a tentative push on his arm. He stirred, and although he didn't awaken, she felt confident that he wasn't dead. She would find out if he was in a coma when she reached Abilene.

Continuing on along the lonesome Texas road beneath the stars and the half-moon, with the stranger's faint scent around her, she wondered about him in the natural way of a woman without a man wonders. How had he come to be stranded along the road? What did he do for a living? Did he have a girl-friend or was he married? What might he be like in bed?

CHAPTER 3

Sweet Circumstance

In Abilene she pulled into a Texaco Star Mart; it was one of those brand-new big ones being built all over the place. Several cars sat at the fuel islands, and several more were parked in front of the store. Rainey pulled her rig to the side, where it wouldn't block traffic.

Thankfully, her stranger's eyes fluttered when she shook him.

"Wake up. We're in Abilene," she said, giving his arm a rather forceful shake.

His eyes opened. They were smoky in the fluorescent light that reached them from outside.

"We're in Abilene," she told him again and studied his eyes, worry rising quickly. At first he looked a little confused, and then he looked frantic.

Giving out a groan, he fumbled to open the door and threw himself out, where he immediately went to vomiting.

She thought to grab napkins from the glove box, stuffed the pocket Bible back inside, and hurried around to him.

He was a pitiful sight, bent over by his cramped stomach. The puppy was hanging way over the side of the truck, sniffing. Concerned that the dog would jump down, she stepped over to shove him back. At that particular moment, she got a good look at the stranger's head in the silvery glow, and her own stomach constricted.

"Did you know your head is bloody?"

It was on the right side, which was why she hadn't seen it in the light of the truck cab. It looked the same as a big grease spot, but she knew it was blood.

He looked at her with a mixture of confusion and surprise. He felt gingerly around his head and then looked at his fingers.

She was immensely glad she had picked him up. At least she had done the right thing there.

Peering harder at the blood spot, she said, "It looks like it's dryin'."

She handed him a napkin to wipe his mouth. He wiped his fingers instead, so she handed him another and suggested he sit on the running board of the trailer, while she got a bottle of water from behind the truck seat.

"Here." She handed him the bottle.

He tilted the bottle upward, swished water in his mouth and spat it out in a forceful stream. She regarded the action as a hopeful sign that he was okay, although the way he dropped his head did not seem altogether positive.

She stared at him, and her mind went far astray thinking how undoubtedly his car had gone off the road in a split second, just as it had been a split second when she had almost run him down while she'd been lost in thought and music.

How quickly things could happen, lives go all askew, when one was just going along.

Bringing herself back to the present, she took the bottle of water from his hand, wet a couple of napkins and handed them to him to cool his face. He said a hoarse thank-you.

Thinking it prudent to get an assessment of the wound, she boldly bent close and gently parted his hair with her fingernails. "You have a pretty good goose egg here," she said.

Blood matted a spot about the size of a silver dollar. Luckily it was on the hard bone well above his temple. His hair was silky, thick and the color of mahogany. She felt the life of him beneath her fingers and her nose.

"We'd best get you to the hospital," she said, quickly stepping back.

"I'm all right. I don't need to go to a hospital."

He spoke in a drained voice that was hardly assuring. She did not think she should take his word for his condition.

"Oh, I really think you had better."

"I'll be all right. I just need a few minutes," he said in a sudden sharp manner that she did not think was called for.

She clamped her mouth tight against a retort. And as she couldn't see wrestling him into her truck to rush him to the hospital, she waited for him to either collapse or to regain what she considered full composure.

Another minute and he took the bottle of water from her and again rinsed his mouth several times, each time spitting out the water in a forceful manner that succeeded in greatly easing her tension. Obviously he had enough strength that he was not likely to die any moment. Although there could be long-term ramifications from a good blow to the head.

"I think you could have a concussion. You passed out in my truck and threw up. Those are definite signs."

"I slept," he said, this time taking a swallow of the water.

She watched him for a long minute, and then she said, "You should go to the emergency room, and the police can be called from there. You'll need to report your car. And possibly we should report about my almost running you down. I might have added to your injury."

It probably wasn't too sterling on her part, but she did think drearily about a big rise in her insurance premiums; undoubtedly his insurance company would find a way to put a lot of it on her. It was seeming like a bigger mess all the time. She imagined a hospital, the empty halls at this time of night, painful fluorescent lights, and reams of forms to be filled out. They would likely be there all night.

The next instant she noticed him looking up at her, his expression saying clearly that he considered her a very bossy woman. She might have jumped in with a good comment that these things really needed to be done, but a Trans Am flying around the rear of the trailer distracted her. The sporty black car, music booming, zipped up to stop with a squeal of tires in front of the nearest fuel pump, an action that irritated Rainey no end. She didn't know why people had to speed into gas stations. Had she been crossing the lot, she could have been run over.

Then her stranger—somewhere along the line she had started thinking of him as *her* stranger—suddenly stood.

"I'll just go in to the men's room there and wash up," he said, indicating the store. He started away, rounding the Trans Am and fuel island with a stiff but steady enough stride.

She snatched her purse from the truck and hurried after him, asking, "Are you sure you should move a lot?" She tried to get close enough to be ready should something happen, like his keeling over, and when he stopped to open the door, she was so close that she bumped up against him.

"I'll be fine, if you don't manage to knock me down," he said and went on into the men's room.

* * *

She took the opportunity to go into the ladies' room, where she combed her wind-blown hair. If she had one vanity, it was her hair, her best feature in her own and everyone else's estimation; auburn, verging on true red in the sunlight, it waved and swirled to her shoulders. It always seemed to draw a man's eye. She checked her makeup to make certain she didn't have any mascara smudges, and she freshened her lipstick, a natural dusky peach. With relief, she noted that the finish on her fingernails still looked respectable. There were few things she disliked more than tacky chipped nails.

When she emerged from the ladies' room, she saw her passenger walking down one of the aisles. Going directly to him, she noted that he appeared to have regained his full strength. His hair was damp, freshly combed back and shiny.

"Do you feel better?" she asked. In that split second she realized she was as disappointed as she was relieved—her ministrations would not be needed.

When he turned to her, she saw that his eyes were a soft brown, like a buckeye seed, with very long lashes for a man. They had cleared completely, but she was somewhat jolted by a shadow of sadness within them.

"I'm okay," he said, averting his eyes. "Except for a headache." He took a box of ibuprofen from the shelf.

"Maybe you shouldn't take any before you see a doctor—in case you have a concussion."

"I'm awake and responsive, and I have a headache," he said, then walked to the counter to pay.

She went slowly after him, feeling a disquieting sensation— a sense of being dragged along by circumstances that wanted to get out of hand. She watched him shake three ibuprofen tablets into his wide palm and pop them into his mouth before she could point out that the directions on the bottle said one, two maximum, unless instructed by a physician.

She halfway expected him to start coughing, the pills lodging in his dry throat. Then she realized that he was very tall. She herself was just over five foot six, and she was looking up at him. A thick strand of his dark hair had fallen down over his forehead. He rubbed his hand over the back of his hair in an absentminded manner.

Still a little concerned about the ibuprofen, she suggested a snack. He tersely declined food of any sort but said he would have some coffee. He stepped to the coffeemaker, but she was closer and got it for him, while he stood beside her. She got herself a Coke. He dug into his pocket for money to pay, but she came up with bills first. After she paid, she turned to see him frowning at her. He said a brusque, "Thank you," and she said equally tersely, "No problem."

Without further comment, they took their drinks back out to her rig. Okay, Lord, now what? Rainey thought. How did she manage to get herself into such situations? It occurred to her that she didn't know his name.

When the puppy yipped at them as they approached, she recalled him with some surprise. He had shown amazing restraint in not getting out of the truck. She thought that if he got out, she could just drive off and leave him. He probably had that all figured out.

Turning, she went to check Lulu, feeling a little guilty for not looking in on the mare first thing upon stopping. Lulu was dozing and disinclined to stir enough to look out the open window, once she saw there was no forthcoming Twinkie.

Rainey returned to her pickup, where her stranger stood looking down the street and again stroking the back of his hair in that absentminded fashion.

"My name's Rainey Valentine," she said.

He blinked, then gave his name as "Harry Furneaux" and offered his hand. She thought the name suited him perfectly.

"Do you remember the accident? Do you know how it happened?"

He nodded. "Deer in the road—a line of them came running across in my lights. I swerved to avoid them, hit the gravel, I guess."

"Deer can total a car. One of my friends had one come through the windshield and almost kill her."

He repeatedly raked his hand through his thick hair. "My head feels like a watermelon."

"Jell-O gettin' old," she offered. "That's what my ex-husband Monte said when he hit his head once. He fell off an oil rig and was knocked out, and when he came to, he was muddled for half the day, wasn't even certain who I was."

Watching him, her anxiety began to rise again. "You really should see a doctor. Vomiting like you did could mean a concussion, and there can be long-term ramifications from a blow on the head. We should make a report to a doctor and the police, so that there's an official record for my insurance company."

"There's no need," he said and downed the final bit of his coffee. "I'm fine. See—one finger, two fingers. I'm at a convenience store in Texas, America, and I don't think I'm the President or God. I'm not, am I?"

"No."

"There. The doctor would say take aspirin and rest, and I'm doin' that, so there's nothin' more to be done."

She thought that he had the best command of sarcasm of anyone she had ever known, not counting her mother.

He also had a stubborn look that she thought was really pushing it, considering the circumstances; however, she had to agree with his point. Rest and aspirin had been about all the doctors had told Monte to do, too.

And she did not consider his attitude about not wanting to go to a hospital uncommon. All the men she had known had an aversion to hospitals. With the exception of her mother's death, her father had steadfastly refused to even set foot in one, even when each of his children had been born. When Robert had had his appendicitis attack, he'd lain around moaning and groaning for half a day before giving in and letting her take him to an emergency room, where he'd had to go directly into surgery. Monte, who had climbed oil rigs for a living and raced Harleys for self-expression, had been inclined to run on seeing a nurse with a needle.

"Look," her stranger said then. "I appreciate you picking me up out there."

"You're welcome."

They gazed at each other. Rainey felt a quickening inside herself, a very strong sense that she did not want to quit looking at him. As she tried to hide it, she wondered what was called for on her part, and what was behind the sad weariness in his beautiful brown eyes. And what it might feel like to kiss his lips.

"What are you goin' to do about your car?" she asked, averting her eyes to sip on her Coke. "Don't you think you need to make a report to the police for insurance purposes?"

"I think it's fairly evident that I crashed." He was looking in the distance again. "The car's not going anywhere. I'll call someone to go get it tomorrow."

So he was not concerned about his car.

"Do you think you could drive me to a motel?" he asked.

"A motel?" She had an odd difficulty imagining any point beyond that moment in the Texaco parking lot.

Then, before they could proceed with their conversation any

further, a fight broke out over at the Trans Am that was still beside the fuel pumps. There were four young men, of the type that wore lots of black clothing and silver rings in their ears and on their fingers. Two of them immediately went to blows. Rainey recognized one as being the driver of the Trans Am.

It was a very short-lived altercation, breaking up before anyone could step in, when the driver of the Trans Am was punched in the nose and cried out and turned away. Two young men drove off in a roaring Mustang, leaving the injured young man on his knees on the pavement, his friend hovering over him.

Rainey immediately got the napkins from her glove box and hurried toward him. A clerk came jogging out of the store. The young man—boy was what Rainey thought—was holding his nose and crying that he was bleeding to death.

"It just seems that way," she told him, pulling his hands from his nose and stuffing napkins in their place. Blood was indeed gushing in an alarming amount.

Then her stranger was beside her. "Here...put this penny under your upper lip," he instructed, and when the boy fumbled, her stranger did it himself, while the young man looked at him with wide, teary eyes. Her stranger told the young man to press hard on the penny and hold his head back and that the bleeding would quickly stop.

Within seconds, the boy said, "It's stoppin'," in a tone that indicated he now believed he would live after all.

Her stranger, straightening, advised the boy to get the earring out of his nose, as it was already swelling.

Once more back at the pickup, they stood there watching the boy leave in his Trans Am. She said, "I don't know what makes boys think fightin' is so much fun."

"He didn't think it was fun, but the boy that hit him sure did," her stranger commented in a knowing manner. And then he was looking at her with a crooked grin. "He'll have his turn…every boy likes to say he has punched some guy at least once."

She shook her head and allowed that it had to be a guy-thing. Then they were standing there again.

"Well, do you suppose you could take me to a motel?" he said.

"Sure," she said. There was nothing else to say.

She asked him what motel he would prefer. He said any one that was convenient. When she suggested the La Quinta, he said that would be fine, and he thanked her with the utmost politeness for going out of her way.

"It's not out of my way," she told him. "I've got to go right by it."

Her mind was filling with all sorts of conjecture about him. Surely he wasn't some sort of criminal, although how could she really know?

As she pulled the truck out onto the highway, she asked him where he was headed. "I might be going near where you were goin'. I'd be glad to drive you, if I can."

"I wasn't going anywhere in particular. I was just driving," he said in a weary voice, his eyes directed out the windshield but seeming to look a lot farther than down the immediate highway.

She thought he seemed to be doing what her mother would have called looking painfully backward.

She did not want to leave him at a motel. She justified this overwhelming urge by telling herself that he should not be left alone, in case he had had a concussion. And there was still the matter of those three ibuprofen he had taken on an empty and unsettled stomach. What if he started to vomit and there was no one there to wipe his face with a cool cloth and make certain he did not choke?

She wore herself out with the worrisome thoughts during the ten-minute drive over to the motel. Her fertile mind drew a disturbing picture of him alone in a motel room, one with bleak off-white walls and a wide bed with a gaudy spread and sheets all tangled, staring mindlessly at a television set until the hotel clerk came pounding on the door, which her stranger wouldn't open, as he was either zoned out from a concussion or contemplating ways to hang himself with his belt.

She was growing quite panicky by the time she saw the La Quinta sign. And then her gaze fell on the restaurant next door, an all-night Denny's, as if it had been plopped down on earth for the sole purpose of being an answer to her worries.

"I'm starved," she said. "I think I'll go over there and get somethin' to eat. Would you like to join me? I really hate to eat alone. I'd sure appreciate it if you'd join me."

She knew he was a gentleman and would not be able to refuse, which he didn't. He seemed, in fact, to take hold of the opportunity. Freddy, and sometimes even Charlene, was forever telling her that she imagined all sorts of things, but in that moment Rainey was certain she was correct in her estimation of the man and the situation. She was here at this particular place in time for a reason, and so was he. Nothing happens by coincidence, her mother had forever told her, and she felt in that moment that her path and this man's were destined to cross.

They went inside and sat at a booth next to the night-black window that reflected their own images. Seeing him wince when he swiped back his hair, she got up and examined his head wound. He probably allowed this because he was so surprised by her boldness.

"It's fine," he told her. "It'll just be tender for a few days."

She was satisfied to see the broken skin already sealing itself.

"You'll need to wash it good, though," she said and slipped back to her seat.

He still did not want to eat, but she talked him into getting a piece of pie, pointing out that he should eat something on top of all the ibuprofen he had taken.

"I'm a pharmacist's assistant," she told him, wanting him to realize that she knew what she was talking about when it came to tending the body. "I've just taken a few weeks off to do a bit of barrel racing."

The way it came out, it sounded like she was on a vacation. She didn't mention that when Mr. Blaine would not give her a leave of absence, she had quit, and Mr. Blaine had been so annoyed that he'd told her not to let the door hit her in the butt on the way out, so therefore she was really out of a job. She was reluctant to sound like an unemployed drifter to him.

The waitress came and took their order, smiling at him as if he were so much candy. He didn't seem to notice. Possibly women always looked at him in such a way, Rainey surmised.

She learned that he took his coffee black—indeed, he raised an eyebrow at how much sugar she put into hers—that his favorite pie was cherry, that he was from Houston, that he was observant enough to notice the name written on her trailer was the same as her own, and that he could sit very still and watch her eat.

When they finished their snack and umpteen refills of coffee, and walked out into the cooling night, she gave in to saying, "Are you sure you don't want to go to the hospital? I really think you should have your head looked at. I'll be glad to drive you."

"No, thanks. I'm fine." His eyes were on hers with some intensity. "I appreciate all you've done."

She thought it was time to say goodbye, but what came out was, "You aren't goin' to kill yourself, are you?" She would rather feel foolish than regret.

He looked shocked, and then he shook his head, "No. It might have crossed my mind in the past weeks, but I never seriously entertained the idea."

He gave an amused grin and gazed at her for a moment.

"I just need a little time away from things for a few days. That's what I was doing when I wrecked my car—getting away. Guess I got pretty far, too," he said, his crooked smile widening a bit.

"Oh. Well, I understand that. I've been doin' that." She knew well what he was saying. She knew it deep down.

Again they were looking at each other. Gazing into each other's face and wondering all the things that cannot be said. For her part, Rainey thought of the bleak motel room.

She asked him then to go with her.

As his eyes widened, she corrected, "I don't mean with me alone, but up to my Uncle Doyle's. That's where I'm goin'. He lives a few hours from here—up just outside of Childress."

She told him that she was going to spend a couple of days with her uncle, and about her uncle's house that sat all alone in the rough country just west of the Red River and how there weren't any other houses to be seen for miles.

He tilted his head and gazed downward in a fashion she could not gauge.

"It's not fancy," she said, "but it will be quiet and certainly away from things. Uncle Doyle won't mind at all."

Her mother would have called this one of those things that seemed to be the thing to do at the time.

And then he sort of nodded and said simply, "I think I'll take you up on that."

Rainey had a sense that he surprised himself as much as he did her.

CHAPTER 4

Driving at Night

Thinking it unwise for him to sleep again, because of his possible concussion, she kept talking as they went north along the dark road. She talked of country songs that she liked, of the good roads in Texas, and of how the puppy had been dumped on her.

He contributed little to her efforts beyond, "Yes," "No," or "Mm-hmm."

At one point she said, "Back home, we have a law about dumpin' dogs and cats, and if caught, you'll pay a fine of a hundred dollars and have your name run in a square box in the *Valentine Voice*. My mother got that last part put through. She thought shame was the best deterrent. Of course, not many people have ever been caught at it. Only one actually, and that was because he was from another town and didn't know what would happen to him in ours."

"Back home," he said and cracked his eyes to look at her. "Where would that be?" he asked.

"Valentine, Oklahoma. Cultural center of the universe," she

added, thinking that rather witty. "Great-grandaddy founded the town."

"Hmm." His eyes were once again drifting closed.

"Are you originally from Houston?" she asked.

He cracked one eye at her.

"Your accent," she said. "It's not as pronounced as some, but I'd imagine you're from East Texas, maybe south Arkansas."

"Mm-hmm."

A few seconds later he repositioned himself and said, "I'm *not* passing out. I'm just going to nap."

"Fine." But worry nagged at her.

He leaned against the side of the cab and grimaced when he hit the tender wound on his head.

"There's a little pillow tucked behind your side of the seat," she told him, feeling quite generous.

He found her mother's pillow, rested his head on it and was asleep so quickly it was like he had passed out again.

She assuaged her worry about his concussion by telling herself that for all she knew, this manner of falling asleep quickly was normal for him.

The miles sped away under the rumbling truck as she drove through the night, the same as if she'd been alone, which she found mildly irritating.

Driving at night encourages all sorts of thoughts. Long ago, she had come to the conclusion that many of the ills of the world could be solved in one month, if more of the people in charge of those ills simply went to driving around at night. Freddy always said this theory on her part showed conclusively that she was a few bricks short of a load.

Unlike her passenger, she had never been one to fall quickly asleep. Her mother had said that from birth she awoke about every two hours and that she could hear neighbors whispering in their own homes.

It was normal for her to lie for thirty or more minutes, her mind wandering from this to that, before falling into a light sleep full of dreams, from which she would awaken several times in the night, worries and wonderings prodding her. She had in the past suffered terrible bouts with insomnia, and her mother had encouraged her to deal with this by going out and driving around. The driving did not cure the insomnia, but it did make her a good night driver. She generally enjoyed driving at night, when she had the road to herself and even her mind was more thoroughly all her own, with no intrusive noise from the collective thoughts of other people.

While she drove now, her mind replayed scenes from the evening, and it came to her that she had on the same evening managed to pick up a puppy and a man.

Freddy, when he learned of this, would have a few terse comments.

The puppy lay just on the other side of the glass, and the man was eighteen inches away, breathing the same air as she did.

She couldn't understand how she had come to have them. She had been going innocently along in her lonely, depressed and confused life when a dog and a man had been thrust upon her.

"Everything in season and for a purpose—even if we never know why," her mother used to say.

What was the reason for this? She glanced over at her passenger and felt a tightening in her chest. Sharp apprehension that something she didn't understand had entered her life. That something was going to be required of her. Commitments she felt unprepared to take on.

She had the explicit urge to pull over and tell them both, "Out! Get out!"

* * *

The bumps jarred her passenger awake.

"We're at Uncle Doyle's," she told him.

It was just after two o'clock. She drove down the narrow rutted drive to the dark, weathered wood house. There was a light on in the kitchen. As the truck rumbled to a stop, the yellow porch light came on, and Uncle Doyle, a man so skinny that he had no shape at all, held open the screen door.

"Who's this you got with you, Rain-gal?" he asked, batting moths away from his head where only a few strands of hair stretched across the top.

"A friend, Uncle Doyle—Harry." She kissed her uncle's cheek as she passed into the kitchen, where a single light burned over the sink and the faint scent of cigarette smoke hung in the air. There were books and magazines everywhere, she noticed, then turned to see her passenger coming inside, blinking and looking uncertain, and as if his head pained him greatly.

"Well, howdy young fella," Uncle Doyle said. "Come in and welcome. By golly, it's the middle of the night. I'd gotten to readin' and hadn't really noticed. Maybe y'all would like a bit to eat." He suddenly looked a little at a loss as to what to do with them.

"We've had a bunch of snacks, Uncle Doyle. Aunt Pauline sent you some praline patties and some reports from her trip to Argentina."

"Ah, yes…" Her uncle's eyes lit up behind his thick glasses, and he immediately opened the file folder Rainey passed him, ignoring the bag of praline patties. "That Pauline is good to her ol' brother-in-law," he mumbled, already losing himself in the papers.

His eyes on the pages, he walked away through an open doorway to a small room where a lamp lit several open books on an oak desk and stacks of books all around it. The room of a studious man.

Harry was staring after her uncle. Rainey touched his arm. "I'll show you to your bed."

Up the stairs and past the small bathroom and into a bedroom with a slanted ceiling and twin iron beds set against opposite walls. She told him to take his choice and went to shove open the dormer window. Then she dug into her purse, pulled out the bottle of ibuprofen she had retrieved from the truck seat and tossed it to him. He caught it, looked at her with a raised eyebrow.

"Clean towels are in the bathroom cabinet. If you're hungry, feel free to look around the kitchen. I have to go take care of my mare."

Not understanding herself why she had become so cool, she left him sitting gingerly on the side of the bed, rubbing the back of his head.

The puppy, apparently concluding that they had reached a safe destination, had gotten out of the truck and was waiting at the back door. When she came out, he met her eagerly and followed at her heels as she got Lulu from the trailer and put her in a paddock off the tin barn and ran water in the narrow stock tank, all more or less by the light of the stars. The single pole lamp was at the far corner of the barn.

Lulu ran to the middle of the paddock, sniffing the air and then the ground. Then she trotted closer to the fence where Rainey was and began to crop grass. The paddock had not seen a horse or cow for a long time, and there was plenty of grass. Lulu stayed near Rainey, seeking the reassurance of a friend in this strange place, while the puppy sat beside her feet, and she stood leaning on the top fence rail, looking up at the stars, her chest filling with the familiar sense of wonder.

"It's like they're all lights, isn't it?" she said to the puppy and the horse. "Makes you know there's a lot in this world that we don't know about."

Thank you, Lord, for another day...for bringing me safely here...and that I didn't run him down. She thought of this with a great relief, then, very unnerved at what might have been, swiftly moved her thoughts along. *What is going on here, Lord? Should I just have left him in Abilene? Please send someone who'll take this dog....*

The puppy followed her back to the house. She shut the door against him, and moments later opened it to set out a pan of water and a crusty biscuit she had found in a pan on the stove. Her hand hesitated, and then she touched the top of his head.

Closing the back door, she stood for a moment with her hand on the knob. The kitchen looked quite messy. Uncle Doyle was still reading whatever Aunt Pauline had sent him and likely would for some time. Rainey called to him, and he smiled at her.

"Guess I'll go on to bed," she said. She was suddenly very weary.

"You look all done in, honey. See you in the mornin'."

She went upstairs to the same bedroom where she had left her passenger. She saw him in the light from the hallway. He was fast asleep in the narrow bed, undoubtedly had fallen there instantly. His expensive clothes lay across the cotton quilt at the foot, and his shoulders were bare.

Rainey wondered what he would do if she crawled in beside him.

Probably go on sleeping, she thought with a smile. He appeared done in.

She turned out the hall light, undressed, putting back on her shirt to sleep in, and slipped beneath the covers of the opposite bed. It was the only one left available, and no one could sleep on the short Victorian sofa in the living room.

CHAPTER 5

Every Heart Has a Story

She slept until the sun was high, a light sleep from which she would drift up at different sounds—the telephone's ring, a squeaking door, the rustle of her passenger rising, when she'd peeked and seen his long bare legs as he slipped into his trousers, then the gurgle of water through pipes, and a truck driving off.

She slept as well in this bed as she did in her own. While she had not been in this house for several years, it seemed perfectly familiar and comfortable. The family—the Valentines on her daddy's side and the Overtons on her mother's—was spread out over southern Oklahoma and Texas, yet despite the distance, as strong a bond remained as if they all lived on the same street. "We carry the family traits in our blood," her mother had often said. "Good or bad, can't be denied."

Uncle Doyle's wife Thelma had been her father's sister, so to all the Valentines, he had become a Valentine, no matter what the legal papers said. Having been an orphan, Uncle Doyle himself often forgot that his name was Smith. When reminded of it, he would say that there were plenty of Smiths, so they wouldn't miss him.

The quilt under which Rainey snuggled bore the characteristic Vs of all the quilts made by Grammy, her father's mother, and there were the same scents in the house from the laundry soap favored by the women of the family, as well as the tendency of the elder men to smoke Camels.

Finally, awakening as slowly as she had gone to sleep, she stretched lazily and then looked over at the opposite empty bed, gazing at it for several long seconds. For some reason she pictured her passenger hitchhiking away down the lonesome highway. Going out of her life in the same strange manner in which he had arrived.

She wouldn't be surprised if he had gone, she told herself, getting up to pad downstairs in her big denim shirt, panties and sock feet, not bothering with either her jeans or combing her hair. Not being a cheerful morning person, even at ten o'clock, she would not attempt any unnecessary effort until she'd had her coffee.

The house was silent, the shades drawn in the living room and dining room, both of which went generally unused. They were neat, if dusty.

The kitchen, annoyingly bright with sunshine, was empty. There was hours-old coffee, thick and strong, left in the pot, and she found a single clean cup in the cabinet. Poured it full, one teaspoon of sugar. She drank deeply and then had to cough.

Another couple swallows of coffee and she became sufficiently awake to see the kitchen in its entirety. She saw with a little shock that it was a terrible mess.

She had noticed a certain disorderliness last night but had been too tired to see the true scope of the situation. Rolled up newspapers not yet read, mail, files and books, dishes covered the table. Food encrusted dishes were stacked in the sink and spread across the counters, along with an open bag of chips and several slices of stale bread, and some little things that looked like tomatoes but might have been shriveled red peppers.

She wondered if Uncle Doyle was depressed. She had recently read an article in the newspaper about older people getting depression, and one of the signs was a letting go of cleanliness.

Well, where was her cousin Neva? Why wasn't she looking after her daddy better than this?

No doubt Neva was busy with her own affairs, Rainey thought, a doleful feeling about life in general washing over her. Everyone was busy with their own lives, and that left people like Rainey and Uncle Doyle all alone in theirs.

Except that she wasn't quite as alone as she had been the day before, she thought, remembering both the dog and her passenger as her gaze lit upon a deep-blue sport coat hanging on the back of one of the kitchen chairs.

She reached out and laid a hand on it.

Seeing no one through the window over the sink, which gave a limited view at best, she went to the door and stepped out on the porch. The puppy was there and came immediately to wriggle around her legs. He did not jump on her, a point in his favor. She hated dogs that jumped on a person, and this one just sniffed and wriggled.

Then she saw the curious sight of her passenger bending down by the front tire of her truck.

"What are you doin'?" she called, going to the edge of the porch. She could see what he was doing, of course, but she wondered if he should be exerting himself like that in the hot sunshine.

He looked around at her, then straightened slowly. "You had a flat tire. I'm changin' it."

"Well, do you think you should be doin' that… since you had a concussion yesterday?"

He was changing her tire in his silk shirt and rayon trousers, but she didn't comment on this, getting distracted by the surprising sight of his muscular shoulders beneath his shirt and the way the sun shone on his dark hair.

Returning her gaze to his face, she said, "I could have done it. You shouldn't be exerting yourself, and you might get your shirt dirty."

"I can do it fine," he said, walking forward and brushing one hand against the other, the gold of his wristwatch catching the light. "I was not diagnosed with a concussion, and the least I can do for you is change your tire."

She saw then that he was looking at her legs, which reminded her that she wore only her shirt and socks. She supposed he'd seen a woman's legs before…and if he could think to look at her legs in such an appreciative manner, his head was obviously okay.

He squinted up at her. "You picked up a nail somewhere, and it gave you a slow leak. You'll need to get it plugged. I'd have sent it with your uncle—he went into town to get some part for his baler—but I didn't see the flat until after he'd left." His gaze drifted back to her legs.

"Thanks." She pressed her legs tight together. "I'll take it to town this afternoon. Have you had breakfast?"

"Had a piece of toast and coffee with your uncle. I'm not much of a breakfast person—and your uncle's coffee is strong enough to stand a person up all day."

"It's strong, all right, but it'll wear off at an inopportune time. I'm a breakfast person, no matter what time I get up, and you really should eat. I'll find somethin' to cook, if you want to come on in when you get done."

She went upstairs and put on her jeans, not wanting him to get some mistaken idea about her. And she combed her hair in an effort to look more proper.

Proper really wasn't exactly her strong suit, she thought, recalling how she had asked a veritable stranger to come along with her. She was very honest, though. Even Freddy said this. He would say, "Rainey is honest, even if she is a dingbat."

Slowly lowering the brush in her hand, she stared long at her reflection in the mirror, her spirit faltering as she wondered if she had once again given in to foolishness. What had she expected by asking Harry to come along?

Things so rarely turned out as one expected.

There was a huge bowl of brown eggs in the refrigerator, and some sausage links that looked fairly fresh, a carton of milk that smelled okay, even though it was out of date. She managed to scrape together a healthy breakfast of scrambled eggs, sausage, biscuits and gravy, and even a tomato that wasn't too old.

"Is that all you're goin' to have?" she asked, concerned by the single scoop of eggs and lone biscuit her passenger put on his plate.

"I'm not all that hungry."

"Breakfast is the most important meal of the day, and it's almost lunchtime, besides. Your body can't make much energy with that little bit."

"What you're having is a heart attack waiting to happen," he said, motioning at her plate.

"People have gone overboard about this fat thing," she said, lifting a biscuit thick with butter. "A body has to have fat to process vitamins."

He took a bite of his biscuit and looked mildly surprised. "This is really good." he said.

"Well, if there's one thing I can do, it's cook. My husband Robert used to say that I could stop a war with my biscuits."

Her ability to cook had always seemed like her saving grace, making up in part for her tendency toward foolish mistakes. Of course, her talent in this endeavor had also indirectly caused a number of her foolish mistakes. Her mother had said that her good cooking was the main reason men had always so quickly proposed to her. Rainey had married only two men, but she'd had at least half a dozen real proposals. For a time she had avoided cooking for a man for this reason—because it seemed that as soon as a man ate one of her meals, he would ask her to marry him.

Remembering this, she suffered a flash of anxiety. What if he was running away from his wife and children and fell in love with her cooking?

This gave her pause. Running from a wife and children was, in her opinion, a much more serious offense than almost any type of criminal behavior. Of course, she was getting carried away with wild suppositions, but the disturbing speculation did serve to point up the fact that she hadn't really considered before what he might be getting away from. She had been so worried about his concussion and felt such empathy for his confusion that she had not gone any further.

"This is really delicious," he said with enthusiasm, reaching for a second biscuit.

"Thank you. You aren't married, are you? You aren't runnin' away from a wife and children, are you?"

He looked up, startled. "No. I'm not married."

"Oh. Well, I guess it isn't really any of my business." She felt silly and rude and wished she had controlled her tongue.

"I haven't ever been married," he said, in a sort of dazed tone.

She looked at him. He blinked and looked down at his plate,

and he sat there holding the biscuit and looking intense, his jaw-line very tight.

She had a strong sense that he was working up to a further explanation, and she suddenly wondered if she really wanted to know what he was getting away from. She didn't want to be disappointed in him. Not truly knowing him, she had attrib-uted to him a very good character, if confused, and now she re-alized that this might not be the case at all. A great dread of being disappointed in him washed over her.

She was certain he would have told her everything at that mo-ment, if she had asked, but she was saved from doing that when just then a vehicle drove up, and the puppy went to barking his fierce little puppy bark.

Through the window of the door, Rainey saw the little puppy dash off the porch, and then heard her Uncle Doyle let out a yell.

"Ye Gods and little fishes," she said, opening the door to see the puppy darting again and again at her uncle's ankles. She hur-ried out to grab hold of the pup.

"That's a feisty little fella you have there, Rain-gal. I left by way of the front door, and I guess he didn't see me go." He touched the puppy's head. "You're pretty good at takin' care of Rain-gal, pooch." The puppy, satisfied that things were now in control, wagged his tail.

"He isn't really my dog, Uncle Doyle. Someone dumped him on me. He didn't bite you, did he?"

"Naw…he's just all show. Probably make a good companion for you while you're travelin' all over creation," he said with some censure, then went on to the sink to wash his hands, adding, "I'm sorry about the kitchen mess, darlin'. I forgot all about it."

Spying a book and the file folder from Aunt Pauline still on the table, Rainey deftly moved them, tucking them behind a canister on the counter. If her uncle happened to spy them, no doubt he would open them, and then he would get to reading and forget to have his meal. And Lord knew that Uncle Doyle didn't need to skimp on meals.

Uncle Doyle's thinness always gave her a little ache in her chest. He was so skinny, he disappeared when he stood sideways. She felt she must *feed* him.

She washed him a plate, and he sat at the table, complimenting her on her cooking so much that she became uncomfortable.

"Been a long time since I had such good food, Rain-gal. Her cookin' is somethin', idn't it?" he said to Harry. "There ain't many women can look like Rain-gal and cook on top of it, but all them Overton gals are like that—good lookers and good cookers.

"When Rain-gal and her mama were here last, I had a fella from the Ag Department down in Austin pull up out there and get the scent and come in, and the next thing I knew, my hand came in and set down, too. Those two men kept eatin' and lookin' at Rainey and her mama, too, even though Coweta was past seventy-five then. By dang, I thought I wasn't never gonna get them men outta here."

"Uncle Doyle, how's your alfalfa this year?" she said to change the subject. When not immersed in his reading, Uncle Doyle could talk a blue streak. "Uncle Doyle retired from being a county agent and is experimenting with improvin' alfalfa," she explained to her passenger. "He's helped put new seed on the market."

She watched her passenger take yet another biscuit and, following Uncle Doyle's example, put a piece of sausage on it and spoon gravy over it. She was pleased, but a little worried, too. She doubted that her passenger was used to rich foods. Little sparks of worry went off in her mind; she had possibly corrupted him with her gravy, which was rich and could be habit forming.

"It was awful wet this spring," Uncle Doyle was saying, "and the alfalfa got a lot of weeds. I'll bet we had as much rain this spring as y'all did down in Houston, Harry," he said.

Rainey realized he was speaking to her passenger. Harry. She stared at him, and he shot her a sideways glance.

"Weather patterns are goin' a little crazy these days," Uncle Doyle said. "Why, I can remember how parts of this country out here used to 'bout go to desert in the summer when I was a boy. Now we got thick grass and even trees growin' all over, and the Red has water in it most of the time. There's some says it's all the radio waves."

She said, "I haven't ever been to Houston, but I hear it is really humid there." She kept looking at her passenger and wondered what all he had discussed with her uncle that morning. What he might have told Uncle Doyle that he hadn't bothered to tell her.

"It can be," he said. "Think I'll get another cup of coffee. Anyone else want any?"

"I'll take a half a cup," Uncle Doyle said. "I clean forgot, Rain-gal, but Charlene called here this mornin'. I wrote a note and put it somewhere...." He looked around with a puzzled frown, then patted his shirt pockets.

"It's okay, Uncle Doyle. I'll call her in a few minutes."

She tried to think of a way to bring the subject back to Houston and find out more about her passenger. Maybe she would just say straight out: So what do you do down in Houston? What are you gettin' away from?

"Here it is," Uncle Doyle said with satisfaction. "I got to write everythin' down, or I forget about it."

He handed her a scrap of paper torn from a paper bag. All that was written on it was: "Charlene called this a.m. Call her back."

Rainey said, "I need to phone in my entry into the Amarillo rodeo, too, Uncle Doyle. I'll use my calling card. Is Neva goin' up to the rodeo?"

"Well, I don't rightly know," her uncle said, folding his arms and leaning forward on the table. "My daughter and I haven't spoken in three months—since she chose to move in with her no-account boyfriend without the benefit of marriage."

"Oh."

Possibly more was called for on her part, but she was surprised and couldn't think of anything else to say. She was a little embarrassed, too, wondering what her uncle must think about her passenger.

"I raised her better than that," Uncle Doyle said. "If nothin' else, she ought to have better sense. She's got a blessed four-year college degree and is an assistant bank manager, and that no-account ain't fit to roll with a pig, works weldin' in the oil fields half the time and rodeo the other half, when he ain't layin' around, which is what it seems like he does most of the time." He snorted. "Her mother'd be heartbroke."

"I thought Neva was goin' with a physical ed teacher," she said, vaguely recalling what Neva had told her at her mother's funeral back in the spring.

"She broke that off and took up with this bum."

"Oh."

It seemed to her that Uncle Doyle was looking at her and her passenger, who was sitting there looking uncomfortable.

"Harry and I are just friends, Uncle Doyle," she said. Then, "I think I'll go call Charlene."

Laying her napkin beside the plate, she left the men. Harry seemed to get on well with her uncle; he could handle any needed explanations.

"You were supposed to call me as soon as you got there," Charlene said, causing Rainey to sit down, feeling like she was wilting.

She sat in the old gooseneck rocker, and it rocked forward, setting her off balance and just about sliding into the floor. She was trying to get straight and listen to Charlene at the same time, which put her at a distinct disadvantage.

"I got really worried last night," Charlene was saying in her sharp tone. "For all I knew you were squashed in the truck along a Texas highway."

"I didn't realize you expected me to call last night. It was late when we got in—about two o'clock in the mornin'."

"And just what is this *we* business? Uncle Doyle said you have a man with you—a guy named Harry. You didn't say anything yesterday about a boyfriend. You haven't gone and gotten married again have you?"

The questions, jumping from boyfriend to marriage, confused Rainey. "No, I didn't get married," she said at last. "I just met him last night, Charlene, when I almost ran him down on the road. He had run his car off the road, and..."

"He ran off the road?" Charlene broke in. "What are you doin' pickin' up a drunk who ran his car off the road?"

"He wasn't drunk," she defended. "He'd just had an accident is all, and he was walkin' along the side of the road in the dark. He was out in the middle of nowhere, and I had to give him a ride, and he'd hurt his head but didn't think he needed to see a doctor, and well, he needed someplace to go for a few days." *Whew!* She'd spoken as fast as possible to avoid another interruption.

"He needed someplace to go?" Charlene sounded incredulous. "You picked up a stranger because *he needed someplace to go?*"

Rainey felt herself wilting a little more. "Well, he had a concussion." She straightened. "I couldn't just leave him there. It's sort of complicated, Charlene."

She began to get irritated. She could try again to explain, but she rather thought she would get nowhere. Her sister did not have the type of mind or heart to understand unorthodox circumstances. Charlene was a black-and-white sort of person.

"He could be a murderer," she said.

"He hasn't murdered us yet," Rainey said practically. "He's really nice. Uncle Doyle even seems to like him."

"Oh, gosh, Rainey, you are just like Mama."

Charlene spoke with great censure and equal distress, and Rainey didn't know what sort of reply was called for. And more disturbing, it sounded as if her sister had begun to cry.

"Oh, Rainey, That Mildred Covington was over at Daddy's *all night*. Helen went by there first thing this mornin', and there they were, sittin' at the breakfast table, That Mildred Covington still in her robe. Helen was embarrassed to death, and That Mildred Covington just sat there, bold as brass. Lord, at her age. I don't know how Daddy can just forget Mama in such a short time. And everybody's goin' to start talking about it."

Apparently Mildred had become That Mildred. Rainey said, "He hasn't forgotten Mama, Charlene. You know he hasn't."

"He sure is givin' every evidence of it. Just like, okay, she's gone, let's get on with things."

Rainey thought that there really wasn't a reason not to get on with things.

"It's like Mama didn't count for anything, cookin' and cleanin' for him, settin' out his paper every Sunday, just the way he liked it." She was clearly sobbing.

"Oh, Charlene, Daddy's just horribly lonely. Mama did see to his every need, and he's at a loss without her. Really, him lettin' Mildred do for him is a compliment to Mama—it shows how much he loved having her that he's lookin' to find the same with someone else."

She was trying to see this thing in the best light. She wasn't nearly as shocked as Charlene, because she had suspected that this was going on. She thought it might help to add, "And they are in their eighties, Charlene. They were probably just watchin' movies all night. You know how Daddy likes to watch that Western channel."

"I don't care what they were doin' all night. It's what it looks like. I wouldn't be lettin' my little Jojo go stay at some boy's house, even if she is only eight years old, so I don't think it is any different for Daddy and That Mildred to carry on like that.

"And another thing, he is barkin' up the wrong skirt. Mildred Covington is a far cry from Mama, that's for sure. She wears those knee-high hose with her dresses, for heavensake. They show when she sits there in that rocker, and it looks so tacky. But I can't seem to do anything with him, Rainey. You are the only one who can, because you're just like Mama."

Rainey was surprised by the hint of helpless distress in her sister's voice. She had never witnessed her sister helpless. Charlene was always so managerial.

"When are you comin' home, Rainey?"

"I don't know," she said uncertainly. "I'm going up to the

Amarillo rodeo this weekend…I think Lulu and I have a good chance of winnin' up there. Lulu came in second down in San Antonio, you know, with seventeen point nine seconds."

She hoped by changing the subject to the rodeo and her plans she would get her sister's mind off wailing over their father, as well as off the subject of Rainey going home. She did not feel up to going home yet.

"I hope you do as well as you'd like. But you've been gone long enough, Rainey. You need to plan on comin' home."

Rainey thought at least she had succeeded in getting Charlene's mind lifted up; her sister sounded much more like her commanding self.

Rainey scraped the leftovers from breakfast into a pan on the porch. There had not been very much left, so she had cooked a bit of cornmeal mush, too. The puppy, wagging his entire back end, lapped it up.

"I thought you didn't want him," Harry said, looking on from where he leaned lazily against a porch post.

She thought of him as Harry now, after Uncle Doyle addressing him as such a number of times over breakfast.

"I don't," she said. "But that doesn't mean I'd let him go hungry."

"Maybe your uncle would keep him."

"He'd likely forget to feed him. In case you haven't noticed, Uncle Doyle is somewhat absentminded. He's very focused on his research, and when reading anything that interests him, he forgets everything else."

Her passenger nodded, looking somewhat absentminded himself. He had beautiful eyes. Long dark eyelashes.

Quite suddenly she realized he was staring at her. She tried to look nonchalant.

"Are you still planning to go into town to take your tire for repair?" he asked.

"Yes...after I get a shower."

"I'd like to ride along with you, if that's okay. I need to get some things—toothbrush and shaving supplies and maybe a change of clothes."

She looked at his clothes. "You might not find anything like what you're wearin'."

"I imagine I can find some jeans that'll do just fine."

He cast her a crooked grin, and his eyes seemed to sparkle for a moment, but back of that sparkle was a heavy sadness. She looked at him for a long second, wondering about his sadness, before she turned away into the house. She might have taken that opportunity to bring up the matter of the life he was getting away from, but she shied from that. She felt she would be prying, and she wasn't certain she felt up to taking on someone else's sadness. And she sure didn't want to be disappointed.

What she wanted was a shower.

CHAPTER 6

Every Story Has a Chapter

As she opened the truck door, she caught sight of the puppy several feet away. He stood poised, with the tips of his ears up, looking at her with longing.

She sighed. "Come on." She lowered the tailgate—easy now with the trailer unhooked—and he jumped inside, big paws sliding on the slick metal bed. Slamming the tailgate, she returned to slip behind the wheel. Harry was looking at her.

She said, "Maybe I'll pass a house with kids in town and have the chance to drop him off," and put on her sunglasses.

It was the sort of day that could be mistaken for August, except that the light, while bright and warm, was thinner. Even the air was thinner. It came in a fresh breeze beating through the open windows, tugging at their hair and bringing the scent of the earth.

They passed a field of cotton, and she pointed it out.

"I know what cotton looks like," he said, with that crooked grin she was beginning to think of as familiar.

"Well, I don't know how much cotton they grow down around Houston."

"They raise cotton a lot of places," he said. He looked at her and then turned his gaze ahead out the window.

She returned her eyes to the road, wondering about him and his life. She wished she didn't wonder so hard.

With a quick movement, she flicked on the radio, and lively country music filled the air. Their glances met, and they smiled at each other, before jerking their gazes away at the same instant.

Then she sneaked a peak at him, saw him rubbing a hand over his hair.

Again his eyes came to hers. "It's a nice day," he said.

"Great day," she said and made herself focus on the road and driving, while very aware that he rode beside her. She figured it felt as it did simply because he was the first person to ride in the truck with her since she had started out on her trip to somewhere.

They dropped Rainey's flat tire for repair at a gas station, and then continued on to a farm-and-hardware store. In the parking lot, she tied the puppy in the back of the pickup, saying that she didn't want him to jump out and get run over. Even though he had not exhibited such behavior before, she looked at the busy street and grew doubtful.

Harry had never been in a farm store and seemed to find the possibility of purchasing a chain saw and antibiotics and syringes at the same place quite fascinating.

"They even have paint," he said with some fascination.

"Jeans, too," she pointed out, amused and fascinated herself by his fascination. "You won't find anything like what you're wearin', but you did say you wanted some clothes." She gestured at the stacks of Wrangler jeans.

Leaving him apparently quite happily engaged in perusing the clothing, she went on to the stock supplies to get the wormer and grain she needed for Lulu. She also picked up some dog food and a rawhide chew bone for the puppy, telling herself that she could toss it down in the yard where she dumped the dog to occupy him when she made her getaway.

Her shopping complete, she returned to the clothing section to find Harry gazing at himself in the full-length mirror. He wore jeans and a faded denim shirt that stretched nicely over his shoulders. A brown cowboy hat on his head, he turned to the right and then to the left, then cocked the hat at an angle the way he surely had as a boy watching Little Joe in *Bonanza*.

"It's great," she said.

He whirled around, snatching off the hat, a blush spreading over the sharp planes of his cheeks. As if it were on fire, he tossed the hat back on the table with the others. "Just thought I'd kill some time."

"Oh, no…you might need it." She took it up and extended it to him. "The next couple of days are to be sunny, no rain in sight. Here, let me see again."

He took the hat and looked at her. She motioned at him. He set the hat back on his head and tested the placement.

"How does it feel?"

He cocked an eyebrow. "I don't think I know how it's supposed to feel."

"Uncomfortably tight far down…there. It should be tight but feel as if it could loosen. It will stretch."

He looked again in the mirror, at first as if sneaking a look, then frankly and as if to make certain he recognized himself. She liked how he had quickly gotten over his self-consciousness.

"It suits you," she said.

His eyes came to hers. "Well, howdy, ma'am," he said, his

soft brown eyes sparkling, and his mouth grinning the first full grin she had seen thus far.

"Howdy, yourself." She jerked the brim of his hat downward over his face and laughed gaily.

He swept the hat off and grinned at her, thoroughly full of himself.

"You should look at boots, too," she said, giving his loafers a doubtful look.

So he bought boots, too, with a bit of her help and a lot of laughing and horsing around. Then they drove to Walmart, where he got socks and underwear, another shirt, and toiletries. She added a jean jacket to his cart, pointing out that they were on the high plains and that the nights would be cool.

He touched the jacket and looked at her.

"I know it's only a couple of nights, but you might be glad for the jacket."

He nodded.

They went through the store, Harry rolling the cart after her. His eyes widened when she tossed four big packages of snack cakes into the cart. She noticed his gaze slip down her figure; she thought he liked what he saw.

She picked up cleaning supplies, saying that she didn't trust her Uncle Doyle to have any. Harry pointed out dog collars hanging nearby.

"I don't need to buy a collar," she said. "I bought him a chew bone. I'll use it the first chance I get to dump him, to keep him busy so he won't chase after us."

"Oh."

He paid for his purchases ahead of Rainey, and she noticed him carefully watching the clerk pass his credit card through the machine. He seemed nervous, and she wondered again about his life, what he might be getting away from. When the clerk passed over his sacks, she thought she could almost hear him sigh with relief.

As they walked out across the bright parking lot, she asked him if he might need cash. "I think I'll drop by the bank where my cousin works. There won't be any trouble for us to get cash there, with a check or our credit cards."

"Why don't we just use an ATM?" he suggested, looking around as if to spy one.

"Well, I've never used one of those machines. I don't have the number or card or whatever it is you need."

"You've never used an ATM machine?" He looked stunned.

"No. I don't like them...they sort of scare me. I mean, they suck in a plastic card and spit out money. Seems way too powerful a machine to mess with, if you ask me."

He stared at her, then furrowed his brow and asked how she felt about a dialysis machine.

"I don't think I could trust one of those, either," she said, making no apologies. "Bank's just up here on our way."

Rainey left Harry walking the puppy on a grassy area next to the bank. He said he didn't really need any cash.

"I'll just keep using the card," he said.

She shrugged and went into the bank.

Her cousin Neva saw her and jumped up from her big desk, coming forward with a wide smile. Rainey was struck. Her cousin had changed greatly in the few months since Rainey had last seen her. Neva's brown hair, usually cropped short and mannish, now curled to her shoulders. She no longer wore glasses, and her dress was two inches above her knees.

The man, Rainey thought in an instant. This was the result of the bum not fit to roll with pigs.

"Good golly, girl, this is a surprise!" Neva said, enveloping Rainey in a big, warm hug.

Joy washed over her. Neva had always been her favorite cousin. She was, as Uncle Doyle had said, very smart. She had attended the university at Austin on full scholarship and could have gone on to any university in the nation for her master's. Instead she had said that four years of higher education was enough for anyone and had come home to work in a small-town bank, where, she said, she could live the simple life, which for her included racing barrels. What Rainey appreciated about her cousin was that Neva never acted superior to those of lesser intelligence.

"I guess you are stayin' out at Dad's," Neva said.

"Yes. We got in there late last night—I've got a friend with me for a couple of days. I've been racin' Mama's horse in barrels the past couple of months, and I'm on my way to the rodeo up in Amarillo this weekend. Aunt Pauline had me bring your daddy some praline patties and some information about alfalfa she saw down in South America."

"I'd heard you were racin' barrels again. Leanne said she had seen you in Wichita Falls. Leanne came through here a few weeks back on her way to the rodeo up at the XIT ranch—she gave me and my horse a lift up there. She sure does have a fancy rig. She's doin' pretty good with it these days, pretty much goin' professional now."

Leanne was a cousin on her mother's side. Rainey agreed that Leanne was very good, then mentioned that Leanne's horse had cost upward of thirty thousand dollars.

"And let me tell you, Leanne was spittin' nails when she came in second to a five-hundred-dollar horse," Neva said, laughing. Then she folded her arms and said, "Well, I didn't know you were comin' by here, cause Dad hasn't been talkin' to me for about three months now. Did he tell you?"

"He mentioned it." Rainey searched her mind for something helpful to say about the situation.

"Well, it's his choice," her cousin said. "He told me not to bother comin' around to see him, so I don't."

"Oh, he didn't mean that. People say things in the heat of the moment."

"He sure did, and he said too much." Neva looked at the credit card Rainey held. "Did you want a cash advance?"

"Oh...yes."

Her cousin took the card and went around the counter to a teller drawer. Rainey told her she would take a couple hundred. "I really think I'm gettin' near my limit."

A woman poked her head out of a glass office and called Neva to the telephone.

"One sec," Neva held up a finger, then counted out Rainey's money, saying, "Listen, we're havin' practice on barrels and poles tonight out at Shirley Trammel's arena. You're welcome to join us. I can't make it to Amarillo this weekend, but I'm probably goin' to a rodeo over in Hereford at the end of the month. My Buck's goin' over there, he rides bulls."

Her cousin smiled brilliantly, giving birth to deep dimples. Rainey had never noticed the dimples. It must have been the new haircut that somehow framed them.

"Shirley's place is a mile north of Daddy's." She cast a wave as she hurried to the glass office. "You come on."

"Come to supper tonight," Rainey called, but her cousin simply waved and shook her head.

When she came out of the bank, Harry told her he'd found out that there was a dog pound. An old man had walked past and told him.

"Why would he tell you that?" Rainey asked, lowering the

tailgate for the puppy to jump inside. She imagined the strange situation of a man just walking down the street and blurting out, "The pound's around the corner."

"I asked him," Harry said.

Rainey got behind the wheel and buckled her seatbelt.

"I don't think I need to take him to the pound. They only give the dogs a few days, and if no one claims them, they put them to sleep."

"The man said he thought the pound killed them in two weeks. He wasn't sure, though."

"You are just a wealth of information," Rainey said and shifted into drive, headed slowly down the road, keeping an eye out for a house with kids playing in the front of it. There were not many houses on the main street, and she supposed she would look awfully conspicuous driving up and down neighborhood streets.

CHAPTER 7

Naked to the Eye

When they stopped at the station to pick up Rainey's repaired tire, Harry made several calls from a pay phone. She saw him walking toward the phone as the attendant was putting her tire in the back of the truck. The sun shone on his new hat and his shoulders. He had nice, square shoulders.

She got into the truck and sat there, watching him. He had a card in his hand—a calling card, she guessed. He bent his head close to the phone. She watched the intense set of his shoulders and head movement.

After a minute, she started the truck and drove over to him, stopping a few feet away. It seemed the polite thing to do. She did not stop close enough to be eavesdropping, but close enough to have a better look at him...and to possibly catch a few words.

She could hear no more, however, than murmuring. He turned, and she saw him give a small smile, nod and say what she thought must be, "Thanks," just before hanging up.

To her surprise, he dialed again. He waited, and in her imagination she heard the ringing across the line. His shoulders looked tensed, and for whatever reason, she felt tension, too, and chewed her own lip. Spying a fingernail file lying on the dash, she snatched it up and began filing her nails while repeatedly glancing up at him in a way she recognized as a little silly, but she could not stop, either.

He had reached someone, pressed the receiver close to his mouth.

He looked skyward, then back down, shaking his head. She caught, "No!" quite loudly.

Then he seemed to listen long, said something and hung up, hard, his hand remaining for a full minute on the receiver, and his shoulders sagging as if he had been shot in the back.

She wondered wildly if she should get out and run to him.

Then, sweeping off his hat and rubbing his arm over his head, he looked around at her. She realized she was staring at him. She quickly looked down and filed like crazy. *Who was he talking to? What was it all about? Well, she didn't like whoever they were. They had hurt him.*

With dismay, she realized she had gotten carried away and filed one nail at a ridiculously crooked angle.

Glancing up, she saw Harry dialing one more time. He paced with this one. It seemed to take him quite a while. She wondered what could be going on, and she was growing hot.

She was debating about getting out and standing on the shady side of the truck, when he called over to her, "Do you have your uncle's phone number?"

"Oh...oh, yes. Just a minute."

She got her little address book from her purse and hurried toward him, holding open the page and pointing.

He repeated the number into the phone. Then, looking intently at her and motioning, he loudly repeated the name Farris Wrecker Service and a phone number, which she repeated to herself until she found a pen and a scrap of paper in her purse to write the number on. She handed him the paper when he hung up.

He looked at it and then squinted at her. "No one had found the car." He spoke as if he was both mystified and disappointed.

"Oh."

They got back into the truck, and Rainey headed it down the highway. She wanted to ask him a dozen questions about who he had talked to, but a reluctance to pry kept her silent. In any case, he did not invite conversation. A mood thick and dark had come over him. He gazed out the window, looking as sad as anyone she had ever seen.

Finally she said, "I'm makin' fried chicken for supper." Good food generally could lift the darkest heart.

He grinned at her, and she was satisfied at her attempt.

CHAPTER 8

Daring Souls

Harry didn't want to hold Lulu for her. He said, "I don't trust any animal whose head reaches above mine."

"Your head appears even with hers," she said, surprised to see him standing rooted to a spot several safe feet away.

"Not even enough...she has at least nine hundred pounds on me."

"She's as gentle as the pup," she told him and held the lead rope toward him.

With a distrustful eye on Lulu, he stepped forward. "I wasn't too certain about that pup at first, but I figure I have about a 130 pounds on him easy and can hold my own," he said in the manner of a thinking man.

Chuckling, she put the lead into his hand. "Here...put your nose next to hers."

He arched an eyebrow.

"See...put your nose to hers, like she does...she's learnin' about me by sniffing." She blew softly into Lulu's nose and kissed the soft tip.

She left him standing there with the mare while she opened the trailer and cleaned it out. She had not had a spare minute to see to that chore since arriving. Glancing over her shoulder, she saw Harry and the mare eyeing each other, Lulu obviously wondering nervously what there was to be afraid of.

Then she took the mare and loaded her into the trailer and they were off. As they passed her uncle sitting slouched in a rocker on the porch, a thick research book in his lap, Rainey slowed and called out the window, "Come on over after a while, Uncle Doyle." But he shook his head.

With a sigh, she headed on down the drive. Glancing over, she saw Harry once more placing his hat on his head, dipping it low over his brow, as they were heading into the sun.

His gaze caught hers. They smiled at each other. She thought how lovely his brown eyes were, and quickly returned her gaze to the view beyond the windshield.

"Go girl!"

"Get his shoulder up!"

"Head for home!"

The horse knocked the rider's leg into the barrel, and Rainey winced. Then horse and rider were racing lickety-split down the dusty arena to the encouraging shouts ringing upward to the wide pale sky.

There were seven barrel racers taking turns using the arena for practice and a number of other riders out for the relaxing fun of riding. Men and women sat around on the tailgates of pickups and fence rails, drinking RCs and Coors, and kids ran around chasing each other and playing in the dirt. No trees for miles, the wide sky above the color of turquoise, and the evening golden sunlight lingering. It was an open and free atmosphere that encouraged spirits to laugh and soar.

Squinting beneath the shade of her wide-brimmed hat, Rainey rode Lulu toward the arena gate. A sense of anticipation rose in her like bubbles out of an uncorked bottle of champagne. There was a part of her that said "Ah" when she mounted a horse and found her seat, and Lulu, having already done a few slow turns around the barrels, was primed.

The mare's ears cocked back and her tail swished high. Heading Lulu toward the gate of an arena was like switching on an engine, and when Rainey tapped her heels, Lulu went into instant turbo drive, not what anyone would expect from a mare so fat. Rainey usually was a little surprised to remain on the horse's back and not be left back in the dirt by the force of gravity.

The mare's mane flying, and Rainey's hair beneath her hat doing likewise, they streaked into the arena and around the first barrel to the familiar encouraging shouts, and to some odd fellow boldly bawling instructions. Rainey barely heard the shouts, though, as she reveled in the power of the horse between her legs and the wind in her face. Tempering her exuberance for the sake of safety, she pulled gently on the reins, and Lulu settled into a flowing pace, rounding each barrel pretty as you please, turning for home at the third barrel and running for the gate. Then, riding right in front of Harry, Rainey let her spirit and the mare fly. She wanted him to see them in all their majesty.

The man with the stopwatch called out to her as she passed, "Twenty even." She nodded at him and headed Lulu off to walk around the outside of the arena and catch her breath.

Neva rode up on her brown gelding. "You hold her back around the barrels."

"I don't see any need to risk an injury in practice. All she needs is to go over the pattern, anyway," she said, stroking Lulu's neck. "She always seems to know when it's practice and when it's the real thing."

"That J.T. annoys the hell out of me," her cousin said. "Sitting up there on his big paint and calling out instructions and criticisms like we're all his private students. Like anyone asked him."

Rainey chuckled. For her part, she had barely heard the man. She had tuned him out. She could do that with anyone, having learned how when her brother Freddy got on his own high horse.

Neva said, "He's Shirley's husband, and everyone puts up with him because of that. I can't for the life of me understand what she sees in him. Shirley is a professor with tenure at the junior college, and she owns the ranch. J.T. really can't do anything, but he likes to act like he knows and does everything. Shirley has to come around behind him and do the job over— basically what he does is give her double work and scare off her friends. Who needs that?"

"Oh, who knows what any woman sees in a man?" Rainey said, her gaze finding her cousin's current boyfriend sitting on the tailgate of his flashy red pickup truck.

She herself had been wondering: What in the world does Neva see in that man? Buck was handsome enough to put your eyes out, she supposed. Or he probably was to some women, although he struck her as someone in need of a shave and a haircut, or at least body-building shampoo. And a bit of gumption, too, if that could be had at the barbershop.

Her gaze slid as if drawn by a magnet to Harry, sitting right beside him.

Neva said impishly, "I imagine there's one thing J.T. can do, just like my Buck...and your Harry."

Rainey glanced over to see Neva gazing at the two men. It was plain to see that she thought Buck had hung the moon and stars.

Returning her eyes to Buck, Rainey tried to see what Neva saw, but again her gaze shifted, and she noticed how the golden evening sun glinted on Harry's thick brown hair.

So far, since getting his hat, he would put it on and take it off five minutes later, as someone not used to wearing a hat often did.

"He isn't *my* Harry."

Harry had obviously liked Buck immediately, in the way that some men who seem totally opposite often gravitate to each other. Looking easy in his denim, sitting there beside Buck, he swung his booted feet slightly, a bottle of beer in one hand, and his other draped atop the puppy, who had displayed a tendency to nip at horses' heels and therefore was confined to the truck.

Rainey was one to let a horse teach the pup with a good swift kick, but others there did not feel so inclined. She had been close to tearing into a guy who had hauled off and kicked the pup with his very pointed boot. Harry had stepped in with a calming hand and taken the pup off to the truck with him.

"He's okay, Rainey," he had said, feeling the pup's side where the sharp boot had struck. The pup licked his hand nervously, as if fearful something else might be going to happen to him. "You're okay, aren't you, buddy?"

"Are you sure? You don't think he could have a broken rib…maybe one cracked?" She felt for herself, as Harry reassured her again, telling her that the man hadn't kicked the puppy nearly as hard as a horse would have.

"Well, a horse's hoof isn't pointed…and it knows how to hit. A horse will usually give a warning blow first, hard but not deadly. And besides, that's one animal dealin' with another," she added indignantly. She was still half contemplating going over and giving the sharp-booted guy a swift kick of her own.

Neva was saying, "You said you picked him up off the highway. I'd say that in some way he *is* your Harry."

"We are not lovers," Rainey said. She wished she had not said anything about how she had come to meet him. It sounded a little foolish.

"I didn't say you were…and there's a lot to being lovers that has nothin' to do with anything goin' on between the covers."

"I've been married twice. I'm tired of being disappointed by men."

"We women of the Valentine blood are a bold bunch, aren't we?" Neva said with a chuckle.

Rainey stared at her cousin, feeling sudden emotion at the term *Valentine blood*.

"I picked Buck up, too," Neva said in a way that made Rainey's ears prick; she knew there was more to come, a confession of some sort.

Neva gazed down at her saddle horn, and then she raised her eyes, speaking in a soft voice. "I know what I'm into with Buck. Daddy thinks I don't, but I do. It's just that what I'm lookin' for isn't the same as what Daddy thinks I should look for. I can earn myself a living, make my own decisions, take my own car to the mechanic—I don't need a man for any of that.

"I need a man to love me," she said, simply and profoundly.

"I know Buck doesn't have an ounce of ambition—not like the world counts ambition, anyway. He isn't much interested in money, as long as he has his truck and his bull-ridin' riggin'. When he gets broke, he goes to work for a while, builds up a nest egg, then slacks off again. He doesn't worry about tomorrow. I know it may sound silly, but that is what I admire about him. He puts the joys of living life today above money. He strives for joy, rather than money. He's there for me, rather than for makin' money."

Rainey saw with some surprise that Neva's brown eyes were beautiful, passionate. She knew that this was what Buck saw in her plain cousin. It struck her that love truly did make a person bloom.

"All day long I see people scramblin' for the almighty dollar," Neva said. "Some runnin' right over their husbands or wives or mothers or fathers to get it. Always sayin' to themselves, 'Got to have money to live, there's time for lovin' and enjoyin' later, after the money is made, the future all secure.' Eugene kept sayin' that to me. We'd get married after he made school principal and was secure. He was thirty-four, for heavensake, and talkin' all the time about retirement. He wanted us to have our house all paid for the day we married.

"You know why I think Daddy approved of Eugene? Because Eugene never was a threat to take my heart away, I'll tell you that," she said.

Rainey thought that Neva might have hit upon a truth. She vaguely recalled meeting Eugene once, but she could not recall what he looked like; perhaps this fact was telling in itself.

Neva said, "You know when I first saw Buck, what he did? It was in a Hardee's over in Wichita, just before last Christmas, and a poor old deaf-mute man was going from table to table, giving out these little notes that asked for money and gave a blessing. I was with Eugene, and he turned up his nose and said the old man was a plague on society and needed to get a real job. I'm ashamed to say I was afraid of his criticism, if I gave the man money. But then, when Eugene had gone to the rest room, I saw Buck take out a ten-dollar bill—'bout all he had in his pocket, I imagine—and he put it right in the beggar's hand. And there were tears in Buck's eyes."

Rainey saw her cousin's eyes glisten, and her own heartbeat ran faster, picturing the scene.

"What did you do?" she asked.

"Well, not anything, then. I watched him walk out to his

truck, and I wanted to run after him, but I was too afraid of being a crazy fool. And runnin' out on Eugene while he was in the bathroom did not seem like the thing to do.

"But when we got out to his car, I told him that I could not marry him, and I told myself that there were a lot worse things than bein' a fool—one of them is living with regrets. I promised myself that if I ever got a chance to meet a man like the one who had given the beggar money, I'd snatch him up."

"And you did get the chance," Rainey said, caught up in the story.

"Yes, at a club I went to with some girlfriends. It was four months later, and at first, when I saw him standin' underneath a light, I thought I had to be imaginin' things. I mean, it was like I heard angels singin' hosannah and God sayin', '*Well, here's your chance, Neva. What are you gonna do now?*' I snatched my courage and went over and asked him to dance. Then I told him about seeing him in the Hardee's and that I thought I might be in love with him."

"You did?" Rainey said, amazed and awed.

Her cousin nodded, saying earnestly, "I know it sounds like I'd lost my mind, but I was desperate. I wanted to have love in my lifetime. Real carrying-away-love, like they write songs about."

Rainey could not take her eyes off her cousin's glowing face. Something inside her answered, *Oh, I know...I know!*

"Buck came home with me, and we sat up all night talkin'... just talking," she said with a chuckle, "and two days later he asked me to marry him."

"Two days? You got married after knowin' him two days?" Rainey glanced down at her cousin's hand. There was a ring on her left hand, one with a turquoise stone. Rainey had thought it a birthstone ring.

"Well, no," Neva said, lifting her hand and fingering the ring. "I got cold feet. It was one thing to be bold with him and another to risk my lifetime—I don't believe in divorce, and frankly, I know Buck is sort of weak in that area. He doesn't like unpleasantness or conflict at all and is apt to run off. You know how men can be."

"Yes," Rainey said, averting her eyes downward.

Neva said, "Right after Daddy was so rude to him—trying to drive him off—Buck did run off for a couple of days, sayin' that he wasn't the man for me. But he came back, and when he was still with me a month later and still askin', I said yes, if he wanted children. He doesn't really care about having kids, but he said it would be okay, if I did. He likes nothin' better than pleasin' me…or anyone, really." She smiled tenderly, then jutted her chin. "But I won't tell Daddy, because he told me not to bother comin' around. He insulted Buck, and he insulted me, and it is up to him to apologize."

"Oh, Neva, I can see your point, but you and your daddy are just goin' round in circles with that kind of thinkin'. He misses you, and he needs you. He is a mess, not eatin' right and growin' mold in his refrigerator. What if he dropped dead tomorrow, like Mama?" She thought Uncle Doyle might do that from food poisoning in his own kitchen.

"There is so much that went with Mama," she said, her voice cracking. "Things that should have been said but had been put off. And now it is too late."

Neva stared at her.

"Don't waste time with pride, Neva."

Then, at the moment that she was thinking, *There; I got that out,* congratulating herself for not missing the opportunity, so enthused at her accomplishment that she was trying to come up with more that would seal the healing between father and daughter, there came horrified shouts from the arena, the type of shouts that caused the blood to run cold.

She and Neva about ripped their necks off turning.

A horse had lost its footing rounding a barrel. For a horrified instant, it seemed the world held its breath as the horse desperately tried to find ground. Then the horse went over on its side, and the small rider shrieked.

"Oh, Lord...that's little Pammy," Neva said and spurred her horse toward the arena.

As she jumped off Lulu and dropped the reins to the ground, Rainey saw Harry sprinting for the fence. It seemed as if she blinked, and he was through the cable fence and running across the arena toward the girl with all his might. The girl's horse, having scrambled to his feet, just about ran Harry down, but at the last minute, not breaking stride, Harry veered out of the way.

He was pushing a man out of the way by the time Rainey and the others got to the girl.

"I'm a doctor," she heard him say and watched him go down on his knees beside the child.

The little girl was crying, "My leg...my leg," and beside her a wild-eyed woman was saying, "My baby! Oh, baby!"

Harry took the girl's hand, made her lie back and leaned over her, seeming to capture her eyes in a hypnotic manner. "We're gonna take care of you, honey. I'm a doctor. It's hurt, but it isn't anything we can't take care of."

She was about twelve and small for her age, Rainey saw. Tears streaked her face, but her eyes locked onto Harry's, and her cries stopped.

He jerked off his shirt and spread it over her and called for someone to get something more to cover her. Rainey ran and got her mother's pillow and sweater, and thought to grab the last of the napkins in case they could be needed.

Returning with her things, she pressed them on Harry and knelt beside him to help. She saw then the full extent of the child's broken leg. A bloody stain was spreading on the girl's pant leg. She looked at Harry's face and could read nothing. Someone, probably J.T., called attention to the blood and said he had a knife for cutting away the pants, but Harry tersely said to leave it alone until they got to the hospital.

He made all his examinations with one hand, never letting go of the child's hand gripping him. This made his effort to remove her boot difficult, and Rainey, seeing his intent, did it for him and reported that the circulation in her toes was okay. Only then did he seem to realize it was she who was assisting.

He said to the girl, "You're gonna be the envy of all the kids at school, with a cast for everyone to sign," making certain to speak to her as he and Rainey moved her injured leg to position a folded blanket between it and her good one, taking her mind off what was going on.

"I need belts, strips of anything to tie her legs together."

Belts and girth straps and rope were instantly produced, as if coming out of the sky. Rainey had done this once before with a cousin, and she was able to work with him and his one available hand to secure the child's legs together.

A Bronco appeared, and Harry swiftly lifted the girl from the dirt and placed her in the back seat. He hopped out and assisted the hysterical mother in beside her daughter, and then rejoined the two at the girl's feet.

The Bronco started off, and Rainey stood there, holding the puppy by the lead, watching the figures through the dusty back window as the vehicle drove away as fast as possible over the clumps of grass.

"He's a doctor," Neva said beside her.

"Yes," she said. Of all the things he could have been, she had not thought of this. She supposed she could understand more why he had been wanting to get away. She could imagine a doctor's life must be very stressful.

It looked like he wasn't getting away far enough, though.

CHAPTER 9

Pennies In Our Pockets

Rainey drove to the hospital in Buck's truck. It had a true truck transmission and difficult clutch. She about ran into the back of a little Fiat when she stopped in the parking lot.

Upon entering through the emergency doors, she was immediately set upon by the child's mother, who pressed Harry's shirt to Rainey and proceeded to thank her in an overwhelmingly sincere fashion for bringing Harry to the arena. The woman credited Harry's very presence as the sole cause for her daughter not suffering any internal injuries. In fact, she seemed to credit Rainey for Harry's very presence in the world and appeared possessed of the belief that Rainey had known he would be needed and had therefore brought him deliberately to save the day.

Rainey thought the woman was either on drugs or needed some.

"Perhaps you should speak to the doctors," she said, trying to guide the woman to a chair in the hall and looking around for a nurse to help. She had a sense that the woman, having held herself together by a thread through her daughter's emergency, was now giving way to her hysteria with gratefulness, in the way of someone who has perhaps been taking her child for granted.

"Oh, I could have lost her," the woman repeated a number of times. She only barely sat in the chair and then popped up, about to grab the man mopping the floor and thank him, too, except that she was taken in hand by a nurse and led away to sign forms.

For a moment Rainey wondered about her mother's pillow and sweater, and then she decided to give them up for lost— her mother would probably have been thrilled to know her old things had seen a crisis—and turned to find Harry.

A nurse at the desk said that she had seen him disappear moments before into the men's room. Clutching his shirt, Rainey went to stand beside the door. She wanted to give him his shirt immediately. No doubt he felt odd walking around a hospital half bare. He would be cold. He had hard, wiry muscles, not an ounce of fat to provide warmth.

She stood there, smelling the hospital smell, which reminded her of her mother breathing her last in a hospital room, when she should have been breathing that last at home. She blinked to clear her teary vision and turned her thoughts to Harry.

It was amazing to learn he was a doctor. And she was a little annoyed that he had not told her, although she could not honestly find a reason why he should have. Would she have been as astonished to learn he was an airline pilot, or an IRS agent? She saw now that in her mind, for some reason, he had absolutely been a stockbroker, which, in retrospect, made her very shortsighted.

A sound reached her. Retching. From inside the men's room.

It seemed pretty silly, but she thought she recognized it as being Harry's retching.

She placed a tentative hand on the door and called through the crack, "Harry?"

No answer, except a cough.

She went inside and found him bent over a toilet. Immediately she soaked paper towels.

"You are in a men's bathroom," he said, straightening.

"I've been in one before." She went to dab one of the wet towels over his face.

"Why does that not surprise me?" Scowling, he snatched the towel from her hand and wiped his face.

"I was only tryin' to be of assistance," she said, swallowing. The sense of needing to fall through the floor swept over her like a wave and made her angry.

A man came through the door and stopped dead, staring at her in surprise, then checking the door plaque, as if to make certain he had the right to be there.

"I was just leavin'," she said, lifting her chin and breezing away from Harry and past the man, resisting the urge to shut his mouth for him.

Harry was right behind her.

"I brought Buck's truck," she said, thrusting his shirt at him and continuing on toward the exit at a pace just shy of running.

She heard his boots tap rapidly behind her on the tile flooring.

"Hey, what'd I say?" He grabbed her arm.

She gazed into his eyes and felt all manner of forceful emotional turmoil, which was both perplexing and embarrassing.

"Why do men always say that?" she asked, taking the offensive.

"What?"

"'What'd I say?' Just by askin', you know that you said an insulting and hurtful thing."

He stared at her with surprise. And then a nurse called to him. "Pammy would like to see you."

Confusion swept his face. Rainey told him that she would wait in the truck and hurried away, pushing out the glass doorway, tears threatening. She walked quickly, thinking. He certainly had not said anything to bring this on. And the child was okay—Rainey herself had had her leg badly broken and knew the child would recover and now have a story to tell.

Her brother's voice echoed in memory: *You're just too sensitive, Rain.* He had told her that since she was a child and always said it with his condemning frown, as if being sensitive was a fault needing to be scrubbed away.

Sometimes she thought that she had worked so hard at not being too sensitive that she had lost the ability to know what she felt at all.

Looking up, she suddenly saw a purple truck in the place where she had thought she'd left Buck's red one. Then she realized that it *was* Buck's truck and that the light from the pole lamp made it look purple. She went over and got behind the wheel, stuck the key in and sat there thinking for several long minutes, all thoughts that, one way or another, ended up being, *Well, I'll be danged, he's a doctor.*

She turned the key, and the truck rumbled loudly. She drove over to the doors, and a minute later Harry emerged, walking with his long-legged saunter out from the shadowed entrance into the dimly lit portico.

"She's going to be okay, isn't she?" Rainey said, as he got into the seat, folding in his long frame.

He nodded. "Her leg has two bad breaks but there's no evidence of internal injuries. She's young and will most likely heal fast." He rubbed a hand over the back of his head.

She searched his face surreptitiously, then looked away

quickly before he could notice. She thought he looked a little pale, but not terribly sick.

She shifted and headed down the drive to the street, telling him that Buck and Neva had taken care of the pup, her horse and her rig, and would get them to Uncle Doyle's, while in her mind she had a running argument with herself, wondering all about him and telling herself that none of it was her business and that she didn't care, either.

Seeing a Sonic Drive-In, she was turning in even as she asked him if he wanted anything to eat. She pulled into a stall, carefully, so as not to knock the extended mirrors on Buck's truck.

"I think I'll get a foot-long hot dog with chili, and some fries."

He studied the menu for a minute and said, "I'll take a cheeseburger with everything, and milk."

"Milk? Do you think that's a good idea, especially with a burger?" she asked.

She had begun to suspect that he had a grave illness. It all fit. He might have some sort of brain tumor or other horrible illness, which had caused him to throw up, not his head injury. Maybe that was why he had come away from his family—to spare them his suffering, which he knew only too well, because he was a physician.

"I'm fine. And I like milk—does a body good, you know."

She frowned, but turned to call their order into the speaker phone, and then they sat there in awkward silence. Rainey drummed her fingers on her open window.

"I sometimes throw up when I see a person in pain," he said.

She looked at him.

"I guess I throw up when I have pain, too...but mostly it's when I see another person's pain. It's no big deal. It's like some people get nosebleeds. They just do."

"That must be a difficult reaction for a doctor," she said.

"It is," he said and turned a bleak gaze out the windshield.

Watching him, she recalled him bending over the little girl, recalled the intensity of his eyes that had been all for the girl and how his voice had been calm and reassuring and his hands capable in the manner of a man who knew what had to be done and had taken hold to do it.

"You didn't appear about to throw up when you took care of Pammy," she said. "You took care of her and got her to the hospital before you threw up. My first husband, Robert, fainted at the sight of blood. Out like a light, no matter what. Once I was chopping carrots and about cut my finger off. I called for him to come help me, and I ended up having to wrap my finger in a paper towel, step over him and drive myself to the hospital. I got blood all over his BMW."

As she had hoped, he gave that lazy, sad smile she had begun to associate with him when he was amused.

"Why do I think you bloodied his BMW on purpose?" he said.

"I didn't…but I was glad."

The girl appeared with their food. Rainey didn't want to put the tray on the window of Buck's truck; some people didn't like doing that to their vehicles. She brought the food into the truck.

Harry produced several bills and told the girl to keep the change.

That the tip was a substantial one was evident from the girl's broad grin and eager nod.

Rainey looked over at Harry, who was carefully unwrapping his hamburger with his long-fingered, broad-palmed hands. Her gaze lingered on his hands, remembering how competently and tenderly they had ministered to the hurt girl.

She had to tear her eyes away from those hands, but their image remained to echo in the back of her mind.

* * *

They were both curiously silent as they returned to Uncle Doyle's. Rainey was wanting a bath and wondering if she would have to drive back into town with Buck's truck, as she had left too hurriedly to coordinate plans, had simply caught the keys Buck tossed her.

When she mentioned this, Harry said he would take the truck to town for her if need be.

"You wouldn't know where you were goin'," she said, somewhat surprised, yet impressed by his willingness.

"How big is the town?" he answered reasonably.

Then the truck's headlights lit upon Neva's pickup and small, two-horse trailer, the horse's tail hanging out, parked beside Rainey's own bigger rig in Uncle Doyle's graveled drive. Her heart leaped with the hope that her cousin and uncle had reconciled.

This proved to be something of the case, if not perfectly correct.

Neva was in the house with her father, with the door open and light shining through, and Buck was sitting out in Neva's pickup truck, listening to the radio, twanging country music that he could, and did, drink beer by.

"That dog don't much like men," he said, leaning out the truck window into the silvery glow of the pole lamp when Rainey went over to give him the keys to his pickup and thank him for the use of it. "Ever' time I go to get out of this truck, he growls."

Harry was bending over petting the pup, who had come running and wiggled his entire body back and forth between Rainey and Harry.

Watching, Buck qualified, "Well, I guess he likes Harry. I must smell bad to him." He gestured with his beer. "Neva's on in the house. I didn't think I should go in. I think I rile that old man just by sight of me. I think he has somethin' against facial hair."

Rainey tried to reconcile the man she stared at with the man her cousin had described. Then Buck was calling to Harry, asking him to have a look at his elbow that was paining him when he bent it a certain way.

Rainey stepped back and watched Harry speak to Buck through the window. He went so far as to have Buck display said elbow. She had the uncharitable thought that Buck's problem was likely from too much lying around and lifting beer.

Turning from the men, she went to the house. Neva met her at the door. Rainey figured she was probably keeping close to the screen door in order to breathe the fresh air. Uncle Doyle sat at the table in a swirling cloud of gray cigarette smoke.

Neva reported that she had given Rainey's mare alfalfa but had not grained her, not knowing how much Rainey usually gave the horse. Then she said that she had just gotten off the phone with Juanita, Pammy's mother.

"She told me Pammy's doin' real good. Her leg hurts some, but they've given her something for it, and she's watchin' the Disney Channel. I think they need to give Juanita something. She sounded on the very verge, I'll tell you."

"Juanita was born on the verge and just went over from there," Uncle Doyle said. "She's a pothead," he explained, then puffed good on his cigarette.

Then Harry was coming in and Uncle Doyle was offering coffee all around. By the small talk that was made, Rainey was certain that her cousin had not told her father about her marriage. In fact, Uncle Doyle seemed to behave as if Buck was not sitting out there a couple hundred feet from his back door, and

Neva, wearing the desperate look of a woman balancing the affections of two men, seemed intent on not calling attention to it, either.

"I bought some cinnamon rolls," Rainey said, unable to think of anything else to do but present some food. She brought the rolls and plates to the table, and the sight of them appeared to jar Neva into motion.

"I can't stay to eat. I gotta go. Are you leavin' tomorrow, Rainey?" Her eyes pleaded with her to stay.

"Not until evenin'. I'll make chicken pot pie for supper. You all come over. Six o'clock."

Neva blinked and then looked at her father. Rainey glanced at Uncle Doyle, who frowned down at his coffee cup but did not make a comment. Neva looked back at Rainey and nodded, hesitated, and then went over and kissed her father's dry cheek before leaving.

Rainey went out the door with her cousin and, standing there, rubbing her arms against the fall chill, she watched Neva hurry across the yard beneath the light of a rising moon to Buck's truck, where he now sat. It seemed like she had to wake him. Then she stuck her head in the window and kissed him in the darkness, where Rainey couldn't see, although she witnessed her cousin's leg come clear off the ground.

She watched until the red taillights of Neva's and Buck's vehicles were getting small down the drive. Then she looked down to see the puppy sitting right beside her feet. She touched his head quickly and gave in to scratching him behind the ears. Satisfied, he settled himself against the wall by the door, as if taking his place. She regarded him for a moment, and then went back inside the smoky glow of the kitchen, where Uncle Doyle was explaining about his weak knee and telling Harry the story of how as a boy he had been run over by a tractor. Harry's being a doctor apparently brought out people's need to speak of their infirmities.

Taking up her coffee, she leaned against the counter, listening to the familiar story of Uncle Doyle almost losing his leg. She watched the enjoyment of the telling on her uncle's lean, weathered face and the way Harry sat forward at the table, as if listening intently, with the quirk of that sad smile on his lips. She wondered what type of doctor he was—perhaps by perfect fate a bone doctor.

When her uncle had finished his tale, she said, "Neva and Buck are married, Uncle Doyle. She is not living in sin with him."

She felt perfectly justified in interfering by both the need for expediency and her experience with what happened when people hid things that needed to be said. She intended to see Uncle Doyle and Neva put to rights before she left the following evening for Amarillo. She had a feeling her mother was right on her shoulder, giving her the words.

Uncle Doyle's head came around, his deep-set eyes widening, a mixture of emotions flying across his face: surprise, dismay, anger.

"There's no use in gettin' all mad over it," Rainey said before he could find any words.

Then she proceeded to tell her uncle how he would surely be needed soon in the capacity of grandfather, which she thought might be just the idea to warm his heart, as he had always wanted a number of boys. One thing that had been a great disappointment to Uncle Doyle, she knew, was having only one child and that being a daughter.

"Well, just think of it, Uncle Doyle…" she said and presented in great detail the picture of boys racing around him, while he taught them to drive the tractor and grow alfalfa and dry and bale it to the perfection for which he himself was known. She saw the anger on his face slip into thoughtfulness.

"It seems to me that Buck will also be just the man to help you with cuttin' and haulin' hay, and he's bound to give Neva a lot of little boys to do the same thing. I think he looks like a man who'll give off boys, don't you, Harry?"

Harry jumped in with the spirit of things and agreed. "Bound to," he said. Rainey was very proud that he didn't let the facts of life get in the way.

About all Uncle Doyle said to everything was, "Well, it's done...and I don't guess I can shoot him." He said those gruff words in a decidedly accepting manner, she thought.

Satisfied that she had things going in the right direction, she left the men at the table talking over old joint injuries and went upstairs to take a nice long hot soak, which for her was the equivalent of tossing back several fortifying jiggers of Jack Daniel's.

Running the water hot enough to fill the room with steam, she squirted shampoo into the stream, filling the tub with bubbles. Shedding her clothes, she swept up her hair and stepped into the sudsy wet warmth. Deeper and deeper she sank her body, until her shoulders were under, only her knees and head sticking out, and inhaled the moist air, relishing being alone. When she was thoroughly warmed, she spread her wet washcloth on the cool enamel back of the tub and reclined with her head resting on a folded hand towel, lazily watching water drip from the tarnished chrome faucet.

Plop...plop...plop. The drips formed, slowly growing silver and plump, like life, until, one by one, they overgrew and fell into the sudsy water.

Lifting her foot, she toed the drop, wiping it away. She watched another form, and when it was about to drop, she touched her toe to it, too, wiping the water from the sharp edge of the faucet. She toed the opening of the faucet, into which her toe wriggled neat and smooth.

She had a moment of panic, when her toe seemed to be stuck, but it came free, and with thankfulness, she sank her foot beneath the warm water, lay back and listened to the water drip. *Plop…plop…plop…*

Pictures plopped into her mind with each drip, coming slowly, one after the other.

Plop, and it was Harry, gazing at her with haunted eyes when he asked to be taken to a hotel.

Plop, and it was Harry at breakfast, digging into her biscuits and gravy.

Plop, and it was Uncle Doyle, all hurt when he spoke of his daughter's betrayal of him with the man of her dreams.

Plop, and it was Harry, running across the dirt to the injured girl, so intent he had almost been run down by a horse.

Plop, plop, plop, and it was Buck in the truck, and Neva running to kiss him, and the pup at Rainey's heels, and her mother's whispered voice, *Oh, honey, I have to tell you…*

We can sure live a lifetime in a moment, can't we, Mama? she whispered, *Whether we want to or not.*

She did not realize that she had dozed off until a knock at the door startled her.

"Rainey, did you fall asleep?"

"Oh. I guess I did."

She sat up, feeling warm and fuzzy and a little like asking him to come in. "I'm okay, though."

"Well…just checking," he said in something of a shy voice. "I'll be down in the kitchen."

"Okay."

She was sure he was saying, "I'm here, and I'm ready to tell my story."

CHAPTER 10

Out Where It Gets Lonesome

When Rainey came downstairs she was wearing her blue robe over her nightgown, and she knew she smelled lovely, as a woman fresh from a bath always does. She had in fact spritzed herself with the expensive perfume Helen had given her. She had done this before realizing, stopped, and been very annoyed with herself and stuffed the bottle way to the bottom of her purse.

She stopped in the doorway to see Harry at the table, his head bent over a small brown box, and his dark hair catching the shine of the overhead light.

He looked up at her. A thick strand of hair fell over his forehead. His gaze quickly swept her from head to toe, and then came back up to her eyes. She jerked the belt of her robe tighter and wished she'd remembered to put on socks.

"Gosh, it's freezing in here," she said, hurrying past him to slam down the window over the sink. "I guess we could light the furnace."

Rubbing her arms, she turned to face him, but he had again bent his head over the brown box on the table.

With some surprise, she saw that the box was the old fifties radio that had sat gathering dust on the second shelf of the microwave cart. Her eyes widened as she saw he was poking inside the back of it, while it crackled with static.

"Shouldn't you unplug it while you do that? You might get shocked. Freddy was fiddlin' in the back of a radio once and got shocked so bad he lost his hearing for three days. Scared us all to death."

Slowly he turned his head to look over his shoulder. "Just how many husbands have you had?"

"Well...two. Why?"

He frowned. "By my count, Freddy is number three."

"You are counting?" This was interesting.

He blinked, and he actually blushed, she was sure of it.

Returning his gaze to the bowels of the radio, he said that he had not been exactly counting, but that he seemed to recall a Robert and a Monte, and now here was a Freddy.

"Freddy's my brother. Robert and Monte are my ex-husbands," she said in a clarifying manner. "Robert was number one and Monte number two and gone now for two years. Well, not my husband for two years, but he does show up every three or four weeks to borrow money."

She bent, peering over his shoulder. "I really think you should unplug that thing."

His brown eyes came round to hers, close enough for her to see the gold flecks in them.

"Then I can't tell if all the tubes are tight," he said.

"Oh."

She came up straight and occupied herself with making certain her robe was folded over her gown. He returned to the radio, as if she were not there.

"Do you know what you're doin'?" she asked.

"Pretty much," he said. He carefully adjusted the tuner, and the music became stronger. "Old radios are a hobby. I have about a dozen—radios, not hobbies. The tubes have to warm."

She thought, A doctor with old radios as a hobby. This is interesting.

The music was blues, out of an Austin station. She remarked about the miracle of hearing music from an album turning so far away, coming over the airwaves, skipping over the hills and flowing across the range and over cattle and right into the box in the small kitchen.

"It is something of a miracle," she said, cocking her head to listen.

He nodded at her with satisfaction. "They don't make 'em like this anymore."

She looked at the radio and then at him. "Is that the kind of music you like?" she asked disbelievingly.

"You need to broaden your musical taste," he said, with that hint of a grin.

She said that she imagined he liked opera, too. "And I bet you drink expensive wine and cappuccino or expresso and whatnot."

"Yeah. *Ex*presso and whatnot."

"I know it is *es*presso," she said into his grin. "I may not drink it, but I know what it is."

At that moment the differences between them were so very stark, she in her cotton and bare feet, with her preference for cowboy coffee and country music. Even in his denim, he would not be taken for any man she had ever known. What did he think of this *thing* between them?

Then she jumped up and went to the shallow pantry, from which she drew a slim, green bottle.

"Dandelion wine. Uncle Doyle makes it every spring. Want to try it?"

"Sure."

She brought glasses, but she could not find a corkscrew. He took the bottle from her, produced a small pocket knife, and within a minute of delicate operation had it uncorked.

"You seem very proficient at that," she said.

"I've taken out a couple of bullets," he said.

"Is this harder or easier?" She thought of him taking bullets out of flesh and wondered if he'd had the same expression.

At her question, he looked surprised. "Actually, I guess flesh is harder, only because one is so conscious of it being alive."

She studied his face, couldn't keep her eyes from it.

He poured a couple of swallows into a glass, and then he tasted, while she watched him with a curious expression. "Not bad," he said, seeming highly pleased. "Not bad at all."

Delight washed over her. She gestured for him to pour both glasses and, watching his deft hand movements and the glistening liquid swirl, she stretched her legs. He passed her a glass and waited to tap his own to hers. She felt him watching her as she took her first sip.

"Uncle Doyle has won awards for his wine," she said.

"Your uncle is a man of many talents," he said. He looked at her a moment, and then he sat back and drank deeply.

"You are a far cry away from where you were this time last night," she said.

"I guess I'm a much farther cry from where I was a week ago," he said frankly, and she knew that he was about to tell her everything, and she was so very glad she had not pried it from him with insistent questions but had waited for him to be ready.

CHAPTER 11

Land of the Living

"Just what would you like to know?" he asked her, his mouth forming his amused, sad grin.

"Well, all of it," she said, causing him to blink. "Start with your family." In her experience, everything in a person's life, good or bad, began with one's family.

With a chuckle, he lifted his glass to tap hers in a silent toast, after which he downed a good swallow and then proceeded to tell her that he and the four generations before him were natives of Houston, Texas. His full name was Harrison James Furneaux—a name that seemed very substantial and to fit perfectly with his expensive watch—and that his father always called him Harrison and his mother called him James.

Rainey felt this was a telling point about his parents' relationship. "Do you have brothers and sisters—and what do they call you?" she asked, her mind fitting puzzle pieces together.

"Two older brothers and one younger sister, and they call me

Harrison," he answered just as rapidly. "Most people call me Harrison."

"I like Harry," she said.

That smile came again. "I took it up recently," he said, and regarded her as if to judge her reaction.

"Good idea." Leaning forward, she propped her chin in her hand, in an attempt to show she was keenly listening.

He shifted his eyes away and took a breath, then told her that his father was a physician, as were both of his older brothers. His mother had a career in charity work and sat on the board of a number of charitable organizations.

"People always come to her when they need money—I've seen her make a couple of phone calls and raise a hundred thousand dollars in fifteen minutes."

Rainey, forming vague impressions of a tall, broad-shouldered father and brothers, and a mother in pearls and slim skirts, asked about his sister. He said she had married a doctor and gone to live in New Orleans, where she was embarking on a career in raising great sums of money for charities in the manner of their mother, producing a duplicate image of a woman in pearls in Rainey's mind.

"What kind of doctor are you?" she asked.

He told her that he was a family physician, had just finished his residency. She took this news with the apprehension of any woman who finds the man she is attracted to is likely younger than herself.

"My father was quite disappointed," he said, folding his arms and leaning on the table. "Family physicians do not, as a general rule, achieve the preeminence required in my family. My father would have preferred I be a surgeon and fit in with the family 'team.' Between them, my father and brothers cut and splice all the available organs."

She watched his expression grow grim, as he explained, with a mixture of sarcasm and sadness, that from birth, it was dictated that he would follow in the family footsteps. As it had been presented to him: *This* is what the men of the Furneaux family do. The men of his family were *physicians*—not simply doctors—and the women of the family married physicians, all of them being notable, of course, and it was expected each of them would hold high the flame and pass it along for the next generation.

"And you don't want to do that," she said, wanting him to get the idea that she understood completely.

His eyes, deep-brown, met hers, and he smiled that sad, crooked smile. "Not exactly."

He frowned thoughtfully, passing his hand over the back of his head in a manner she had come to associate with him pondering, and began to tell her that one of his brothers had broken ground when he had dared to show an interest in family practice, too.

"Actually," he explained, "I believe my brother had always wanted to be a veterinarian, but he couldn't bring himself to go that far astray. And after my father worked him over, he decided he had made a mistake with his family practice leanings and that he really wanted to be a surgeon after all. I guess Dad thought I would go along the same way and eventually decide I wanted to be a surgeon, too.

"But I get a little too queasy," he said in an amused confessional manner, "and I simply don't have the inclination." He breathed deeply. "I realized this, and it was a pretty big disappointment to my father, but he could have handled it sooner or later. What he couldn't handle was my conclusion, after going all the way through residency, that I don't really have the inclination to be an especially stellar physician, period."

She broke in with, "Oh, but I think you are a very good doctor. You might not do well for yourself when you have a head injury, but you were very good with Pammy tonight."

Again the crooked smile. "Ah, but a good doctor is not equal to a stellar physician in my family."

He splashed more wine into their glasses, then sat back, saying, "I went to my father and told him I had decided not to continue in general practice…and further, committed pure heresy, by telling him that I had decided to pursue the practice of psychiatry."

"Oh."

"Exactly. You must understand that, to my family, all forms of emotional anguish are a weakness not to be tolerated, and emotional therapy is quackery. In fact, they don't believe in emotions at all. Emotions are not allowed in my family—one leaves them at the door, along with muddy shoes."

Beneath his cavalier tone was the strain of it. The deep hurt. The scene played like an old black-and-white film in her mind, his broad-shouldered giant of a father rising up in his double-breasted suit, while his son stood before him in a collarless silk shirt.

"I imagine your father was rather upset," she said.

"Oh, yes, I'd say that he was upset. You see, this was not the first time I had disappointed him. Two years before this, in the midst of my residency, I had a nervous breakdown."

He watched her, and she looked him in the eye.

"My family is very emotional," she said.

"I had imagined so," he commented with a crooked grin.

His gaze fell to his glass, and he continued. "When I told my father that I had already resigned from the hospital that bore a wing named after our family, I think he would have shot me, if he'd had a gun."

Watching him throw back a good gulp of the wine, she saw etched into the handsome planes of his face the painful disappointment of a son who has fallen short of fatherly expectations.

"He hated that he could not control you," she said.

"Oh, I guess he still manages to control me to an extent," he said. "But not as he wishes."

"So what happened?" she asked after a moment of silence. "He obviously didn't shoot you. Did he disinherit you?"

"Something like that," he said, grinning at her expression. "I think he said something like, 'No son of mine is going to toss his future down the toilet....'"

He looked at the glass in his hand. "I was wise enough to get out of his sight. I spent a few days holed up in my apartment not answering the telephone. My father came over once, to yell at me some more, and then I figured I needed to get out and drive around and think it all over."

"Oh, driving is very good for that," she said.

"If one stays on the road," he said. Then he drank from his glass, his brows knotted with thought. A second later, he leaned forward, his eyes intense.

"For weeks now, I've been struggling to figure out what I really want—to make certain I'm not simply rebelling against my father."

"I don't think you are doing that. I think you are much too careful to do that. You know too much."

She saw appreciation of her comment reflected on his face. Then he sat back, and his gaze drifted to the table. She watched the pondering expression come over his features again. She thought that his eyes were beautiful. He had very long dark eyelashes that a woman would like to kiss.

"How old are you?" she asked.

He blinked, looking a little surprised. "Thirty-one."

"I'll be thirty-five next month."

He looked at her with curious confusion. Then his eyebrows went up, and he ran his gaze over her face, as if both assessing her physical attributes and wondering why she should point out their ages.

Rainey turned her head, reached for the bottle and boldly splashed the last of the wine into each of their glasses, saying, "Well, I think you are already a good doctor. You care. I've always thought that what makes a good doctor is simply wanting to help. Anyone can look up facts in a medical book, but treating the person as a human being is what doctoring is all about."

He inclined his head. "In psychiatry, I can use my training to treat the entire person, body and mind. The deepest wounds are those you can't see, the ones people carry around with them every day."

"Yes, I think so," she said.

"I have to be sure," he said, almost as if he had not heard her agreement. "I know I'll figure it out, and right now I'm going to give myself the time I need to think about it. About what I really want."

He leaned forward and looked at her with those beautiful brown eyes. "You see, this is the first time in my life that I've really thought about what I want to do. I know that sounds strange…but I…well, I guess it's been a lot easier to follow the road mapped out for me by my parents and grandfather. All those physician Furneauxs, you know. Not that it's their fault— my actions are all my own. But my father and the others, they're pretty powerful sorts, and it is a little difficult to question the wisdom of those who have achieved what they all have."

She liked the way he didn't just slip the blame for his lapse all off on his family. She thought of his father. She had seen fathers of the sort she imagined his to be and knew it couldn't have been easy for a son who very naturally wanted to please. A son who marched to a different drummer. What courage it must have taken. She wondered how a father such as his had managed to produce such a special son.

He said, "Once, when I was about fifteen, my father discovered that I wrote music lyrics. Several of us guys at the school I went to had formed a band—I played guitar, not well, but I did play. I wasn't a good student, and I'd already lost a year, because of a car accident just before first grade, and so my father was always pushing me. He tore the paper with my lyrics into pieces and said I was wasting my time. He made me stay at school over the Thanksgiving holidays and study in order to bring my grades up."

His jaw was tight, his eyes far away, as if being drawn back into the past. She imagined the cruelty of it, a child away at school, alone and abandoned by an ambitious father with no charity. She wondered at a mother who would allow such treatment of her child. She saw his father in the double-breasted suit, making a martini after work, standing over his wife, Harry's mother, who wore pearls and a perpetually distracted expression, probably considering whom she could next prevail upon for charity money. Probably his father always stood while insisting everyone else sit. People of power always did that. It was Freddy's habit to pace in front of them all. Of course, their mother had always seemed to emit quiet power, and eventually Freddy would have to sit down, would sort of plop down in disgusted capitulation.

Somehow she found herself telling Harry about her family, first about how Freddy would get so aggravated at the way their father always deferred to their mother.

"In my family, the women generally run things," she said.

"Now why doesn't that surprise me?" he said, his voice low and filled with amusement.

She gave him a condescending look, and then went on to tell the funny story of how, when her mother's sisters would all gather at the house, her daddy would go out back and stay in his workshop that he'd fixed up with a bunk and stove, because he said the women didn't leave him any air to breathe. He might sit out on the porch and when anyone came he'd say, "Better take a good breath now, afore you go inside. The women are suckin' up all the air."

She was pleased to see him smile a true smile.

"It isn't at all that Daddy is weak or passive," she explained, wanting to correctly portray a man she thought was about the best in the world. "What Mama said was that Daddy's easygoin' way was his strength. She said that strong, rough waters can carry a person away and drown them, but still waters run deep, and that still waters will hold a person up."

He gazed at her, and she at him. He said she obviously had special parents.

"Yes," she said, "I did…I do."

She related that her parents had married later than most and that her mother had been thirty when she'd had Freddy and thirty-seven when she'd had Charlene. Then, at forty-seven, her mother had turned up with another baby, which of course had been a shock to everyone.

"Freddy always calls me the 'late child,'" she said, her gaze on the glass in her hands. "I think it was hard on him, another girl in a family where the two women already dominated, not that Charlene is as domineering as Mama was, but she isn't any wallflower, either. And Freddy was in his teens and the type that it probably embarrassed him to death that his mother gave concrete evidence of havin' sex."

He was gazing at her, listening intensely and as if hearing down beyond the words. It was very natural for her to tell him the rest of it—that Freddy and her mother had always seemed to have this battle of wills, and of how she now suspected Freddy's resentment of her stemmed from his having known all along that their mother had conceived her with a lover, instead of their own father.

It was the first time she had spoken the bald truth aloud.

"Mama told it all as she was dyin'," she said, as mystified now as she had been then. "Right there with her dyin', I found out that my real daddy was an oil geologist who'd more or less been passin' through and not the man I called Daddy at all."

She played with her glass as she spoke of it, the words spilling out and rolling away like a string of broken beads.

"We have a lot of emotion in my family," she said. "We acknowledge it, and then what we do with it is try to stamp it out."

She tried for a grin, and then she found herself on her feet and stepping to the counter. She might have gone right out the door into the night, had she not gotten a hold of herself.

"Would you like some coffee?" she asked. "I don't think I ought to filch any more of Uncle Doyle's wine. He usually saves it for Christmas presents."

Harry looked startled. "Yes, umm…yes, coffee sounds good."

As she went about preparing the coffee, getting out the cups, she sensed him behind her, his eyes on her back. And then he came up beside her, leaned on the counter. She glanced at him, saw he was looking at her as if he wanted to say something but didn't know what.

"Did your father know?" he asked finally.

She glanced at him through a stray curl and nodded. "Oh, I'm sure of it. Mama wasn't a person who would lie about somethin' like that to her husband. You know how some women might sneak a less expensive brand of coffee in on their husband by puttin' it in the expensive can? Well, Mama wouldn't even do that."

He looked a little surprised, as if he had never considered that someone would do that.

"Women do stuff like that all the time," she told him. "You know, go out when they are by themselves and buy exactly what their husband told them not to but never let on. Daddy never would tell Mama what she could or could not buy, and she never hid what she paid for anything, either."

She saw them again, her mother and father in those last moments. "I could tell he knew it all…by the way he sat there with his head bent but still holding her hand. I'm sure Freddy knew, too. I saw it on his face, you know, the way you know somebody knows somethin'."

He nodded.

"Charlene was stuck over by the door, cryin'. I myself had to lean close, with Charlene makin' all that racket."

He awoke her from the memory when he very gently tucked the stray curl behind her ear. She gazed into his sympathetic eyes, then dropped her gaze to his throat and to his chest, where it crossed her mind to lay her head.

He asked, "Why do you think your mother told, after holding the secret for so long?"

She sighed. "Well, I guess it really wasn't a secret, was it? Daddy and Freddy both knew. Maybe Charlene, but Charlene never can keep a secret, so I think it more than likely she didn't. She was makin' such a fuss, she still may not know it."

She turned from wanting to lay her head upon his chest and pushed the button on the coffeemaker.

"We haven't talked about it. Charlene hasn't mentioned if she knows or not." She thought about that, then said, "I think

Mama knew that Freddy would tell me just as soon as he could after she died. She knew Daddy wouldn't. Daddy can't ever talk about anythin' so intimate. He can't even say the word *pregnant*. But Freddy…oh, he wouldn't dare say anything as long as she was alive, because he'd have to deal with her, but no doubt he'd have been glad to tell it all when she was gone, and she didn't want it to come to me like that. She wanted to tell me herself."

She realized she had been staring at the floor for some moments, when a thought occurred to her. She looked intently at him.

"How did you come to be out on that road last night?"

He looked confused at her abrupt question. "I'd wrecked my car…I'd been visiting a friend, and…"

Just then the puppy started barking furiously outside. Then came the sound of him running away, barking.

"Ye gods, that could be coyotes!" Rainey cried and ran out the door.

Vaguely she heard Harry call her, but she kept on going, anxious to see to the safety of the puppy. This was as wild a country as was left anywhere in her estimation, and she'd heard numerous stories of coyote treachery.

Racing out across the yard toward the alfalfa field and fading sound of the puppy's barking, she called, "Puppy! Here, boy!"

"Rainey!" Harry caught up to her.

"The coyotes will kill him!" Keeping going, she peered as hard as she could into the darkness toward the sound of the puppy's barking growing ever distant. She could faintly see the corral to her left. She heard Lulu snort, heard the mare's hooves thump the ground. She expected any moment to hear the sound of a dog fight…the puppy being set upon and torn to pieces.

"Oh, pup…come here, pup." Then she stepped into a patch of stickers. "Ow ow! Dang…ouch… ouch!"

"Rainey?" His dark shadow appeared to her left this time.

"I've stepped into a bunch of stickers," she said, trying to stand on one foot.

"Jeez, you're out here barefooted." His hand took hold of her arm.

"Well, I didn't have time to get my boots. Oww...dang!"

"Here, I'll pick you up."

"Oh...he's quit barkin'," she said, divided by pain and worry. "Come here, pup!" Then, "Ouch...ooh... I hate these dang stickers."

"If there had been dangerous coyotes out here, I suppose you were goin' to fight them barefooted."

She did not appreciate his tone. "You don't need to get in a snit. Coyotes are scared of people. All I had to do was come out here yellin'."

"You did that. Now, are you gonna let me carry you back, or are you gonna be stuck here all night?"

"I can pull them out...." She gave off several ouches and ows in between calling again for the puppy.

"He probably doesn't know to come to a call," he told her.

Then he stuck something in her hand. A butcher knife.

The next instant, he took hold of her arm and jerked her up and threw over his shoulder.

"I am not a bag of potatoes."

"No, you sure aren't. You're more like a ton of bricks." He stumbled and struggled for footing.

"Don't drop me!"

"Then be still."

Realizing she held the butcher knife, she worried that he might fall and one of them would get stabbed. She shut her mouth and hardly dared to breathe the rest of the way back to the house, where he deposited her in a chair with a very audible "Whew!"

"See if the puppy is comin'," she told him.

He cast her a raised eyebrow. "I might have a heart attack, and you're still worryin' about that dog." He was gasping for breath. "You are no feather, you know."

She didn't reply to that nonsense. Sometimes a good look was sufficient.

He stepped to the open door, gazed out, said, "Not yet," and then closed the door.

She said, "It could have been a pack of wild dogs. They are worse than coyotes."

"It might have been a skunk or racoon or a deer," he said reasonably.

"We would have smelled a skunk. And a racoon might drown him in the creek. They do that."

As she looked at him, tears suddenly welled up in her eyes. It was the silliest thing. She blinked, but they kept coming.

"You wanted to get rid of him," Harry said.

"I don't want him to get eaten up alive, or shot with a wild pack of dogs."

He crouched in front of her and brushed her hair from her face. "It's all right to want to keep him, Rainey."

She brushed the tears from her cheeks. "I'll stop in a minute. It's just…oh, just a bunch of stuff."

"Okay," he said calmly.

She breathed easier when he stood and stepped backward. Bringing one of her feet across the opposite knee, she began to pull out the sandspurs. She had always hated this. Sandspurs had a sort of hook, and she tried to minimize the pain by squeezing them out.

"Here, let me do it," he said, again crouching in front of her and brushing her hands aside. "Look over there at the sink."

"Don't just yank them."

"Why?" he said and yanked one.

"Ow! Dang. They have hooks on them."

"They do?" And he yanked another and another in quick succession. He had the sharp nodules removed from both feet practically before she could get a good breath. Two left thorn slivers embedded beneath the skin. When he would have used his pocket knife to remove them, she jerked away and said she would get a needle and do it herself.

"You didn't want to be a surgeon, remember?"

He asked where he could find some glue.

"Glue?" She looked incredulous. "Well, there in that drawer, I think there's a bottle of Elmer's."

He put a dab of glue on each sliver and told her when the dried glue was pulled away, no doubt the sliver would come, too. She looked skeptical.

As they waited for the glue to dry, there came a sound on the porch. Instantly, Rainey was hopping on one foot to the door and opening it.

"Oh!" Sinking to her knees, she gathered the panting puppy to her, crying a little again.

CHAPTER 12

All Sorts of Desires

She decided the puppy had to stay inside, to eliminate the chance of him being killed by coyotes or running off with wild dogs. This had suddenly become a very imminent possibility to her.

Taking the rug from the back door, she put it in front of the bookshelves crowding the corner and had the puppy lie down. "That way Uncle Doyle won't stumble over him when he gets up."

Straightening, she looked at Harry, who stood looking at her. Shyness seemed to come over both of them.

"It's really late," she said, shadowed thoughts of an exciting nature flittering at the corners of her mind.

His gaze shifted away from her, and he rubbed his hand over the back of his head. "Yeah, well, I think I'll just sleep down here…in the living room."

Oh? "No one can sleep on that couch."

"I'll sleep on the floor."

On the floor? "Now, don't be silly. There are two perfectly good beds upstairs and a perfectly respectable four feet between them. In case you are worried."

She felt her cheeks flush. Now that he'd said he was going to sleep downstairs, she was suddenly aware of all sorts of desires.

He shifted his gaze from hers. "I'd just as soon sleep down here. I think I'll read for a while."

Pulling her robe tighter around her, she said, "Well...I'll get you some blankets."

Upstairs, she tore the blankets and pillow from the twin bed he'd slept in the previous night, took them down and made him a pallet on the carpet, wall-to-wall and thick, fortunately.

"There, that will beat the couch, anyway," she said, straightening.

"Thanks." He stood in the archway, looking at her quite frankly.

They gazed at each other.

"I'm leavin' for the Amarillo rodeo tomorrow night," Rainey said, her mouth going dry. "You're welcome to come with me, if you want."

He blinked, then said intently, "Thanks. I guess I don't know yet what I'll be doing."

"Suit yourself." Disappointed that he had not leaped at the opportunity, she turned quickly, not wanting him to see her face. "Good night."

"Good night, Rainey," came his warm voice after her.

She paused and looked back at him. He gazed at her with an amused grin and very warm eyes. She whirled and raced up the stairs, away from him.

She jumped into the bed and pulled the covers up tight, as if to hold herself there and all together. She squeezed her eyes closed, but she couldn't shut out the feeling of being a fool.

Oh, it was the way a woman without a man was given to thinking.

It had happened so quickly, the passion rising until it seemed to explode in full bloom between them. She supposed it had been building there all along, since she had picked him up off the highway until they were sitting looking at each other across the table in the warm light of the kitchen and the further warmth of the dandelion wine.

He was not married, but did he have a girlfriend? Someone waiting back home for him? She was annoyed with herself for not asking. On second thought, she was glad she had not asked. It would have seemed far too obvious on her part.

Why in the world had she gone and told him all that stuff about her family and, further, asked him to go to Amarillo with her? Had she totally lost her mind?

Just then she remembered the coffeemaker. *Good heavens!* They had totally forgotten to drink the coffee, and she could not recall switching the maker off.

She thought of him lying on the living room floor, where she would have to pass by, and no telling what that would look like…what he would think.

But she could not leave the coffeemaker to burn the house down, so finally, with annoyance and dread, she got out of bed and stealthily slipped down the stairs. A lamp burned in the living room. Then she saw with relief that he was asleep, with a book lying open facedown across his chest. She imagined how it had been, how he had read for all of thirty seconds, before dropping instantly to sleep. Not one minute spent ruminating about raging emotions.

She had the urge to go over and give him a good whack.

And then her gaze fell to the foot of the blankets, and she saw the puppy lying there.

The puppy and she regarded each other for long seconds, in which the puppy kept his head down but softly thumped his tail. *Two of a kind.*

Turning, she went along the beam of light from the living room, through the kitchen and to the coffeemaker, switched it off and made the house safe. Then she slipped back up the stairs, sat on the bed and rubbed her feet with lotion, soothing where the sandspurs had been.

The glue had worked very well to remove the tiny splinters. He was a clever person, she thought.

Turning out the light, she slipped beneath the covers and lay staring up into the darkness, so dark without a moon.

Her mother had been so white, lying against the white hospital sheets, and telling it all in a raspy desperate voice, and then, in the end saying, "I have loved you all with all the love I had to give." Her voice so faint, and so amazingly happy.

She shut her eyes against it all, pushed the useless anger aside.

Her eyes popped open. She shut them again, and her mind whirled like mice chasing themselves on a wheel. Uncle Doyle and Neva...make chicken pie for tomorrow's supper...the puppy...Charlene would not appreciate the puppy...Harry.

She had the covers as tangled as her mind and was considering going out and driving around, when she heard her mother's voice, "Now, Rainey hon, why worry when you can pray?"

Oh, Mama, who are you to tell me any of that?

Her mother's face, with its patient and persistent expression, seemed to stare down at her from the darkness.

The psalm came to her: *The Lord is my shepherd, I shall not want...He restoreth my soul....* She repeated it over and over, drifting into sleep and dreaming of her mother's hand upon her brow.

CHAPTER 13

Reach Out and Touch Someone

"I'm takin' the doc here out to learn 'bout puttin' up hay." Uncle Doyle cast her a wave as he headed across the yard. "Don't worry 'bout lunch—we'll go in to the café in town and get us a chicken-fried steak."

Harry waved with his hat and grinned the grin of a boy going off on an adventure.

She stood there a moment at the porch screen door, blinking in the bright light, watching the battered blue pickup truck drive away, realizing it was just as well the men were leaving. She again wore nothing but a big shirt.

She had drunk Uncle Doyle's strong coffee, made herself and the puppy scrambled eggs and toast, which to her notion was not a very substantial start to the day, and cleaned the entire kitchen before she remembered she needed to get some pants on.

The phone rang as she passed it on her way up the stairs.

It was Charlene. Rainey sank down into the unpredictable gooseneck rocker, careful to slide all the way back.

"I'm glad you haven't been murdered yet," her sister said. When Rainey was confused, she explained, "By that guy you picked up."

"Oh. No, we're all fine. He's a doctor." She instantly regretted the absurd prompting that had made her say that, knowing her sister would jump on it.

"He is? Well, why didn't he have somewhere to go? I never heard of a doctor not havin' to go somewhere, like to the golf course. Why was he out on the highway?"

"He had wrecked his car. I told you."

"Well, I imagine a doctor would have Triple A or somethin'."

"He might have. I didn't ask."

"So, here we have a doctor with still no place to go?" Her voice was ripe with suspicion.

"Right now he's off with Uncle Doyle, to help load hay," Rainey answered, getting stubborn.

"Why is a doctor going off to help Uncle Doyle load hay? I've really never heard of such. What is the story on all this?"

"Have you never heard of someone needin' to take time off and have a vacation?" Rainey said. "He's been under a lot of pressure, and he needs to have a little getaway. That's all."

"Well, you don't have to get snippy. I was just thinkin' that you need to be careful. I do worry about you."

"Thank you, Charlene," she said, feeling guilty but not knowing exactly why.

The line hummed for several seconds, and then Charlene said, "Well, Mr. Blaine took me aside yesterday when I stopped in the drugstore. He wants you to come back to your job."

"He does?"

"Yes. He is desperate. Della Mayes is messing up people's prescriptions and generally driving everyone nuts. Mr. Blaine said he'd give you a fifty cent raise. I told him he'd better think in the range of two dollars, at least."

Rainey was surprised to find a homesickness for the drugstore slice into her. She remembered the smell of the old wood and how she always liked to fill her basket with the prescriptions, then go out and deliver them. She'd just had a cardboard box at first to hold the prescriptions, but then she'd found a big picnic basket on sale at Wal-mart, with a red-checked liner and lid. She loved the basket, and she loved waking to a planned day each morning, where she got to chat with other people. It made her feel somewhat personally responsible for helping heal people by delivering their medicines.

It struck her then, how much she had in common with Harry.

"Monte was here, too, for the third time," Charlene said. "He looked desperate, too. I gave him twenty-five dollars for you, so you'll owe it to me. He doesn't ever pay you back, does he?"

"Sometimes he does." Mr. Blaine and Monte were marching across her mind, and it was a couple of seconds before she realized that her sister had gone on talking.

"Freddy and Helen are havin' a little dinner party on Sunday night. They originally wanted it on Saturday, but Daddy refused to come because *Bend of the River* is playin' on the Western Channel, and he didn't want to miss it."

She paused for effect and added, "Freddy told Daddy to bring That Mildred Covington *as a date.*"

"Oh."

Rainey thought of her father, picturing him in one of his white starched shirts and the way he always pulled at the neck. Surely he would not wear a good shirt for Mildred. He wouldn't hardly wear one for Mama.

"Is Daddy goin' to?"

"If Freddy has anything to do with it, he will. He does not care that Mama has been gone less than six months. You know what he said to me? He said, 'Mom is gone, and it won't do Dad any good to stay alone. He might need someone to take care of him soon, anyway.'"

"Is Daddy sick?" Rainey said, alarmed that she might have missed something Charlene had told her.

"No. Freddy's just lookin' ahead, anticipating. He doesn't want to be havin' to take care of Daddy."

It made Rainey sad to think of her father getting sick, and of Freddy saying it like that, like money and convenience were his chief concern, above their father's happiness. *Her father? Did she have a right to think that way?*

"But if Daddy is happy with Mildred, Charlene, that *is* all that matters."

"That Mildred is makin' certain Daddy is happy with her right at this moment," Charlene said in a tone that said she knew how the world worked. "Kaye Upchurch told me That Mildred did this same thing with Dwight Lowe last year after his wife died. That Mildred would have hooked him, too, but he moved to a fancy senior living center out in California with his sister."

Rainey pictured Kaye Upchurch. She was the mayor's wife and knew everything about everyone in town. Rainey also knew that Kaye had had a terrible time with menopause and had for some time taken an antidepressant, which had been a blessing to her. She clamped her jaw shut. She was always careful not to tell what she knew about customers.

Charlene said, "I'll bet if we ask around, we'll find out there's a few more men that widow has cozied up to at one time or another."

"Well…" Rainey looked for a positive response. "She's been widowed for five or six years. She's probably really lonely."

"Oh, Rainey, everybody's lonely at least half the time. She should just get a hobby."

"Well, I guess she has," Rainey said before she thought.

At least that made Charlene laugh full out.

"Oh, Rainey, I know it's true," her sister said, her voice now pliable and warm. "I know Mama is as dead as she'll ever be, but I just do not like this thing with That Mildred. I just don't like it. And it gripes me to pieces to see Daddy actin' like a silly old fool. Freddy thinks he's an old fool, but he isn't, Rainey. Well, except about this stupid Mildred."

"Daddy isn't a fool, Charlene. He never was with Mama."

Charlene sighed heavily. "He's eighty-two, Rainey, and Mama's dyin' has knocked the stuffin's out of him," she said in a mournful tone that slid into desperate. "I just don't know what to do to help him. I just don't know what to *do*."

Rainey thought that if Charlene didn't think she knew the answer, then no one else was going to have a clue.

She found herself saying, "I'll be comin' home, Charlene, Sunday, after the Amarillo rodeo."

"What? You're whisperin', Rainey."

"I said, I'll come home on Sunday."

"Then try to get here in time for Freddy's dinner. It's at seven o'clock. Well, this is long distance, you know, and my story is fixin' to come on. Bye."

"Bye…"

She heard the line click and the dial tone return before hanging up.

For quite a few minutes, Rainey sat in the gooseneck rocker, staring, seeing her sister, her father, the drugstore and the town, with its wide main street and sidewalks, colorful seasonal signs flapping from the streetlamp posts, the Main Street Café and Blaine's Drugstore and the bank on the corner, and the tree-lined neighborhood streets where children and dogs played. Valentine, where she had lived all of her life, except the two years she had been married to Robert.

Quite suddenly, she wished she hadn't told Charlene she was coming home. She didn't feel ready. She thought she might never feel ready. She had the awful fear that maybe she didn't belong in Valentine anymore. Maybe she didn't belong as a Valentine.

Then she realized that she was staring at the thirty-year-old console television set and remembered her sister had said, "My story is comin' on."

All My Children. Charlene had watched that forever.

Wondering if the old television set would even work, she got up and switched it on. The picture was a little hazy and blue, but right there was Erica smiling that brilliant smile, the one she had when she was about to do something wiley.

Rainey had seen the program while visiting their Aunt Pauline down in San Antonio. Aunt Pauline taped it each day while she worked and saved one or two weeks of episodes to watch at once in marathon viewings. She liked them best in bursts, Aunt Pauline said. Rainey had watched with her aunt and gotten caught up on all she had missed in two years of working at Blaine's.

Slipping back into the gooseneck rocker, Rainey thought she would watch, even if the picture was hazy and off-color. The people on the program had much worse problems than she did.

She telephoned Neva at the bank. "I told Uncle Doyle that you and Buck were married." She had begun to worry that her cousin would be annoyed that she had stepped into her business.

"You did?" Neva sounded surprised and relieved at once. "What did he say?" her cousin, the high-powered bank executive, asked breathlessly.

"Not really anything. I guess I didn't give him much of a chance. I pointed out that this meant he would soon be a grandfather. I hope you guys get on that real soon, because he's sure to come around then. Will you pick up some strawberries and bring them out? I bought the cream and then forgot the strawberries."

"Oh, Rainey…maybe it'd be best to cancel. Buck said he might go out with the guys tonight."

"Neva, you manage that bank, don't you?"

"Yes."

"Then manage Buck just a little. You bring him tonight. I can't leave here until I know things are started in the right direction with y'all."

"And what if we come out and things go off in the wrong direction?"

"They won't. Don't even think that way. And you might suggest to Buck that he shave. That might be a help. Tell him, just until you guys have some babies, and then he can have as much hair as he wants."

When she hung up, she thought that she really was her mother's daughter. She was able to correctly arrange everyone's life but her own.

When the phone rang that afternoon, she thought immediately of Charlene. She didn't want to talk to her sister again, but then she told herself to quit being silly. This was Uncle Doyle's phone; anybody he knew could be calling.

A gruff voice on the line said, "This is Farris Wrecker Service. We got Mr. Furneaux's Porsche out of that wash. Is this the right number?"

"Yes, it is. Only he isn't here right now."

A Porsche? She hadn't realized it had been such an expensive car. She pictured him racing down the highway in it, his brown hair blowing in the breeze.

"Well, tell him it's bunged up good, but I don't think it's totaled. Anyway, we got it yeste'dy evenin' and brought it to our lot. We'll keep it thirty days, and unless he notifies us of what he wants done before that, we'll start sellin' parts."

"Can you do that?"

"We do."

"I'll tell him. You better give me your number, just to make certain he has it."

Harry and Uncle Doyle came in about midafternoon: Uncle Doyle went straight up to take a shower, and Harry flopped down on the shady porch. He looked worn slap out. Sweat glistened on his face and dampened his shirt, and a fine layer of dust covered him. After one look, Rainey brought him a glass of iced tea and the note she'd written about the call from Farris Wrecker Service.

"They said if you did not notify them in thirty days what to do with the car, they would start sellin' parts off it. I don't think they can do that, but the man said they would." She eased backward and sat in one of the rockers.

"I guess they can do anything they want. They have the car."

His throat bobbed as he swallowed large gulps of her tea. She hoped he didn't get a headache from drinking the cold liquid so fast. He had an indentation around his head, so she knew he'd worn his hat, but he still looked to have gotten a lot of sun.

Setting the glass aside, he lay all the way down on the porch. She watched his chest rise and fall.

"I just think that is high-handed, saying they'll start sellin' parts," she said. "How can they do that without the title?"

"Most people can do anything they want to, if no one objects." After a minute, he added, "Don't worry over it, Rainey. I'll take care of it. I'll call my insurance agent in a few minutes. Did the guy say how badly it was damaged?" He cracked his eyes at her.

"Bunged up good but not totaled. I still imagine it'll take a lot to get a Porsche fixed."

He nodded and closed his eyes again, eyelashes long against his cheeks.

"My parents bought that car for me as an early present for finishing my residency," he said, eyes still closed.

"Oh," Rainey said. Relationships were all quite complicated, she mused.

She watched him, his chest rising and falling, the hair that blew across his forehead. The puppy got up from his place against the wall and slunk over and lay next to him. A breeze drifted nicely over all of them.

"You know," Harry said, not opening his eyes, "I see now the value of physical labor in chain gangs. I have never physically worked so hard, and now I can see that when you do that, you stimulate your mental energy. No conscious thinking, beyond lifting the bale of hay and stacking it. The mind is able to focus and give forth all sorts of enlightened thoughts."

She was a little surprised. "Such as?"

"Such as what is important and what isn't. Such as giving away your soul because you don't ever deal with things."

He did not elaborate on that, and she thought of his term: giving away your soul. She thought there was such a thing as getting lost from your soul. Of maybe never really finding it in the first place.

He said, "Do you know your Uncle Doyle has thirty years on me and I had to hustle to keep up with him? And he knows the names of all sorts of birds and grasses and bugs."

"He's been doin' it all his life. I think you could say you know the names of some bugs—cold and virus bugs."

She went into the kitchen and brought back a wet hand towel. Easing down, she sat beside him and began to wipe his face. He peeked an eye at her and then closed it again. She boldly wiped gently at his eyes, over his long silky lashes, his cheeks and up on his forehead and down to his ears and on down to his neck, and then she traced his lips.

His hand, strong, bleeding in a couple of places, came up and caught her wrist, and he gazed up at her. She did not look away.

He let go of her wrist and caught the back of her head.

"Something else I thought about while I was out there," he said, his voice husky and his eyes seductive. "A lot." He tugged her down to his parting lips.

She went willingly, eagerly, and he kissed her hard, with passion that lit her up and made her moan. Kissed her until she could not breathe.

Shaking, she pressed a hand to his chest and raised her head. She looked at him a long moment. Felt her cheeks burning, felt her body wanting much more.

Then she got up and went inside the house, letting the screen door bang.

Harry fell asleep on the porch. She saw him through the screen door, and then she tiptoed away, as if that was necessary not to wake him. Every time she passed the door, she would look out at him.

She felt as if his kiss was permanently on her lips. How was she going to act toward him now? She was no doubt making a big deal out of nothing.

He awoke some twenty minutes later and came inside. He stood there looking at her, until she looked at him.

"Would it be all right if I used Doyle's phone to make some calls? I'll use my card."

She'd thought he might have been going to say something other than that. She was a little annoyed that he hadn't.

"I'm sure Uncle Doyle wouldn't mind either way," she said. "I heard the water stop in the pipes a little bit ago. He's probably out of the bathroom now."

He rubbed his hand over his head and nodded. He went into the living room, and when she came into the dining room to start setting the table for the evening, she heard his voice. She moved quietly as she spread the lace tablecloth, not wanting to disturb him. And listening. Oh, it was only the insurance agent he talked to. Sounded like they were friends. She couldn't hear a lot of words, but his tone sounded friendly. She heard him say thanks and goodbye.

She got the good dishes out of the china cabinet; they clinked. Then she put them around on the table. Harry was speaking again. His tone had changed. It sounded strained. She stilled, holding one of the desert rose china plates.

"Dad, I'm sorry to disappoint you. But this is something I have to do, and I'm the one who has to make the decision."

Silence.

"I'm sorry, Dad."

Silence again.

Tiptoing to the entry, she looked beyond the narrow stairway. She saw him sitting there, his hand lying on the receiver he'd replaced, his shoulders slumped. She wanted to go to him, but she worried that might not be the thing to do. Sometimes when you know you've disappointed another person, you don't want anyone to see you.

And maybe she wasn't the one who should be comforting him. They were just getting into all sorts of complications here.

She went quietly back into the kitchen, got the plate of scraps she had saved for the puppy and took them out on the porch. He wagged his tail at her and sat down, waiting.

"Well, you have manners," she said, setting the plate on the porch floor.

Lifting her eyes from the dog, she looked out across the field of alfalfa and the rolling land of mesquite, in the direction of her home. She thought of her father. Winston Valentine. It took a lot more than conceiving a child to be a father. Suddenly she was so very grateful to him. She wondered why she could not settle the questions in her mind with that one answer: he had been a father to her.

Buck had shaved. His hair was still shaggy, but he had it combed neatly back. For an instant, with Uncle Doyle looking at him, Rainey thought Buck might back out the door, but then Uncle Doyle nodded at him through a wreath of cigarette smoke.

Rainey whispered to Harry to get the old radio he'd fixed and face it into the dining room, and to turn it low on the blues station. "Maybe it'll soothe their tempers."

She served supper on the long table covered with her aunt's lace cloth. Candles flickered on the old oak sideboard.

"Oh, Rainey, I haven't seen the table like this since Mama," Neva said. "It is just lovely. Isn't it lovely, Buck?"

"Yeah."

"And everything smells so good. Let me help you get things." Neva followed Rainey into the kitchen.

"Get back in there with the men," Rainey whispered. "Harry can't do it all alone."

Uncle Doyle asked the blessing with five chopped words. Things looked awfully strained, until the food started being dished up, sending steam and aromas rising.

"Oh, Rainey, this is delicious." Neva grabbed hold of something to say. "Isn't it delicious, Buck?"

"Yes, it is." The napkin tucked into his collar bobbed as he cast Rainey an appreciative grin.

"There's no doubt that Rain-gal can bring a person back to life with her chicken pot pie," Uncle Doyle drawled, his tone slipping into warmth. "I imagine her cookin' could be a prescription for sick folks, wouldn't you say, Doc?"

Harry nodded. "I'll bet it could stop wars," he said and very deliberately forked a piece of chicken into his mouth, while his eyes remained on hers.

Rainey felt a funny response in her chest and thought of how he had kissed her. But he had not said a thing about going to Amarillo with her. Besides, their kiss wasn't anything. Though it had been quite a kiss, she supposed.

"Rainey could give me her recipe, and I'll give it a try, Daddy," Neva said.

"It's Mama's recipe," Rainey said. "She always made it for family gatherings."

What her mother had told her was to always rely on the pie's cream gravy to put everyone into a mellow stupor.

An uneasy silence fell over the table again, and Harry broke it by asking Buck about his experiences in Desert Storm. It turned out that Buck had been in the army—which Harry had no doubt learned in chatting with him the previous night—and this brought out Uncle Doyle, who had himself been in the army for a number of years early in his life.

It seemed that every time conversation lagged, Harry had a way of getting it going again.

CHAPTER 14

Back Out on the Road

When Harry slipped upstairs, and Uncle Doyle and Buck were engaged in after-supper smokes and a discussion of how Buck could weld the broken spring on Uncle Doyle's hay wagon, Rainey left Neva finishing the dishes, got her bags, which she'd already set by the back door, and carried them out to her horse trailer.

She didn't want Harry to see her taking her things. She had become increasingly agitated about the prospect of saying goodbye.

For one thing, there were too many questions. Should she offer her address and phone number? What for? Was she going to hold out her hand for a shake, or was she going to hug him? Was she going to go for one magnificent goodbye kiss?

She felt she might cry, which was plain silly. The urge to simply slip away became stronger and stronger.

The puppy padded along with her to the trailer, beside and then in front, casting back looks at her and causing her to about stumble over him.

"You are gonna break my leg, dog," Rainey said in a tone

that caused the puppy to skitter out of the way, although not far. He knew in the manner that animals know things that she was leaving, and he didn't want to be left behind. Sorry for her short temper, Rainey touched his head.

The sun had slipped away, leaving a thin band of gold on the horizon and deepening turquoise sky above. The handle to the trailer's dressing room was cool. She threw her bags inside. They landed with echoing thuds.

Grabbing a halter and a Twinkie cake she had bought for the purpose, she went to get Lulu. While she was putting the halter on the mare, Harry came to the gate and held it open for her. She felt his eyes on her. She didn't look him in the face, but she saw he had on the Levi's jacket. The air was getting nippy.

Stuffing his hands in his front pockets, he fell in step beside her as she led Lulu to the trailer. Her heart did this crazy thing of pounding hard. She told herself to stop being silly.

"Looks like you got them together," he said, inclining his head toward the house, where the windows were yellow squares in the growing dimness.

"I guess we did our part—I really appreciate your help through supper. I don't think those two would be talkin' yet, if it hadn't been for you."

He shrugged.

They reached the back of the trailer, and Harry jumped ahead to open the door. Rainey loaded Lulu, who entered as slowly and deliberately as an elephant, her hooves going *thump-thump* on the rubber mat. Giving the horse a pat, Rainey closed the divider, came out of the trailer and closed the door.

Still without looking at Harry, she walked to the truck and threw the lead rope in the back. That was when she saw the maroon nylon bag, sitting there behind the rear window.

She turned her head so quickly around to him that she about broke her neck.

His eyes met hers, and he came toward her. "Doyle gave me the bag. I forgot to buy one the other day."

"Oh. Well, that was good he had one."

They gazed at each other, her golden-green eyes searching his brown ones. She saw suddenly that the sadness was gone from his eyes. And then she heard very clearly, before he spoke, *I'm going with you, if you still want me to,* and she answered, *Yes.*

His lips quirked into a small grin. "I thought I'd go on to Amarillo with you, if the offer's still open."

She could not help smiling. "You're welcome to come."

For another moment they stood grinning at each other, and then she turned and slipped behind the wheel. She stuck the key in the ignition to start the diesel engine so it would warm.

Then, with her hand on the key, all manner of fearful doubts took hold of her.

"Harry?"

"Yes?" He stepped closer, propping an arm on top of the open door.

She wet her lips. "Look, I don't want you to have the wrong idea...about me...about me askin' you along. I'm not lookin' for a hot weekend or anything. I've been married twice, and I think that's enough foolishness for any woman. I'm not looking for a quick weekend affair."

Only when she'd finished did she lift her eyes to look at him.

His brown eyes were intense on her. "I didn't think of it like that," he said, his voice sharp. "If you thought I thought that, then I'm the one who is sorry."

She had hurt his honor, she saw. She certainly didn't know what to say now.

He lowered himself into a crouch and looked up at her for

long seconds. He said, "Rainey, as I see it, two things are going on here. One is that for the first time in my life I'm stepping out in my own direction. I'm daring to find some things out, and it feels more right than anything ever has before. I need this time to understand what I really want, and I know I'm doing right in that regard."

His lips quirked in that crooked grin. "The second thing that's going on is what I never in my life imagined, and that is a lovely woman has come into my life. A woman who fascinates me, who I'm feeling something for that I never felt for another woman. I don't think I'm wrong to believe that there is something going on between us."

There was no other answer but to shake her head. "No. You're not wrong."

"We get along well. I like being with you, and somehow you are helping me figure things out. Amarillo is as good a place as any for me to spend the next few days, is what I thought—" he paused and breathed deeply "—and also that I can't just let you go out of my life without seeing where this may go."

"Oh, Harry, I don't know." His boldness put her off balance. With him being so straightforward, she could not pretend to herself. She felt more for him than she had for any other man in a long time. But that scared her pants off.

"No promises and no strings," he said in a calming tone, then added, "In case you haven't noticed, Rainey, you are a woman traveling alone. Maybe you will need me."

She felt a dawning surprise. "I've been travelin' alone for a long time. I know how to take care of myself. I have Daddy's gun."

"And I know that any man who hassles you would have a hard time of it, too, but there are some men out there equal to you," he said with thick sarcasm.

He gazed at her, waiting.

"I would like your company," she said.

There was a lot more she might want to say, such as: I may be falling in love with you, and are you falling in love with me? How can you do that when I don't even know who I am? I have nothing to give you…but I feel like I do need you.

Those things could not be said, however, at least aloud, although she wondered if he could hear her thinking.

With this disconcerting thought, she turned back into the truck and started the engine.

Rainey turned on the headlights and waited while Harry put the puppy in the truck bed. He slipped his lanky body into his seat and slammed the door securely.

"Enjoyed the visit, Uncle Doyle. See you next go-round!"

"I sure appreciate the hospitality, Doyle. Very glad to have met you."

"Well, you folks know where we are. You come on any time."

Neva peered at them from next to her father. "Good luck in Amarillo, Rainey! Thanks for the recipes."

"Just remember what I told you about the cream gravy. Bye!"

"Goodbye!"

Rainey and Harry waved at the three people on the porch, who waved back, and then the truck was heading down the drive. Slowly, mindful of Lulu, she turned the truck north along the blacktop highway. The light was fading away in the west and the moon rising in the east. She caught sight of the puppy in the side-view mirror, pressing his face into the wind. She glanced over at Harry, who was easing his long legs.

With a vague feeling of déjà vu, she returned her eyes to the road and paid sharp attention, in case something or someone should unexpectedly appear at the ragged edges of her vision.

* * *

On the way to Amarillo, Harry told her how he had come
to be out on a country road far from Houston. He had gone to
visit a dying friend, Thurman Oaks, who had lived in Cool
Springcreek, one of those small towns a person missed if they
blinked while going through.

"Thurman was a patient in the hospital during my residency," he explained, going on to talk about a man who stood
six-two, his age of eighty-five having brought him down from
six-four, and who had been a farmer, a cowboy, a wildcatter, a
newspaperman and now a preacher of "The Word." "That's
how Thurman describes himself," he said. "And he sure went
around talking it to everyone."

She couldn't clearly see Harry's eyes, but she felt his passion
and his caring for the elderly man.

"What did he look like?" she asked, wanting to picture
the man.

"Look like? Well...he was big, like I said, and what hair he
had left was white and sort of shaggy down on his collar. He
wore a mustache and a thin beard along his jawline."

"Sounds like Santa Claus."

Harry grinned. "Yes, I guess he did look like Santa Claus.
He was jolly like that." He went on to explain that Thurman
had had cancer, and that the doctor in charge of his case had
more or less dismissed him as being a lost cause.

"He said Thurman was too old, and there wasn't any use
in doing anything for him. He just tossed him aside," he said
in a bitter tone. "I couldn't cure Thurman," he admitted. "In
a man of his age, the treatment would have brought on death
quicker than the cancer, but with the proper support, he
could live several good years, not simply exist. One of the
things is to manage the pain. If the pain is managed, the

human body can go on functioning for a lot longer. Too many doctors today just don't count in the pain, both physical and mental."

Harry would count in the pain, she knew, glancing at his intense face and remembering how he had been with the child, and before that the young man and his bloody nose. Remembering how he would get so very nauseous and yet continue.

"Were you able to do that for him? Manage the pain?" she asked.

"Pretty much," Harry said with a slow nod, shifting himself in the seat and easing his long legs. "But I think it was mostly Thurman himself. He had such a strong state of mind. Despite his age and infirmity, he had a purpose in his life. He said God gave him life, and it was up to him to do the living as long as he was here."

She glanced at him, saw his face illuminated by the dash lights, his brow furrowed.

"My mother used to say something like that. She used to say, 'I'd best live today. Tomorrow I might be dead.' Mama used to have all kinds of sayings."

She experienced a sudden longing for her mother. She imagined running into the kitchen, where her mother might be sitting with coffee, and telling her mother all about Harry. But she couldn't do that, would never be able to do that again.

"Thurman called for me, when he knew his time was near," Harry said. "There I was, all messed up in my apartment, and I got his call. I was so messed up I barely wondered at him calling me, I just went running over there to see if I could do something for him, but you know what he wanted? He said he felt called to give me a blessing and a ten-dollar bill. He said it was the first ten dollars he'd made when he struck out wildcatting."

She could picture it, the strangeness of it, and was thoroughly caught up in the story, gripping the wheel and listening for the why of it.

Harry said, "I looked at that ten-dollar bill, and I knew that I wanted to be a therapist to the elderly. I wanted to help them go wildcatting, like Thurman had done with life. You know, when people get old, they get forgotten, as if they and their problems don't matter."

She said to him then, in so many words: tell me about how you will do this. Tell me all. And he did, which got them a long ways down the road.

They stopped halfway to Amarillo at a small convenience store to get snacks and use the rest room. The store was old, one that had once been a chain, back when oil was high, but was now independently owned by a local person. Probably Iranian. It seemed that in the past few years Iranians were buying up half of West Texas. They came to study oil at southwestern universities and then stayed, probably because of both the headiness of freedom and the landscape, which no doubt resembled their own. The clerk was definitely a person of Middle East extraction, with a thick accent, perfect teeth and a beautiful, instant sort of smile that compelled one to smile back.

Rainey appreciated that, and she was also highly approving of the rest room facilities. To encourage such cleanliness, she made certain to compliment the man on the bathroom when she came out. Then she requested the last corn dog she saw beneath the warming light, a package of fig bars and a bottle of Lipton tea.

"Wouldn't want to take a chance on you starving," Harry

said, coming up behind her with his own purchases. He pushed aside her hand with money and paid.

"You know a man likes to pay sometimes," he told her as they stepped out the door.

"Two things I have learned as a woman—that if I pay my own way and drive my own vehicle, I can pretty much lead my own life."

He gazed thoughtfully down at her. "Is that what you want most? To lead your own life?"

She didn't know exactly what he meant, and her mind turned his words over with some agitation.

Then, at that fateful moment, she saw the puppy fly out of the pickup bed, land on the ground for a split second and race off growling. She had forgotten to tie him in the truck.

"Oh, puppy!" She raced off after him into the adjacent dark field, gripping the paper sack with the corn dog. Beneath a distant pole lamp, she saw a cat streaking ahead, the puppy not far behind. "Come back here, puppy!"

He didn't, of course.

He disappeared into the deep darkness. And she wished she had named him. She thought that somehow, if she had named him, he would come to the call.

"Well, he's gone," she said, coming to an abrupt stop.

Pivoting, blowing right past Harry, who had come behind her, she stalked back to the truck, understanding in that moment that she had been abandoned. It did not matter that she had been giving up the puppy since he had come to her. He had abandoned her, and that was different than her giving him up. But it did not matter, because he was gone, and once they left, they didn't come back. That was how it was, and there wasn't any need to cry over it. Being hurt never fixed anything. Being hurt only hurt, and she simply could not stand being hurt.

It was an old familiar feeling. She felt she could hardly breathe, and that someone was drilling a hole in her heart.

Getting into the truck cab, she slammed the door, thinking hotly, If he knows what's good for him, he'd best not say, "You wanted to get rid of him."

Realizing she still clutched the paper sack with the corn dog, she smacked it onto the seat. Her throat got all tight. She didn't want to cry and make a fool of herself in front of Harry.

She squeezed her eyes closed. *Please, God, take care of that dog. I'm sorry...sorry for being so stupid.* She swallowed and commanded herself not to cry.

When she opened her eyes, Harry was gazing at her through the window. He reached out and opened the door. She sure hoped her eyes didn't look like she wanted to cry. Possibly he couldn't tell in the dimness, anyway.

"Come on," he said. "Let's go call him again. Just give him a couple of minutes." When she didn't immediately move or reply, he added, "We aren't in any rush to go, are we?"

"No...I suppose not."

"Come on, then." He motioned with his head, his hands being tucked into his pockets, and hunched his shoulders a little against the night cool.

She got out reluctantly. She didn't think she could face the puppy not coming back. She thought of her mother lying in the casket, never coming back.

Then he took her hand in his, which was warm and secure.

They went back across the field, calling, "Here, pup! Here, dog."

"Oh, he isn't gonna come," she said.

"You don't know that."

"Yes...I do."

"No, you don't." His hand tightened on hers.

"We'll probably get all sorts of dogs showin' up," she said drearily, and no sooner had the words cleared her mouth than, sure enough, two others came—a hound dog of some sort and a cocker mix.

"We are goin' to be accused of stealin' dogs," she said. "Shoo...get!"

They succeeded in getting rid of the strange dogs and didn't dare go to calling the puppy, for fear of bringing the wrong ones back.

Then, just when Rainey felt the last of her hope slipping away, there came a yip. Hope flickered anew. She looked at Harry, who was a black shadow, then stared into the darkness, holding her breath.

Harry whispered, "Here, boy."

The puppy appeared, wriggling around their legs.

Rainey swallowed, squeezed her eyes closed and sank down on her knees, gathering the dog to her. Then she scooped him up and carried him back to the truck, leaning backward to balance his weight. There she broke off a piece of her corn dog and gave it to him.

"I guess I'm gonna have to keep you after all this trouble. I'll have to give you a name."

"Roscoe," Harry said at her shoulder.

She raised an eyebrow at him.

"He looks like a Roscoe."

She looked at the pup and said she thought he looked more like King or Duke.

They argued about the name as they got back into the truck. Rainey maintained that something of some substance was needed so that the puppy could live up to it, and Harry said he found the name Roscoe to have plenty of substance.

As she headed the truck once more down the highway, she glanced over at Harry. "Thanks," she said.

"No problem," he answered.

Then he motioned toward the dash, saying, "Mind if I find some other music?"

He tuned until he found what suited him—blues or jazz, Rainey thought with some consternation. Robert had really liked blues and jazz.

CHAPTER 15

Our Own Corner of the Universe

"Are you going to tell me about your husbands?" he asked, holding out an open bag of Cracker Jack.

Surprised, she glanced at him. Then she dug into the bag, saying, "I don't know. Are you going to tell me about the women you've been involved with?"

"That would be a short story."

She cast him a look that said, So tell it.

"I suppose I've had one sort of serious romance. Amy. My mother had these hopes for us since we were kids, because Amy was the daughter of my mother's best friend. I liked Amy, and she liked me, and for a while there we worked up to something that was sort of serious, but then that turned into absolutely nothing except annoyance.

"I always had an idea that Amy was disappointed in me. She could see my father and my brothers and was really impressed, and she had these ideas of what could happen with her life attached to mine. But she began to see the truth of me a long time before my family or I could. Amy wanted a man who had a lot more ambition than I was ever going to have."

"Ambition for what?" Rainey asked, already forming her own ideas.

"Oh, Amy wanted to host a lot of important parties with important people, and she pretty well figured out I wasn't going to come up to that. She ended up marrying a senator. Biggest wedding I've ever seen. Governor came, and television news anchors. My mother was really disappointed not to be the mother of the groom at it."

She glanced over to see him thoughtfully popping Cracker Jack into his mouth. "You are tellin' me that you have not had anyone in your life but this Amy?" Who sounded pretty much like a gold digger and not his type at all.

"I've had dates…a couple of wild ones, too. But, no, Amy was the only one that might be considered important. So tell me about these fools who let you go."

She looked ahead at the beams of light on the road, then glanced over at him, seeing his face in the silver glow from the dashboard. The atmosphere lent itself to bringing things out of hidden places, sitting there as they had been for miles and miles, only a foot from each other in the dimly lit truck cab. Breathing the same air and hearing the same sounds. He regarded her patiently.

"Robert was a lot like you," she said, and his eyebrows went up.

She thought about this for several seconds and shot another glance at him. "No, he wasn't anything like you," she said, revising her opinion.

"Well, I think I'm relieved."

She said, "He liked fine things—watches, designer clothes, European sports cars…and blues. He liked blues and jazz."

"I probably don't want to say this, but he had taste."

"Oh, yes, he did. If he had not, I wouldn't have fallen in love with him."

"You did love him, then."

"Well, of course. I married him. I'm not somebody who would go around marryin' somebody if I didn't love him."

"No, I wouldn't think you were."

She popped the rest of her handful of Cracker Jack into her mouth and focused on the road illuminated ahead. "Robert was very particular. It was never goin' to work with us from the get-go. We were so very different," she said, not wanting to sound critical of Robert.

"Opposites attract, so they say."

"Well, they certainly did—at first, anyway. We were crazy for each other. But in the long term, we got annoyed with each other, too. I think he got disappointed before I did, and then I got disappointed that he was disappointed. I never could give Robert what he wanted." She sighed. "I guess I was pretty much of an embarrassment to him."

"An embarrassment?" he asked, holding the Cracker Jack bag toward her again. "Couldn't be. He had to be a foolish fellow."

She dug out another handful of caramel corn. "I'm so glad you are so much on my side."

He almost grinned.

"Robert's sophistication was what I liked about him in the beginnin'. He was a such a contrast. Physically he looked rough, but he dressed and talked very suave. He knew exactly what to say, what wine to order, drove a Mercedes and read all these highbrow books. I met him in my first year of college, so I was all impressionable and everything, naturally."

"Very naturally. And you were perfect to stoke his low self-esteem."

She glanced at him with a raised eyebrow.

"Sorry. Sometimes the stuff I learned in therapy just naturally comes out."

She inclined her head. "I suppose it was like that a little. The thing about Robert was that he'd actually come from a little town over in eastern Oklahoma and from dirt-poor parents he wouldn't even go back to visit. Once he'd told me that his daddy had beaten him and that he had escaped that kind of life and would never go back."

A glance at him, and she saw understanding flicker over his face. He looked ahead out the windshield.

"Robert had made himself over into this sophisticated kind of guy, and he thought I would want to do the same thing. I did, sort of, at the time. He tried to help me, but I never really could do it. He'd get so annoyed that I found the books he wanted me to read boring, and he just about pulled his hair out at the way I talk. Whenever I said, 'Well...' he'd say, 'That's a deep subject.' He made great fun of my accent.

"The instant it ended—after I'd put him through his last two years of schooling and he'd gotten a position on the university faculty, I might add—" she heard the pain in her voice, after all this time "—was when I wrecked the Mercedes, and he came yelling at me for that, never askin' how I was."

She gazed at the headlights on the road, remembering, feeling again how small and worthless she had felt when Robert had yelled at her like that, while the nurse put a bandage on her head. She had felt herself shrinking, even as she realized that Robert had been making her feel worthless for a long time. In her panic that she might completely disappear, she had yelled at Robert, "Screw you," which had given her enough strength in that minute not to disappear.

She laughed in the telling of it. "You know what he said to

me? He said, 'That is about what I would expect you to say.' Oh, I was already so embarrassed that I'd said that and right in front of the nurse. I screamed it," she admitted, wincing.

"Then I looked over and saw the scissors right there. I jumped off that emergency room table, snatched up those scissors and cut Robert's fifty-dollar tie right in half, then handed him the cut half and walked out, leaving him standing there with a stunned expression and his half a tie."

Harry laughed at all of this, and she thought that was great of him.

"I think that's the first time I've heard you really laugh," she said.

"It's a great story," he said.

"It is, isn't it?" They laughed again and she felt a warmth washing over her. She realized she had let go of the embarrassment at the memory.

He told her, "I've seen a number of marriages break up in an emergency room. It's a really good place for it. If there's any violence, it can be handled, and if anyone collapses, that can be handled, too. What about your second husband? What happened with him?"

He shot her a raised eyebrow. He was an incredibly handsome man.

"Monte? Oh, Monte was just one of those foolish mistakes a woman makes when she's in a terribly low period, seeing the years slip by and wishin'…oh, just wishin'." She sighed. "What a girl ought to do when she finds herself in such a condition is to lock herself in her kitchen with lots of herb tea and study the Bible and all those self-help books that tell a woman how to find herself. Perversely, what most of us do is what I did—I went crazy over Monte and got pregnant and ended up marrying him."

"Pregnant?" he said, obviously startled. "You have a child?"

She hadn't meant to tell it. She had meant to skip that part, because even after all these years, she sometimes cried.

She shook her head. "No. I miscarried at four months." She blinked rapidly as the glow of the headlights on the road blurred.

"Oh."

She felt his eyes on her; he was that way, didn't try to hide his curiosity.

"It was hard on Monte. He had been so excited. We hung in there for almost two years, but it just never worked. I couldn't fill the hole in Monte, and he couldn't fill the hole in me. You know what I think causes divorce? I think it is not a lack of love but way too much disappointment. You have so much hope for someone's love to conquer all, to help fill you up, but then you find out that it doesn't. That is hard to love through."

She glanced at him, somewhat amazed at herself for revealing such intimate thoughts.

"I never would have thought I would be married twice," she said. "I mean, I really don't believe in divorce. Sometimes I wonder if I know myself at all. My mother used to say, 'It seemed the thing to do at the time.' That seems to be how it is, at least for me."

"I think Robert and Monte were fools."

"You do?" She glanced at him, surprised at his words and his tone. It was decidedly intimate. His gaze was, too.

"Any man's a fool who lets you get away."

"Well," she said, not quite certain what to say to that, "I suppose we were all fools, but I have learned. I learned mainly that married love had better be much more than a feeling. The feeling—the fire—burns out, but real love is an action. It is something you do. And in marriage *both* people have to do it, even when they'd rather not."

She motioned for him to pass across the Cracker Jack bag, and they shared what remained. When he dug out the last kernel, he offered it to her, put it right in her mouth.

Just outside Amarillo, she pulled beneath a pole lamp and got the puppy up in the seat between them. She did not want to take a chance that he would see something on a city street and jump out, and she didn't feel like tying him. The night air had cooled considerably, and she had begun to get tired, to experience a strong sinking sensation. Whenever she got tired, she did so very quickly and wanted nothing but to lie down. This tended to make her a little impatient, and peevish, too. She tried not to be this way, but she didn't seem to make much headway. She was too tired to make headway.

"So far Roscoe hasn't jumped out while the truck is moving," Harry said, petting the dog's head.

"The key words are *so far*," she said. "He ruined my confidence back there, and now that I have settled on keepin' him, I don't want to lose him, which is probably exactly what will happen, but I'll do my best anyway. And his name is not Roscoe."

The dark streets were nearly empty, the most traffic coming as cars left the fairgrounds that grew up behind a tall chain-link fence. The colorful lights were lit, but the Ferris wheel was still and empty.

Slowly turning into the entry for participants, she lowered her window to speak to a man in a thick coat, who took note of her truck and trailer, then told her to park where she found room, but advised that all the camper hookups were already taken.

She drove past trucks and trailers looking for a space. The only space she found was far from the barn and the rest rooms, and she had to back the trailer into place. She had to ask Harry to get out to help guide her. Inexperienced, he gave her all sorts of confusing hand motions and looked more like he was directing an orchestra.

"Just yell 'stop' if I'm about to hit that trailer there," she told him.

She suddenly wondered what Harry thought of the primitive accommodations and felt very self-conscious. She knew what Robert would have said. As long as she'd been divorced from him, she thought, he could still haunt her.

"I usually just sleep in my trailer until the morning," she said, more forcefully than she had intended, "rather than go to all the trouble of unhooking to drive to the motel. I have a reservation over at the La Quinta for tomorrow. For now, you can have the entire front seat, and I'll get you a blanket and pillow."

She didn't look at him. She was annoyed with the way she felt, all defensive, and this made her all the more annoyed with him. She thought that if he hadn't been along, she wouldn't have this feeling, and she would be free to simply be how she was. That was the problem with entanglements. One had to accommodate oneself to others—and so many times, once one did that, the other one up and left.

"Okay by me," he answered smoothly, drawing her gaze to see that it really did seem okay with him.

"Well, good."

Outside the truck, the high-plains breeze was downright cold, ruffling their hair and whispering through their jackets. It brought the aroma of greasy fair food, and the scents of animals and damp earth. From the carnival on the far side of the fairgrounds, music abruptly stopped, and colorful lights began to go out.

By the light in the trailer and the glow of sparsely placed pole lamps, she got Lulu out and led her to a stall in the barn. Harry and the puppy followed along. It was all new to both of them, and while Rainey readied Lulu and the stall, they avidly investigated the block walls of the stalls, the other horses, the small arena in which a few people rode even at this time of night. He helped her to get the hay and water for Lulu and was in such good humor that Rainey had to remark on it.

"I'm used to odd hours," he said. "I can pretty much drop to sleep or wake up at an instant's notice."

"Well, I'm tired, and when I get tired, I can't hardly stand anyone in a good mood." She felt that if she didn't lie down, she was going to fall over right there. Possibly she would not go directly to sleep, but she needed to get off her feet.

She got the things from the room of her trailer. "I think this is all you'll need. Oh, and the keys are in the ignition. That way I have light back in the trailer. You might want to listen to the radio. The battery's real good."

She felt anxious now to please him in any way that she could, since she was in such poor humor.

"Thanks."

"I'll take the pup. I have more room."

"Okay."

She called the puppy to come with her, trying out the name of Duke. The puppy, pricking his ears, looked from her to Harry, who was opening the truck door. "Here, pup," she said more firmly, and he came, wagging his tail.

She threw a towel down for the puppy to lie on, took off her boots and turned out the light, then climbed up onto the quilt-covered mattress that served as a comfortable bed in the gooseneck of the trailer. She thought of the need to remove her makeup but was too tired.

Out the narrow window at the front, she could look down

into the rear window of the truck. She saw his shadow. He was still sitting up. The light from the dash showed he had turned on the radio; she thought she could hear it, but there was music playing from somewhere else, too. There was the sound of cars on the road, the squeak of metal from somewhere.

His shadow moved as he lay down in the seat. She stared at the window another minute, and then she rolled to her back and lay there thinking about him and how he looked at her and the way he made her feel.

But she could not trust her feelings when it came to men. And she was way too tired to be thinking on it, anyway. She had enough trouble thinking rationally without being tired.

Pulling up the blanket, she closed her eyes.

CHAPTER 16

First Light After a Long Night

A voice and the puppy whining and scratching at the door awoke her. It was first light, barely. There was a thump on her door, and then recognition of Harry's voice came through her foggy brain.

"Rainey...I got coffee."

Harry and coffee! That got her up, falling from the mattress up in the gooseneck and stumbling over her boots, making a great deal of noise and trying to smooth her hair as she went to open the door. The puppy jumped out, and then she was staring at Harry, who stood there holding two white foam cups.

She winced inwardly at the cup, but she was desperate for the coffee and took it immediately, sipping from it, while he got the puppy and brought him back.

"What happened to the warm weather?" he said, as he and the puppy came into the trailer.

"You are now in North Texas," she said, "and it isn't even daylight."

"It's daylight," he said, glancing out the window with puzzlement, as if making certain he had not mistaken things.

"It may be light, but the sun isn't up yet. That qualifies as not yet daylight."

"Oh."

She told him to have a seat on the trunk, the only other place to sit besides up on the mattress in the gooseneck. He would not have fit up there; his head would have bumped the ceiling.

She sipped the steaming coffee again and decided it definitely had a foam taste. Riffling around in the cabinet in the corner, she found her favorite ceramic mug. She poured the coffee into it, and then she happened to look over at him. He was watching her.

"I only have this one ceramic cup," she said, holding it with both hands. "I had another one, but it broke."

She rather heard the voice of Saint Peter prodding her to offer him her cup, but she held on to it. She figured that, as a doctor, he probably drank out of foam cups a lot and didn't mind it. She managed to climb back up on the mattress, where she held the warm cup in both hands, inhaling the aroma of the coffee.

"You're pretty much a mess in the mornings," he said.

She looked up to see him grinning at her. "This is still night to me. And you need a shave."

Then she saw him rubbing his chin. "Maybe I'll grow a beard."

She shook her head. "No. Won't fit you."

"You don't think so?"

His voice brought her eyes to him again. He looked as disappointed as a boy. He was wanting to be new and different, and she had dampened him.

"Well, you might try it. Just to see. I could be wrong. I am on rare occasions." The burst of energy that drummed up the answer faded, and she went back to sipping her coffee.

"This looks pretty cozy," he said, looking around.

"Mama had it fixed up for sleeping comfortably. It has an air conditioner." She pointed. "But she didn't want cooking equipment or a portable toilet. She said that's why there are restaurants and gas station bathrooms."

"Sounds reasonable."

That made her think how Freddy had said on a number of occasions that the words *reasonable* and *Mama* did not go together. She didn't comment on that, though. She felt as if her mind was too weak for her to trust speaking much of what came out of it.

He told her that he had found a great place to get breakfast. "They have biscuits and gravy." He seemed eager about the prospect.

"That's good." She sipped her coffee, yawned and sniffed her runny nose, self-consciously keeping her eyes from his because of the disheveled way she knew she looked.

"Are you sure you're going to live?" he said, chuckling now.

"Well, if I start to go, you are a doctor. Surely you could do something to revive me."

Their eyes met.

He said, "I imagine I could do something."

A little startled, she looked into her cup and drank deeply.

A mischievious inner voice whispered, You're sittin' on a bed. Why not haul him up? And suddenly the image of them both entwined bare naked popped into her mind. It was very disconcerting.

They went to the barn to feed Lulu and to wash up in the rest rooms. That took Rainey some time; she thoroughly washed her face and brushed her hair, pinning it up, and then she reapplied her makeup. She felt enormously better when she came out.

Harry was nowhere in sight.

She walked outside the barn and looked around. The fairgrounds were coming alive. The first of the morning sun's bright rays shone on the fall-colored trees and yellow-block buildings and the Ferris wheel skeleton poking up against the pale sky. A number of trucks and stock trailers were arriving. A woman wearing chaps and a fancy shirt led two beautiful horses into the barn where the cutting competition would soon begin. Men could be seen stirring over at the carnival rides, beginning their inspections and maintenance.

Then she spied Harry over in the area behind the stock barn, where fencing was being set up. She knew him because of his height, and the way he stood.

"It's pig racing," he told her when she joined him.

"Yes."

Nearby sat a truck and trailer that had Jernigan's Racing Pigs emblazoned on it.

"Are they going to ride them?" Harry asked. "How fast can they go?" Clearly he was fascinated with the prospect of racing pigs.

Rainey told him that no one rode the pigs, they just raced on a course, and that it was quite a lively act, too. "But right now, I'm hungry," she said, tugging his arm. "Let's go to that café you were talkin' about. We can eat some pigs."

He looked startled, then glanced from her to a single pig, which had been unloaded into a pen. The pig was huge, pink and cute.

"Now I don't know if I can eat sausage," he said, coming along.

"Oh, they aren't that cute close up. They're really ugly."

He led the way to the café he had found, acting, she thought, quite proud of himself. Rainey was not familiar with it and judged it to be a new addition since she had been to the fair. She was immediately relieved to see coffee served in mugs and food served on plates, even if they were plastic, and with stainless silverware.

"This is a great place," she told him, when they sat down.

He looked pleased.

She ordered scrambled eggs and hash browns, and a big cinnamon roll and orange juice. Harry ordered two eggs, hash browns, and biscuits and gravy, and sausage, too, after a moment's thought.

"I have corrupted you." She looked at his plate. "All that fat and salt…a heart attack waiting to happen," she added, using his own term.

"What?" he said, stretching up and looking down at his skinny self. "Do you think I need to worry about my weight?"

She looked at his slender body. "I guess not. In fact, here, have some of my cinnamon roll. You know, you may have met me just in time."

His reply amazed her. "Yes, I think I did meet you just in time."

Her gaze flew upward to see him slowly taking a bite of the rich biscuit, while his brown eyes held a decidedly sexy light.

She averted her gaze to take up her coffee cup, thinking, *Oh my Lord, what did I say and what are we doing?*

Rainey purchased three sausage biscuits to go, for the puppy. When they stepped outside, she said, "I guess we can look around, if you want. I'll need to let my food settle before I exercise Lulu."

First they walked around the carnival. It was early, and none of the rides were in operation, but people were stirring. This time was used for maintenance and relaxation, too. While people would soon begin streaming into the fair exhibits, most would not come to the carnival until afternoon.

Harry looked at it all in that curious manner he had of looking at everything. He said he had never been to a carnival, nor even the state fair. "I have been to Six Flags…back in college," he said.

Rainey, on the other hand, had been to many a carnival. "There's a small circus that comes to Lawton every year, and they have a carnival, too. Mama and Daddy and I went most years. Daddy used to work with a carnival, back in his early twenties."

Her father had explained the dynamics of each carnival game to her, she told him. While the games looked more modern, the basics of them had changed very little over the years.

"See the ball toss. Well, first off, it's difficult to get balls in the glasses because the balls are of a perfect size just to barely fit, and they're plastic, which makes them want to bounce over the rims. And that ring toss on the bottles…some of the rings will be made a hair smaller than others, and you can't tell it just by lookin'. They will hardly fly over a bottle. And see those glasses for tossin' in coins—some will sit a hairbreadth lower or higher. Anymore, there isn't much out-and-out cheating—the police watch for tricks—so mostly it is all these little dynamics, so that when you win a prize, you put out enough money to pay for it."

As Harry and Rainey walked past, a few of the carnies in the booths called lazily for them to come and try the games. Rainey kept shaking her head.

Then they passed a dart-throwing booth. When the round man there called, "Hey, come give it a try. I'll give cut-rate this early in the mornin'!" Harry grabbed her hand and tugged her over.

He plunked down a dollar, and the man handed him five darts. Harry cut his eyes to her and then focused on the board of balloons for a full minute. So long, in fact, that Rainey had begun to wonder if something was wrong when, in quick, smooth succession, Harry threw the darts. Five times and five broken balloons.

The carnie looked at him and put five more darts on the counter. Harry plunked down a dollar, picked up the darts, stood there and looked at the board, and then did it again.

"Now I got to blow up a bunch more balloons," the carnie said. Apparently having been entertained as much as he could stand, he waved his hand at a row of prizes.

"The mouse," Harry said, pointing. He immediately handed the stuffed gray mouse to Rainey, took her elbow and led her away. "I used to play a lot of darts in school and early in my residency days," he said. He was, she could tell, extremely pleased with himself. He was quite irresistible that way.

On the way back to the truck, she led the way through the stock barn, where people were preparing their animals for the day's shows. Today it was cattle of various breeds.

"Be careful where you step," she cautioned. She held her stuffed mouse close. She didn't want to drop it in the dirt, and she also had to remember not to rub it against the greasy paper bag of sausage biscuits for the dog.

It was clear that Harry had never seen cattle so close up. He was amazed at the cows' big soft eyes and the rings in the bulls' noses, a little disturbed by those that were chained to posts and more disturbed by those that were not.

"What if they run off?" he said, eyeing intently an enormous bull that was not chained, and that eyed him back in a lazy manner.

"Where are they gonna go?"

To his raised eyebrow, she explained that these show animals were not like wild ones. "They've been handled all their lives. It isn't likely they will break into a sudden spree of terror. Doesn't he seem content lying there?"

She gazed with warmth at the bull, whose long lashes entranced her. She had gone through a period in her life when she refused to eat beef, because of the animals' lovely eyes.

Then she look over to see that Harry still had a skeptical expression on his face. She pointed to another bull farther along.

"Even an animal considered dumb knows when he's well-off," she said as they came to that bull. His owner was grooming him, scratching the bull's head in the process. The nameplate nearby read: Big Babe.

"Just don't wave nothin' in his face," the man told Harry. "He doesn't like to be teased...no animal does. You want to scratch his head?"

Harry, clearly delighted, did so and ended up in a full discussion about the animal and its grand attributes, according to his owner.

Watching the light in his eyes and the way he tilted his head to listen, Rainey suddenly experienced a disconcerting feeling in her chest. She turned and stepped away. Seeing the open doors to the rodeo arena that was attached to the stock barn, she walked toward them. She thought it would be a good idea to refresh her mind about where she and Lulu would be running. As she stood there gazing into the cavernous building, Harry came up beside her.

"Is this where you'll race tonight?"

"Uh-huh, and tomorrow night, too, if we're lucky." She walked out atop the dirt. "It's a little small, and the entry is off center. That won't bother Lulu, but a lot of professional racers won't come to these arenas with off-center entries anymore.

They have their horses trained for entering straight in, and an off-center entry cuts their times.

"This place is perfect for bull and bronc ridin', and ropin', though. And the people sittin' in the front rows get a really good view."

He began to ply her with all sorts of questions about the rodeo. As she answered, he nodded thoughtfully and roamed his eyes over the pens and the seats and the tall ceiling, as if trying to picture it all. He went to look at the bull and bronc chutes, bending and peering through the rails, then climbing up to get a better look.

Encouraged by his avid interest, she pointed out the old wooden ceiling and spoke of what the building must have seen in its time. They speculated on the building's age.

"Daddy rode broncs a couple of times here, and my mother almost won the All-Round Cowgirl title at an all-girl rodeo here in the fifties. She had to ride a bronc in tryin' for that, and Daddy told her that if she was goin' to give it a try, she damn well better not come off. She did come off, though, and the horse stepped on her hand and broke it in two places. Cost her and Daddy over a thousand dollars in medical bills. Mama began and retired from bronc riding at the same event."

She had not recalled this history in a long time, had had no reason to do so. Now she thoroughly enjoyed the telling of it all to Harry. And she enjoyed the way he looked at her and cocked his head, listening intently, as if he wanted to know everything she could tell him.

She simply adored looking at Harry.

CHAPTER 17

Kinship

"I really need to get him a bowl today," Rainey said, crumbling the sausage biscuits on the paper bag for the puppy. She had been using Uncle Doyle's dishes when she had bought his food.

"I imagine ol' Roscoe would appreciate that, wouldn't you, buddy?" Harry said, petting the dog.

He and the dog seemed to have grown quite close. Rainey experienced a little slice of jealousy, followed by panic. What if the dog went off with Harry, when he went off? At the thought of Harry leaving, her mind seemed to short-circuit and go blank.

She took a breath and said, "His name is not Roscoe," as she put the food down. She was pleased with the way the puppy politely sat and waited and didn't bump her arm. He ate very delicately, too.

"Then what is his name?"

"I don't know yet. I have to wait for the right one to come to me." She gazed at the puppy. "Duke. Duke is a good honorable name."

"Duke is the name of a hound dog."

She looked at Harry with some surprise. "Why would Duke have to be the name of a hound dog?"

"It just is. In all the movies, the hound laying on the porch is always Duke."

When they went into the horse barn to get Lulu, they saw that the cutting competition was in progress in the arena there. Harry was keenly interested.

"I haven't actually seen cutting," he said, "but one of the doctors at the hospital had cutting horses and was always talking about them."

"Well, let's go up and sit down for a while. I have plenty of time to work Lulu."

The stands were not very crowded. Rainey led the way to the middle, which she thought gave a good view of the goings-on in the arena. She explained the happenings and gave her opinion as to the ability and performances of each horse and rider. Harry got so caught up that he leaned forward and appeared to be trying to help the horse in its challenge with the steer.

Rainey looked at the back of his head. He kept taking his hat off and holding it, then slapping it back on his head, all in unconscious motions. She gazed at his thick, lustrous hair, at it curling down upon his collar. Imagined putting her fingers into it and playing with it.

She was so confused about Harry. She couldn't let herself care for him. They were just friends spending a weekend together. Mutual need. He needed her company, and she supposed she needed his, although she didn't want him to know that. She didn't even want to know it herself.

She wondered if she was going to get foolish and sleep with Harry.

Almost as if he heard this thought, Harry glanced over his shoulder to see her gazing at him. "What?" he said with little-boy innocence.

"You," she said, grasping at so many impressions at once. "I thought you didn't much like horses."

"I didn't say I didn't like horses. I said I didn't trust them. I can trust them when I'm not having anything to do with them."

"That makes good sense, fella," a man sitting on the other side of Harry said.

Rainey glanced over to see a man, alone, one boot up on the bleacher in front of him. He was one of the old cowboy type common in that part of Texas, wiry and hunched over, pant legs tucked into his boots, the brim of his straw cowboy hat turned up sharply at the sides, and a cigarette hanging out of his mouth.

"Don't ever trust a wild animal," the man said around the cigarette. "And horses are wild animals, no matter how much they've been kept up. You can ride one and pet it and love it, but you'd better not trust it one hundred percent."

"My father always said that," Rainey said, feeling called on to say something to be polite.

"Well, he's right. I been run over by a number of perfectly tame horses. Not out of meanness, now I don't mean that, but a horse can get spooked or just throw a plain ol' hissy fit. The dang thing is a thousand pounds, and half the time he don't know his own power. He's like a little spoiled kid, and he can get scare't of the least thing. The son of a buck might have seen a hundred blowin' paper bags, and then one flies past and suddenly he's higher than a kite and comin' down on you.

"You're Coweta Valentine's girl, aren't ya?" he asked.

The question startled her. She had been trying to watch the current horse and rider cutting in the arena, while appearing to listen to the man's exposition. She had not expected him to say anything important, certainly not to make a reference to her mother. For an instant she felt she'd been caught not paying attention, and then the full import of the question hit her.

"Yes," she said slowly, searching his face. He peered intently at her with blue eyes shining like lights out of his darkly tanned face.

"You must be her last one...Rainey?" he asked, as if bringing the name up from deep in his memory.

"Yes, I am. You knew my mother?" She wondered all about it, felt her blood coming fast.

He nodded, squinching his blue eyes. "From a long ways back. Dang, if you ain't Coweta made over. You look just like she did at yer age."

"People say that."

She saw that Harry was looking at her, a curious expression on his face. She sort of smiled at him, and very conveniently a cheering rose up for the horse that had just completed its go, so it was natural for her to turn her eyes to the activity in the arena. Still, all her attention remained focused on the old cowboy.

Was he her father?

Oh, Lord, it was crazy. But he could be. That was just the thing of it. He could be. Stranger things had happened in this world.

She saw then quite clearly that the thought had been with her all these months. While she'd been traveling all over looking for herself, a part of her had been searching for the man who had sired her, too. Oh, maybe not searching, but keeping an eye out, just in case.

She heard the man move, saw him out of the corner of her eye stretching his bony leg. Was he someone her mother would have fallen in love with?

He looked a little short for her mother, but then, her mother never had looked on the outward man.

"I imagine you ride horses, like your mama," he said. She looked over to see him stamp his cigarette out on the footboard. "Barrel racer?"

She nodded. "I'm ridin' Mama's horse right now. Lulu. Mama died last spring," she said. It occurred to her that he might not know, and she spoke gently, not wanting to bring him a shock. He looked pretty old.

He nodded, his old face going long. "I heard that back in the summer, and awful sorry to hear it, too. Your mama was real special. Real good with horses...and people." He spoke thoughtfully, as if holding a secret, she thought.

"What's your name?" she asked, heart beating fast.

"Herb Longstreet."

He had a beak nose and high, flat cheekbones, lots of Indian in him, no doubt. Her mother might have been attracted to him some thirty-five years ago.

He leaned over and stuck out his hand, and she shook it; it was thick and rough. Then Harry did the same, introducing himself.

"Are you an oil geologist, Mr. Longstreet?" Rainey asked, unable not to.

She saw Harry's raised eyebrow out of the corner of her eye.

The old man looked surprised. "Why, no, ma'am. I guess I done a lot of things in my life, but I ain't never messed with the damn oil. No, sir." He laughed, showing worn teeth.

"How did you know my mama?"

The man's lips quirked. "Sold her a horse I should have kept once." He shook his head and chuckled. "I thought I was gonna put one over on her, and she put it over on me instead. Coweta made somethin' of that horse, and ended up makin' five thousand dollars in the bargain. It was all a long time back, when I was down around that country 'round Valentine. We'd see each other from time to time, though, over the years. She done me many a good deed, too."

Rainey thought: He loved Mama. For certain he did.

Then he asked, "How's Winston doin'?"

A little surprised, she said, "He's okay. Misses Mom." She didn't suppose she needed to mention that the widow Mildred Covington was taking up the slack.

The old man nodded, coughed hard into his hand and pulled out a package of cigarettes. Quite suddenly the look on his face was very sad. Probably he was thinking about Mama being dead, and how old he himself was and that he could go any minute.

Maybe she had gotten the facts wrong, Rainey thought. Maybe her real father had not been an oil geologist. She wished her mother would have said a name. She should have asked, but it had not seemed the thing to do at the time, to grab her dying mother and yell: "Tell me!"

Harry had sat back up straight. He watched the cutting but kept glancing at her. She didn't want him to know she was upset. It was silly of her to be upset. She watched the horse and rider cutting and commented that the horse had trouble turning left.

"That horse ain't never gonna be able to turn left," Mr. Longstreet commented.

Rainey wondered about Mr. Longstreet and her mother. Men had all the time been in love with her mama, she knew. She felt as if her breath was squeezing out of her lungs, as if she might at any minute jump up and demand that the man tell her about his relationship with her mother.

She got so afraid she might do this that she touched Harry's leg and told him she was going to get Lulu. "I need to work her for tonight," she said, striving to act perfectly normal while she practically jumped to her feet.

"Okay." He started to get up.

"You go ahead and stay here," she said, touching his shoulder. "There isn't anything you can do." She looked at the old man. "It was nice to meet you, Mr. Longstreet." Her voice croaked.

Mr. Longstreet nodded, his eyes intent on her for a second, before she turned to make her way down the bleachers. She had to pay close attention not to step on any hands or trip over someone, and not to shake, which she had begun doing. She had not realized her mental state was so strained.

She also didn't realize until she reached the bottom that Harry had followed her. She wished he hadn't. She felt really funny, not herself at all. She didn't trust herself around people right that minute.

"You didn't need to come with me," she said to Harry, more sharply than she had intended. "I'm just goin' to exercise Lulu, and you'll be bored."

"I can watch," he said calmly. Right that minute his calmness annoyed her.

"I've got to go to the bathroom," she said and ducked into the ladies' room.

She stared at herself for a minute in the mirror. Her eyes were golden-green. Sort of hot looking, she thought. She thought that she looked exactly like Mama, not whoever was her father. She knew that Mr. Longstreet had cared for her mother. She wondered if her mother had cared for Mr. Longstreet. She wondered if she'd known her mother at all.

Turning on the water, she wet a towel and then wiped beneath her eyes, to get any mascara smudges. She couldn't tolerate mascara smudges. Then she noticed one of her fingernails had a bad chip. She dug a bottle of polish from her purse, quickly touching up her nails, thinking that she might ask Mr.

Longstreet about his relationship with her mother. She could do that. She could find a gentle way to do it, so as not to embarrass Mr. Longstreet. She wouldn't do it around Harry, though. He would think she was a mess, if he didn't already.

She was standing there, waving her hands to dry her fingernail, when the most startling thing happened: her cousin Leanne came bursting through the door.

Leanne glanced at Rainey and kept on going without a word, into a stall and slamming the door.

Rainey, as amazed as could be, stood there, her hands frozen in the air. She had not seen her cousin in a year, maybe two. She certainly would not have expected to see Leanne show up at this rodeo; Leanne was a professional barrel racer so successful that she mainly kept to high-stakes barrel racing futurities and the major championship rodeos.

With a burst of motion, Rainey threw her cosmetics back into her purse, intending to slip out the door. Such action was a little low, but apparently Leanne hadn't recognized her, so she wouldn't know. Leanne had a personality that wore Rainey out, and right then she did not feel at all up to her cousin.

Just then Leanne called from the stall, "Rainey? Good golly, girl, is that you?"

In a flash Rainey considered just not answering and leaving, but she also thought about Leanne being her cousin, flesh and blood. She said, "Well, is that you, Leanne?"

"Yes, honey! I just now realized that was you standin' there. I bet I looked like a crazy woman racin' in here, but I've had to go for the last hour and Clay wouldn't stop. He just won't make pit stops."

Rainey wondered what this Clay expected a person to do, but she said, "Leanne, hon, I'm glad to see you, but I've got someone waitin' for me. I'll see you later, though."

"Wait, Rainey! Give me a dang minute, will ya'?"

"Well, okay." She felt ashamed of being rude. And she thought Leanne's voice sounded a little desperate, although this was natural, considering.

A minute later, Leanne came out of the stall, zipping her turquoise jeans. "Whew! I feel better. Clay wanted me to pee in a paper cup."

"Why didn't you just make him pull over?"

"Oh…" Leanne gave a vague wave of her hand as she turned the water on in the sink. "It wasn't any big deal."

Rainey would have considered it a big deal. But everyone had their own ideas, she guessed.

"I'm goin' with Clay Lovett now," Leanne said, drying her hands on a paper towel.

Rainey figured she was supposed to be impressed. "Oh?"

Leanne looked at her. "He's one of the top bull and bronc riders," she said. "This is a good rodeo for those men's timed events. Pete Lucas is here." Apparently Pete Lucas was someone else she should have heard of, Rainy thought. "Clay and Pete are good buddies. And Clay's Mr. November on the cowboy calendar this year."

"I haven't seen the calendar," Rainey said.

"Well, Clay and I have been together for almost nine months now, and we're really serious, but he's been married before, and there's all sorts of complications. He's a little gun-shy."

Rainey could understand that. She wondered if anyone in the world ever stayed married anymore. She also wondered why Leanne felt the need to speak straightaway these intimate details of her life.

Right that minute, Leanne was bent close to the mirror, inspecting herself. Rainey figured that Leanne must have turned thirty-one over the past summer. She had never married, being very involved with her career in barrel racing. She looked as beautiful as ever, even with smudged mascara and uncombed hair, the way a woman looks when she's traveled sleeping in a vehicle. Leanne was an Overton, a first cousin by way of her mother, who had been Rainey's mother's younger sister. Rainey and Leanne favored greatly, although Leanne's hair was more brown and she was smaller, more finely built. Rainey always thought Leanne could stand to gain a few pounds, but Leanne said being small was her edge in barrel racing.

"I heard you've been runnin' barrels on your mama's old horse," Leanne said, turning to face Rainey.

Rainey nodded. "I guess we've been makin' a stab at it. Havin' some fun."

Leanne's eyes went up and down Rainey, as if comparing herself. Rainey felt a little flat in her blue jeans and blue denim shirt. Leanne wore stylish Western clothing, colorful and sharp. Her expression turned very satisfied.

"You never were the professional horse-show type," Leanne said flatly. "It's a lot of work, believe me. It takes a lot of competitive spirit."

Excuse me? Rainey thought. But that was Leanne. Charlene said you couldn't take offense at Leanne or you'd be in knots all the time.

And there was truth in what her cousin said. Rainey had never been highly competitive. She wasn't sure what she was. She always felt that she had one foot in the horse world and the other somewhere else, only she didn't know where that was.

"Would you have a lipstick?" Leanne asked.

Rainey handed over her flowered cosmetic bag. "Use what you need."

"I heard that Aunt Coweta left you all her Mary Kay. I used

to get a lipstick from her that I loved. A peach color…can't remember the name right off."

"I have a peach mocha in there."

"This isn't it," Leanne said, frowning at the lipstick, "but
it'll do."

Rainey said she would look in the boxes at home. "If I find
any other peach ones, I'll save them for you."

Leanne also used Rainey's powder and blush. She leaned toward the mirror, explaining all about how she probably
wouldn't have come to this rodeo, that it didn't really pay
enough—as if this were okay for Rainey, though—but Clay
had wanted to come and do it with his buddy Pete Lucas, and
her horse was so great that he could race anywhere and win.
Her attitude was pretty much that Rainey should be prepared
to lose.

The entire time Leanne talked, Rainey was thinking: Harry
probably figures I fell into the toilet or something. He might
poke his head in here…or he might have just given up and gone
on. Who the hell is Pete Lucas? And Clay-who-won't-stop-for-
his-woman-to-go-to-the-bathroom Lovett? I just don't keep up,
and what's more, I don't care. I wonder if Mr. Longstreet is still
sittin' on the bleacher, thinkin' about Mama. I should have
talked to him about her. I let the chance slip right by me. Maybe
I'll get another chance, and I'll be ready.

Leanne tossed the lipstick back in the bag and zipped it up.
"I'm glad to run into you, Rainey," she said, in an un-
characteristically sincere tone that touched Rainey. "I wanted
to tell you that I was sorry about your mama. I apologize for
not gettin' home for the funeral, but I was at a big show out in
California and had a couple of expensive horses up for sale."

"It's okay," Rainey said. "Everything was pretty much confusion at the highest."

Maybe Leanne would stay in the rest room, she thought, maybe comb her hair or something. If she followed Rainey out, Rainey would have to introduce her to Harry...if he hadn't gotten tired of waiting and gone off.

"It was sure sudden, wasn't it?" Leanne said. "My mother said about half the town formed the procession to the cemetery."

"They said it looked like it. I really didn't think to turn around and look right then." She was aggravated at Leanne for bringing it all up. It was like the wound had been hit and busted open.

"I really need to go now. I need to get my horse exercised." She reached for the door, hoping Leanne would stay in the rest room.

"I really miss Coweta," Leanne said, following Rainey out the door.

Rainey was startled at the tone of her cousin's voice. She looked over to see her cousin's eyes tearing up.

Leanne continued, "I used to talk to your mama when she and I met up at different rodeos and shows. It was a lot of fun tellin' people that she was my aunt. I mean, your mama was really somethin'. Everybody just loved Coweta. She'd come over and sit underneath my awning with me, and she'd always bring me that lipstick I liked, and we'd just talk and talk. Then, after she quit barrel racin', I'd stop to see her whenever I went home. I could talk to her, and I never could my own mama." She had folded her arms about herself and rubbed her upper arms.

Rainey felt as if something had been going on behind her back. She had not known about her mother being so close to Leanne.

"Well, she wasn't your mama," she pointed out. "It's different than with your own mother. There's some things you just can't tell your own mother." But Rainey had talked easily to her mother, too.

She pushed through the front doors, and there was Harry, standing to the side. Immediately she thought that she would not tell Leanne that Harry was a doctor. Telling someone like Leanne that a man was a doctor was like waving chocolate right in front of her face.

Harry's eyes jumped with surprise, moving from her to Leanne, obviously struck by the resemblance.

Rainey made the introductions, and Harry inclined his head and smiled at Leanne, offering a handshake.

"I'm glad to meet you," he said.

And Leanne said, "I'm very glad to meet you," in a way that seemed to mean: oh, boy, I'd like to run away with you. "And where did Rainey find you?" Leanne said, bold as could be, and rather as if she were surprised at Rainey knowing some-one like Harry.

"She picked me up off the highway," Harry said.

"Well, she ought to tell me where this highway is," Leanne said.

The talk went along this stupid vein for a few more comments, and then Rainey said she needed to go work her mare.

"I have to see to my Blackie, too," Leanne said.

She pointed to her trailer. Rainey had already seen it, a fancy aluminum rig with living quarters, the sort that cost as much as a brick house. At that very minute, a man, thick shouldered in a red shirt, came out the door and stood looking in their direction.

Leanne started edging away. "Clay's probably ready to go get somethin' to eat, too. He doesn't like to be held up when he's hungry. Y'all come on over later, hear?" She broke into a run for her trailer.

Watching her, Rainey thought there seemed something out of kilter with Leanne.

Then her attention was drawn by Herb Longstreet coming out the door to her left.

"Good luck tonight, gal," he said.

"Thanks."

She watched him walk away, thinking that this obviously was not her chance.

Harry's hand came to the back of her neck, and she looked at him. Suddenly she was so thankful that he was there with her. For just an instant it seemed like he gave her something to hold on to.

Rejecting this foolishness, she turned her head. "I'd better go work Lulu. I'd rather get her worked before Leanne comes over with her horse."

But she did not step away from Harry. She let herself remain with his hand on her neck, and she leaned toward him, just a little bit.

CHAPTER 18

At the Fair

Harry stood with the puppy at his feet, his forearms resting on the fence rail, and watched her ride Lulu in the outside exercise arena. She thought he looked good in his hat. *Good* was not exactly the right word, but close. There was something about him in that hat that made Rainey feel like smiling and jumping into his arms. She had to be very careful not to reveal this and make a pure fool of herself.

It was quite trying to keep every blessed impulse to herself. She was supposed to be paying total attention to riding and training Lulu; that was why she had come to the fair, after all, in order to race barrels. And she really needed to pay attention in the practice arena, because it was filled with horses and riders. Because she was so preoccupied with Harry in his hat, she almost had a head-on collision with a big man on a bay horse. It was the big man's fault—he was too big to even be riding that horse, and he rode right in front of her—but she should have been prepared for his stupidity.

Telling herself to settle down and get to business, she went to riding Lulu in circles, working to limber her neck. The mare had stored up a lot of energy in the confines of the trailer and the stall. For a good ten minutes she loped around with her nose tugging at the tie-down and her tail flying. Rainey let her fly and then pulled her down, let her fly and pulled her down again.

Harry kept standing there watching, and Rainey's mind kept being drawn away, and every time she sensed Rainey's concentration slip, Lulu took advantage of it by making slow turns and casting her own attention all over the place.

Finally Rainey rode over to Harry at the fence and asked him to leave. "I can't concentrate with you watchin' me like that."

He looked surprised, of course. "I didn't mean to distract you."

"I know that. It isn't your fault. I'm just havin' a hard time with Lulu today." And with herself, she thought. "Maybe you'd like to go over and watch the pig races or something."

He blinked. "Okay…"

"Would you take Fido with you? I don't want to have to worry about him, either."

"Fido?"

"The puppy—I'm tryin' out names. It means faithful." She thought she might like it. The puppy looked up at her, his face a question mark, as if he might be trying out the name, too.

Harry looked a little perplexed, then he said, "Come on, Roscoe," and he went off, with the puppy right at his heels.

Rainey worried that she may have hurt his feelings but forced herself to pay attention to the job at hand. She never got her concentration going, however, and felt that both she and Lulu were just very out of rhythm. After another forty minutes, she gave up. She thought then that she really hadn't come up to the fair to race barrels, but had simply been coming up here for someplace to go. But she hoped she didn't make a fool of herself, now that Leanne was here.

"Leanne is goin' to race tonight," she told the mare, as she led the horse toward the barn and the wash rack. "I'm tellin' you to get yourself ready. I don't expect us to kill ourselves to win, but we dang sure don't want to come in last."

She looked around for Harry and began to regret asking him to leave. It had not helped, him leaving, and now she wondered if he would return. Maybe he'd gone for good. No...he still had his bag at the truck. But he'd gone off and left his stuff in his Porsche, so likely he wasn't concerned with stuff like that.

As time passed, she began to get anxious. She washed Lulu and brushed her and brushed her, and he still didn't come back. She began to really be irritated. He had taken her dog. He had better bring the puppy back before he went off for good.

She had decided to at least walk over to the pig races and see if he was there, when here he came toward her. She saw the puppy first, running toward her, and that was how she recognized that Harry was the man walking forward with his head jutting up over his arms loaded with stuffed toys.

The next thing she noticed was that he looked as if he'd conquered the world.

He said, "I'm gonna have to go to an ATM. I spent all my cash."

The look in his brown eyes went clear through her. His eyes shone with pure happy delight in a way she had not before seen. It was a delight in himself, she realized. And then she saw that he was looking directly at her, and the light in his eyes grew warm and smoky.

Gazing back into those wonderful brown eyes, she thought that she could fall in love with him so very easily. Likely she already was in love with him.

* * *

They dumped all the stuffed toys on the mattress in the gooseneck, left Lulu tied to the trailer and soaking up sun, and went to see the fair.

"If we want to see it, we'd better go ahead," Rainey said, "because I'll need to get a nap later to be ready for tonight. And let's go get something to eat. I like to eat a lot in the middle of the day and not hardly have any supper, because I don't want to race with food in my stomach."

"I didn't think you ever went without food in your stomach," he said.

Making no comment to that, Rainey fixed the puppy into a makeshift collar and lead, because she realized how negligent she had been in letting him run loose, and they took him along.

They stopped at a booth selling fry bread filled with spicy lamb and rice. Harry was eager to try it, the same way he was eager to try everything. They carried their food and cups of Coca-Cola over to a bench underneath a gnarled elm. People were filling the fairgrounds now, and they sat watching all manner of men and women and children walking past. There was a man with three children all over him, literally. He had a tiny baby in a sling on his chest, a toddler in a pack on his back, and a little one by the hand. Then there was an old couple, eighty at least, walking hand in hand.

Harry got up and walked over to throw their trash in the barrel. Rainey saw the warm sunlight on his hat, and then he was looking at her.

As they started off, he took her hand.

Walking hand in hand, as if they both weren't contemplating a lot more, they went through the exhibit buildings, looking over all the displays of pies and breads and canned peaches and grape jelly, clothing designs, beautiful quilts, and knitted items, and photographs. Rainey did her own judging, and she put forth that everything should get a ribbon, simply for showing up.

"Then the ribbons would be meaningless," Harry pointed out. "No one would care."

"I just think all this competition is needless. Look at those who didn't get a ribbon. They'll feel hurt. And who are these people who hand out the ribbons, anyway? Who set them up as judges?"

She realized that what Leanne had said about her not having a competitive spirit was churning around somewhere in the back of her mind.

Harry looked at her as if she were a little cracked. "Somebody set them up as judges," he said. "They probably didn't want the job but had to do it. I had to be a judge once at a chili cook-off. One of those affairs my mother arranged to raise money for the hospital. She had a state representative, the mayor and a couple of hospital bigwigs cooking chili. She can get anyone to do anything. She made them cook, and she made me and a couple of other doctors judge."

"Did your father judge?"

He frowned. "He's the only one she can't make do anything."

"Well," Rainey said, turning the conversation a little, "what is it about everyone always wanting to beat the other fella? Look at all that football. They have kids of five playin' football. Good grief. I think it is a major sickness of society, all this competition. People need to learn how to cooperate, not compete."

"Why do you race?"

"For myself. I race to have fun and see what Lulu and I can do. And I almost hate to do very well, because that means someone else has to lose, and it's my fault, and I always feel so bad."

She got a little carried away then and told him of her fantasy about maybe beating Leanne, which she couldn't ever do, but just in case it looked like she would, she would have to throw the race to Leanne, because she could handle losing but Leanne would simply die, or kill herself, if she lost to Rainey. Then she realized how silly she was being, getting all worried about something that was never going to happen.

She said, "I guess I am as warped as everyone else."

Harry laughed, and the next instant he pulled her to him and kissed her quickly. Then he said, "Everyone should be as warped as you."

She didn't know what to say and had to look away.

After they finished perusing all the exhibits, they went over to the vendor booths, where they saw everything on sale, from pottery to jewelry to specialty animal feeds. The man at that booth gave the puppy a sample of the dog food, and he did it before she said he could, which she thought was a little rude. But the puppy seemed to like it, so she bought a small bag.

Down a few more booths, they came to one selling shiny tin-and-tile mirrors. Rainey thought they were lovely. They looked very Mexican, and she loved things with that tone, the color and earthiness of it.

"Aren't they pretty?" she said.

"Well, I guess so."

"They are a little gaudy, I suppose." She was a little disappointed.

"Colorful...they're colorful. I was just trying to picture them on a wall."

"It depends on the wall," she said. "They'd probably go well in my cottage, or Mama's house. She has all sorts of things in her house, but I wouldn't think they'd go very well in your house."

"How do you know? You haven't seen my house."

"You have a town house." She had a picture of his place in her head, probably lots of leather and chrome and glass.

"Why do you say that?"

"Don't you?"

"Well, yes..."

She looked at him, and for an instant she saw all those prominent doctors and society women behind him. "Would these mirrors go in your town house?"

He smoothed the back of his head. "A person could get scared in the night by one of these things," he said, then took her hand and tugged her on.

Feeling the warmth of his hand against hers, she wondered what his hands would feel like all over her body. About the time she had that thought, he turned his head toward her and met her gaze. She thought then that they might have been very different in many ways, but she was fairly certain he was thinking some of her same thoughts.

It was a statue, and the mind knew that no animal could hold itself with its back legs shooting up in the air, but the bull sure did look real. A photographer was taking people's pictures on it. Harry and Rainey watched while he took a picture of a little boy, wearing his daddy's black cowboy hat. The hat fell down over the boy's face, and he kept pushing it up and peeking out. He was really cute.

Rainey looked over at Harry and saw his eyes were zeroed in on the boy. The expression on his face unnerved her, and she noticed that his hand was gripping hers very tightly.

Then his gaze flickered down to her, and he said, "I lost a little boy about that age, back in March."

"You lost him?" Her first thought was that he'd misplaced

a little boy, and to wonder why he would have a little boy to misplace.

"He died," he said, pain flashing across his features and his eyes returning to the boy on the bull. "It was just the flu…but by the time his parents brought the boy to the emergency room, he was really dehydrated. Still, we started working on him right away. I'd had other kids like him a hundred times. But then suddenly…"

He swallowed and looked really upset, and she didn't know quite what to do, other than stand there and hold his hand.

He said, "The thing is, complications pop up that no one has any experience with. New stuff all the time, and medicine has limitations. Sometimes, no matter what you do, a person dies."

All she could think to do was put her head on his shoulder.

Then the boy was off the bull and walking away with his parents. The photographer asked Rainey and Harry, "How about one of you two?"

Harry wanted to do it, but Rainey hung back. She never liked having her picture taken. Photographs rarely flattered her; she usually ended up with a silly grin or her eyes half-closed, making her look drunk. "Even Mama would say that I was so much prettier than any of my pictures," she told Harry. "What does that tell you?"

"Aw…come on. It'll be a great souvenir."

"You don't have any money," she pointed out.

"Okay, lend me a twenty. Come on."

She did want a picture of him, and it suddenly occurred to her that getting a picture of the both of them would be a good idea. Something she might like to have after this weekend was over.

Handing over the money, she told the photographer she wanted two shots. She asked Harry to tie the puppy to a table leg, because she didn't like the idea of trusting him to sit there.

The table wouldn't exactly stop him from running, but it would slow him down.

The two of them getting up on the bull was a comedy in itself. Harry had to hold her to keep her from sliding forward. He held her pressed against his chest, and what held him in place, she wasn't quite certain. While they struggled to get situated, a line began to form. The photographer got in a hurry, snapped two shots and told them, "That's it." Rainey had little confidence in how her image would appear.

Much to her relief, however, the pictures turned out very well. She looked a little surprised in one, but not drunk and not too silly. And in the second she looked downright good. She gave Harry that one, because he looked his perfectly handsome self in both of them.

CHAPTER 19

Giving Fate the Third Degree

They started off for the carnival rides—Rainey had been attracted by the Ferris wheel turning against the blue sky—but on their way they passed the petting zoo, where Harry was like a kid, and Rainey remembered that he'd said he had never had a pet. Then, when they passed the pig races, they stayed to watch two complete races, and then they went back to the horse barn, where they caught the tail end, so to speak, of the Western pleasure riding, which Rainey likened to watching concrete set but Harry enjoyed, so she set herself to enjoy it, too.

Time had slipped away, and it was nearing three o'clock when Rainey said she had to go to the motel to get some sleep. Exhaustion had hit her with a suddenness, and she wanted to lie down so badly that she almost left Lulu tied to the trailer and went off to the motel. Thankfully Harry remembered the mare as Rainey was unhooking the trailer from the truck. He even walked the horse to her stall. Apparently he had sufficiently overcome his fear, at least of Lulu, who went along docilely.

On the drive to the motel it occurred to Rainey that she had forgotten to call and reserve a room for Harry. It was possible that the motel would be booked solid, with all the fair atten-dees and the rodeo people flooding the area. If they couldn't give him a room, she would have to share her room, which was the only practical and polite thing to do, and if that was the case, she knew she couldn't be trusted.

She didn't mention any of those concerns, of course; she didn't want Harry to know the nature of her thoughts at all. She sought to act perfectly cool, going on the theory that passion denied became nonexistent. This sometimes seemed to work, al-though she was perfectly aware that passion very often behaved like that unpredictable spark from the fireplace which can some-times light unnoticed in just the right place and burst into a full blaze to burn the house down. Probably all she had to do was take a full look at Harry in his cowboy hat, or maybe have her gaze accidently light on the hollow of his throat, and she would end up throwing herself at him.

She was balancing precariously between anticipation and fear, and keeping her gaze downcast, when the clerk handed them each a key, separate rooms side by side.

"I'm goin' to sleep for at least two hours," she told Harry, as she opened the turquoise door to her room, letting the puppy go on in, which he did, as if to check it out and make certain it was safe for her.

Harry was looking at her. "Sounds good," he said.

"I don't want to eat any later than six-thirty, though. I like my stomach to be pretty empty when I go to race."

He nodded, still looking at her. She thought she was saved from her uncertain passion because he had left his hat in the truck. And, too, she was simply too tired to face passion and all the fears it generated.

She picked up her bags, went into her room, shut the door and leaned against it, holding herself back from calling after him, listening to him go into his room and shut his door.

She set the bedside radio alarm for five o'clock. Then, down to her bra and panties, she slipped between the bedsheets, all parts of her body voicing relief. She didn't, of course, fall directly asleep. She lay there listening for sounds from Harry's room, but she didn't hear anything. The people on her right came in and began arguing, something about where they were going to eat. The puppy jumped up on the bed, and she told him to get off. There was no sense starting that habit, but he looked so downcast that she put her jeans on the floor for him to lie on. He seemed pleased.

The phone rang in the arguing couple's room, and this reminded her that she needed to call Charlene and check in with her location and motel phone number. She thought she would have to defend herself immediately, because she had not telephoned her sister sooner, but Charlene started right in with the latest episode of Daddy and That Mildred.

"Get this," Charlene said. "This morning before dawn, That Mildred Covington twisted her ankle while she was gettin' out of the bathtub, and she had to sit back down in it and call for Daddy to come help her out."

"Was he in her house?" Rainey was a little shocked. It wasn't like her father to stay at anyone's house. He hardly visited inside someone's house, although he would go up to the porch or stand in the yard and talk. If Mildred Covington had gotten him to go over there all night, she was making good headway.

"No. He was at home. That Mildred is apparently practical and takes her cordless phone in by the bathtub each time she bathes. And she just as apparently doesn't have any girlfriends she can call, so she calls a man to come over and help her naked self out of the tub."

Rainey pictured Charlene's head going back and forth for emphasis.

"The phone is practical," she said. "She probably should get one of those call buttons. Mr. Blaine helps a lot of his customers set those up."

"Uh-huh."

She thought she could hear Charlene drumming her fingers.

Charlene said, "Daddy had to help her out of the tub and take her to the doctor, too."

"Well, it's good that he could help." Rainey didn't volunteer the information that sprains couldn't be firmly diagnosed, and it could have been every bit the farce Charlene obviously thought it was.

"Oh, that woman makes me just want to go over there and jerk her head off," Charlene said.

Rainey was beginning to feel the same way, which she thought was a silly sentiment. "Charlene, it is good That Mildred Covington can give Daddy something to help him through his time of mourning."

"Oh, yeah. She's gonna end up givin' him a heart attack, that's what, makin' him haul her big naked butt all over creation."

"If she hoped to titillate Daddy, I doubt she succeeded. His eyesight is pretty poor these days," Rainey said, and jumped to change the subject by telling her sister about running into Leanne. "She's racing here, too."

"Then I hope you weren't plannin' on winning. Last I heard from Joey is that Leanne can't be beat with that horse of hers."

"That's what I hear, too."

"How's Leanne doing? I have not seen her in...gosh, probably a year."

"She's pretty, just like always. She tried to be nice. She said she was sorry about Mama, and she about started cryin'. Did you know she and Mama were good friends?"

"Everybody was Mama's friend. She didn't know a stranger," Charlene said. "And one time I went over to the house to visit with Mama and Aunt Vida, and Aunt Vida went on and on about what a good smart daughter Peggy was and what a no-good foolish daughter Leanne was. Mama took up for Leanne so strongly that I was a little surprised, but Aunt Vida is so thick she never noticed. I understood Leanne a lot better then. I guess she has to act stuck-up, with her mama always down on her. Peggy had her picture in the paper the past week. She's been voted best teacher in the school district."

"Leanne's had her picture in the last three issues of the WPRA."

"A rodeo publication is not the same thing in Aunt Vida's eyes. For one thing, it is not a home paper, so none of Aunt Vida's friends read it."

"I met another friend of Mama's, a Herb Longstreet. Did you know him?"

"No…I don't think so. But good golly, Rainey, Mama would start talkin' to anybody like they were a long-lost friend, and later, when I asked who was that, she'd say, 'I don't know. We were just talkin'.' I don't know how she managed to never get robbed. Speaking of robbed, what happened to your doctor?"

"He isn't a robber."

"That's good. What happened to him?"

Rainey shifted up on the pillows and gripped the receiver. "He came on up here to Amarillo with me." Her voice came out hoarse.

"Oh?" Charlene waited, and when Rainey couldn't get anything else out, she said, "How deep are you?"

"Deep enough to need a lifeline." She was a little surprised at her answer. Until that minute she had not realized the depth of her emotion for Harry. She gripped the phone receiver as emotion swept her—doubts and fears, mostly.

"Well, my goodness. Well. This *is* a development."

It was a development, all right. Now that she was looking at it, she was startled. She had not felt anything of this sort in a long time. After her failure with Monte, her passion for anything had pretty much dried out, and she had believed this was for the best. When one did not feel deeply, one could not be hurt deeply.

"Do you think you might marry him?" Charlene was saying, although it took a few seconds for her question to penetrate.

"No—good grief, Charlene. I've only known him for a few days." The impression of her family seemed to be that she was flighty and irresponsible. Freddy had called her a dingbat, and Charlene had used the term *free spirit*.

"That's long enough to get married. Joey's cousin Mel got married to a girl he knew for just a week."

"Well, with my track record, I don't think I have any business thinking about gettin' married again."

She sat up, bending her legs. The puppy, who was now lying on her boots, turned and looked at her, as if seeking a cue to get on his feet. She thought that she didn't have any business keeping a dog, either, and she was pretty certain Charlene was going to be annoyed when she brought him home.

She said, "It's just that my vow of celibacy seems to be slipping."

"Celibacy? When did you come up with that?"

"When I got divorced from Monte. It seemed the thing to do, with my record. And I wasn't much interested in men, anyway."

The line hummed, and then Charlene said, "Oh, my gosh, then this one—Harry, isn't it? He's the first since Monte?"

Rainey nodded, as if her sister could see her. "Yes...and, Charlene, this is so stupid."

"Feelings are never stupid," Charlene said in a scolding manner. "Feelings just *are,* neither good or bad of themselves, just troublesome. Are you sleepin' with him? Is he there now?" She dropped her voice to a wild whisper, like that mattered over the telephone.

"Of course not. I wouldn't call you if he was." She looked over to the empty side of the bed, and Harry's image swept through her mind. "But I wish he was. Oh, Lord, Charlene...I never thought I'd feel this way again. I know that sounds a little silly, but since I haven't felt like this all these years, I figured I was beyond it. Now...oh, I'm just so confused. I don't want to turn into a woman like Lila Hicks and have a path worn to my back door by men comin' for a sample, and giving away so many pieces of myself until all I have is this horrible bleached hair and desperate eyes with bright-blue shadow."

"No, you don't want that," Charlene agreed readily. "Even though I don't think I should criticize poor Lila. And I think you are a far ways from it, since you haven't been with anyone since Monte." She sounded as if she were still mesmerized by that fact.

"Lila Hicks probably started because she kept thinking she was in love," Rainey said. "That's how I got married twice."

"I think if he is the first to get you in this state since Monte, you can be certain you feel something genuine for this man."

Rainey considered that. "Yes...but I don't see that it makes a difference. I felt genuine love for Robert and Monte, and look how that turned out."

"I see your point. And you really haven't slept with anyone else?"

"No," Rainey said. She was a little annoyed that her sister

kept belaboring that particular point. "What do you think of me, Charlene? I have never slept with anyone but my husbands, which is probably my entire problem. I am hung up on feeling such a commitment about sex."

"I didn't think anything, except that you are thirty-four and really pretty and healthy, and it just seemed natural that you'd have a man now and again."

The line hummed.

"I never really thought about it at first," Rainey said. "I was just so upset at messing up with Monte, knowin' the reason I had gotten tangled up with him was because I had let myself go in regards to sex. I'd just been so *needy* in that department. Later, I would feel needy sometimes, but mostly I've just cried myself to sleep, or gone driving or riding. Really, there hasn't been much temptation. I don't meet lots of eligible men."

"No, Valentine does not contain an abundance of available men," Charlene agreed with a sigh. Then, "Oh, Rainey, you must have been so frustrated. Sometimes I've gotten so worried about what I might do if I lost Joey. I haven't ever admitted it, but I just can't imagine goin' for years without sex. I do believe the teachings of the Bible—it is practical advice to have restraint—but a healthy woman going without sex is one thing that seems beyond me. Maybe if one loves God so much, sex with a human doesn't matter. I can understand that, and I can understand gettin' old and outgrowing the need for sex, or maybe goin' crazy and not needing it, but by and large, most healthy women need it. I love Joey so much that sometimes I can't keep my hands off him, and sometimes at night I've gotten so scared at the thought of what would happen if he died that I've woken him up to make love to me."

For a minute Rainey had a bit of panic, thinking that her sister was going to go on with details, which would not help her at all, but thankfully, Charlene stopped.

Rainey said, "Charlene, time just gets by, and finally you come to see that you don't want a man for just physical things, and you can make it without one for almost anything else."

Charlene said, "I guess. But it seems that if you've met a man who sparks your heart, I believe it is a blessing. He could be the one you have been longing for."

"No. He's just passin' time, passin' through." Her heart didn't want to accept that, she thought, which was the entire problem.

"Well...I guess you might end up being glad you let it all go right by you," Charlene said. "A good rule of thumb is always to do nothing until you are certain. And I would say that I've heard a lot of people say they had regrets about havin' an affair, but I've hardly heard anyone say they regret *not* havin' an affair."

"How many people do you know who have had affairs?"

"A few," Charlene said in a knowing manner. "And look at all those people on the soap operas. If a person has half a brain she can sure learn from a soap—those people are hardly ever happy, and what they do most is jump from one affair to the next.

"Oh, my gosh, someone is pullin' up...it's Mary Lynn's car...and she's brought Jojo home...I wonder what's happened, Jojo was goin' to spend the night with Sarah over at their house. Mary Lynn looks serious...and she's carryin' somethin'. I've got to hang up now."

Charlene's voice had been steadily rising until it vibrated with high agitation. Rainey said, "Goodbye," quickly in order to give her sister freedom, but as she went to hang up, she heard Charlene yell.

"Rainey, wait! Thanks for calling me, honey. And you are

not like Lila Hicks and never will be. Trust yourself. Don't be afraid of your feelings. Don't be afraid of *yourself*."

She rather startled Rainey with her hurried stream of words, and it was several seconds before she got out, "Thanks, Charlene." She didn't know, though, if her sister heard, because quite quickly there came the hard click of the phone being hung up.

As she replaced the receiver, she wondered about Jojo. Her niece was the sweetest little girl, but she could do unpredictable things. One time she had taken twenty dollars from the jar in the kitchen, money Charlene was saving for Joey's birthday party, and bought ice cream for all the neighborhood kids, and another time she had hidden a little neighbor boy under her bed for an entire night.

Rainey supposed it was this little quirky bent of Jojo's that made her one of Rainey's favorite people.

Slipping down in the bed, she rolled over and closed her eyes, feeling relaxation wash over her. She mused that the talking hadn't settled anything, but at least it had gotten her jumbled emotions out. As she fell asleep, she thought of how she could be unpredictable, too, like Jojo. But she was all she had. And she was tired of being afraid of herself.

A knock sounded on the door while she was using the curling iron on her hair. Her heartbeat did a little jump. She whipped open the door, and there was Harry, as she had known he would be. But she was surprised to see him holding a small arrangement of flowers toward her.

When she just stood there staring, he pushed them closer, saying, "These are for you."

"Oh." She took the vase of flowers. "Thank you."

She realized she needed to step backward to let him in.

"Where did you get these?" she thought to ask. The flowers were in fall colors, mums, little lilies, carnations, all her favorites.

"Florists deliver. So does the pizza parlor, and I hope you like yours with mushrooms. It should be arriving any minute. I thought we could have pizza in and avoid rushing and the crowd, and after the rodeo, we could go over to this restaurant the clerk told me about and get dinner. I didn't think you'd be able to go much longer than four hours without food."

He went over and sat himself down in the blue upholstered chair. Sat all the way back in it.

Rainey set the vase on the table and thanked him again.

He said, "I wanted to show you I appreciate what you've done for me."

"I haven't done anything special. I've appreciated your company." Then she turned quickly, saying, "I just have to finish with my hair." She was going to pull it back in a ponytail at her neck, but the ends needed to be controlled.

Looking into the mirror, she heard him click on the television, and then her gaze drifted to see his reflection in the glass. He had the remote in his hand as he watched CNN.

She kept glancing at him in the mirror, quick little glances that she didn't think he could see, and she saw him glance at her, but they each went on pretending as if neither felt the pull between them. It was a magnetic pull, one that suddenly was so strong that she imagined if someone tried to walk between them, they would get bounced right off the magnetic waves.

She would glance at him and then at the vase of flowers. She told herself that the magnetic pull was probably her imagination, but then she saw him repeatedly looking at the floor in her direction, and she realized he was looking at her feet, which were bare.

This caused her to became inordinately aware of her bare

feet. She felt naked. The pull continued between them, so strong that she could not meet his gaze for fear that a blaze might occur in midair.

She began to think that maybe she should bring it out in the open, say something like, "Listen, we have got to get this settled. Are we going to make love?"

Or maybe she would simply turn around and go to him and kiss him.

But of course she couldn't do that. There wasn't time, for one thing. She had to get herself together and get over to race Lulu around barrels.

She was all wrapped up in these thoughts while Harry watched television and looked at her feet, and then she dropped her earring as she pulled it from her jewelry pouch.

It was her habit to wear the silver disks with Indian designs when she rode; she felt they were her lucky earrings, even though she didn't really believe in luck but in God. Maybe she believed mostly in her mother, because it had been Mama who had given her these earrings.

When she dropped the earring, it bounced in a most peculiar way, and she didn't see it anywhere. The carpet was a gunmetal color, and her earring was antiqued silver. She went down on her hands and knees, and then Harry came over to help her look. He got down, too.

"I don't see how I could lose it in this little space."

"Maybe it bounced into the bathroom...I don't see it."

"Well, it couldn't have disappeared."

"Here it is." He had moved the trash can and found it lying next to the baseboard.

"Well, that is strange...bet I couldn't do that again."

Then he was looking at her ear and saying he would put it in for her. She stood stock-still with anticipation. His hands were gentle, and he knotted his brows in concentration. She tingled from her ear down her neck at his touch. Then the magnetic force took hold of both of them and brought their eyes together. There really was no need for words, because they were both asking the same question.

Rainey looked at his lips, and the memory of when he had kissed her flashed across her mind. The next instant, she said, "Thank you," and turned away and began throwing all her cosmetics and brushes back into their case, clinging to ignoring him for all she was worth.

Then the young man arrived with the pizza. Rainey hurried to get into her purse for money, but it turned out that Harry had cash. He said he'd found an ATM at the convenience store half a mile down the road. Apparently he had been getting around while she'd been sleeping.

CHAPTER 20

Rodeo Gals

Rainey almost missed the grand entry.

It took more time than she had imagined to stop and get a collar and leash for the puppy, and she felt that had to be done, since he was going to be left tied to the trailer while they attended the rodeo. They selected the collar and leash quickly enough, but then had to stand in a long checkout line, made longer because the cash register decided to get confused. Pretty soon three people had to work it over. Rainey might have just left the collar and leash, but she worried that because of her procrastination in getting a proper leash and collar, and then her impatience, the puppy might get hurt.

Then she discovered Lulu had thrown a shoe. She found it in her stall. The mare had probably kicked the stall wall, in the way she had of doing when she got annoyed at being confined. The only farrier was backed up with serious difficulties with two roping horses, and slowed by a handy bottle of Jim Beam, too. If Lulu had thrown the shoe right before the race, Rainey would have raced with it like that, but since it had happened early enough to get corrected, she felt it her duty to do so, even if it meant she could possibly miss the grand entry.

As she awaited her turn, not wanting to miss her place in line, feeling disappointed because she wanted to ride out in front of Harry, who had gone off to get them box seats and would be looking for her, might even worry about what had happened to her, Leanne came by, saw her predicament and said she would ask Clay to fix it.

"Clay's daddy was a farrier, and he's shod horses since he was a boy. He does all my horseshoeing. I won't let anyone else touch them."

Rainey appreciated Leanne's generosity. Her cousin obviously was confident that there was no way Rainey was going to come close to being competition for her.

Leanne went off and came back with Clay, who was terribly handsome and likely looked great bare-chested on a calendar. Her next impression, however, was of a surly individual.

"Come on over to the trailer," he said in a gruff voice, directly after Leanne had made the introductions.

Pivoting, he started away in long rapid strides. He might not have been overly tall, but he had long legs. Leanne, tugging along her horse, ran to catch up to him, and Rainey tugged Lulu and broke into a jog to follow, going out into the twilight, leaving the riders gathering for the entry and the music pouring out of the arena. They had to pass right by her own rig, and the puppy wagged and barked, and she felt mean not stopping, but she hurried on, having the sense that if she so much as slowed down, Clay was going to whirl on her and yell, "Come on."

Clay reset Lulu's shoe in the manner of a man who could do it in his sleep. While Rainey could not fault his ability, she did not approve of his impatient manner toward Lulu.

Rainey stood there paying attention in a way that let him *know* she was paying attention, ready to jump in if he got too rough with her horse. Leanne ducked into the trailer and came back out and stood nearby, and she and Rainey chatted, the sort of talk you have when you really aren't paying attention.

"Lulu is pretty as ever," Leanne said.

"She's reached her prime."

"I have a gelding you might be interested in, if you want to keep racing and get somewhere with it."

"I don't know. I'm goin' home on Sunday." It occurred to her that going home had nothing to do with it, but it seemed to.

Leanne said, "Oh, well, maybe when I get back there I'll give you a call."

Then they both fell silent. Leanne seemed to fade inside herself. Although she didn't say anything to Clay, it was like she was listening to him. She stood watching him with her arms sort of wrapped around herself. There was something about the two of them that made Rainey nervous. Of course, Leanne usually made her a little nervous.

Clay finished and dropped Lulu's foot, saying, "You'd better get her shod all around pretty quick. That'll be thirty dollars."

She was so surprised that at first she wondered if she'd heard him correctly.

"Oh, Clay, don't be silly," Leanne said in a surprised and annoyed tone. "This is my cousin…no, Rainey, do not worry about it."

"I think all I have is a twenty," Rainey said, digging into her pocket.

"I said don't worry about it," Leanne said, her voice sharp. "I'll cover it."

Clay hadn't said anything. He was putting his tools away.

Leanne had her eyes glued on him, while giving Rainey a dismissing wave.

Rainey, uncertain, held out the twenty, and Clay took it with a nod, and then the three of them started back to the arena, Clay again walking quickly and Leanne double stepping to keep up with him. Rainey was just as happy to follow more slowly with Lulu, to put a distance between herself and them. She could hear Leanne's angry whispers and Clay's deeper ones. She was a little embarrassed to think she was the cause of them arguing.

Thirty bucks for ten minutes work, she thought. It was the expertise that cost, not the time, she supposed, mulling over the fact that back home she could have had Lulu completely shod all the way around for a top price of forty-five dollars. But she wasn't back home, and this had been an emergency, so she supposed she should be grateful. A man was worthy of his hire. And he wasn't a relative of hers. Thank heaven.

She had always loved rodeo grand entries. She liked the lively music that played and the way, at the small, hometown rodeos, that everyone rode around, from fat grandmothers to little bitty cowboys about falling off their mean old Shetland ponies.

This rodeo, being professional and a little higher on the scale, had only the professionals riding around. Men who worked for the rodeo company and a rodeo queen did a routine with the Texas flag, the rodeo company flag and the Stars and Stripes. The rest of them—Leanne and Rainey managing to make it in at the tail—just rode around them, a flamboyant rush of colors, pounding hooves and flowing tails.

Perhaps Lulu was not the fastest barrel racing horse, but it was Rainey's belief that her mare was one of the prettiest out there, and Rainey had dressed carefully, keeping in mind as she always did to wear colors to match her saddle blanket and

Lulu, too. Charlene had been the one to teach her to do that; she called it having flow. Rainey knew she was a good sight, and she rode around with confidence. *Cocky* would be a good word. There on Lulu she knew she was okay and in control of herself.

She missed Harry the first time she went around, but she found him on the second. He sat right in front, almost in the middle of the arena. He had his hat on. She waved, and he waved back, with that grin of his.

The Amarillo rodeo arena was old and small and great for people in the box seats around the rail, who got a close-up view of the contestants trying their hearts out and breaking their necks.

"Oh…I can't look!" she cried and covered her eyes with her hands.

She heard the buzzer, and Harry said, "He's okay," and patted her thigh.

"He is? Oh, good."

She let out her breath. Harry was regarding her curiously.

"I get so excited, no matter how much I see all of this. And in these seats, we could end up watching someone get his neck broken right in front of our faces."

Right then, as she spoke, a pickup man rode in front of her, and she could have reached out and plucked the Skoal from his back pocket, if his pants hadn't been so tight.

She saw the bronc rider dusting himself off in the arena not fifteen feet from their seats. He raised a hand to the crowd, but he was limping. A boy, he appeared to Rainey, when he'd come bouncing past on a thick bucking horse, bouncing so hard that there was a foot of daylight between his bottom and the bronc saddle, until he slipped sideways and then clean off and was dragged along with his hand still wrapped in the rope. It was a wonder his arm had not been ripped clean off before the pickup man managed to get alongside to rescue him.

"I'll bet his mother is having a good cry somewhere," she said, watching him until he went out of sight behind the chutes. The thought that she could have a son that age startled her.

"I've seen them as young as that mangled from car wrecks while they drag raced."

Harry's comment reminded her that he was a doctor, which she guessed she tended to think little about. He leaned forward, his gaze swinging back to the chutes, and she looked at his dark hair curled over his collar. Itched to put her hand there. That he was a doctor seemed strange to her in that moment, although she couldn't say why. She had thought he was on the edge of his seat from interest, but now she wondered if maybe it was his habit to stay ready for any sort of contingency.

After the grand entry, she had put Lulu in her stall and come to join Harry until it was time for the barrel racing. That was the definite advantage of not being a champion. Leanne wouldn't leave her horse alone and was very careful in whose care she did leave him when she had to, because she was afraid someone might steal or drug him. She was right this minute riding her horse quietly around in the area behind the arena.

The announcer was giving the names of the bucking horses coming up and telling a little about each one, to take up time while the next entrant prepared to ride. When the announcer called the name Pete Lucas, Rainey recognized it as the one Leanne had mentioned in connection with Clay's. He appeared to be having a bit of trouble getting settled on his bronc, because the bronc—called Texas Tornado—kept trying to climb over the rails of the chute. All the bucking horses were named— the bulls, too—and generally lived a well-fed and even pampered life when they were away from the arena. When they proved to be good stock, they got to be well-known and thought of fondly in many cases.

All this Rainey explained to Harry as Pete Lucas tried to get himself atop the bronc. Then the chute opened and Texas Tornado jumped out, clearing the ground with all four feet, and she almost put her hands over her eyes, but she got so caught up that she didn't. The bucking horse sunfished before taking off across the arena, with Pete Lucas bouncing right in the middle of his back and pumping his legs in rhythm with the horse, perfectly balanced, reclining so far he was about lying down. He made such a ride that it brought people to their feet and cheering.

Rainey and Harry clapped and cheered as hard as everyone else. He grinned at her, and she did the silliest thing. She leaned over and kissed him quickly.

Undoubtedly it was the lively look in his brown eyes, and she was certain that being only a few feet away from the possibility of witnessing death affected her, because she suddenly felt extremely alive.

Harry didn't look surprised. Pleased, but not surprised. Probably he had often been near death and not a lot surprised him.

She was surprised at herself, though, and turned quickly away to watch the next rider.

It was as if she were seeing it all through new eyes, as she explained the rules and objectives to Harry. He really liked the steer roping, but the bulldogging appeared to be his very favorite. At first he got awfully upset about the way the steer was jerked around by the neck, by both the rope and the man's hands, but when each time the animal got up and trotted away unhurt, he relaxed. Rainey decided not to tell him about the one time she had seen a steer that did not get up and trot away after being roped. All sports have their fluke accidents. If people didn't accept that, she supposed elementary school football would have been stopped a long time ago.

"I have to go get ready."

She really hated to leave him. They were having such a good time, and the intermission clown act was wonderful, but she couldn't sit still any longer. She had begun to worry about her performance in front of Harry, and to anticipate it, too.

"I'll go with you," he said, standing.

She looked at him. "You won't be able to see the races much from the entry door, but you could run back up here, I guess…if you want to do that."

He said he would, and suddenly she was very glad he was coming with her. She reached over and took his hand, leading him along.

The night had turned sharp, and they stopped for her jacket at the truck, and to pet the puppy.

The horse barn had people coming and going, but it was a different atmosphere, illuminated by light fixtures dropped from the ceiling. More intimate and expectant somehow. With Harry walking alongside, she led Lulu to the outside training pen. As she mounted to ride the mare in a few warm-up circles, Harry, no doubt recalling how his watching her disturbed her concentration, casually went to the truck, ostensibly to quiet the puppy from barking.

As she rode into the staging area, he walked along beside Lulu. The other barrel racers were waiting there, and one said that the clown act was about to wind up. The Dodge truck was ready to drive in and set up the barrels.

She glanced down to see Harry's bright eyes upon her. He reached up and put a hand on her thigh, letting it rest there. She was aware of his warm palm clear through the denim fabric of her jeans. Aware of his long legs as he stood casually, his wide, wiry shoulders under his denim jacket and his intent brown eyes shadowed by his hat.

Rather than a distraction, his presence was at that moment a comfort. The knowledge came full upon her how sweet it felt that he was there and sharing it all with her. Pulling for her. And then she was swept with sadness, thinking of her mother and that this was what her mother had wanted, each time she had asked one of them to come watch her. Mama had wanted to share her experiences, her trying, and just whatever happened with something that she loved to do.

Rainey felt great regret that she had let slip past so many of those times she could have enriched her mother's life and had her own enriched, by sharing. She wondered if these regrets would ever quit washing over her.

Loud explosions came from the clown act in the arena— clown acts relied heavily on smoky explosions—and then out came the clowns and in went the Dodge truck with the barrels.

Harry gave her thigh a squeeze. "Good luck." And then he left to go back to his seat. She watched him walk away, but it was as if a part of him remained, and she wasn't alone.

She breathed deeply and spoke to Lulu, telling her that they had to settle themselves and think about the ride. Get prepared.

Just then, as she was trying to concentrate on preparedness, Leanne appeared, thrusting her reins at Rainey and requesting her to hold her horse while she ran to the rest room.

"Ever since I got pregnant, I have to pee about every half hour," she said in a very aggravated tone and hurried away.

Pregnant? Rainey was shocked.

But then she thought her shock was quite foolish. Pregnancy was a very natural thing and did tend to happen when a woman had a relationship with a man. As the shock faded, jealousy inched over her. She was going to be thirty-five and had let her opportunities for a child pass right by her, along with her failed marriages. She would gladly have put up with having to pee every half hour, she thought, if she could have a child.

She told herself to let that go and get ready to ride. She didn't want herself and Lulu to embarrass themselves. And then, as life would have it, right when the announcer was calling the first barrel racer, her gaze lit on Herb Longstreet. He was near the arena door, looking in. She thought to go over and speak to him, but there she stood holding Leanne's horse and trying to get herself prepared.

She was fifth to go. Things were looking good; only one woman ahead of her had made any time at all. Of course, Leanne hadn't yet run.

Screwing her hat on her head, she headed Lulu toward the entry. The mare was a growing ball of eager energy between Rainey's legs, swishing her tail and champing at the bit. Rainey watched the girl ahead of her run around the barrels; she knocked one with her knee, but it didn't fall over.

The girl came racing out of the arena, and Rainey danced Lulu up to the entry. Watching an official, she took three deep cleansing breaths and offered it all up. Then she tapped Lulu's sides, and they were off.

Bursting out into the bright lights, heading for the first barrel, Rainey urged Lulu, who reached for ground. Scooting neatly around the first barrel, digging earth, and across to the second barrel. Hooves and hearts pounding. She and Lulu seemed to take wings and fly.

Look at me, Mama!

Around the third barrel and heading for home like a flow of

wind, everything a blur to her eyes and the roar of the crowd in her ears and Lulu a grand power bearing her along, and as she came bursting out of the arena, blowing right past the next rider with her determined brows, laughter bubbled up and out, as it always did, and she knew with the certain knowing that the reason she did this was for the incredible exhilaration of it.

Whew! It hovered there, that glorious feeling, like a glow swirling around herself and Lulu. She set the mare walking in a circle. Several people smiled at her, and she knew she wore that grin that causes people to smile in return. Then she saw Harry heading toward them across the sandy ground.

She flung herself right off Lulu and into his arms.

CHAPTER 21

One-Way Rider

She was amazed when it finally got through to her that she had scored a time of seventeen seconds. This was the fastest time she had ever achieved on Lulu, and it put her tied for second with a girl named Martha Reed.

"Maybe it's because I held Leanne's horse for her while she went to the rest room," she told Harry. "He and Lulu exchanged breaths, and maybe he gave her some hints in the process."

Harry chuckled at this, but she was halfway serious. Something had happened. Maybe it was the clear high-plains air. Or perhaps it was as simple as all the practice finally coming together. Rainey got so caught up in the excitement of the achievement, and in praising Lulu as she walked her to cool her down, that she forgot all about the rest of the barrel racing and missed seeing Leanne's performance. No doubt after Leanne raced, she and Martha Reed would be tied for third, which was still really good, in her estimation.

Returning to the arena after settling Lulu in her stall with some alfalfa, they came upon Leanne outside the back door, leaning against the wall. She had the reins of her gelding in one hand and her other hand pressed across her stomach.

"Leanne…are you all right?"

Her cousin gave a little weak nod. "I think so. I just felt faint. I think it is probably the hard ridin'."

"Leanne's pregnant," she said to Harry, as she automatically felt into her jacket pocket for a napkin, in case it should be needed. "Why are you holdin' your stomach? Are you hurting?"

"No…I didn't know I was." She dropped her arm.

"Why don't you sit down," Harry said, but it wasn't a question. As he spoke, he took her arm and led her over to a stack of hay bales nearby, jerking one off the top and plopping it down for her. Easily, probably from all the practice he'd recently gotten with Uncle Doyle.

Leanne sank down on the hay, while she held on to her horse's reins. She removed her hat, without any regard as to how her hair would look, which was a definite worrisome sign to Rainey.

While Harry took Leanne's wrist to check her pulse and asked her if she was having cramps, Rainey went to find a faucet to wet the two napkins she'd found in her pocket. When she came back out, Harry was telling Leanne that she probably should have something to eat and put her feet up.

Rainey gave her the damp napkins, and Leanne pressed them to her temple.

Harry said, "I think it was the hard riding—got her out of breath. But it wouldn't hurt her to lie down."

"I'll just sit here," Leanne said. "I'm feelin' a lot better, but I'll just sit here for a few minutes."

Rainey suggested tying Leanne's horse to a nearby post, but Leanne said he wasn't one to stand tying and might jerk away and get hurt. Rainey thought it was a good sign that her cousin was strong enough to remain protective of her prized horse. And he wasn't any trouble, anyway; occupied with snatching alfalfa out of the bales, he wasn't likely to wander, even if Leanne let him go.

"I'll miss Clay's ride," Leanne said. "Would you go watch, Rainey, and tell me what happens?"

"Maybe I should go get him."

"No," she said with some alarm. "I'll be fine in a minute, and Clay will be disappointed that I missed his ride. If you'll go watch and tell me, I can tell him that I saw."

Rainey closed her mouth against the comment that Leanne's pregnant state was a little more important than Clay's bull ride. "Harry will go watch and come back and tell us," she said.

Harry was willing, as he always was. He went off, and Rainey sat down beside Leanne.

"What is he—a doctor?" Leanne asked.

"Yes."

"Well, for heavensake," Leanne said, blinking in surprise. Then, looking away, "He's awfully nice, Rainey. The kind you just want to hug all the time. You're lucky."

"Yes…" Then she added, "We're just spendin' the weekend together. Friends."

"Awfully friendly," Leanne said with amusement.

Rainey's self-consciousness was quickly overcome by worry about Leanne, whose amusement, which had not been all that much anyway, had faded. For once Leanne didn't seem to be sucking Rainey's energy. She appeared too weak for that.

"Feeling any better?" Rainey asked, wanting reassurance.

"A bit, yes," Leanne said, again pressing the damp napkins to her temple.

Rainey thought maybe her cousin's body was better, but her spirit was low.

"What was your time?" she asked, thinking it would boost Leanne to talk about how quickly she'd run around the barrels.

"Sixteen-three," Leanne answered, absently, not seeming to care.

"Well, that puts you in first place, doesn't it?"

"Yes. I knew I would be…I didn't have to work at it."

Rainey supposed Leanne's comment was more fact than cockiness.

The sounds of cheering reached them. Rainey said whoever was riding was doing good. She wondered about Leanne needing to lie to Clay about seeing him ride. Rainey did not think her cousin's relationship with Clay was at all on stable ground, but she thought she should restrain herself from comment.

Just then Leanne said, "Clay's real sensitive. He always wants me to see him do well."

Rainey was a little startled that Leanne should pick up on her thoughts. She said, "Oh…well," which was the best she could do, and that with great restraint.

"Clay wants me to have an abortion," Leanne said.

"Oh…well," she said again, all manner of emotion rolling up inside of her. She rather thought Clay did a lot of wanting. "What do *you* want, Leanne? It is a baby in *your* body."

Leanne sighed deeply. "I don't know," she said wistfully, then added, "Clay'll hate me havin' this baby. It'll tie us down, and he doesn't want that. And I don't want to lose him."

Rainey's first question was, why not? She bit the words back for fear of sounding critical, but her feelings rather came out anyway, when she said, "You don't want to lose a man who wants you to abort his child?"

"Don't go gettin' righteous on me, Rainey. Your closets are pretty dusty, too."

"I'm not being righteous," she said. "I know I've made plenty of mistakes in regard to men—in regard to my entire life, really—but I don't think that precludes me from asking a practical question."

"Pre-*cludes?* Only you would talk like that. I don't even know what it means," Leanne said in a sarcastic manner.

After a moment, Rainey said, "I'm not being righteous. I think because I've made so many mistakes, maybe I can pass to you something I've learned. You don't seem all that hot to have an abortion, and it seems to me you need to think a lot more about your choices."

Leanne played with the end of her horse's reins, and Rainey sat next to her, thinking her cousin was being stupid, and also that she shouldn't be judging. For his part, Leanne's horse caused a lot of rustling, having loosened a bale of hay enough to get big, full bites.

"I lost a baby," Rainey said.

Leanne swiveled around to stare at her. Rainey turned her gaze to the shadowed ground.

"I married Monte because I was pregnant," she said, "but I lost her at almost five months when I was in a car wreck. Wasn't a big wreck, hardly anything...but enough, I guess. It was a little girl." She looked at Leanne, at her pretty face gazing so intently back. "Yes, I lost her, didn't have an abortion, but the results pretty much add up the same. I didn't have her, and there isn't a day that goes by that I don't wish for her, Leanne. You think I'm righteous? I guess maybe I am, because I do not have my daughter, and I may never have another child, and I get really annoyed at women who just wipe out their babies because it is inconvenient."

Leanne looked away. "It isn't because it's inconvenient. It's…oh, Rainey, I don't even know how to be a mother. And Clay probably won't stay around to be a father. I don't know how I'll support a child. How can I bring a baby into a life so uncertain and messed up?"

"Who does know how to be a mother? It's like barrel racing—you read manuals, and you try until you find what fits. Only motherhood isn't competition, Leanne. You don't have to do it perfectly, you just do the best you can. And it's up to Clay, if he doesn't want the child, but you can't overlook that it's growing inside of you. You're thirty-one. How many more chances do you think you are goin' to get?"

Leanne looked down at her boot.

"You can put the baby up for adoption, Leanne," Rainey said hesitantly, feeling she was overstepping all sorts of bounds. "If you really feel you can't be a mother, that things aren't right, you can put her up for adoption. There's lots of people who want babies so badly."

"And how am I goin' to survive in the meantime? Go home to Mama? Not hardly. She's goin' to hate me over this. I never have been what Mama wanted. You know what she told me when I was last home? That I was a tramp. I guess this will prove it."

"I don't see why a child should prove it any more or less," Raine said. This line of thinking had always provoked her. "Why put that much on a child, who is a blessing, not a condemnation?"

She realized she herself had always sort of considered Leanne rather trampy, and she was ashamed of this. Lord only knew Rainey had no room to be pointing a finger.

"I have no savings," Leanne said. "Every bit I've earned these last years has gone into building my career and my horse business. Clay owns part of that, too. I just don't have anywhere to go, Rainey."

Leanne's desperate voice went clear through Rainey. Casting around for some hopeful thing to say, she considered the point that perhaps Leanne had underestimated her mother, but on second thought, probably Leanne knew her mother full well. Aunt Vida could be hard as rock.

"Anything you want badly enough can be worked out," she said at last. And then it hit her. "Daddy's in that big house all by himself. You could stay there."

Leanne's head came round, her expression startled, but then it softened, as if maybe she was turning the possibility over in her mind.

"You know how Daddy is. He loves babies."

Leanne shook her head. "Rainey, you live in a fantasy world. You think you can solve everything by finding me a place to live, but there's so much more to this. I have a life."

"I know. I know that," Rainey said. She probably should have let it go, but more came out anyway. "Don't let Clay bring you down, Leanne. Raise him up, if you can, and if he doesn't come up with you, then you go on without him. Don't let him be the reason you abort your baby. Think this over really good and decide for yourself."

She guessed she was as bad as Mama and Charlene about controlling her opinions.

Leanne said with annoyance, "Don't you think I am, Rainey? Don't you think this is breakin' my heart?"

"How you feel now is nothin' to how you're goin' to feel if you get an abortion. I have seen plenty, working at Blaine's pharmacy."

"Just shut up, Rainey."

She thought then that she did need to shut up, although she had a real struggle doing it. The wild idea to say, "I'll take it. Give it to me," came to her, and she might have blurted that out, but just then a pickup truck pulled up, and a man got out and said they were sitting on his hay and he needed to load it up. He wasn't happy when he noticed how much Leanne's horse had eaten, but she told him that he shouldn't have left the hay sitting there where anyone could have at it. She had apparently sufficiently recovered herself.

While the man was still loading up his hay, Harry came out and gave a report of Clay's ride. He described what he had seen in great detail. Rainey imagined it was because of his profession as a doctor, trained to notice every little thing.

Leanne thanked him all over the place and took the opportunity to touch his arm a lot. Being pregnant didn't stop her from coming on like gangbusters.

CHAPTER 22

A Woman's Heart

As she stepped out of the dressing room of her trailer and into the glow of the pole lamp, her heart beat with anxious expectancy. She wore a long-sleeved sweater with a neckline so wide it was almost off the shoulders, requiring a strapless bra as it would on occasion slip off one or the other shoulder in an especially sultry feminine way she liked, although she shivered in the cool air. The sweater was over a flowered silk skirt and fancy custom-made boots, and she had done up her hair.

She had not dressed for a man in a long time. She had not gone out with a man in a long time, and this was a bona fide date. Harry was taking her to a place he had gone to the trouble to seek out, a place he said would have Spanish guitar music—in her mind very passionate—and Mexican food—hot and spicy—and wine—enticing and sweet.

He looked at her, and she was thrilled by the way his eyes were eating her up.

He said, "You look beautiful."

"You're awfully handsome yourself," she replied.

They gazed at each other for a few more seconds, and then the puppy's yipping drew their attention. He wriggled at the end of his leash tied to the trailer. She didn't want to leave him tied there while they were gone. He'd been there so many hours already, and there was a chance of rain, maybe a storm that would frighten him.

"I think I'll put Sergeant in the dressing room," she said, going over to release his leash.

"Sergeant?" Harry said.

She was trying out another name. "He is a police dog...at least mostly."

"Don't you think you might confuse him with all these different names?"

"I want to get just the right one. That's really important."

"I agree, that's why Roscoe is good."

She cast him a skeptical look. "It sort of sounds like an old bum," she said as the puppy clambered happily into the room.

"I think a comment like that would offend the Roscoes of the world. You're operating from some sort of prejudice."

"Oh, well..." She laid a pair of her jeans down, and the puppy curled up on them immediately. "I have never met anyone named Roscoe," she said, leaving the light on as she shut the door. Hopefully he would be content enough that he wouldn't tear up anything.

They had driven about five blocks, following the directions to the restaurant, when seemingly at the same moment that it began to rain, the truck suffered a flat tire. The right front, this time, a blowout causing the wheel to pull hard but conveniently over to the curb.

"Maybe this rain will pass quickly," she said, still gripping the steering wheel and gazing at the drops on the windshield.

But Harry, already removing his expensive sport coat, said, "I'll get it changed quick."

She insisted the rain would pass in a few minutes, but he wouldn't listen. Slipping into his denim jacket, he buttoned it up, snugged his hat on his head, shot her a smile and told her to wait in the truck. "No need for both of us to get wet."

She watched him slip out of the truck and sort of duck against the rain. He stepped back to the truck bed, where, luckily, they had left the spare and jack after leaving Uncle Doyle's. It didn't seem to be raining too hard, and maybe it would not get worse.

Harry disappeared downward beyond the front fender. She looked through the rain-spattered glass and nervously watched traffic going past, worrying that someone could crash into them and push the truck right over Harry.

Then the rain began to come down harder, until it was streaming over the windshield. Lightning forked the black night sky, and thunder cracked sharp enough to cause her to jump. Then lightning came again, hitting just one street over, she was certain.

She grabbed her mother's old brown sweater and held it over her head as she popped out into the storm and went around and yelled at Harry, "Get in the truck. You're gonna get electrocuted!"

"I'm already wet now," he yelled back at her. "You get back in the truck." He was having a fight with a lug nut and cast her only a glance. He had only succeeded in removing three of them.

She could not get back in the truck and leave him out in the rain, possibly to be struck and killed by lightning. It seemed the least she could do was stay there and brave it out with him. She pleaded for him to get into the truck, but he ignored her, and she saw a stubborn streak in him that he must have been saving up all these years of giving over to his daddy. He put both his hands and one foot to fighting with the lug nut. The lightning cracked and rain poured, while she stood there with a sweater over her head, watching water dribble off his hat, knowing clearly that in the days since she had met him, she had been so preoccupied with her own inner struggles and reactions to him, that she had not truly seen *him*.

Another particularly close lightning strike, and Harry grabbed her arm, propelling her to the passenger door.

"Get in there." He opened the door and shoved her inside.

Stunned, she sat there a moment. He had not fully closed the door, and rain spattered on her arm.

Throwing Mama's sopped sweater to the floorboard, she opened the glove box. The Bible popped out at her, reminding her to say a few hasty prayers as she dug under the napkins for a small can of WD-40. Again getting out of the truck—she could be just as stubborn as he could—she hurried around Harry to spray the lug nut, although it seemed a fruitless gesture in the pouring rain. Harry watched her as if she were crazy, but then he went to work on the lug nut again, so she figured he was crazy, too.

There in the pouring rain and with lightning hovering overhead, he kept at it until he was able to remove the flat tire. She lifted the spare to roll it toward him. He pushed her hands away and took the tire from her, and she watched him put it in place before she went around and got back into the cab behind the wheel.

Her wet sweater sleeve did little good when she pressed it to her runny nose. She sat there waiting, sniffing, shaking in her clothes, the sweater hanging off her right shoulder, dribbles of water tickling her neck. Reaching out, she turned the heat on full. She was digging out a towel she'd remembered was stuffed behind the seat when the passenger door opened and Harry came in with wind and rain.

He slammed the door closed and removed his hat, and when he tipped it, water streamed to the seat.

His gaze came over to meet hers. Then she glanced up at his hair. It was dry, perfectly dry, while the rest of him was sopped. Pointing this out, she started to laugh. His dry hair seemed as absurd as what they had both done.

"What were you thinking?" she asked and passed him the towel.

"To change a tire. What were you thinking?"

They gazed at each other a moment and then went to pointing fingers at each other and calling each other stubborn and crazy.

"I think your father should see you," she said. "I'll bet he never knew you could be this stubborn."

"Oh, I think he knows," he said, patting his thighs with the towel. "That was the whole problem."

She didn't know what to say to his comment. She was a little overwhelmed by him. There was something she saw in him now, a rod of steel that put her in awe and admiration and even made her a little afraid, in an excited sort of way.

"I guess you wouldn't want to go on to the restaurant," Harry said, disappointment echoing in his voice as his eyes swept over her hair and down her clothes, lingering distinctly, she saw, on her wide neckline and breasts.

"Well, I think I do. I'm hungry, and I'd just as soon go, if you don't mind me goin' with how I look."

"You look great to me," he said, which she thought was wise of him. But he did seem to mean it.

So they were off again, her driving and trying to see through the rain, and Harry reading the directions on a now damp scrap of paper. The ink had run, and Harry couldn't be certain at one point if they were to turn left or maybe the clerk at the hotel had written "Rt" for right.

They ended up lost in what looked to be a rather tough neighborhood. The rain had stopped, and they could see better, but reading the addresses didn't help a lot, as the clerk had not written down a street number, only the name of the restaurant and the street it was on. At least driving around so long gave them time to drip-dry down to damp.

After circling one block twice and still not finding the restaurant, Harry pointed to a couple of men standing on a corner underneath a streetlight, out in front of a seedy-looking little bar. "I'll ask them where this place is."

She didn't think that was such a good idea, as the men looked decidedly questionable, as any two men would, standing like that at such a late hour in front of such a bar. She pointed this out to Harry and cited that he and she were outsiders in such a neighborhood. "I could fit in," she said, "but you are definitely a Yuppie."

"I think, riding in this truck, I am fitting in quite well," he told her.

She overlooked his disparagement of her truck, cautioning, "They could be drug dealers or something." They definitely looked like the sort she had seen on television.

He said, "I don't care what they do for a living. I just want directions."

He gazed at her expectantly. Still reluctant, she nevertheless directed the truck to the curb in front of the two men. She thought of her Daddy's gun in its pocket, but a safer course seemed to remain in gear and ready to drive. She thought that if the men made any type of threatening move, she could hit the gas and get out of there.

In response to Harry's question, one of the men stepped forward. He was a black man, with close-cropped hair, a tough-looking face, a neck as thick around as his thigh, and a threadbare coat. She kept her feet ready to switch pedals.

Then he spoke and came out with the mildest voice, saying, "Well, son, you're a little off course." He smiled at her and nodded. "Evenin'."

"Good evening," Rainey said, surprised.

The man rubbed his stubby chin, saying, "Let's see now...how many blocks down do you reckon it is, William?" He looked at his friend, and they discussed in lazy drawls and decided all Harry and Rainey needed to do was to keep going in the direction they were pointed for about four blocks.

"You'll see it off to the right in the middle of the cross street. Has the name in magenta neon lights. Real good place, too. Sometimes Spanish music, sometime jazz. Good."

Her mind was going over his use of the word *magenta*. Whoever used that word?

Harry thanked him politely, and the two men told them to enjoy themselves. Rainey waved happily at them as she headed the truck away, and the two men waved in return.

They found the restaurant exactly as the men had said.

To Rainey's relief, the ladies' room was very near the entry, and she zipped in there to repair herself. Her hair was her biggest problem. She managed to pile it atop her head in a helter-skelter but very feminine fashion.

As it turned out, she need not have worried overly about her appearance, as the dim atmosphere of the restaurant was completely on her side. She thought surely the place broke all fire-safety codes. The only electric lights were low green-and-red ones at the edge of the musicians' area, which wasn't a stage but simply a cleared area at one end of the room. Everywhere else, the room was lit by candles, on the tables, in sconces on the walls, on shelves, all casting a warm and flattering glow.

The restaurant was one of the most romantic places she had ever seen in her life. It was small, decorated like a patio in Mexico City, or what she imagined a patio to be in Mexico City, with vines and flowers winding upward and hanging from overhead beams—artificial plants, she felt sure, but they looked very real in the dim candlelight. At every white-cloth-covered table, couples gazed at each other over red candles. Except for one table next to a wall, where two gray-haired wizened men played chess in the light of three candles they had taken from other empty tables. Tonight the music was Spanish, acoustic guitar played with passion and beauty, a lively style to make a person tap his toe, and slower, emotional ballads of life that touched the heart and brought tears to the eyes. That most of it was sung in Spanish she couldn't understand didn't matter; the music transcended language.

Harry could speak Spanish, she discovered, when he ordered quesadillas and wine. His accent leaned toward East Texas, but still, she was impressed. Very impressed when they danced and he held her close and sang the romantic words in her ear. He was thoroughly romancing her, and she gave herself over to it in the manner of a woman who recognizes a rare, precious time in her life.

"I've never been in such a wonderful place," she told him, pulling back to look into his eyes. "I'm so glad we came."

"I'm glad you like it."

He was eating her up again with his dark eyes, in a way that caused all the womanly parts of her to answer.

As they sat at the table, she laid her hand upon his strong forearm, and as they danced, she let her hand feel the hardness of his shoulder. She put her cheek next to his and inhaled his male scent deep into her body, and when their thighs brushed, she didn't pull away. They danced and talked and ate quesadillas and some sort of cake-and-ice-cream dish the waiter said was a specialty, and then they danced some more—just to be able to hold each other—and clicked their wineglasses in a salute to themselves and remaining alive after their foolishness in the storm, and they told each other important things, such as things they had seen thus far at the fair and rodeo, their birth signs and places they had been and things they had seen and laughed at.

Neither of them spoke about what they would do when the weekend was over. How she would head for home and likely drop him at the airport to head for wherever he needed to go, his own homeward journey, she guessed. Such thoughts did enter her mind, but she kept brushing them aside. She didn't want to tarnish this time with thoughts of reality. She figured this time was a gift. She was in his arms and felt happier than she had been in ever so long. Thinking just did not seem a wise thing to do.

And then he said to her, "I may have fallen in love with you."

He said it clearly, after they had not spoken for some minutes, during which time they were simply gazing at each other and holding hands across the table, and she was having the fantasy of kissing him and pressing her body naked against his.

For a moment, in great surprise, she gazed into his eyes lit by the candlelight. They were warm, hot and intent.

"There's no need to go off in that direction," she said.

Thoroughly jangled, she pulled her hand from his and tried to act as if she passed it off as a joke. She was confused and doubtful and disappointed for some reason that she didn't understand. She had not expected him to dabble. It did not fit the picture she had of him, although, of course, it was a very male and human thing to do.

"What's wrong?" he asked. "Is it that you don't believe me? Do you think I'm just handing you a line to get you into bed?" At least the directness was like him.

"What sort of response do you expect to such a statement?" she asked, matching his directness, annoyed that he had started in on this and spoiled the wonderful time they had been having.

He looked surprised at her attack, and this just made her more annoyed.

She said, "You want some response from me. People don't say things like that—" she could not say the word *love* "—unless they want a response. Just exactly what response do you want?"

He gazed at her with a perplexed expression. "I guess maybe I did hope you would say you cared for me, too…but mainly I just wanted you to know what I feel."

She composed herself, seeking to be rational. "I care very much for you. I'm attracted to you, and you well know it. But I know, too, that this is a special time, and a lot of what makes it special is that this is something of a stolen interlude for both of us. Come Sunday afternoon, it will be over. You'll head on your way, and I'll go home. I'll remember this time, and you'll always be dear to me, and I don't want to spoil it all by tryin' to twist it into something that it isn't."

He frowned and looked down at his wineglass, and then back at her. "Why do you think this is just an interlude? Why can't it be a beginning of something for us?"

She did not know what to say to that.

He waited, though, so she tried to come up with something.

"Well, you are just taking a few days away. You have a life to return to, and so do I. I have to go home on Sunday."

"Houston isn't on another continent," he said, with that familiar echo of sarcasm. "I know where Oklahoma is, and how to get there. And I know you know how to get around, so you could find your way to Houston."

She dropped her gaze to his glass. It was hard to get her breath. Very frightening to speak of her fear.

"I've been married twice, Harry. I don't know if I can let anyone in ever again. I'm going to have to be very, very sure."

"I don't think that is going to stop me from falling in love with you," he said, his voice so warm that it enveloped her.

Next he rose and took her hand, and saying in a husky tone, "Come here," he pulled her up and into his arms and danced her out onto the small floor.

Alone on the floor, his arms around her waist and her arms up around his neck. The filtered red-and-green lights that lit the musicians flickering faintly over their faces. She gazed at him, and he at her, as their bodies moved lazily, seductively, together, brushing harder and harder.

I'm so scared, Mama. I can't go through another broken heart.

Then she pressed her cheek against his and let herself lean upon him, let her heart beat against his. And her heart whispered: *Maybe.* Yet still she could not say the word *love.*

They closed the place down. They danced and had another glass of wine, and then another, and gazed at each other in the candlelight some more. They didn't talk much, simply listened to the music. Rainey was glad to do this, to stay where no decisions had to be made.

But finally everyone had gone, and the last musician got up from his stool and left.

"I guess that means we need to leave, too," Harry said.

She rose with him, not saying anything, slipping her hand into the crook of his arm.

Outside, the sky had cleared, and stars could be seen even there in the city. On the high plain, the vast sky dominates even the city lights. The air had turned sharp, whispering of winter. She shivered, and Harry quickly jerked off his sport coat and put it around her shoulders. It was warm from his body heat. His scent engulfed her.

They walked slowly across the small lot to the truck. She handed him the truck keys, saying, "I've had a little more wine than I'm used to."

For some reason she felt he was used to drinking wine. Also, she was shaking clear to her bones.

He guided her to the passenger door and put his hand on the door handle. But he didn't open it.

She looked up at him, seeing in an instant the hot desire sweep his face, just before his lips came down upon hers. Oh, Lord, the sweetness of his kiss! Tears sprang into her eyes, and she began to quiver with wanting so much that she could hardly stand up. The next instant he pushed her back against the truck and pinned her there with his body, while he kissed her for all he was worth. For her part, she kissed back in the same manner, and they went at each other all hot and hard and wild.

When he finally lifted his lips from hers, she was not only breathless but she could hardly see.

She blinked, seeking focus, and found herself gazing at his throat, upon which a slice of light from the pole lamp fell. She saw his heart beating there. He still held her against the truck with his body. She throbbed against him, and he against her. She wished they never had to move, and in her passion-fogged state she might have believed that they never would.

His fingers tilted her chin upward, and she looked into his dark eyes, which regarded her with certain intent. Then he kissed her again in a deliberate manner that drew a moan from her throat and brought dampness springing to intimate regions. He didn't stop until she was out of breath and totally incapable of standing on her own.

Holding her up, he again gazed into her eyes.

"I am falling in love for the first time in my life, and I want to see where we go with this," he said. "I mean all of it, not just the sex."

"Oh, Harry," she said, because nothing else would come, and dropped her head against his chin.

He lightly kissed her hair, and, still holding her up, he opened the door and slid her inside on the seat. She watched him round the truck and slide in behind the wheel.

As he started the truck, she scooted over beside him. She laid her hand on his thigh and her head on his shoulder, rather melting against him. Her heart seemed to beat in the juncture of her legs.

Do you think this could really be the one, Mama? God? How can I know what is real?

On the way back to the motel, with Harry's thigh flexing beneath her hand, she seesawed, one minute daring to believe that it could be true, that a miracle really was occurring in her life and she had found her man at last, and the next minute telling herself to have some sense, and keep hold of the pieces of her heart.

She wondered, too, how it would go when they reached their rooms. She would have to make a decision. Her self-control was not at a high point, and she felt Harry was in the same situation, never a good position from which to make a decision.

She actually found her sexual response to Harry very gratifying. She had found that she was alive, and surely there was hope for her to feel emotion again. Harry had brought her hope that she could indeed care for someone.

Then they were passing the fairgounds, and she remembered the puppy and Lulu.

"We have to get Sergeant," she said, coming up off his shoulder. He looked surprised. "And Lulu—I always check on Lulu in the night at a public barn."

"Okay."

He turned the corner and headed for the contestant entry gate. Remaining sitting up straight, she took a good breath, and her eyes drifted downward to her hand on his thigh. She was at once relieved and annoyed at having to stop at the fairgrounds. In fact, she wasn't certain she would be able to get out and stand up. She felt as if unfulfilled passion had weakened her bones.

"Wait here, and I'll get Roscoe," Harry said, and she gladly did so, taking the time to gather her strength.

Quickly he returned with the puppy, who bounded up into the seat, and the three of them drove over to the horse barn. When Harry drew to a stop in front, she looked over and saw there were lights inside and out at Leanne's trailer and for the first time gave her cousin a vague thought.

Then Harry was reaching for her hand, and she scooted out of the truck, glad to find her footing more stable than she had anticipated. Holding hands, with the puppy happily leading the way and glancing back at them, they trooped inside to see about Lulu.

After having been so long in dimness, Rainey blinked in the bright light. She was self-conscious about how she must look; her lipstick possibly smeared, and her hair in thorough disarray, wearing a large sport coat which did not match her skirt and sweater. She wondered if her inward craving for sexual fulfillment showed. She wouldn't look Harry in the face, but with a glance she noticed he looked just fine. Any man with a good haircut can go through anything and still look fine.

There were several other people checking their horses, a couple of men playing cards outside a stall, and some riding and cutting up in the barn arena.

At their approach, Lulu lifted her head and even whinnied, but when she discovered no Twinkie cake was forthcoming, she dropped her head back down and shifted away with disgust. Rainey felt badly about forgetting a Twinkie cake. She petted Lulu, but the mare kept her head turned. Checking Lulu's ankles, Rainey found them fine and was convinced that Lulu had not been kicking the stall walls. Satisfied that Lulu was at this moment in perfect comfort, Rainey edged out of the stall and closed the gate.

Stuffing her hands into the jacket pockets, she looked at Harry and saw he was looking at her.

He reached up and gently took a stray strand of hair hanging against her cheek and tucked it behind her ear. Then he caressed his thumb over her bottom lip, his eyes asking all sorts of questions. Feeling a rising heat and urgency, she dropped her gaze to his chin. His head came down, and he kissed her in a quick, driving manner, to which she hungrily responded, tears coming to her eyes.

Then, almost before she had realized, she had put her hand to his chest, pushing gently. Turning, she headed away down the aisle. She had the urge to run far and fast.

The next instant, Harry was walking beside her. To her surprise, he took her arm and looped it through his. He smiled down softly. A sliver of pleasure slipped down her back. With the puppy sniffing along in front of them, they walked to the front doors and out into the night.

CHAPTER 23

Love, Crazy Love

Harry opened the passenger door for her. She guessed now that she'd let him drive, they both were going with it.

"Ah…maybe we should stop for coffee," he said, his eyes hopeful.

"Yes. That's a good idea." She didn't want to part from him, yet she didn't want him to know the full extent of her longing for him, either. It was a very precarious position.

Just as she started to slip into the truck seat, a yell and a bang jolted their attention toward the line of trailers and campers across the lot.

Another bang, which she immediately placed as being from Leanne's trailer, possibly her horse kicking the trailer wall. Leanne had a small pen set up beside her trailer, but the horse was not there. Rainey figured he had to be in her trailer, as Leanne was too paranoid to put him in one of the public stalls.

But then there came a scream, and a figure resembling a strawberry-haired baby doll—it was Leanne, bare legs catching light—came flying out the door of the camper to land on the ground with a thud Rainey was quite certain she heard. Next, Clay, bare-chested, came out the door to the ground with one long stride, yelling at Leanne and jerking her up and beginning to beat the tar out of her, while she screamed back at him, trying to get away.

At the same moment, Harry and Rainey started running toward them.

"Hey!" Rainey yelled, sending her voice where her hands couldn't reach as Clay went to shaking Leanne like a Raggedy Ann doll.

She came to a halt, though, when she got close enough to see his face, the skin tight over his cheekbones and his eyes pure mean. At that sight, fear shot down her body and planted her in her tracks.

Luckily Harry wasn't deterred. "That's enough," he said, attempting to get between them in a reasonable manner.

Unfortunately, reason made no dent in a madman, and Clay swept Harry aside and kept hold of Leanne's arm, dragging her toward the trailer, yelling something about it wasn't anyone's business.

Harry went at him again, and the puppy started barking around at their feet. Seeing the brave puppy and then Leanne's terrorized expression at last propelled Rainey into action, and she jumped into the fray, trying to pry loose Clay's hold on Leanne.

Panic gave her the idea to bite his hand, but just as she was about to do that, Harry threw himself on Clay, at last freeing Leanne's arm. As Rainey caught her cousin, she saw Harry draw back and punch Clay. For a second time that evening Harry shocked her. The power of his punch was such that Clay's head snapped backward, his body stumbling along with it. Then Harry took a stance in front of her and Leanne, legs apart and hands clenching.

She was now on the ground with Leanne, who had sunk to her bare knees, and between Harry's legs she saw Clay scrambling to his feet, like a mad bull. But then a new figure jumped on him, and the next instant there were people all around.

Leanne had blood pouring from her nose, and Rainey felt handicapped to help as she did not have any napkins.

Someone said something about calling the police.

"Oh, don't call the police," Leanne said, her voice muffled from her hands wiping her nose. "Don't let them call the police, Rainey," she said to her, as if she thought Rainey could order the world.

"I think they already have," she said, pushing away the puppy and helping Leanne get to her feet, anxious to get her out of the cold wind, as all she had on was a shirt and panties.

Harry came up on the other side of Leanne, and they got her inside her trailer and sitting down on the cushioned bench. It was bright in the camper, everything all sparkling chrome and shiny vinyl wood. Jerking off Harry's jacket, so as to not get blood on it, Rainey turned to the sink and found paper towels, having to move several whiskey bottles to do it, while Harry attended to Leanne, doing that penny thing beneath her upper lip and having her tilt her head back. He took her pulse and looked her over.

With the wet towels, Rainey wiped the blood from Leanne's face, wiping around her bloody hand that held the penny. At least Leanne appeared to have all her upper teeth. Her bottom lip was battered good, and hopefully she hadn't lost bottom teeth; Leanne had lovely teeth. There was a swelling on her cheek.

The urge to take a two-by-four to Clay's head welled up in Rainey.

Harry asked Leanne if she felt any pains, if anything seemed to be broken. Rainey took it as a good sign that he wasn't immediately dialing for an ambulance.

Leanne moved her arm, testing. Then she shook her head, mumbling around the penny, "My arm is pretty wrung, but it's not broken. I'm okay."

Just then the trailer door was jerked open, and Rainey whirled, preparing to smack Clay, if it was him, but it wasn't. It was a shorter figure, with dark blond hair, and when Leanne said, "Oh, Pete," she knew it was Pete Lucas, and that he was obviously a friend.

Catching sight of the puppy through the open door, Rainey squeezed around Pete Lucas to let him in. A woman outside asked if they might need to send for an ambulance, but she told her Leanne seemed okay. She closed the door and looked around to see Pete Lucas crouched in front of Leanne.

"Are you okay? I'm so sorry…." He looked pained, as if he wanted to reach for her but held himself back, and Rainey knew at once how it was. He was in love with Leanne.

Leanne nodded and took the penny from beneath her lip. "There isn't anything for you to be sorry for," she said weakly, trying to give him a smile.

"He was gettin' so riled, and it seemed to me that my bein' here just added to it. I thought it'd be best if I left. I guess I should have stayed."

"You didn't have anything to do with it," Leanne said, shaking her head sorrowfully. "He was upset about his ride is all. And all I got is a few bruises. I've had worse horse wrecks."

Then she shifted her eyes to Rainey, and suddenly great tears welled up and spilled over in silver streaks. "I wouldn't let him hit me in the stomach, Rainey. I protected my baby."

"Oh, honey…" She sank down and took Leanne in her arms. "You did real good, honey." Then both of them went to bawling, while Harry and Pete Lucas looked on.

After a minute of all this, Harry brought more wet towels and began wiping both women.

The police came, but Leanne wouldn't press charges, so they didn't waste much time on any of it.

"He didn't mean anything by it," Leanne said. She had recovered her normal coolness. "Clay gets down sometimes, is all, and if I had kept quiet, he'd have been all right."

"Has he done this before?" Rainey asked, alarmed.

"It isn't somethin' that goes on all the time, Rainey." Leanne was examining her face in the mirror.

Rainey sent a questioning eye to Pete Lucas, who was sitting beside Harry on the little couch, both men leaning forward, forearms resting on their thighs. Pete returned a look that said Leanne wasn't exactly telling the truth.

"There's no excuse for anyone losin' their temper like that, Leanne," she said.

"No one is perfect, Rainey. Clay is goin' through a rough time right now. His ex-wife won't let him near his kids, and she's taken just about everything from him. He's doin' the best he can. Tomorrow, when he's calmed down and realizes what he did, he'll be really sorry."

While she spoke, Leanne studied the blue bruise beneath her eyes. Rainey was fairly certain Leanne's right eye was going to be downright black.

"I think I'll go take a shower," Leanne said and laid down the mirror. She got up and went to the small bathroom. As she started to close the door, she paused and said, "Rainey, you'll be here for a while, won't you?"

Her face was pinched. She looked so small there in the door, spatters of blood on her shirt.

"Sure. I'm going to make some coffee."

The minute she heard the water start in the shower, Rainey turned on Pete Lucas for the entire story.

"I understand you're a friend of his. What kind of man is he? Does he do this sort of thing on a regular basis?"

He looked startled to be so questioned, and she watched him, trying to figure him out, how he could be friends with the type of man who would beat a woman.

He wet his lips and said, "He's shook her up pretty good a bunch of times, but this is the first time he ever hit her like that." Then he added, "That I know of, anyway. His ex-wife, she got a restraining order against him. That last split up they had, Clay tore up their house. I've known him a long time, and he's always had a temper, but this past year he's been gettin' a little crazy."

Harry was regarding her; he didn't look surprised at all. It occurred to her that he must see a lot of this, being a physician.

Pete asked Harry, "She's really okay, isn't she? The baby…"

"As far as I can see, she and the baby are fine," Harry told him. "She needs to take care, of course, but a healthy fetus is actually pretty tough to dislodge. He really didn't beat her, just slapped her around."

"He gave her a black eye," Rainey said, surprised at Harry's attitude.

"I've seen women who couldn't be recognized."

At that, she had to turn from him. She went to get cups from the cabinet, and a weakness, a great sorrow, washed over her. For an instant she was swept back in time to when her baby died inside her. Mama had said it was meant to be, and even the doctors had said they had suspected a problem with the baby's heart. None of that had been a consolation to her.

She leaned against the cabinet, and then Harry was there, his arms enveloping her from behind and his warm lips pressing the cool bare skin of her shoulder.

She felt obligated to stay with Leanne through the night. She had the belief that if she stayed, Clay would not return. He was in all likelihood passed out in the room of another one of his friends—Pete and Leanne both assumed this was the case—but she still felt responsible for being with her cousin. Pete felt the need to stay, too, and as she was there, Harry and the puppy—which Leanne started calling Buddy—stayed, too.

In the early hours of the morning, Rainey's and Leanne's womanly talk about pregnancy and how it felt to have babies moving over the bladder and the breasts getting tender drove Harry and Pete Lucas outside. Both men had seemed a little cramped in the small camper anyway. Harry kept having to keep his tall frame ducked down, and Pete just seemed too thick, his shoulders bumping into something every time he turned around. With the puppy's presence, it seemed each time one person moved, another had to move, too.

Harry went to get the truck from in front of the barn, and Pete went with him. The two of them sat in it, parked in front of Leanne's trailer, rather like sentries on guard, slouched down in the seat, dozing, while the puppy, unable to understand human female conversation, lay happily on Rainey's foot.

Peering out the window at the shadows in the truck, Rainey thought to go out and tell Harry to go on to the motel to sleep in his bed. But she didn't want him to go. She liked knowing he was right within calling distance.

When she pointed out to Leanne that Pete had remained out there, too, Leanne nodded and said, "He's really sweet."

"It is obvious he is in love with you."

Leanne shrugged, averting her eyes. "I guess."

They were sitting across from each other at the little table, doing their fingernails. It was something to do in the early hours to keep their hands busy, and apparently Leanne was as particular about her nails as Rainey. She had a very extensive manicure kit, containing a dozen different nail colors.

"Why do you prefer Clay to a guy like Pete?" she asked.

Leanne looked at her and blinked. "Pete is nice, and I like him a lot, but it wouldn't work between us. And I don't appreciate you bad-mouthin' Clay."

"I'm not particularly bad-mouthing Clay, but I do wonder why you think it works with a man who beats you around, and say it wouldn't work with a man who comes with his heart in his hand to see if you are okay." Leanne's continual defense of Clay provoked her.

"There's a lot you just don't know, Rainey." Leanne shot her a frown, then focused on painting her fingernails. After long seconds, she said, "Pete is nice. Too nice. I'd drive him crazy in no time. And nice can get a little wearing, tryin' to live up to it day after day."

"I might rather try that than gettin' beat up day after day." Rainey wondered if Leanne meant that Pete was boring, or maybe that she didn't feel nice enough to match him.

"That may be how you see it, Rainey, but that doesn't make you right." Then she said, "There's just somethin' about Clay. We are a lot alike, he and I. He takes me just like I am...and he needs me."

Rainey understood such logic. Need spoke to a woman. Right then Rainey felt that even if she didn't like Leanne very much—and she suspected Leanne knew that—she needed to help her somehow.

She said, "Women get burned up by men like Clay. Men like Pete keep a woman going."

Leanne tilted her head. "Maybe...but Clay won't let me go off with another man while I have his baby."

"But he wants you to abort it?"

Leanne gave her a look that clearly said she would not understand. "He's afraid of losin' me. When his wife had their two kids, she didn't pay him any attention anymore. And we do have our careers. A baby is a big consideration. Very soon I'm not goin' to be able to ride."

"Are you still thinkin' about gettin' an abortion?" She had thought that surely Leanne had changed her mind, considering her efforts against Clay.

"I don't know," Leanne said, a little vaguely. Then she threw down the tissue she had been using. "I just don't know, okay?"

Rainey did not know what possessed her, either, but the next moment she was saying, "Leanne, I'll take the baby."

Immediately she thought of her little cottage, not much bigger than this camper. Precious little room for a crib. Maybe Daddy wouldn't mind if she moved back home.

Leanne's eyes came up, shocked at first, and then defensive. "I don't know as I want to give up my baby, Rainey. And I'm just as capable as you to be a mother."

"I didn't say you weren't. You are the one sayin' you aren't sure you want this baby, and I'm telling you I do want her."

"We don't know if it is a her."

"Her or him, I don't care. I'm offerin' you an option, Leanne."

She was a little surprised at herself. But she figured she had surprised herself before.

And then suddenly she thought of Harry. What would he say? Well, it probably wouldn't work out with him, anyway, and the baby would be a comfort. Someone to love, to care for. Good for Daddy, too. She saw him holding the baby. Maybe caring for a baby would bring them closer, and he wouldn't need That Mildred.

"It is a good solution, Leanne. You could still see her and everything."

"Don't go makin' plans for me, Rainey. Don't push me. I get enough of that from Clay and Mama. And if you want a baby so much, go have your own."

Rainey could not think of anything to say to that, at least, not anything nice.

After a minute Leanne said, "If I have this baby, I'm goin' to be unable to ride for months. There's nothin' good about that.

"And nothin' good about havin' to go to the toilet every ten minutes, either," she added, getting up and going into the little bathroom.

Slowly Rainey replaced the cap on the bottle of polish. She had only put one coat on her nails, and they looked streaked, but she felt deflated and had no heart for pretty fingernails. In the face of Leanne's predicament with Clay and the fate of a baby, painted nails seemed a little inane.

The night had turned out to be awfully confusing.

She moved the curtains and looked out to see the two shadows on either side of the truck cab. There was such a lonely aura about that.

Just then movement caught her eye. A man. He came out from between two horse trailers and stood looking their way. She couldn't be certain if it was Clay, but she thought it was. She froze, hoping he couldn't see her, but of course he could, there in the light.

A few moments, and he turned and went back into the shadows, leaving her thinking about him. No doubt Clay had a lot of internal demons. He certainly didn't need another child. He was too big a child himself.

Somehow, when dark night lifts, so do human fears. It was as if, when dawn came, they were all safely assured that Clay was not going to return drunk and go wild some more. This was Rainey's and Leanne's reaction, although the guys had no doubt come to that conclusion long before.

Leanne, who had curled up in her bed in the gooseneck, fell into a deep sleep. Rainey got up from where she had been dozing with her head on the table, slipped into Harry's sport jacket and nudged the puppy awake with her foot.

"Come on, Buddy."

The puppy and she stepped out into the gray dawn of a crisp morning. There was no frost, but she could see her breath.

Pete Lucas's head was against the passenger window of her truck. She walked around to the driver's side, where Harry sat with his head back on the seat. Gently she opened the door.

"Everything all right?" he said, coming awake immediately, his eyes opening clear and focused, although he moved slowly.

"Yeah." She nodded. "I need to feed Lulu, and then we can go to the motel." She felt herself sinking into exhaustion.

Harry reached over to shake Pete Lucas; he had to shake him robustly to get a reaction. At last Pete came semiawake.

"Do you want us to drive you somewhere?" Harry asked him.

Pete shook his head and pointed and mumbled that he would just go into Leanne's. He stumbled inside her trailer, probably taking advantage of Clay's absence to simply be with her and look upon her. Rainey thought that maybe he would be lucky and Clay would be gone forever, although she sincerely doubted this happening.

Harry got out, and she scooted into the seat. The puppy came bounding up beside her. Then Harry got behind the wheel again and drove over to her trailer to get the grain and hay for Lulu.

"I'll take care of feeding her. You two stay here," he said, leaving Rainey with the puppy's head in her lap, the engine running and gradually heating the cab.

That she let him feed Lulu was testimony to her exhaustion. And to her trust in him, she supposed. She leaned back against the seat and watched him through the window. Bucket of grain in one hand, flake of alfalfa in the other, he disappeared into the barn.

He did not look at all like the man she had picked up along the side of the road all those days ago, the one who had worn loafers and slacks and a silk shirt. The one who had professed to be afraid of horses. Since she had not known him before, she could not be certain of her assessment, but he seemed changed from that man. He remained slender and handsome, and sarcastic, too, but he was no longer the lost man she had first found. There was a certainty about him now, a peace about him. Of course, he could have had that all along, and she might not have seen it, being preoccupied as she was with her own concerns.

She had met him in midchange, she thought. The change had begun before she met him, at the moment he had dared to face his father and follow his own desires.

Suddenly came the whisper of a thought, like a breath on her heart. Maybe the somewhere Rainey herself had been looking for was as simple as finding the courage to accept herself and go for what she really wanted.

She knew then, with that particular knowing the spirit has, that all of it, Robert and Monte, and all the mistakes she had ever made and all of the good choices, too—such as picking up Harry—were a part of her life and to be valued. Yes, even the mistakes were to be valued, because they were each valuable pieces of what made her.

Thinking of this, she drifted into sleep and roused only slightly when Harry slipped again into the seat. He put his arm around her and drew her close, and she snuggled gladly into his warmth. She felt the truck rumbling over the road.

The next thing she became aware of was Harry's voice saying, "Rainey. We're here."

He shook her gently, and then he was helping her out of the truck. He had already opened the door to her room. They stopped there in the opening, and he handed her her purse.

"Get some sleep," he said and kissed her quickly, before going on to his own door.

She went inside, closed the door and leaned against it, listening to his door close.

CHAPTER 24

Heart with a Past

The first thing she saw when she opened her eyes was the bouquet of flowers Harry had brought her the day before.

The light-blocking drapes were parted, letting in a stream of ethereal sunlight that illuminated the flowers from behind, and she lay there looking at them, dragging up from sleep like she always did.

She thought that maybe waking would not be so difficult for her if she always had flowers to gaze at first thing upon opening her eyes.

She reflected that it had been just yesterday evening when Harry had showed up with the flowers. Not even twenty-four hours.

It seemed at least a week ago, because enough had happened in the hours since to fill a week. Her mind skimmed over all those events, going back to seeing Harry standing at the door with the bouquet.

This was the first gift of flowers she had received from a man since...since Monte had wrecked her Mustang and tried to apologize with a bouquet, flowers which she had suspected he might have swiped from the cemetery, as they had been definitely greenhouse cut flowers clutched bare in his hand.

She recalled how Harry had looked when he handed her the bouquet, so pleased and hoping for her pleasure. She worried that she had not thanked him enough. She had been so surprised at the time. And afraid to let her feelings show when they really did come over her.

Various images of Harry, like snapshots, streamed across her mind and filled her with wonder. She saw a quiet man whose gentleness masked a steely strength. He was a man who continually turned his face fearlessly—or foolishly, as the case might be—to the wind. He did not laugh easily, but he was easily amused. And almost nothing shocked Harry, she supposed from all he had seen as a doctor. This was a very comforting quality.

This singular man, Harry, had said he thought he was falling in love with her.

She grabbed a pillow and clutched it to her chest, feeling all manner of desires and fears. They overwhelmed her to such a point that she rolled over to reach for the phone and call Charlene, moving so quickly that she startled the puppy, who looked up from where he lay on a pair of her jeans, ready to jump to his feet, should that be required.

Three rings, and Charlene's answering machine picked up.

"If you get this in the next hour, call me at the motel," Rainey said into the receiver.

She hung up, feeling sharply disappointed at not being allowed to discuss her thoughts with her sister. Sometimes thoughts not given voice tended to get jumbled up again. In fact, her thoughts already seemed to be crumbling. Where she had for a split second experienced clarity and a rising hope, she now had doubts trying to crowd in as fast as ponies crowding around the feed trough.

She took hold of the prospect that Charlene could return her call any minute. Flinging back the bedcovers, she went to shower, leaving the bathroom door open so she could hear the phone if it rang.

It occurred to her that she was at last becoming closer to Charlene, from a distance. She wondered if their newfound relationship would continue when she went home. Maybe whenever she wanted to talk over anything deep with Charlene, she would have to telephone her.

The phone did not ring while she was in the shower. She checked it when she got out, but there was no message light.

Standing there with a towel around her, she dialed Harry's room, hearing the ringing both on the line and through the wall. Maybe he was asleep, although he normally would come awake immediately. When he did not answer after eight rings, she clicked off and dialed the front desk.

"I just dialed Mr. Furneaux's room, but there was no answer. Has he checked out?"

"No, ma'am," the voice seemed surprised. "I believe I saw him drive away a few minutes ago."

"Oh. Thank you."

She went to the window and peeked through the curtains. The space where her truck had been was now empty, the sun shining on a grease spot on the concrete.

Of course this was not strange, she told herself. Harry had walked a number of places yesterday morning, while she slept. He had her keys from last night, so this morning he could drive himself where he wanted to go.

She wondered if he might have gone to buy her more flowers.

Her heart was pounding furiously, and she pictured Harry walking along the highway, away from her. Or, in this case, driving away.

It had to do with her poor experiences with men, she knew, and took herself by the scruff of the neck and got dressed, did a complete makeup job, and even put a new coat of polish on her nails. Then she took the puppy out for a walk. There was a nice grassy field at the rear of the motel. Coming upon a stick, she threw it, attempting to teach the puppy to fetch. When he got it, she called to him. He looked at her, stick between his jaws, and cocked his head this way and that.

"Come, boy. Here, Buddy."

He remained poised, gazing at her.

"Here, Roscoe," she said, and he came running. "Oh, Roscoe…good boy, Roscoe," she murmured, burying her face into his fur, filled with thankfulness for him.

Then standing and holding his leash, she urged him to run, and she ran with him, over the stubbly fall grass and rock, far out of sight of their room.

Maybe if they were gone long enough, she thought, Harry would have returned when they got back.

Finally, out of breath and growing hungry, the puppy with his tongue hanging out, they walked back across the grass and to the rear of the motel, along the covered walkway. When they came to the corner, she peered anxiously around it.

Yes! Relief swept her as she beheld her truck sitting in its space, the bright afternoon sunlight hitting the roof.

Then her gaze fell on Harry, leaning against the fender, the sun shining on his brown hat and denim shirt. Looking like a Levi's jeans advertisement, waiting for her.

When she got close enough, he looked into her eyes and said

hurriedly, "I just went to get your spare tire fixed. I got you two new front tires put on, too."

He regarded her with apprehension.

The puppy pulling her forward, she went to him. He opened his arms and enveloped her against his warm chest that smelled of cotton and sunshine.

"I'm sorry," he said, stroking her hair. "I didn't mean to worry you. I didn't want to call and wake you up…. I thought I might get back before you woke up."

She shook her head against his chest, unable to get words past the lump choking her throat. He rubbed her back and kissed her hair.

"I think I'm fallin' in love with you, too," she finally managed to get out.

Although she didn't lift her head, she felt his body smile.

"Don't be so sad about it," he said, a hint of amusement in his tone.

"It's crazy, and you know it's crazy." She hit his chest with her small, balled fist. "You live all the way down in Houston, you have school…a career to get goin'…we can't go anywhere with this." She supposed, having blurted out her growing love, she was just going to babble about everything. She was crying now.

"You picking me up was the best thing to ever happen to me," he said softly, tilting her face to look into her eyes. "We'll work it out."

"It scares me to death."

"I know," he said. "Me too."

"Oh, Harry." She gazed at him, at his beautiful, soft brown eyes, searching them for what, she wasn't sure.

"It does not have to be all or nothing right from the start," he said. "We'll just take it a step at a time, and find each puzzle piece and put it in place before we go on to the next. We'll just see what happens, okay?"

He arched an eyebrow.

She regarded him a moment, and then she leaned toward him, and he met her, and they kissed. It was enough to bring her left foot swinging up clean off the ground.

CHAPTER 25

The Knack for Knowing When

It turned out that Leanne had accepted Clay back faster than a train to New Orleans. Rainey, walking with Harry to the barn to get Lulu, looked over and saw Leanne leading her horse across the lot, and Clay, in a skintight T-shirt, walked beside her with his hand resting at the back of her neck in a claiming manner. Leanne, wearing dark sunglasses, acted like she didn't see Rainey. Clay glanced at her, probably because she was staring a hole in him, but he did not acknowledge her.

"It won't help for you to start a fight, Rainey," Harry said, giving her a tug along. "You might end up getting me beat up."

"Why in the world did she take him back?" she said fiercely.

It made her feel very sad to think of all the hurting hearts making desperate choices all over the place.

"I should have talked more to her about this," she said. "I should have gotten her to leave last night."

"Do you really think you could have done that?" Harry asked.

She looked into his brown eyes. "I guess not." Even if her

cousin had agreed with her about Clay, she wouldn't have missed that night's racing.

"She has to do what she feels she has to do," Harry said. "And she may be right—maybe she can help him."

Then his arm came around her, drawing her close to him, as if to draw her out of her dark, preoccupied mood and to remind her that he was near and their own lives needed to be attended to. She could practically hear him: Don't keep running from your own life by focusing on the lives of others.

It was her own thought, of course, and it startled her. She pressed closer to him, if that were possible.

When they reached Lulu's stall, she fed her the Twinkie cake she had brought for her. Then she turned to Harry and said, "I'd rather not exercise her while Leanne's there. Let's just tie her to her trailer so she can be in the sun, and you and I can go over to the carnival and get somethin' to eat...and then we can go over to the dart booth, and you can see if you can pop all their balloons."

He looked so pleased at her suggestion that she had to glance away.

Her own fears were so much harder to deal with than trying to lead Leanne's life for her.

"Hit me," Harry said, putting another bill down on the counter of the dart booth.

The carnie placed five darts on the counter, and they all watched as Harry proceeded to rapidly pop five balloons. It seemed he could not miss. In fact, since he had begun playing, he had not missed a throw, and he popped the balloons so quickly that the carnie would stare at the board a minute, counting to make sure that Harry had not managed to pocket a dart without being seen.

A small crowd had gathered. A round of applause ensued now, and Harry gave his slow grin at everyone, saying, "Thank you," and drew her forward to choose a prize.

"I'd like the clown." She'd had her eye on the china-faced clown.

The carnie cut the clown free and plopped it on top of the four other prizes in her arms. She was also holding the end of the puppy's leash, and luckily the puppy was content to lie right at her feet.

A cocky but good-humored-looking young man stepped forward and said, "I bet twenty that you miss before I do."

"I'll take that bet," Harry said.

The two passed bills to the carnie, who was very happy about the situation, and each went to popping balloons to much applause. Things continued in this vein until Rainey was struggling to see and breathe under her load of stuffed animals. The little blond girl standing beside Harry's cocky challenger was amassing a decent collection of her own. Although the young man had missed once, he had immediately bought more darts and again bet Harry. When a harsh-looking young woman in black leather pushed herself up to join the men in their duel, the boy who had been off to the side blowing up balloons could not keep up, and at last a pause was forced until the balloons could be replenished.

At this point, and to some groans of disappointment, Harry bowed out. The crowd quickly transferred attention to Harry's cocky young challenger, who proclaimed he would keep trying until he had beat Harry's record of consecutive hits, which the carnie had written on cardboard and pasted up, trying to encourage business.

"Best to stop while I'm king," Harry said low in her ear, as he guided her away from the booth.

"I think you've already made the carnie's profit for this carnival, anyway," she said.

She was having trouble seeing around all the stuffed animals—she had lost count along the way but estimated at least fifteen—and the puppy was tugging at the end of his leash, which she could not hand to Harry, as it was buried beneath her armload.

"What are they going to do with all these?" she said, when Harry had taken half of them from her—there turned out to be sixteen. "There's already those ten you won yesterday on the bed in my trailer. There won't be room for me."

Harry looked at her, then at the toys, and then at a small boy passing by with his parents. Quickly he stepped over and gave a bright-green dinosaur to the boy, turning away before the parents could say a word of protest or thanks.

Immediately they went through the carnival giving away the stuffed toys to surprised and delighted children, who undoubtedly had been told repeatedly not to take anything from strangers, and to two startled silver-haired women sitting on a bench, who reacted with the same surprised delight as the children.

They gave away all except the china-faced clown, which Rainey told Harry she adored.

"Maybe I'll save it for Leanne's baby," she said. Then she looked at him. "I told Leanne I would take her baby if she didn't want it. Clay wants her to have an abortion…did she tell you that?"

"No, I don't believe so," he said with a somewhat surprised expression.

So she told him all about it, and how she would very much like to take Leanne's baby, pointing out her age and ticking biological clock.

"It seems a solution," he said in a way she could not gauge.

"Will that be a problem for us?" she asked point-blank. Her mind was racing ahead to consider all manner of possible complications. Harry might not want to continue with a woman who already had a baby, and he might be a man who did not care for adoption.

"I don't see that it should," he said, seeming a little surprised at the question. Then he added, "I like kids."

"Oh, I know you do," she said. "I just thought I should tell you that I may very soon be having one. Leanne's still making up her mind. I guess the best thing would be for her to keep the baby, but really, I hope she decides in my favor."

"I think I'd like to have two children at least," he said and cast her a questioning look.

"Two is good."

They walked a bit farther, both of them thinking.

"Well, what if we don't have any?" she asked. "What if I can't have a child?"

"That's fine with me, too," he said.

They had come to the carousel and decided to take a ride. They tied the puppy to a post, and every time they revolved around into his sight, he would yip. Then suddenly there he was, chasing around the carousel after them. This about gave her a heart attack. She had not tied him securely enough, and he had pulled his leash loose from the post, and it was dragging after him. She was afraid he was going to get it caught and choke himself to death right before her eyes.

"Oh, Roscoe!" she cried, stumbling from pumping horse to pumping elephant in her anxiousness to meet the dog, who had now jumped up on the spinning machine, and grab the leash that was dragging on the ground.

"Come here, Roscoe!" With great relief, she drew him to her and captured the end of his leash.

Then Harry was there, helping her to her feet. "Roscoe?" he said with a little smile.

"Don't go there," she said.

The carousel operator was so affected by the puppy's devotion that he told them if they wanted to ride again, the puppy could ride, too.

Harry thought they could not disappoint the generous man, nor the puppy, and she agreed, so they went three more times on the carousel, Harry on one pumping steed and her on one beside him, with the puppy at the end of his silver leash, sitting happily in front of them. In just the few days the puppy had been with them, he seemed to have grown by amazing proportions, and he appeared a regal sight when sitting like that. Full of themselves and the spectacle they made, Rainey and Harry waved to people, until the carousel operator's boss came over and yelled at him for allowing a dog on the machine.

Harry hurried over and told the man, "My wife is almost blind. She and her dog are learning to work together, and he can't be separated from her." This bold lie, even if it was met with skepticism, appeared to save the carousel operator his job.

As they went away, Rainey did her best to appear dependent on the puppy, and as if he understood perfectly, the puppy went straight and proud at the end of his leash. "Good boy, Roscoe," she told him.

They were sitting on a bench eating hamburgers and drinking Cokes when her eye caught a jet flying in the clear blue sky. It was rather close, obviously having just taken off from the airport that was not far away.

"Do you want me to take you to the airport tomorrow, on my way home?" she asked.

"I guess that'd be a good idea," he said.

This reply annoyed her, as she had expected more. Just what more, she couldn't have said, but she was still annoyed.

Then she realized he was looking at her. He said, "We should exchange phone numbers and addresses."

She didn't think this was exactly what she'd had in mind for him to say, either, but at least it was something, and she felt comforted. Since neither of them had paper or pen, Harry said that his phone number was listed in the Houston directory, and she told him hers was in the Valentine directory, just in case.

The distance between the two places seemed awfully long to her.

"I've been considering this past week," Harry said. "I'll have to go back to school for psychiatry. Two or three years at least."

This did not surprise her.

"Well, I think it is a perfect field for you," she said, wanting to be encouraging, yet wondering where this would leave their relationship.

"I don't want it to put a wedge between us," he said.

She looked at him a long time. "What *do* you want?" she said at last.

"Well, maybe you'll come down to Houston some."

"Maybe," she said.

It all came back to her, what she had gone through with Robert, and suddenly she was thinking of Valentine.

He was studying her, and she thought she saw disappointment flicker over his face. She might have imagined it, but she don't think so. It was probably becoming as plain to him as it was to her that they had gotten carried away with thinking they could have anything more than this interlude. They would separate at the end of this weekend, and it was difficult, if not impossible, for two people to develop a relationship with a distance of five hundred miles and vastly different life-styles between them.

She got up very quickly and walked over to throw the hamburger paper and empty cup in the trash barrel, giving herself time to gather what she could of her good humor. There was no need to let doubtful sadness over the future ruin the beauty of this day.

"Come on…I need to go exercise Lulu now," she said, forcing a lightness into her tone and onto her face when she returned to him. "I may just come in second tonight and make some good money. If I do, dinner's on me."

He responded with one of his charming smiles and said, "I'll buy champagne, either way."

They would return to the Mexican restaurant, they agreed, and have the Spanish dessert and champagne and dance until the place closed.

When Harry prepared to leave while she worked Lulu, she told him to stay and watch. He looked surprised but pleased, and he stood at the railing the entire time, with the puppy at his feet. She thought his showing this attention was awfully nice of him, as it could not have been all that exciting watching her ride around and around, and turn this way and that.

When she was satisfied that she had worked Lulu enough, she suggested Harry go off and get them a couple of cold drinks while she cooled Lulu down.

She was watching him walk away, taking note of his attractiveness from the rear, when the young woman who had tied for third place with her the night before rode up next to her. Her horse was a flat-brown with a lovely silver mane.

"He's awful cute," the young woman said, her gaze on Harry.

Rainey agreed, although *cute* was not a word she would use to describe Harry. He was handsome, or attractive, or good-looking, or maybe even a stud.

"Leanne's in there measurin' placement for the barrels," the woman said, nodding toward the arena. "She always does that. Then she'll put special marks for her horse."

"How does she do that?" Rainey thought of all that goes on in an arena before they ran the barrels.

"Well, she'll put a mark on the wall and note the length from the wall in pencil. Last night she marked with a piece of tape. I think she uses that to gauge her turning point."

Rainey wondered if this wasn't all sour grapes on the part of this young woman. She told her then, in case she didn't know, that Leanne was her cousin. By the young woman's expression, she gathered that had been the case.

"Good luck to you tonight," the woman said, and then rode away.

Rainey thought that she would pay careful attention to Leanne and look for her marks. She experienced a rising expectation for her and Lulu's performance, and then she realized that, with all her other concerns, she had somewhat forgotten about the possibilities of tonight. Now, after exercising Lulu, she thought them both in top form, and excitement about the competition rose. It was enough to cover over her present dread of parting from Harry tomorrow. It was enough to help her tell herself that tomorrow was a long way off.

As she led Lulu to the wash rack in the barn, she came upon Herbert Longstreet. He squinted at her with his weary eyes from beneath his hat with the sharply turned-up brim, and then he looked at Lulu, and his expression turned soft.

"Coweta's mare...yes, sir, your mama used to win on this one a lot. I was pullin' for you last night, and you two did well," he said. His tone was not critical of her, but it was as if nothing would equal her mother.

"I doubt I can do as well as my mother, but I try," she said.

"You do fine. Just need more experience, is all, and you got the mare here to help you."

She didn't know what to say to that. She was preoccupied with trying to figure a way to ask if he was her father. She watched him stroke Lulu's neck and tell her that she was a good old gal.

"Yep," he said. "Coweta knew how to train a barrel horse."

"Yes, she did."

"Well, it was good to have seen you, gal. Good luck to you."

"Thank you. Nice to have met you, too."

He nodded, his eyes all squinted up, and walked with his stiff gait, out of the barn into the bright sunlight. She watched him and saw Harry, a drink cup in each hand, stop and speak to him, although she could not hear their words.

Then she quickly returned her attention to bathing Lulu, knowing she had let her chance slip by, and glad and sad about it at the same time.

"I will be ready in an hour," she told Harry at her motel room door. "It would only take me thirty minutes, but I just have to wash my hair."

She paused with her hand on the doorknob, her attention lingering on him for a precious minute while the evening sun slanted on him. By unspoken agreement, they had both made certain their time at the motel was limited. It seemed a good idea. They entered their rooms and slammed the doors in unison.

Undressing quickly, she threw her jeans on the floor for the puppy, who curled up immediately on them, and went to the shower. Her mind insisted on lingering on Harry and warm sensuous fantasies, but she thought that if she hurried, she could outrun the foolish urges. She also reminded herself how much more appealing she would be after a shower. While bathing and grooming Lulu, she had managed to get herself very damp and dirty, and surely she smelled of horse.

As she scrubbed her hair and her skin, she kept pushing thoughts of going to bed with Harry that night out of her mind. She had decided she absolutely should not have sex with Harry, and she was firm in her reasoning, which was that she only had so much of herself left after Robert and Monte, and she needed to take care of that self carefully. She refused to be some sort of weekend stand, no matter if she was falling in love with Harry.

Still, every once in a while her resolve on this matter faltered, the way any woman's would, and she would have to think it through all over again. She wondered what she would do if Harry made any attempt to seduce her. She was just a little annoyed that he had showed little inclination to do so when they came to the motel.

When she turned off the water, she heard the phone ringing. It had stopped by the time she got her hair wrapped in a towel, which she immediately ripped off, as she thought perhaps it had been Harry calling and listened to hear him knock at her door. She wrapped a towel around her body and shook her hair to let it fall in its normal curls.

But no knock sounded at the door. She checked the phone, and there was no message light, either, which puzzled her. Just as she reached to lift the receiver to call Harry's room, the phone rang again. That startled her, and she jumped.

"Rainey. Thank God you answered," Charlene said, when Rainey at last did pick up the receiver. "The guy at the desk said you were in, so he tried again...."

Recognizing the crisis tone in her sister's voice, Rainey fairly screamed into the phone: "What's wrong?"

"Daddy has had a heart attack, and is in the hospital."

Rainey's first coherent thought was that she was awfully glad she'd had a shower. Having a shower meant she was prepared for action. The first action she took was to run out her door and over to Harry's, wearing nothing but her towel, and pound on his door. It never occurred to her to use the phone.

CHAPTER 26

Homeward Bound

After bursting out with, "My father's had a heart attack," she erupted into sobs.

Harry took her in his arms, and she cried against him. Against his chest, which she finally realized was bare and was being smeared with her tears. He was wearing his denim shirt, but it was unbuttoned and hanging open. Taking hold of each side, she pressed the fabric over her eyes.

She knew she had to get a hold of herself. On some level she was shocked at herself for standing there in a towel and crying hysterically. She had often gotten overwhelmed, but she was not normally a person to get overwrought. She had not cried like this when her mother died, not out of control, which this felt to be. Quite suddenly she found herself in the midst of saying, "Oh, God, please," and unable to get enough air.

Harry set her on the bed and produced a paper bag. "Breathe into this bag…here…breathe. Thatta girl."

She thought she did breathe into the bag. She must have, because she smelled donut. She really wasn't certain of anything, however, until she found she was staring into Harry's brown eyes.

"Better now?" he asked, gently pushing her hair from her face in the way he would a little girl's.

She nodded, struggling with the inclination to be totally a little girl and curl into his arms. She feared that another emotional bomb might explode in her any second, and she didn't know what she might do.

He sat beside her and pulled her against his chest. "I'm sorry, honey. Losing your mother, and now your dad...I'm so sorry."

It came to her in that hugging and rocking that Harry thought her father had died.

"Daddy isn't dead," she said. This jolt was what she needed; she came upright and took a good breath. "He's in the hospital, and I have to go home right away."

She sprang to her feet, sensible instinct compelling her to grab her towel, which had started to slip. "I have to get the trailer and Lulu and go home. Can you check us out?" Barely recording his okay, she raced back to her room.

In ten minutes she had dressed and was throwing things into her bags. Snatching up her cosmetics, she caught sight of herself in the mirror and paused. She heard Mama: "In a crisis, you find strength in two things, good manners and presentable appearance."

Immediately she took her brush to her hair and fastened it at the back of her neck, put on her silver feather earrings and applied color to her lips, then stuffed the lipstick in her jeans pocket. She would not face her father without her earrings and lipstick.

Harry came out from his room at the same time she did and took her bags from her hands. She stood there and watched him fling them over into the back of the pickup, for the first time realizing she had assumed he was going along.

He opened the passenger door and called the puppy, putting him in the seat. "Ready?" he asked, looking at her. "I'll drive you."

She shut the door behind her and slipped into the seat of the truck. Harry slammed the door and checked to make certain it was caught. She watched him round the hood and slip behind the wheel. She thought that she needed to ask if she was to drop him at the airport, but she didn't. She had a big lump in her throat and was afraid she would start crying again. She was not at all herself. Herself seemed to have deserted her.

"What's going on? Are you leavin'?" Leanne asked.

Leanne came running beside Rainey as she hurried Lulu to the trailer that Harry was hooking up. Rainey told her about her father having had a heart attack and then remembered to add that he was in the hospital, not wanting Leanne to think, as Harry had, that her daddy had died.

"Oh, my gosh. How bad is it?"

"I don't really know. Charlene said he's awake and aware, but they have him in intensive care. They think he had an attack early this morning, but no one found him until almost noon. He was sittin' at the table by then, slumped over, sayin' he had indigestion real bad. He could have had several small attacks." As she said this, she imagined, horribly, his heart in shreds.

Jerking her mind from the thought, she handed Lulu's lead to Leanne so she could open the trailer door.

Leanne said, "I know this is distressing, Rainey, but your daddy is at the hospital. They're takin' care of him, and there isn't anything you can do. There's no need for you to give up your ride tonight. You stand to do really good and make some money. Why don't you stay and run? You can leave right afterward and be home by one, two at the latest."

"Oh, Leanne, my father has had a heart attack. What do I care about runnin' barrels?"

She took the lead rope from her cousin's hands and led Lulu into the trailer. Roscoe was at the mare's heels, giving small yips, trying to be of help. He had never done that before, but she imagined he sensed her urgency and wanted to help. Lulu did not care about urgency when she went in a trailer; she was smart enough to be careful with the placement of her first step.

"Roscoe, no!" Rainey said, worried that Lulu would get aggravated and kick him.

Lulu heaved her body into the trailer, and Rainey removed her lead and fastened the rail that held her in the middle. When she stepped out, Leanne closed the door for her. Rainey immediately walked around looking at all the trailer tires, then checked the hookup to the truck. Harry was inexperienced in connecting, but even if he had been experienced, she would have checked. Her mind was clicking rather frantically with the necessary steps for safe travel. She even checked to make certain Lulu was still on her feet. She was afraid in her distracted emotional state that she would forget something important and maybe the trailer would come unhooked, or they would run over the puppy, or something horrible like that. In fact, her mind seemed to be filling with dire thoughts faster than she could empty it. She looked around to see if any horses were tied to either of the nearby trailers, afraid that somehow they might manage to run over one, or cause it to bolt and choke itself.

"You need any cash?" Leanne asked, momentarily distracting Rainey from her worrisome thoughts. Leanne was sort of following her around.

"No...I'm okay."

She didn't see the puppy, she realized with alarm.

"Where's Roscoe?" she cried and bent to look under the truck and trailer.

"He's right here, Rainey. I have him," Harry called to her, popping up from the other side of the truck, where he'd apparently been bent over with the puppy. He set Roscoe in the back of the truck and proceeded to fasten him there with a rope from either side.

She got in the passenger seat, and Leanne came to her window and thrust a card at her.

"You call me," she said, and Rainey saw her reflection in Leanne's sunglasses and realized she had not seen her eyes. "Soon as you know somethin' about your daddy, call me at this number and leave a message."

"I will, soon as I get a chance," Rainey said, and a minute later they started off.

She glanced into the side-view mirror and saw Leanne looking after them and thought about her suggestion that Rainey stay and make the run. She thought then that Leanne might have needed her to stay, and she felt a little guilty at leaving her cousin. She felt as if she needed to split herself in two.

Then she looked over at Harry.

"Harry."

His eyebrow went up, and he pressed the brake. "Forget something?"

"I can drop you at the airport," she said, making herself say it. "You don't need to be goin' with me...you have your own life to see to."

He looked stubborn. "I'm driving you. You don't need to be going all that way by yourself, not like this."

She did not argue, as selfish as that was. She was simply too relieved. She did not feel up to driving. And she wanted Harry with her, could not bear the thought of being without him.

She looked out the windshield, in the direction of home, her mind's eye going past the city streets and buildings and down the highway through the grassland and rimrock.

As he drove out of the fairgrounds, Harry cut too soon and bumped the trailer tires over the curb.

"I'll do okay on the highway," he said immediately.

She was not critical, didn't say anything. There was no way she could drive. She was again blinking back tears and throwing her heart down the road to home.

"I hope Daddy doesn't die before I get there," she said, her lips trembling. "I have so much to tell him. I don't want him to die before I do."

Even though she neglected to direct Harry and he ended up taking Interstate 40 over to Oklahoma instead of heading southeast right away, they made it in under four hours, with only two stops, three if you counted the time she had Harry pull over on that long stretch of back road down west Oklahoma so that she could relieve herself. There just wasn't any place to stop out there for about a hundred miles, even in the daytime.

Before they put Amarillo behind them, Harry had stopped at a Texaco Star Mart. Impatient with the stop, Rainey stayed in the truck while Harry topped off the fuel tanks and went inside. When he came out, he handed her a sack of snacks.

"I can't eat anything," she said, shaking her head and setting the sack aside.

He took the sack and pulled out a container of milk and then several packets of pills, which he opened and held out in his palm.

"What are those?" She stared at the pills in his hand, wondering if he had managed to buy drugs, if maybe drugs were being sold now in convenience stores and she hadn't known about the new practice.

"Calcium, vitamin D, magnesium," he said and thrust them at her. "Drink the milk and take these. It'll calm you."

By the way he was looking at her, she wondered how she appeared. Apparently in need of calming.

She took the pills and drank most of the milk. When she opened the glove box to get a napkin to wipe her mouth and apply fresh lipstick, Mama's Bible popped out at her. She opened it and attempted to read a couple of places in the Psalms that Mama had marked with snips of paper, but the rocking of the truck made the print jump and caused a nauseous feeling. She set the book on the seat rather than put it in the glove box, though.

Mama, can you do anything? She wondered if Mama could talk to God and persuade Him to let Daddy live. She wondered if she was being punished, but she knew this was silly thinking on her part, the weird thoughts one has when one is under strain. God wasn't about to end her father's life simply because she had neglected him. She did keep thinking a whole lot of 'if onlys'…if only she had said things, said she loved him, asked the questions she needed to ask, been more open. If only she had been home.

"If I had been home, I would have found Daddy earlier," she told Harry and went on to relate how she had "known" her mother was in distress and gone running to find her beneath the apple trees. Although she admitted that maybe she wouldn't have known, since she did not carry Daddy's blood in her veins.

"But I would have been by earlier to see him. I work most Saturday mornings, and I almost always stop by to check on him on my way to work. I should have been there."

"*Should* is the wrong word," Harry said. "You can use *could* but not *should*. Why should you have been there? You are a grown woman with a life to lead. You could have been there, but you were not, because you were leading another part of your life. What would have happened to Leanne if you had been at home? And take it back further. If you had been home, you probably wouldn't have picked me up on the road last week, and where would I be?

"There is no blame here, Rainey. It is something that just happened, something that likely could not have been avoided, even if your father had been at the hospital. Placing blame never helps," he added.

"I know," she said, which was why she had not placed blame that he had taken a different route than she would have taken. She looked out at the grassland that was growing exceedingly dim, a golden dim with the setting sun.

"He misses Mama," she said. "And isn't it strange that he had a heart attack just like her? Mama had had a bit of heart trouble, but Daddy never has." She paused and added, "He has now. I guess without Mama, we are all sort of falling apart."

After another minute of watching the sun go down upon the land, she said, "I wish I had been there, because I wish I could be in control. But we aren't, are we? We think we are, but we can hardly control ourselves, much less anyone or anything else in this world."

He took her hand and pulled her over next to him. She laid her head on his shoulder and asked him to tell her all about what happens to the heart in an attack. He accepted this strange request readily and launched thoughtfully and in detail into all sorts of medical jargon. She would ask him the definition of the terms, and he would reply at length. This helped pass the time, and it must have bored her a little, too, as she fell asleep for fifty miles.

She chose to go straight to the hospital, even though this meant Lulu was stuck traveling with them, and Roscoe, too. To take the animals home, though, would cost nearly an hour, and she was not willing to wait any longer than necessary to see her father. She also figured that at night there would be plenty of parking room, and there was. Charlene's Suburban was there, but she didn't see Freddy's Lincoln.

"Freddy and Helen went home," Charlene told her, when they came upon her in the ICU waiting area. Larry Joe, her eldest son, was with her, no doubt having driven her. Charlene had given up driving after the car wreck she and Rainey had had, the one in which Rainey had lost her baby. Charlene had been driving at that time.

"Joey's down in Fort Worth, and Mary Lynn has the kids. Daddy is doing good. The doctors think he had two small heart attacks, but he is through that now. His heart rate is a little low, but they're givin' him something for it. He's sleeping."

In spite of Harry's lengthy lesson in heart attacks, Rainey still wondered what a small heart attack was compared to a large one. She supposed the difference was life and death.

Charlene looked awfully pale, tired, but in her normal control, especially considering her abhorrence of hospitals. She, too, had remembered their mother's admonition to be presentable in a crisis. She had on a flowing blue skirt and a loose blouse cinched at the waist with a concho-decorated leather belt, and her hair was neat as ever, even though when they came in she had been reclining on the couch with her eyes closed. Charlene had always been careful about her appearance, and she could rest without smudging one bit of mascara; she often lay back and looked dead, but this ability on her part had saved her face—she could pass easily for ten years younger.

Now she was eyeing Harry, and Rainey made the introductions quickly, then said, "I want to see Daddy."

Charlene pointed out a room across the hall. "Don't wake him, though. The doctor wants him to sleep."

This was not a big hospital, and things were a lot more relaxed there than she imagined they were in the big city hospitals. She'd known exactly where they were going upon entering, so they had breezed past the nurse at the desk, who had not even looked up.

Right this moment, she dragged Harry along with her. She had a hold of his hand and simply did not let go. She was apprehensive about seeing her father with tubes and cords attached all over the place.

But there wasn't much. Her father lay there in the dimness, the only thing attached was an IV in his arm. She moved closer and saw he was also hooked up to a heart monitor. It was beeping with a reassuring rhythm, and her father was doing his regular nasal breathing.

Once she reached the bedside, Harry wiggled his hand from hers and moved away. She saw him reach for the record chart, and then she looked back at her father.

Daddy?

She stood there and felt sort of like she used to back in high school, when she would come to her parents' bedroom upon arriving home from a date. They did not wait up for her but commanded that she come and wake one or the other to tell them she was home. She always woke Daddy, because he faced the door, and all she had to do was touch his hand and say, "Daddy..."

She was afraid to touch him now, afraid she might wake him and cause him to go directly into another heart attack. So she stood there staring at him, studying his features to make certain they were all as they were supposed to be and then watching his chest rise and fall.

She whispered, "I love you, Daddy."

Harry came back beside her and put his arm around her. "He's doin' really good, honey," he said in a low voice and kissed her forehead.

She studied his face to make certain he was telling her the truth. She supposed she was as uncertain as she had ever been in her life.

He said, "He is. His vital signs are plenty strong and steadily improving." He sounded confident.

"I want to stay until he wakes up," she said.

Charlene agreed to trade vehicles, to leave the Suburban and to take Rainey's rig to her house, where Larry Joe could unload Lulu and Roscoe.

"Will he chase my cats and guineas?" Charlene wanted to know about the puppy.

"I don't know, so you'd best keep him tied or penned up," Rainey answered. She really didn't want to see dead chickens all over the place right after her arrival.

She also suggested that Harry go with her sister and nephew. "You can get some sleep in my bed at the cottage," she told him, her hand on his arm.

"I'll stay here with you," he said, and she leaned her head on his chest for half a minute.

Harry let down the metal side to her father's bed and pulled a chair over for her to sit on. While he was doing this, a nurse came over, and Rainey thought they might be told to leave and got herself up to argue, but the nurse just looked a little surprised. She saw then that the nurse was Karen Millhouse, a girl she'd gone to school with. The woman had gained about thirty pounds, which made her face even more pleasant than it always had been.

"I imagine it will do your Daddy good to see you here when

he wakes up," she said in a whisper and patted Rainey's shoulder. "It's real quiet in here tonight...plenty of room for y'all."

Harry slipped out and left her, and she sat there gazing at her father, wishing a lot of things. She prayed some and talked to Daddy in her mind. Harry slipped back in with a cup of coffee for her. A bit later, she finally laid her head down on the side of the bed and slept off and on, coming awake when a nurse or Harry entered, the nurse to check on Daddy and Harry to check on her.

Daddy awoke at four-thirty, his normal time, and he said, "Well, hello, Little Bit."

"Hello, Daddy." She took his hand then, at last. It felt rough, like always, but more frail than in the past, which upset her. She smiled, so he wouldn't know this.

"I'm sorry you got dragged home," he said, looking mournful.

"I didn't get dragged, I came flyin'," she said. "And I guess I've been headin' home ever since I left, Daddy."

They looked at each other and said a number of things without any words. Maybe right that minute words could not convey what her being there and holding on to his hand could.

Then she guessed her father had had enough of emotion, because he began to shift himself up in the bed and said, "You'd better get out of here, because I have to get up and go to the bathroom." He pointed to the lavatory door all the way over in the corner.

"Daddy, I don't think you are supposed to get out of bed.... I'll get a nurse."

"I'm gettin' up," he said and started plucking at the monitor tabs stuck to his chest. This behavior on his part had the curious effect of alarming her and reassuring her all at once.

She flew around the curtain to get help, but no one was in

sight. She ran out the door and spied Harry—apparently he never slept—a silhouette leaning back against the wall, one knee bent and his foot on the wall, and a cup of coffee in his hand. She stopped, knowing she was interrupting some powerful thoughts.

But then he saw her.

"It's Daddy—he's tryin' to get out of bed."

He went immediately into the room, where Nurse Karen had already appeared from somewhere. Daddy was setting off all sorts of alarms. Rainey backed away toward the door, feeling overwhelmed and not at all helpful. Then Nurse Karen came flying around the curtain, threw up her hands and said, "I guess your friend Dr. Furneaux can best handle him. He is really a doctor, isn't he?"

"Oh, yes," Rainey said with a nod.

As she watched the woman walk away, though, Rainey reflected that she really had no proof of Harry being a doctor.

"Daddy, do you know who my father is? Do you know his name?"

"John Elam," her father said, looking at her fingernails.

They held hands, her again in the chair beside his bed, while beyond the window, dawn was turning the sky pink and there was the silence that comes just before the sun comes up.

She was a little relieved that he had not said Herbert Longstreet, and doubly relieved that she had held her tongue in Amarillo.

Her father continued, as if going back in time. "He was a little man, but handsome, I guess. He left this state and never came back. A year after he left, he sent a postcard to your mother, told her he was workin' down Lus'iana."

"Did he know about me?"

He nodded. "Yes. But there never was a question of how we would handle it. Your mother and I decided, and she made it plain to him. I guess he wanted her to run off with him, but she wouldn't do it. He never knew your mama, really," he said with a hoarse chuckle.

"Daddy, why didn't Mama ever tell me?"

"Now, Little Bit, how was she ever gonna tell you somethin' like that?" He regarded her with sharp pain in his eyes and a trembling smile on his lips.

"Freddy knew," she said.

He sighed, in such a way that she had a moment of worry that maybe she was upsetting him. But then he said quite strongly, "Your mama and I handled it as best we could with our limited choices—those bein' the truth and us bein' afraid of the truth."

He looked squarely at her and told her everything. "Your brother knew because he was old enough to figure things out, and because he unfortunately overheard me and your mama one mornin' discussin' things. I don't know if Charlene knew. I tried to get your mama to tell you. She wanted to, but she could not bring herself to do it. She was afraid.

"Can you understand that? To tell you meant she had to admit her great shame and risk how you might judge her, and how it would hurt you. She could not bear to do any of that. You know, and your sister and brother should know, that your mama would have died for each one of you."

"We know, Daddy."

He looked again for a long minute at her fingernails, running his thumb over them. "Do not judge your mother. I guess I always wanted to come off good in this deal, but the Almighty does have a way of openin' our eyes. I've come to see my own part of this. I was workin' all the time...oh, I was the big dealer, sellin' cattle here, land there, buyin' into oil wells and watchin' them come in. Your mama would beg me to come sit with her in the swing, or go out dancin'." He smiled. "She was a lively, beautiful woman, and she needed me to attend to her, and I pretty much ignored her. She went weeks without a man touchin' her, and she just got swept off her feet by this yahoo, who gave her an afternoon of romance that never would have amounted to anything, except she came up pregnant with you. She came to me and told me straight, and said she'd give me a divorce, but she would stay right there where her children were.

"Life don't always go how you think it will, and even you yourself don't always behave like you wish you would. If you got the grit, like your mother, what you do is pick up and make the best of what you've done. Your mother and I both tried to do that. I'm sorry for so much of what we had to deal with fallin' over you kids.

"But I'm proud of what your mother and I made. Let me tell you, your mother spent the rest of her life tryin' to make up for about one hour of foolishness, and she more than succeeded. There wasn't no one a better wife or a better mother. I didn't make that plain in the past, but I'm makin' it plain now."

Rainey's vision blurred with tears, and she saw tears run down her father's withered cheeks. She put her head down on the bed.

He said in a husky voice, "Your mother and I loved each other enough to build on it, and we never regretted stayin' together, and we neither one never regretted that she had you. When I look at you, I see her. I love you, Little Bit, just like you're my own. That seems like all that should count."

"Oh, Daddy…thank you for tellin' me everything."

He stroked her hair, and after a minute he said, "I want some coffee with a lot of cream. Go see if you can find me some, will you, Little Bit?" Just like the Daddy she had always known.

The nurse, a stranger, this time, tried to tell her that her father was in ICU and wasn't supposed to have anything the doctor didn't order for him, but Harry showed her where the coffee was, and she fixed up a cup and took it to him.

CHAPTER 27

The Blood's Country

Rainey wouldn't leave her father until someone else was there to be with him. Leaving him in the care of the nurses might have been all right while he was asleep, but now he was awake and agitated, wanting to go home. Rainey supposed that by someone else, she meant Charlene, who, although very uncomfortable with hospitals and sickness, had managed to mother three children and her own husband.

Freddy had never had child; Helen had a daughter, who had left home early. Rainey didn't think of either of them as caretakers. They were the sort who came to family gatherings and parked themselves on the couch to be waited on.

Rainey was faintly surprised when Freddy appeared at the hospital at barely eight in the morning.

"I was on my way to the store," he said, the store being what he called his car dealership. "When did you get here? Where's Charlene?"

"She went home when I came in last night."

He was frowning at her, as if angry to find her and not Charlene. But she went and hugged him, and he made an effort to respond. Sadness washed over her that he had to make an effort and couldn't seem to feel naturally toward her. She'd always felt this sadness in connection with him.

"Freddy is just a little prickly," she explained to Harry, after her brother had gone in to see their father with hardly more than a nod to Harry when she introduced them.

When Freddy came out, he looked surprised to see her waiting. She told him she thought someone should be there with Daddy, and when he gave her that you-are-silly look, she reminded him of how people in hospitals had been known to have received the wrong medication or even have the wrong leg whacked off.

"Dad's not havin' a leg cut off, and this is a small hospital with nurses who have enough time to see to their patients."

"It's not the same. We know him and what he might want. And one of us should speak with the doctor when he comes." She really wanted to speak to the doctor herself, but she was beginning to feel woozy from exhaustion.

"Dad obviously isn't on death's door, but I'll stay," Freddy said. "You go on home."

She hesitated, not quite certain if she should trust him, not quite believing that he perceived how tired she was.

"I will stay," he repeated with impatience, "and Helen is going to drop in, too. You aren't the only one who is capable of taking care of him, Rainey. I may not be the favored late child, but I do know him and what he might need." He turned and went back through the door.

Harry was gazing at her. He'd heard the exchange. She didn't know what to say, and she was too tired to come up with something.

* * *

"That's my cottage back there. It was the old farmhouse on this place."

She pointed at the little frame house, which looked a lot more run-down in the morning sun than she had recalled. Gazing at it, she realized, with something of a quivering in her chest, that while she thought of the cottage as where she resided, what she really thought of as her home was her mother and father's house. It was there she wanted to go.

When they stopped in the drive in front of Charlene's brick ranch, Roscoe came immediately, wagging his tail. Harry and she both greeted him joyously. She kept thinking, Well, here I am, and Harry and the puppy with me.

Larry Joe came forward from a garage too cluttered to even get the door down, where he was apparently working on a riding mower. She was struck by how he had grown. She had not noticed at the hospital the night before, but he seemed to have grown so much taller in the time she had been gone. He was seventeen now, she remembered, had celebrated a birthday in July.

"Growing mostly in the feet, is what Mom says," he said in a deep voice that Rainey found rather startling. "She's still asleep. I took your mare over to Gramma's—Dad has everything full-up here, and I didn't think you wanted to put her in a corral with three others."

"No, she isn't used to that. Thanks...you didn't tie the puppy? He hasn't eaten any hens, has he?" She looked around, vaguely anxious about possibly seeing blood and feathers.

"Those hens can run under a place in the barn. I hate the dang things anyway. You want some donuts and coffee? I went to the bakery."

Rainey shook her head. "We're beat. We're goin' over to

Mama and Daddy's." She realized she still said Mama and Daddy's, even though Mama was gone.

She did take time to poke her head into the living room to speak to Danny Joe and Jojo, not wanting to ignore them. Everyone thought the Joe on the kids' names was for Joey, but Charlene's middle name was Jo. The kids were watching television, a documentary about the desert. Jojo wrapped her thin arms around Rainey's neck and said, "I'm glad you're home, Aunt Rainey." Rainey almost cried. She went over and hugged Danny Joe, and she thought that, at thirteen, he was sweet to hug her back.

Then she and Harry, with Roscoe in the seat with his nose out the window, were driving away and through town. She had Harry drive, because she wanted to look as they passed along Main Street, to drink it in, yet glad to do so at a distance. She kept the window down, so she could smell it. She pointed out Blaine's Drugstore where she had worked. Roscoe seemed as eager to see everything as she was.

It struck her that she was as glad to be home as she had been anxious to leave all those weeks ago. Eager to see her parents' house, the house where she had grown up and still kept returning to, she looked ahead, as if her eyes could see around corners. She wanted Harry to see it, wanted to show him the front porch, where they would sit on a summer night when Mama had been alive, and Mama's old Motorola radio that Daddy had managed to keep working, and the kitchen that was so good for visiting in, and her bedroom, with the tree close enough to climb out on and to the ground.

She just had to be there.

Around the corner, gazing up the street and there it was, with the big bushes framing the drive. "Lilacs," she told Harry. "They smell so good in the spring."

She was out of the truck almost before he had completely stopped, and Roscoe came right behind her. He ran out across the yard and then right up onto the porch, where he sat and watched them approach. Almost as if he had been coming here all along. In fact, she stopped and looked at him, looking hard, because she had the oddest feeling that Mama would be standing next to him.

Then she turned and saw that Harry was observing the house with appropriate appreciation. He smiled at her and put a hand to her back as they went up the stairs and across the porch.

"Rainey…Rainey!"

Turning she saw that it was Mildred Covington hurrying up the yard from the sidewalk as fast as her pudgy legs would propel her. The woman had obviously seen them arrive from her house down on the corner. Although she never admitted her age, Mildred was surely in her late seventies. She always did herself up well, except for that strange habit of wearing knee-high stockings with a dress and ignoring that they showed when she sat down.

"How is your Daddy, Rainey? Have you been to see him? They told me this morning that he was doin' good, but they wouldn't let me talk to him. Said he was sleepin'."

"I was with him last night. He is doing really well. They'll probably move him to a regular room today."

"Oh, that is good news."

Now Mildred was eyeing Harry with high curiosity. Rainey introduced them, and then, rude as it might have been, said, "We'll see you later, Miss Mildred," and led Harry and Roscoe into the house, which was not locked, and closed the door after them.

In the foyer, she inhaled the familiar scent—the mixture of Daddy's Camels and Old Spice and Mama's rose lotion and lemon furniture polish.

Just then her attention was caught by Roscoe, who went bounding up the stairs. He reached the top and disappeared. There came the sound of his toenails tapping on the wood flooring.

"Well, my goodness," she said, going up and Harry following.

They found Roscoe in her old bedroom, curled up on the braided rug. Rainey looked questioningly at Harry.

"He followed your scent," Harry said and continued down the hall to find the bathroom, saying immediately that he was going to take a shower, removing his shirt even as he spoke.

Her eyes landed on his bare, hard-muscled back. She felt a sort of shimmer of possibilities. She was, however, absolutely too tired to entertain them.

Stripping to her bra and panties, she crawled beneath the cool sheets of her old bed, onto the mattress that retained the indentation of her body. She thought that she had not fully appreciated that her bedroom remained just as it had been when she'd moved away. She listened to the water running in the pipes, then heard it shut off, and as she drifted into sleep, her last thought was that Harry was smart enough to choose a bed in one of the other three rooms.

She slept for three and a half hours and awoke to Roscoe sniffing at her face. She reached for him and nuzzled him as he did her, and then she caught the smell of coffee and cooking meat. Slipping into a terry robe hanging in the closet—a little musty but clean—she wondered who in the world could be here cooking, and she thought of her mother in a blue way.

Glancing into the guest room, she saw that the bed was rumpled but Harry was not there.

It was Harry in the sun-lit kitchen. She and Roscoe both stopped and looked at him. He was at the stove, frying ham, hair rumpled, shirt unbuttoned, as was his habit, showing his tanned chest, and barefooted, too.

"I knew the smell of food would get you up," he said, glancing over at her.

"You can cook?" So many things she did not know about him, she thought, as she gazed steadily at his chest, which had at the most a couple of hairs.

"I can heat things up." He gestured to the pan. "Ham slices, toast, opened a can of pineapple. Your brother called. They moved your father to room 215 in the south wing. Charlene will be there about one. Bring your father's whittling knife and wood when you come."

"Oh."

The next second she went to him, wrapped her arms around his middle and laid her head on his warm skin, listening to his heartbeat and inhaling the particular male scent of him.

"Thank you for being here," she said, while the image of what it would have been like to be alone, drive home alone, be in this house alone, flitted through her mind. She began to tremble. "Thank you for being there all these days, with Neva and Buck and that child, and Leanne and Clay…and for bringing me here."

He kissed her hair, and then he tilted her head upward and kissed her lips. A kiss that started comforting and gentle but quickly turned passionate, leaving her breathless and throbbing and ready to sink to the floor with him.

"Hey…don't make me burn the ham," he said, abruptly letting her go and turning away.

Calming herself, trying to keep her balance, she went to the refrigerator, staring into it until her vision returned and she saw oranges, which she took out to squeeze for an afternoon breakfast.

"Daddy never would abide bottled orange juice," she told Harry, and upon reflection, she added, "I guess Daddy can be as prickly as Freddy."

The following afternoon her father underwent angioplasty to clean the arteries of his heart. The doctor came to them afterward in the waiting room and said that all had gone well; in fact, their father's arteries were not as bad as tests had indicated.

"He'll be out of here day after tomorrow, but he'll need to take it easy for a week—not bed rest, but off his feet most of the time. Then I want to see him begin a routine of regular walking. Start slow, of course, but the goal will be to work up to at least three miles a day. I'll give a sheet of instructions to you when he's discharged."

The doctor left, and they all looked at each other.

"Well, we need to figure out what we're gonna do about Dad now," Freddy said.

"What do you mean, do about him?" Rainey asked, watching his face.

Freddy answered with all he had been thinking for some time. "Off his feet for a week, which means someone's goin' to have to be with him day and night for that week, or he'll be out and drivin' down to the café at the sale barn. And he's goin' to fight that walking routine. Dad's never stuck to a routine in his life, and he isn't about to start just because a doctor tells him to.

"He can't be livin' alone any longer, and let's be honest here. Helen and I both have busy lives and don't have the time to take care of him. Charlene and Joey have their kids and can't do it, either."

Rainey waited for him to mention her, but his eyes passed right over her.

"I think we should think about gettin' him into Prairie View Manor," he said.

She looked over at Charlene, who slowly sank down to the blue vinyl couch beside Joey, who'd come in that afternoon. Joey kept his gaze where it had been for an hour, on the gray tile.

Freddy apparently had looked into Prairie View Manor at great length. He went on to extol the attributes of this wondrous facility as if he had memorized the brochure. He told them how Daddy could have a kitchenette apartment and still have people looking in on him, and, if and when he needed it, they had a nursing home facility, too. Helen stood beside him, giving a nod now and again, her expression clearly saying, "Yes, sir, yes, sir."

When Freddy finally appeared to be finished with his oration, Rainey said, "I'm movin' back home with Daddy."

Then she looked over at Harry, who was gazing at her intently, although expressionlessly.

CHAPTER 28

The Only Thing That Stays The Same

Charlene burst into tears in the Kmart parking lot.

Rainey had just stopped the Suburban and put it into park but had not turned off the engine. She sat there with her foot on the brake, pressing it even though it wasn't needed, gazing with surprise at her sister, who had covered her face with her hands. One minute Charlene had been cautioning about the close proximity of the Oldsmobile on the right, and the next she was sobbing.

They had come to buy their father some khaki slacks and a new shirt for him to come home in. When Rainey had gone through his clothes, she had found them all terribly worn. She had thought it would make him feel better to have some new clothes—rather like he had a reason to live, if he had new clothes. And she thought it necessary, too, to show him there was still someone to buy them. Their mother had always bought their daddy's clothes, all those years. Rainey recalled that the previous Christmas their mother had bought the khakis, the only type of slacks their daddy would wear, at Kmart. She had gotten the name on the label of his old ones, hoping to get the same kind, since he was so picky about them. She hoped to please him and lift his spirits.

She felt a little desperate to boost her father. She had left Harry shaving him, because she felt he was more up to the job than anyone else.

There was a way about Harry. He could boost anyone, even though he himself did not seem an especially jolly person. He was an accepting person. She had begun to think that, faced with an armed robber, Harry would probably say something like, "I'm sure you need to rob me, and I'll help you."

With this thought, she put her hand over on Charlene's shoulder and patted, thinking maybe what her sister needed was for Rainey to accept the crying and let her go at it, purge herself.

After a couple of minutes, Charlene sniffed and dug into her purse for a tissue. Rainey found a napkin in her glove box and handed it to her.

"Thank you," Charlene said and blew her nose. "This is just such a bad time for all of this with Daddy."

"I know."

"My hormones are leaking out my toes, Rainey," Charlene said dolefully and screwed the rearview mirror around to have a look at herself and dab underneath her eyes. "Look at my hair. Look at all that gray. Joey asked me if I was goin' to dye it."

"I think it's pretty. I thought you liked it."

"I guess I thought it was sort of distinguished, but really all it says is that I'm getting old. How many pregnant women have you ever seen with gray hair?"

"Are you pregnant?" Rainey asked, a little surprised, but being careful to appear neither positive nor negative, until she knew the leaning of Charlene's emotions.

Charlene shook her head and gave out a little sob. "Oh,

Rainey, I can't get pregnant—" some more sobs and head shaking "—and Joey and I are havin' problems, and I need to pay attention to my marriage. I just don't have much left to help with Daddy."

Rainey was startled by her sister's revelation. Charlene and Joey had been married for so long. From the time she had met him, Charlene had been crazy about Joey. Rainey could not imagine a threat to their marriage. She didn't want to imagine it. It seemed that if Charlene and Joey could not make it, there was no hope for any marriage. Most especially any marriage Rainey might consider.

"It's all right, Charlene," she said, trying to control a frantic feeling welling inside. "This is just a hard time for everyone, but it will work out. Daddy is going to be fine. We'll get him home, and he'll get back to his old self. You don't worry about him."

"Rainey, Daddy is never goin' to be like his old self," Charlene said, wadding up the wet napkin and tossing it into her purse. "That went when Mama did. We all have to face up to the fact that Daddy is weakening now, too."

She gazed for long seconds at Rainey, who gazed back.

"I know he is weakening," Rainey said. "But he isn't dead yet."

Charlene sighed. "Of course he isn't. I didn't mean it to sound like that. What I'm saying is that we do have to look at things as they are. I know you think that Freddy is unfeeling, but he isn't. There's a lot to what he's sayin'. He's bein' honest, and he is putting forth what he thinks is best for everyone."

Rainey looked out the windshield, at the sun glinting on the red hood.

"We all have lives to live, Rainey. We can't put them on hold or change them all around just for Daddy. You just can't give up your life for him. I don't like the way Freddy says it, but you being their late child, Mama and Daddy sort of gathered you to them. You were their special child, yes, but a lot of that was them using you to heal their marriage. You tied them together, and you were tied to them. But you can't just stop your life and go home to take care of him."

It seemed like Charlene was gathering back her strength by attacking a tender spot in Rainey.

"I'm not stoppin' my life," Rainey said. "I want to go home to live."

Charlene again checked her reflection in the mirror. "What about Harry? He seems awfully taken with you."

"Harry and I are still tryin' to find out about us."

"And how are you goin' to do that if you set yourself to takin' care of Daddy? If you try to hold on to what is passin' away? Things are changing, Rainey. It's the way life is—the only constant in life is change, and you can't stop it. No matter how hard you try, you cannot keep Daddy and the house and everything like it was."

"Freddy and Helen want the house," Rainey said. "They are just goin' to scoot Daddy out of there and take it, and you're goin' to let them."

"That is not so. I am not going to let them do any such thing. I'm just facing that Daddy could fare well at Prairie View Manor, maybe a whole lot better than rattlin' around in that big old house. He'd have good companionship for one thing. More than That Hussy Mildred."

When Rainey didn't reply, Charlene said, "Rainey, you'll focus so much on Daddy and on tryin' to hold on to what is passin' that you won't have anything left over for a relationship with Harry. Don't do that, Rain. Don't let this opportunity pass you by."

"I don't really know what sort of opportunity I have with

Harry," Rainey said with impatience that seemed to swell as she spoke. "But I know what I have with our Daddy. I know what I have to do there. Either it will work out with Harry and me in the midst of all this or it won't, but right now I want to go home to live, okay?"

"I think you should keep in mind one question," Charlene said, having always been intent on getting the last word. "What will you do with yourself when Daddy dies? What will you do, if you have made him your life?"

"And how can I abandon him, Charlene?" She had begun to shake. "Maybe you and Freddy don't want to see it like that, but that is how I see it. I can't just walk away, not from Daddy, and not from our family's home. Now, can we just go in and get Daddy some pants?"

Immediately she regretted sounding so hateful. Charlene looked for a minute like she was going to start crying again. Upset herself, Rainey started to get out of the Suburban and then realized she had still not switched off the motor. She sat back down, turned the key, got out and slammed the door, and headed toward the store with rapid though shaky strides.

She had not realized how depressing her family could be until that minute. Likely Harry could have an entire career simply psychoanalyzing her family.

And she and Charlene definitely did better talking on the telephone.

Rainey walked down the corridor, carrying the paper sack with her father's new clothes. When she came to his room, she found the door ajar. Through the opening she saw her father sitting up in his bed, and Harry sitting in the vinyl upholstered chair pulled up close.

She stopped and stepped back out of sight. She hesitated

about eavesdropping, remembering what her mother always said about people who eavesdropped generally hearing what they deserved.

"You in love with Rainey, son?" her daddy asked.

"Yes, sir, I am."

Her heartbeat picked up. She hugged the sack of clothes close.

"Hmm…well, you aren't the first. Ever since she was a baby, boys been comin' around Little Bit. Them Overton girls are lookers."

"I can imagine that."

Rainey smiled.

"Well, I'm pretty certain she's in love with you, or you wouldn't be with her now. I hope you aren't gonna break her heart."

"I don't plan to."

"We never plan those things. We just manage to do them. I'll give you some advice, and that is, don't take anything for granted. We do that too much in this life, take things for granted, think we're gonna live forever. You know, I never knew I was old until my wife died."

Hearing her father's voice sound so sad, Rainey squeezed her eyes closed.

"Widowhood ain't really any enjoyment," her father said. "You remember I told you that, and you'll appreciate Rainey more while she's alive. Now, there are less men widows than women widows, and so I do get a lot of women comin' after me." He sighed again. "But they're all old."

Clutching the shopping bag against her, Rainey clapped a hand over her mouth. Feeling any moment that she was going to burst out into either sobs or laughter, she turned and hurried back outside. *Oh, Daddy…oh, Daddy…*

It was tears that came, not laughter.

CHAPTER 29

Swimming That River

At sunset they walked, hand in hand, out to the corral to give Lulu a Twinkie cake. Her pale gray coat had a golden tint in the sunset light. Golden rays shone on their faces, on the trees, on the fencing. Roscoe ran sniffing around them, and then sniffing around Lulu, who ignored him. Harry's shirt, the silk one, was unbuttoned halfway down. Rainey had come to realize that Harry simply hated the binding of a shirt. She wore a flowing cotton knit dress that fell softly over her curves down to just above her ankles, total femininity, which she had planned, of course, and the only things she wore beneath were a lacy bra and barely-there panties. There were sensual thoughts in the back of her mind, which she kept trying to keep tucked aside, while she spoke of apple trees.

"Daddy planted these trees when he and Mama moved into this house," she told Harry as she leaned on the corral fence. "They moved here when Mama's mother and father needed care. My grandfather died in the living room." She glanced at him. "You're good for my father."

"I like him. He's tough, like Thurman. I admire people like that."

"You're tough."

He raised an eyebrow. "I guess I'm learning to be," he said, with that amused dry tone.

"I love you, Harry. I love you, and I need you, but right now my father needs me. I don't know what to do."

The words burst from her unexpectedly, causing her heart to pound and all manner of feelings to swell in her chest.

Harry nodded, reached out and took her hand. His sad expression made her quiver and hold his hand tightly.

"He's my father, and he's old and alone," she said. "I can't just let them move him off to a home. It's fifty miles from here, from the place where he's lived for most of his life, from his friends…from everything he knows. He will die then."

"And this is your home, too," Harry said. His gaze was direct, and disconcerting.

"Yes, it is."

She pulled her hand away, turning, looking toward the house. "I grew up here. I came running here when I got hurt as a child, when I lost boyfriends, and when each of my marriages failed. And Mama and Daddy were always here for me, putting me back together.

"I can hardly stand the thought of Helen moving in here. She won't have a vinyl cloth on the kitchen table. That's too cheap-looking for her. She'll move the dining room set out, and Charlene won't take it, and I don't have anywhere to put it, and it is ugly, but I grew up eating at it, and I can't let it go."

She realized she was getting a little overwrought and tried to keep calm. "I can't run away with you, Harry. I simply can't let go of any of this. Not yet."

She dropped her gaze, embarrassed at the unnamed fears churning inside.

He reached for her and drew her against him. She breathed in the scent of him, a scent she had come to adore. She heard his heart beat beneath her ear.

"I'm going to have to leave tomorrow," Harry said.

They were in the kitchen, and the entire time they had walked back to the house, Rainey had known he was going to say that. Probably she had heard him thinking about the best way to say it, but really, there wasn't a best way.

"I know. You've postponed your own life for me long enough."

He had to get on with things, with dealing with his family and with being a psychiatrist and all the other things he might wish to do.

"I don't think of it like that," Harry said, seeming a little startled. "I haven't postponed my life at all. I think I have been truly living for the first time in my life. I've wanted to be with you. I still want to be with you, but I have a need to pursue my path, too."

"I know that."

She gazed at him and thought that she could not bear to have her heart broken again, and that she didn't want to begin some pattern of foolish living.

"I'm not exactly certain about what I'll be doing," he said, stroking the back of his head as he usually did when thinking. "I hope I can get into psychiatry school pretty quickly. I already took a number of courses…guess it was always in the back of my mind. But I'll call you, Rainey, and we can write, and as soon as one of us can, we'll fly back and forth."

She looked away, turned to get a bowl of water and set it down for Roscoe.

"I don't want it to end here, Rainey. Do you?"

"No." But she wondered how it *would* end.

"I love you, Rainey. I've never felt like this before...but I know I love you."

"Oh, Harry." She had made such poor decisions with Robert and Monte. "We're so very different, Harry."

"Not that different...not in any way that matters."

They gazed at each other for a long moment.

"Oh, Harry, what if we don't make it?"

"Why look at failure before we even begin?" he said in that amused, dry tone.

He waited for her.

Another moment of being overcome by doubts all around, and then she went to him.

They kissed hot and hard and long, and Rainey thought that no man she had ever kissed had done so quite as wonderfully.

When she broke from him, her chest heaving, she turned and led the way to the stairs, tugging him along by the hand.

At the bottom step he jerked her to him and kissed her again, causing her blood to flow liquid and hot and burn up any hesitation she might have had left. Two more steps up, she turned and kissed him, and another three steps and he kissed her in such a manner as to cause her to take hold of the bannister to remain on her feet.

She continued upward with shaky legs, while behind her, he began stripping out of his shirt.

At the top of the stairs, he sent the shirt flying across the hallway and shoved her against the wall, pressed himself against her and kissed her until every cell in her body was singing and sweating.

"Harry…"

"Rainey?"

He kissed her neck, ran his hands firmly up and down her sides, and then cupped her bottom and brought her against him.

"Ohh, Harry."

His dark hair was silky beneath her fingertips, his body hard and urgent against her.

Her legs began to buckle. He surprised her by scooping her up into his arms and carrying her to her room, managing, probably strengthened in his passion, to do so quite easily.

He sat her on the bed, and the next thing he was down on the floor, slipping off her shoes and caressing her feet and causing all sorts of sensual sensations that Rainey had never associated with feet. With surprised curiosity, she watched him kiss her instep and then proceed to taste his way up the inside of her bare leg. Her leg began to quiver.

"Harry," she said breathlessly, her leg jerking of its own accord.

"Rainey?" He shot her a grin and continued.

When he reached her thigh, she cried out.

He lifted his head and smiled softly, promisingly, and his eyes were so eager she thought she could not stand it.

She reached for him, crying softly with the sweet ache of wanting, and he came to her, kissing her lips and her cheeks and her neck, unfastening the small buttons at the front of her dress, and all the while whispering tender words of love.

He proceeded to find every tender spot on her body and to play it in such a manner as to bring forth hidden passions that caused her to spread open her body and her heart and to call out his name again and again. Then, when she lay spent and thankful in his arms, he very slowly and gently proceeded to begin all over again.

"Harry?"

"Hmm?"

"Where did you learn...all this? For someone who says he never had a serious girlfriend, you must have had a lot of practice."

He chuckled. "I paid attention in anatomy class."

"Well, it was never like this before...with Robert or Monte."

"It wasn't?"

"No. With them, it was like somethin' they went after." She thought hard. "With you, it's like something you are giving."

His response was to kiss her breast as if he were worshiping it.

"I love you, Harry," she whispered and dug her hand into his thick hair.

And she thought that if this was not true and lasting love, then she would never find it.

They gave themselves to each other all night, and in the morning Harry left.

"I'll just take a bus to Wichita Falls and catch a commuter down to Houston," he said.

"No. I'll drive you down."

"You have enough to do with getting your father. I'll rent a car and drive home."

"You cannot rent a car in Valentine. Maybe Freddy would lend you a car. I imagine he would rent you one."

"I'll take the bus."

"I'll drive you."

In the end he took the bus, saying that he really wanted to

try it. One more new experience. Rainey thought that they were getting their first lesson in the inconvenience of traveling between Valentine and Houston.

The Main Street Café served as the bus station, and they had breakfast there. Rainey could tell Harry seemed anxious to leave now. To get back to his life and get on with things. A number of times he talked of this therapist or that doctor with whom he wanted to talk and study. Now that he had made the choice of pursuing psychiatry, he was enthused and focused. She tried to pay attention and be supportive. She felt supportiveness was her talent, although as the minutes ticked past she felt herself getting wound tighter and tighter, and she really wanted to just jump up and say, "Give it up and stay here and we'll go back to bed!" Her emotional state was not helped by all the people who kept stopping at their table and inquiring about her daddy and looking Harry over, so as soon as they finished their meal, Rainey suggested they go outside, where they could have the last few minutes alone before the bus arrived.

Unfortunately when they stepped out on the sidewalk, the first person they ran into was Monte.

"Hi, Rainey."

Monte's eyes were on Harry as he spoke the greeting, and Rainey made the introductions.

Always polite, Monte shook Harry's hand, apparently feeling the need to say, "I was Rainey's last husband."

"She told me," Harry said with his dry amusement.

"Oh." He looked at Rainey, crossing his arms and sticking his hands up under his armpits, as if he intended to stand there and converse for some time. "I heard about your daddy, and you comin' home. How's Winston doin'?"

"Very well. I'll bring him home this afternoon. How's Janna?"

"She's doin' okay, I guess. Maybe I'll stop in to see your daddy tonight. I always enjoyed your daddy."

Just then, over Monte's shoulder, Rainey saw the sun glinting on the silver bus coming down the street. She looked anxiously at Harry.

"The bus is comin'."

"Oh, are you leavin' on the bus?" Monte inquired.

"Yes," Rainey and Harry answered at the same time, having eyes only for each other.

Rainey forgot all about Monte then, forgot about everyone and even where she was. She got lost in Harry's brown eyes, thinking, I must remember them…in case this is the last time.

Harry draped an arm on her shoulder and bent his head, blocking the sunlight and the world with his hat, and kissed her softly, seductively.

"We'll work it out," he said, his brown eyes reassuring her.

She nodded.

"I love you, Rainey."

Words choked in her throat. Men had told her they loved her before.

"Can you say it?" he asked.

"I love you, Harry."

He pressed her head to his chest, and she gripped his shirt, inhaling the scent of him and pressing it into memory.

And then here came the bus, stopping in the street with a whoosh of brakes and a squeal as the doors opened. Several people got off.

He kissed her boldly right there in front of the doors, a kiss that lifted one of her feet off the ground and almost made her faint.

"I'll call you tonight," he said in a husky tone, and then he turned, swinging the maroon bag that Uncle Doyle had given him over his shoulder and mounting the steps in the boots he had bought. His hat was shoved backward on his head, showing his thick shiny hair.

Then he was gone into the bus, a shadow moving along behind the dark glass. He knocked on the glass about halfway down the bus, and she moved to peer at him, and to wave.

And then the bus was going away down Main Street, and she was left standing there, watching it go in a puff of exhaust and dust and thinking, "Well, we'll see what happens."

"Rainey, you okay?"

Monte rather startled her with his question. She had forgotten all about him and had gone directly to her truck, opening the door with blurred vision. She saw him now, peering to look at her face.

"Yes." She wiped her eyes with a napkin from the glove box.

"He's somebody special, huh?"

"Yes…he is."

"Well, I hope it goes okay for you."

"Thanks."

"I've always been sorry we couldn't make it," he said, looking sorrowful. Monte could look very sorrowful.

"I know, Monte. I have my regrets, too. There's a part of me that will always love you…you know."

"Yeah," he nodded, his face very long. Then he said, "Do you suppose I could borrow a couple of twenties until payday?"

She stared at him. Then she dug quickly into her purse, pulled out the bills and handed them to him, telling him not to ask for any more in the future. "It's over, Monte. I don't have anything left to give you."

He looked a little confused as he walked away in his run-down boots, but she thought he would understand after he thought about it.

She started her truck, backed out and drove to her parents' house, where she went straight to her traveling bags in her bedroom and got the framed photographs of Robert and Monte that she had been hauling around with her for over two months. She carried them to her truck and drove quickly to her cottage, raced into the stuffy rooms which had not been opened for weeks, gathering all her pictures of Robert and Monte that she had tucked away, along with some early poems Robert had written for her during his literary phase, tied together and stuffed in her lingerie drawer, still, after all these years. She also got her marriage certificates and copies of her divorce decrees.

She took all these things out to the gravel drive and burnt them in a pile.

"What *are* you doin'?" Charlene asked, coming up to see.

"Leavin' yesterday behind," Rainey said, feeding a picture of Robert into the fire. She thought that he would find her actions foolish, but, at last, she did not hear his critical voice.

"Are you goin' to marry Harry?" Charlene asked.

"I don't know what's goin' to happen with Harry. He just left on the bus." She added, "He said he'd call."

She wondered if he would. People so often changed their minds. So often things just fell apart, she thought, looking at the small fire of memories.

CHAPTER 30

Long Stretch of Lonesome

From the minute that she came into the house with her daddy, Rainey began to listen for the phone. Since Harry had departed, Rainey vacillated from believing she would hear from him to believing she had lost her mind to think he would call. And either way, some bit of heart was required of her, and she wasn't certain she had any to spare. She felt herself getting wound tighter than a spool of thread, and if anyone jerked too hard, she was going to snap in two, a state that was not helped by the emotional turmoil all around her.

Because of Rainey taking the time to burn away her history with men, she and Charlene were late getting their daddy from the hospital, and he was not at all happy about it. The nurse told them he had been dressed and waiting since before breakfast and long before the doctor had formally discharged him.

He grumbled all the way home, saying things like, "I could have had another nap, if I'd known you were goin' to be late," and "I'm almost too tired to go now, and it is lunchtime," and

"I could have called Bill Yearwood to come get me, if I'd known it was goin' to be so much trouble for you."

With the last statement, Charlene rather exploded. "Oh, Daddy, Bill Yearwood lost his license last month. He can't see to drive anymore."

Rainey thought Charlene needn't have said that, as it just pointed up their father's own dependency.

"He still drives, which is more than you do," their daddy said, surprising Rainey with his sharpness.

"I could, if I wanted to. I keep my license current," Charlene said in a defensive tone.

Rainey hoped Charlene wouldn't start crying; she didn't know what she would do if her sister broke down. If her sister started crying, Daddy might have another heart attack, and even as she thought this, Rainey realized she had to cut off that foolish line of thinking.

She was relieved when Charlene left right after they got Daddy situated on the couch, where he could lie and watch television. Charlene fairly raced away down the porch steps, saying she was going to get her hair done and did not want to be late. Larry Joe would pick her up from the beauty shop.

Then the telephone rang, and Rainey hurried to answer, knowing it was not at all logical to expect the caller to be Harry—who surely wouldn't be any farther than Wichita Falls—but even so, he might call her.

It was Freddy.

Rainey informed him that things were in hand, and, with a sigh, he said, "Well, I guess you'd better let me talk to him."

Rainey passed the receiver to their father, who listened for a full minute and then said, "I'm here on the couch, and all I'm gonna do is watch television, if everyone will leave me alone to do so."

He extended the receiver to Rainey and went to clicking television channels.

"You brought this on yourself, you know," Freddy said to her and hung up.

Rainey carefully replaced the receiver, wondering how all of their lives could be falling apart, and wishing very much for her mother, actually listening for her mother's movements in the kitchen.

"I guess it'd be easier all the way around if I'd go to Prairie View Manor," her daddy said.

Rainey sank into the chair that had been her mother's favorite. She gazed at her father, who stared at the television. After a minute she asked, "Daddy, do you want to go to Prairie View Manor?"

He didn't answer, kept his eyes glued on the television.

Rainey set herself to force a conversation, but this intention was interrupted by the doorbell. It was Mildred Covington, the first of a stream of visitors who came in perky and smiling to cheer Daddy. Unfortunately, Daddy resisted cheering and focused completely on the Western Channel, so none of his visitors stayed more than ten minutes.

"Rainey?"

"Harry?" she said in surprise.

"Were you expecting someone else?" He sort of laughed.

"Well, people have been calling to talk to Daddy all day. Are you in Houston already?" It was only three o'clock, she saw by the clock on the oven. And her heart had begun to pound as she thought, *He called.*

"No. I'm in Dallas, at the train station. I only have a couple of minutes."

Much to her surprise, he went on to tell her that he had continued on the bus because it was so easy, and now he was going to take a train to Houston, because he had met a man on the bus who was doing that, and he thought he would take the opportunity while it presented itself to try the experience.

She did not know what to say to this. His inclination to embrace new activities was both impressive and daunting. She wondered if she was some sort of new and novel experience Harry was trying out. She guessed their relationship was that for each of them. She wished him a good time.

"It'll be late when I get to Houston. Will it be okay to call you?"

"There's no need. You'll be tired." This was what she thought she should say...not be too demanding, when she really wanted to reach through the phone and pull him back to her. She felt her control was nothing short of spectacular.

"I want to call you, Rainey," he said with some urgency. "I want to hear your voice."

"I like hearing your voice, too," she said, giving way. "Call when you get to Houston, no matter what time. The phone never wakes Daddy."

The phone rang, waking her.

"I just walked into my apartment," Harry said.

"You did?" Then, "And you called me first thing?"

"I did go to the bathroom first." He chuckled. "Did I wake you?"

"I had just dozed off." She was trying to come to herself so that she wouldn't say something she regretted.

"Were you waiting for my call?"

"Well, sort of." She had the phone on the bed with her, afraid that in her exhaustion she would not hear it.

"That's good news."

"Is it?"

"Rainey, I'm crazy about you. I have plans for us, and I'm goin' to make you believe it."

"I can't seem to have any plans."

"I know, but you will. I'm beat, and I know you must've had

a hell of a day there, with getting your father home. Get some rest. I'll call tomorrow night, and we'll really talk."

"Okay.... Harry?"

"Yes?"

"I'm awfully crazy about you, too."

The next afternoon, after her father had made the comment that he might as well go on to Prairie View Manor about three more times, Rainey plopped herself down in front of him and requested that he explain himself.

"Do you want to go to Prairie View?" she asked, to prod him into speaking. This was a new father before her, one who looked and acted very much like a child.

"I don't like bein' dependent on my children," he said at last. "I might as well get to the inevitable."

"Do you think that is inevitable...and is that what you want?"

"Who gets what they want in this world? I'm a widower, I didn't want that."

"We don't get everything, but we don't have to jump in front of a train, either," Rainey said.

"If I wasn't here, you'd be free to go off with your fella."

"Oh, Daddy, I don't want to go anywhere. And I guess Harry and I are still findin' out if he's my fella."

He gazed at her.

"Daddy, you have never been sick, and so you are letting this bit of heart trouble take wild proportions. Yes, it is serious, but, Daddy, lots of men younger than you have heart trouble and go on to live many, many active years. You are not sick. You will be on your feet in three more days and take up a walkin' program, like the doctor wants. You'll be drivin' back down to the sale barn and doin' anything else you want. This thing now is about like Freddy having his gall bladder out.

"I'm here because I want to be, Daddy. And I guess you

needin' me came at a good time. It gave me a reason for bein' here. I can't go away with Harry until I'm certain it's for real. Maybe I can't ever go. I don't know, I'm so messed up about men. Maybe I can never trust him, or maybe him bein' from Houston will make it impossible for us. This is my home. Even if you move off to Prairie View, I can't leave here, not right now. Freddy would have to come haul me out. I just need to be home right now, Daddy, and you needin' my services makes it easier."

Her father accepted all this with several nods and then told her to go make him a sandwich. When she brought it to him, she noticed he sat up straighter. After his sandwich, he asked her to bring the phone so he could call Bill Yearwood to come over and watch a Dale Robertson western. Bill had once done a little horse business with Dale Robertson, and he liked to call him Dale.

While the men watched the movie, Rainey busied herself in the kitchen, making three kinds of burritos and elaborate Spanish rice and sopapillas, the batter made from scratch. She had never cooked much Mexican food beyond tacos, but Harry had said Mexican food was his favorite. She decided she should make an effort, in case their relationship did work out.

She had, she thought as she cooked, begun to at least get a glimmer of an image of herself and Harry together on a more permanent basis, and she tried to practice this sort of planning as she cooked. The one stumbling block she kept bumping against was the fact—all burnt pictures aside—that she had been married twice and failed twice. Fear of another failure held her tight.

When she blurted this out to Charlene, who stopped in to show her new hairstyle, Charlene said, "Well, why don't you look at it this way—you've been divorced twice, so if you have to get divorced again, it'll be a snap. You already know all the steps."

Harry telephoned every night for a week, and they spoke for over an hour each time, telling every minute of their days.

Rainey would be waiting in the privacy of her bedroom and snatch the phone immediately, as if to snatch Harry and pull him into the room with her. She would also listen carefully for an extension being lifted, as one time her father tried to listen in. When she caught the click on the line, he said, "Sorry, I just wanted to make a call."

"At eleven o'clock at night, Daddy?"

"Yes. Let me know when the phone is free."

She poured out to Harry her concern about her father's unusual and often brooding behavior. "He keeps saying that maybe he should go to Prairie View Manor, so that I will tell him he does not need to think that way."

"A lot of this is grief work," Harry told her. "He's mourning the loss of your mother and the change in a way of life he's known for so long, and he's also mourning the loss of his physical vitality. He's got a lot of confusing false guilt and anger to get through."

Harry always managed to make her feel better. She tried to find encouraging things to say about his own father's behavior, but could not come up with anything very helpful. What could she say about a father who continued to refuse to speak to his son, all because the son's views were different from his own? And then there was Harry's mother, who consented to have lunch with him but wanted the meeting kept secret from her husband, fearing the repercussions.

Rainey thought that Harry had better get his psychiatry training done as soon as possible, because his family needed his services as much as did her own.

Harry always ended their conversations with, "I love you, Rainey." Her response was, "I do you, too," or "I miss you." She knew this was unsatisfactory to him, but he did not, as he had when he'd left her, ask her to say the words he longed to hear. He was waiting for her to be ready, in her own time, and she was trying so hard to get to that time.

CHAPTER 31

In the Meantime

"Rainey?"

At his surprised tone, she suddenly felt very vulnerable. The thought flashed across her mind that he could have a woman with him.

She said, "I thought that it was time I paid for a call. Did I catch you at a bad time?"

"No. No...I just got out of the shower, but it's okay. I'm really glad you called." Now his voice sounded pleased, and pleasure swept her. "I went to work today," he said.

"You did?"

"Yep...my brother put in a word for me, and I got a position filling in at a clinic for a doctor who decided he needed some time off. He got shot, actually."

To her inquiry about this rather odd pronouncement, Harry explained that he would be filling in at a hospital clinic for low-income patients. The doctor he was replacing had been an unfortunate victim of a domestic disturbance that had taken place at the clinic; he'd been shot and had since been very reluctant to return to work. He was at this moment readying himself for a Caribbean cruise and contemplating turning his hobby of photography into a career. Harry had casually known this man for a couple of years and said he was quite a good photographer, had had pictures published in travel magazines.

"It may not be widely recognized, but doctors quitting being doctors is not uncommon," he added.

She asked about his brother's help in getting him the position and what his father felt about this.

"My brother simply let the head of the clinic know I was available," he said. "And quietly, so that my father will never know."

Still, Rainey thought this was good of the brother, and she could tell that Harry appreciated it. And yes, it was the same brother he had described as having wanted at heart to be a veterinarian.

He went on to fill her in on a few of his cases, a number of the type he had not encountered before on a large basis, and the patients he thought could more benefit from psychiatric help than from the medication he could prescribe. In his way, Rainey knew, he did his best in the emotional area, too.

He asked about her day, and she told him that her father had walked twice around the house. "I told him if he would do that, I'd drive him over to the sale barn to have lunch at the café. Everyone was glad to see him, and he had a great time."

"Rainey, I miss you."

"I miss you, too, terribly." She gripped the telephone and paced, hardly knowing she was doing so.

"If I were there, you know what I would do?"

"What would you do?"

He told her in intimate detail, making her inordinately aware of every part of her body.

"Oh, Harry, I cannot stand this," she said and hung up, her face on fire, her heart and body longing for him.

The phone rang beneath her hand.

At her answer, Harry said very seriously, "I'm crazy in love with you, Rainey."

"I you, too," she said.

She was out at the corral, grooming Lulu, when her father walked out and extended an envelope. "You got a letter from Harry."

"Really?" She took the envelope and looked at the handwriting. It was the first time, she realized, that she had seen Harry's handwriting…yes, it was his address. Her father walked on back to the house, and she opened the envelope.

Dear Rainey,

I'm doing duty at the clinic—did I tell you we are open until nine at night? Part of the hospital. Right now it's quiet, and it's a weeknight, so things aren't so bad. On weekends, though, we often get stab wounds or things of that nature. Earlier this evening I had a guy in here with an arm broken in a fight. He told me he used to be a professional bull rider and had had many broken bones. The X ray of his arm proved him out. I would have liked to have talked with him about the love of danger that drove him, but we were a little backed up at that time. He said he knew your cousin Leanne. Tough guy, works as a bouncer in a club right now.

It's beginning to look like I won't be able to get into a psychiatry residency until after the first of the year. I think my father may have something to do with it. My younger brother hinted this is the case but won't say straight out.

He tried to put the situation in a positive light, saying that at least he would have more time to come up to see her that winter, but Rainey knew he had to be sorely disappointed. He told of a bird on his windowsill, there at dark, which seemed rather odd, and described in great detail how the bird peered at him and he peered back, until it flew away. He signed the letter, "Harry, who loves you."

Rainey looked for a long moment at those words. Then she hurried to finish with Lulu and went back to the house, found her mother's fine linen stationery and a flowing blue pen, and sat at the kitchen table to write.

Dear Harry,

I know it is a disappointment to you not to get going right away on your psychiatry studies, but the clinic does seem to be providing a certain amount of experience in the area of the human psyche. You seem to be finding some satisfaction and even fascination with the work.

On my end, this afternoon, when I went in to get Daddy a bottle of aspirins, Mr. Blaine about fell all over himself offering me my old job back with a two-dollar raise. When I accepted, he requested that I start right away, so I did and worked for a couple of hours. I was very gratified by how many of our customers said they had missed me.

For the next couple of weeks, I won't go in until around ten each morning and work no later than three, because I need to keep an eye on Daddy and get him in the habit of walking. He walked up and down the block today, and Roscoe walks right with him. I think he seems happier. He wasn't bothered at all about Mildred Covington now keeping company with Charlie Blevins, a recent widower. I think he might have been relieved.

You would not believe how big Roscoe is suddenly getting. He weighed in at seventy-five pounds at the vet's the other day.

She thought for a minute and signed, "Love, Rainey." It seemed a standard ending and not any type of solid commitment.

For some minutes she continued to sit there and wonder why she should be afraid of admitting in writing that she loved Harry.

"I'm calling from a pay phone at the 7-Eleven," Harry told her. "My phone is dead, and I didn't want you to try and not be able to get me. Did you get my letter from Wednesday?"

"Yes, and I got my phone bill in the same mail."

He chuckled and said his had come, too. "The clinic isn't in the high-paying category, and all the other doctors there want to know how I drive a Porsche. I told them I just had to take a loan against it to pay my phone bills to my girl."

Rainey felt a warm flush at the term *my girl.* "We'd better get off the phone right now," she said, getting a little worried. She didn't want to make things hard on him. "You'll need your money for when you go back to school."

"No, it's okay. Really," Harry said quickly. "I'm using one of those prepaid cards. I'm covered for thirty minutes...well, twenty-five now. How's your father and everything going there?"

"Daddy's doin' real good. I tell you that in the letter I sent right back to you, and I guess you didn't get it yet. There isn't any need for me to tell all that I wrote you, or you won't need to get the letter."

"Then tell me what you didn't say in the letter. I want to hear your voice," he said in a warm husky tone.

She imagined him bending his head and speaking very intently into the phone, and her heartbeat picked up tempo.

"I think about you a lot, Rainey."

"I think about you, too."

"Well, that's getting somewhere," he said.

Dear Harry,

Leanne came yesterday. She broke up with Clay and is going to stay here with me and Daddy for a little while. But she is no longer pregnant. I was heartbroken to hear this. I've been so busy with Daddy and going to work again that I haven't thought much of it, but in the back of my mind, I guess I still hoped for her baby.

She says she lost the baby in a fall from her horse. I don't think it is my business to question her, but I do wonder if she had an abortion, or if perhaps Clay beat her up. She has a number of bruises on her back. Clay drove by our house already. Daddy was sitting on the porch, and he now takes his rifle out there, to give Clay something to think about, he says. Freddy, of course, is fit to be tied over this, and I know it is rather outlandish behavior, but Daddy is getting such a kick out of it. He seems much invigorated with the thought of shooting someone. I thought it might be a good way to get out his anger—not to actually shoot Clay, but to feel aggressive.

And when Bill Yearwood came for supper this evening (I think he's about to take up residence here, too), he fell in love with Leanne. Leanne doesn't believe me, because Bill is eighty-five, but I said he is still a man, and he fell immediately. He can't hear her, is probably why he fell in love with her.

Leanne wants me to go to a barrel racing futurity

with her this weekend, and I think I will. I find I miss the barrel racing more than I had thought I would. What would a psychiatrist have to say about that?

I have been thinking lately that maybe instead of trying to see your father in person, you should write him a letter, or call him on the phone. I do better with Charlene on the phone, and I sent her a sister card the other day, so she sent me one back.

I will call you Sunday. I want to hear your voice.

With love, Rainey

P.S. I taught Roscoe to sit and shake hands, and Daddy is working on getting him to bring the paper. He's lying at my feet now.

Dear Rainey,

I suppose I could try to write my father. It may be best to wait a few weeks for him to cool off, though, because my brother Malcolm—the brother who should have been a veterinarian—just took a position at a small hospital down in Mexico. An out-of-the-way place with no notoriety at all. Really, I think he's going there to escape his life here. His wife refuses to go, and Dad is furious, of course, at this defection on the part of another of his sons.

I think I may have had something to do with this, and I feel a little guilty, but I guess a little proud, too. Malc has come over here a couple of times to talk to me, and I did write him a letter and tell him he needed to do what was right for him. I guess since I've been writing you, I sort of started getting in the habit of writing notes to people. And my patient reports are a lot more thorough—one of the secretaries praised me for this. In the case of my brother, though, my mother called it inciting to ruin, or words to that effect.

I saw this woman today with the same color hair you have, and I almost called out to her. It made me want to see you so much.

Have a good ride this weekend. I wish I was there to watch.

Harry, who is still crazy in love with you.

Dear Harry,

I'm sorry I missed your phone call this evening. That scrub filly we got at the barrel race in Ardmore coliced. I had the vet out but felt called upon to help. The vet thought I had lost my mind when I laid hands on her and prayed over her. Maybe you will think I am crazy, too, but my mother and I had success with that method several times in the past, and I felt compelled. The filly did get better almost immediately, even if the vet says it was all his medicine.

I am certainly glad that filly pulled through, because Jojo was over here, right there watching and in tears. She already loves that filly and is making quite a little horsewoman. Her father could be proud; unfortunately, she won't have much to do with him. She's already gotten the filly saddled. I'll probably let her get on it next week. That filly is something for her to focus on right now. She can feel the tension between Charlene and Joey and knows things are precarious. Tonight is the second night she has slept with me. She looks like an angel there in my bed.

I tried to call you back, but I guess you've gone out. I wonder if you can see the evening star there in Houston the way I can. Daddy says we're going to have a hard winter because of the way the sky looks to him—hard, he says. I guess winters in Houston aren't much, are they?

I pray you are over your cold.

And guess who warned us the filly was in trouble? Roscoe. He ran back and forth from the house to the corral, like Lassie on television.

With much love, Rainey

Dear Harry,

I just now tried to call—you'll hear my message. I think I missed getting a letter. What do you mean about driving a Mustang now? What happened to your Porsche? And did you mean you are getting into the psychiatric program after all? I went down and had Grady Snow look around the post office, but he says if the letter was lost, it was not by anyone at his post office.

Well, Jojo is staying over here more than at home now, because she ran away when Charlene and Joey had a fight. And Daddy asked Bill Yearwood to move in with us. He might as well, as he's over here all the time anyway. But Leanne is gone. I told you I thought Leanne was speaking secretly to Clay on the phone. Well, she went back with him while she was down at the women's rodeo in Fort Worth. He probably promised her he would never hit her again and all sorts of fantasies like that. I didn't know she could be so stupid, but she says she loves him and owes him her faith. Bill Yearwood is heartbroken. He's hardly eaten all day.

I guess when you come up here in a couple of weeks we'll have to rent a motel room up in Lawton if we want to have any romance. It is the weekend after this one that you are coming, isn't it? Let me know for sure and I'll take that Friday off of work.

I miss you, Harry, and when I read that you are coming, I cried.

All my love, Rainey

Bill Yearwood hollered at her, "Rainey, that Harry is on the phone." Then he yelled into the phone, "She's cookin'. She'll be here in a minute." Rainey thought with some alarm that Bill might have ruined Harry's hearing.

Rainey hurriedly wiped her hands and picked up the receiver in the kitchen. "Harry? I'm sorry about Bill's yelling. Is your ear okay?"

"I held the receiver away from my ear, but it's still sort of ringing."

"Well...guess what I'm making? Tortilla soup. Daddy and Bill just love it, and they rave over my sopapillas, too. I'll make both when you come up, and we'll have a nice dinner before we go off to Lawton. Daddy and Bill are takin' Jojo and having Larry Joe drive them up to Oklahoma City for the Quarter Horse Show finals, so they won't be back here until late. Daddy won't spend the night up there. He does not like to stay away from his own bed."

"Rainey, I can't get up there this weekend."

"You can't?"

"No, honey, I'm sorry. It turns out that Friday afternoon I have a meeting over at the med school to submit my application for the psychiatry residency program, and I'm pulling duty at the clinic Saturday. The guy who was supposed to be working just had a baby. Well, his wife did, early, and there are complications, and the only other doctor is getting married."

"Oh." Disappointment fell over her like wet wool. "Well, it's good that you are gettin' your application in to the school." She pulled herself up straighter and tried to sound positive.

"Yes," he said in a tired voice. "I'll have to go through the interview, though, and get accepted."

"Do you think there'll be a problem?" He hadn't mentioned this before.

"I don't know. No. My dad has a lot of pull, but not so much he can keep me out of school forever. I'm just down right now. I had a woman in today whose mind is going, could be Alzheimer's but possibly she's getting overmedicated by her husband, who I'm pretty certain beats her. He admitted tying her to her bed. She's sixty-two, appears ninety-two, and isn't about to find any aid. The both of them have only each other, are ignorant and trapped there. It makes me feel helpless."

"I'm sorry, Harry." Tears welled in her eyes.

"I sure miss you, Rainey. I wish you were here. I think if you were here, I could believe, you know?"

She knew exactly what he was saying, but she didn't understand how he could say that about her. She had such a hard time believing most of the time. How could it be that she could help him believe?

"I miss you, too, Harry. You help me believe. Can you come next weekend?"

"I think so. I'll try for that."

"I can't come this weekend," Harry said. "Fuel pump's gone out in the Mustang."

"Oh."

"Rainey, I want you to consider marrying me. I want you with me. I love you, Rainey, and I believe you love me."

Rainey didn't know what to say. His frustrated and anxious voice echoed in her ears.

"Will you think about it, Rainey?"

"Yes."

CHAPTER 32

By and By

Harry called and spoke about marriage a couple more times, and because they were both under strain, they had a few sharp words over the subject. Then Harry didn't call for two days.

Rainey worried about this. She knew she had disappointed him in not saying yes immediately to his proposal. Her father, who since his heart attack had developed both a good ability to know what was going on and to speak his mind about it, said that men did not like to be held off.

He said, "You'd better know Harry takes your hemmin' and hawin' as rejection."

"Daddy, I'm just bein' practical. I don't want to be rushed."

To Rainey's mind, love had only a small part in her decision, because love could die, she well knew. She did not intend for that to happen ever again. Any further marriage on her part was forever.

Then she began to believe she was being totally selfish, requiring Harry to be the one to travel up to Valentine, simply because she was most comfortable here now. And possibly she was being very foolish, letting the chance of a lifetime pass her by because she was afraid of the future. She felt she and Harry needed some in-depth, face-to-face discussion about marriage.

After coming firmly to this conclusion Thursday morning, she went right in and asked Mr. Blaine if she could leave at noon and have Friday off, as well. As she had been steadily working past quitting time for some weeks, and he had once experienced what happened when he said no to such a request, he agreed. He would have his daughter come to fill in and pay her a pittance, saving the overtime he had been paying Rainey; he was thrilled with his idea.

"Daddy, I'm driving down to Houston to see Harry for the weekend," she told her father when he stopped by on his daily walk, which was now up to a mile down to the drugstore, where he sat at the soda counter and had coffee before walking the mile back.

"It's about time," he said. "I'll get your truck filled up and the oil checked."

She waved to her father and Bill Yearwood and little Jojo standing side by side, with Roscoe sitting at their feet. "I'll feed the horses," Jojo said.

It was over six hours to Houston, windows rolled up tight, country music on the radio and a sack of snacks in the seat beside her. On leaving Valentine she ran the heater, but by Dallas she turned it off. She was heated by anxiety, she supposed, driving through the city at seventy and about bumper to bumper, too. Rainey thought no one worked in this city; they just drove around.

Upon stopping at a Texaco, she considered phoning Harry. She had planned to surprise him, but she worried a little about her sudden appearance being more of a complication to him. She decided against phoning, however, wanting to see his happy

surprise when she arrived. He would know she was not rejecting him then. That her reservations had nothing to do with not
loving him, but that there was so much more to consider than
that. It would be good for him to see her in his environment,
to make certain he liked what he saw.

It was dark and raining when she came into Houston. She
peered at exit signs and eventually pulled off the highway to
turn on the light in the cab to read the map. While she found
her way to Harry's apartment, the rain stopped.

It was the sort of town-house-style complex where one had
to drive past an entry guard building, although there was no
one in the building. The little building did not look terribly invit-
ing, just a box, really, so possibly the apartment people had
never been able to get a guard on a lasting basis and had simply given up. It would have been nice to have someone there to
direct her, but eventually she found Harry's apartment and
pulled nose-in to the front curb.

Her truck did not at all fit in these surroundings, and love
would not change that, she thought. It could overcome it,
though, she told herself in a positive voice.

She didn't see a red Mustang, which he'd said he was driving now. Maybe he parked it over beneath the shelters, and it
was too dark over there to identify cars. Drapes were pulled over
his front window, so she could not see any light within.

All during the drive down, her mind had drawn up in great
detail how Harry would greet her with a happy cry and sweep
her into his arms. She thought of this now, shaking, as she got
out of her truck and went to his front door. There was a bell,
and she rang it and waited.

She heard no sound from within. The door did not fly open.
She checked her watch, saw it was before eight. Perhaps this was
his night to work until nine at the clinic. She had known this
could be the case but had dismissed it with a hope.

She rang the bell again, waited, and then went back to her truck, trying hard to hold her shoulders up.

With some difficulty, she backed her pickup, much too large for the small parking arena. She saw only two other pickup trucks, parked down at the end of the row of sporty, low-slung, expensive-type vehicles.

The thought that maybe she should not have come tried to take hold and she banished it.

At a 7-Eleven down the street she asked directions to Harry's hospital, which entailed driving through quite a bit of the city and took her some time, as she made at least one wrong turn. At last, with great relief, she pulled into the lot in front of the clinic, where parking was a lot easier. That she did not see a red Mustang caused her some concern.

"Dr. Furneaux isn't here," the young woman at the desk told her and gazed at her curiously.

Rainey explained that she was a friend from out of town. "Do you happen to know where I might find him? I've tried his apartment."

"I'll see." The young woman stepped out a rear doorway, calling someone named Charlie.

Rainey looked at the big clock, and then over at a man reading a *People* magazine. It was odd because the magazine was upside down. The waiting room was nicer than she had imagined.

The young woman returned and said that she could not say where Dr. Furneaux was. "All we know is that he isn't on the schedule until Monday at noon.

"Oh. Thank you."

She went back out to her truck, got into the seat and sat there for some minutes. She could not believe this had happened. He had off until Monday at noon. Why hadn't he told her that?

She drove back over to his apartment, rang the bell again and knocked hard. He could have been out to supper or shopping, or visiting a friend. There was no reason to panic.

But she *was* panicking. She could feel a tightness taking hold of her spine and spreading across her shoulders. Tears threatened, and she breathed deeply to stave them off.

When no one answered the door, she got back into her pickup and sat there for an hour. Then she drove back to the 7-Eleven and used the pay phone to call home. Bill Yearwood answered, and she had to yell into the receiver; she did not know why he insisted on answering the telephone. Bill put her father on the line, and Rainey asked if Harry happened to be there.

"Why, no."

"Has he called?"

"No, he hasn't called."

"Did you check the answering machine? Maybe he called when no one was there and left a message."

Her father checked. "Nope, no messages. Are you in Houston? Isn't Harry there?"

"He wasn't at his apartment. But he may come any time."

When she hung up, she began to shake. She was very close to tears. She went back to her truck, wishing very much for Roscoe to be there waiting for her. Then she thought of calling Harry and went back to the phone.

When his answering machine picked up, she hung up, not knowing what to say. She got back into her truck and started off, not really knowing where she would go. She ended up going back to Harry's apartment and sitting in the truck in front of it, hoping he would show up and forming a new picture in her mind of how it would go—unless he showed up with a woman, a horrible suspicion she wished would leave her alone. She began to wonder a little if one of the neighbors might call the police on her. After sitting there for an hour, she gathered what strength she had left and drove to a La Quinta she had seen on the way into the city.

From her room there, she telephoned Harry's apartment and when his machine picked up, left a message that she was in town and gave the La Quinta phone number and her room. Then she telephoned home, her heart hoping that Harry himself would answer.

"I'm sorry, Little Bit, but Harry isn't here, and he hasn't phoned."

"Did I get a letter from him today?"

"No…let me look at the mail again. No, hon. Are you all right?"

She told him that she was, using a very capable tone of voice, and gave him the number of the La Quinta.

Then she flopped down on the bed and cried. Eventually she lay there wondering where Harry was and going back over their last conversation, which had been tense. But they hadn't fought. If he had been going on a trip, surely he would have told her. Maybe he started up for Valentine and his car had broken down. Or maybe he'd had another wreck. What if it had been a bad wreck and he'd been killed? Who would know to tell her? Had he told anyone about her?

She got the phone book out to look for Furneauxs. There were four, but she did not call any. Midnight was not a time to be calling people, and likely, if any of them turned out to be Harry's family, they would think she was nuts.

If he had gone off without telling her, she supposed he hadn't wanted to tell her. What if she had needed him for something? What if she had suffered a car wreck or turned up with some serious disease? If they had a relationship close enough to speak about marriage, wasn't the relationship close enough to keep in touch, just in case something like that happened? It seemed that if that was the case, he should have called her and apprised her of his plans.

If she didn't hear from him by Monday, she would call the clinic, just to make certain he was alive. But she would not speak to him. She would never speak to him again.

Sometime in the night she fell asleep, still in her clothes, and when she awoke the next morning, well after eight, her eyes were nearly swollen shut from crying. After placing a cold cloth over her eyes for five minutes, she was able to dial Harry's phone number but only got his answering machine again. She didn't leave a message.

She showered, got dressed and touched up the chipped paint on a thumbnail, and went to the restaurant next door for breakfast. There was no message waiting on her return. Still, she called Harry's apartment once more, and then called home, where her father again said that Harry had not called.

"I guess I'll come home, Daddy," she said.

She drove straight home without calling again. From down the street, she saw there was no red Mustang in her drive. When she pulled into the driveway, Roscoe came to greet her. Her father came out the door with an anxious expression on his face, so she didn't have to ask if Harry called.

Telling him she was very tired, she went straight to her room and went to bed. Maybe Harry felt rejected because she had not immediately accepted his proposal, but she did not think he needed to behave in this fashion. This just showed his true colors. The least he could have done was call her.

She hoped he had not been killed in a car wreck.

She could not believe that she had driven round-trip to Houston for a man.

"Oh, Mama, I am heartbroken. I wish you were here." She wondered if she would ever get over longing for her mother.

She wondered if she would ever get over Harry.

Late the following morning, Charlene came into her room with a cup of tea and told Rainey to sit up. "Drink this tea, and I will give you a manicure." Charlene did beautiful nails.

"There's no need to think the worst, Rainey," Charlene admonished her.

Rainey simply looked at her, which didn't stop Charlene from expounding on how Harry had not known she was coming, and he might have done something as simple as gone fishing.

Rainey acknowledged that this was true, but she could not imagine Harry fishing.

After Charlene was done with her nails, Rainey felt sufficiently capable to take Jojo out back for a lesson on the filly. Later, when Charlene and Jojo had left, her father came into the kitchen with two yellow roses. He told her they were the last ones for the year and remarked on how the roses seemed to produce heavily and long this year.

"Your mother always said smelling roses lifted her spirit," he said, putting the roses right under her nose.

Rainey obligingly inhaled. "Thank you, Daddy."

She listened for the telephone, but it did not ring, not even once for Daddy or Bill Yearwood, or even a wrong number. She thought of telephoning Harry's apartment but refused to allow herself to do so.

Harry never did call.

He came, at sunset.

She was out at the corral, feeding Lulu and the filly, when something caused her to look up. There he came, walking toward her across the dead grass. She had to look twice to make certain she truly saw him and that he was not a figment of her imagination, like one of those scenes out of a romantic movie. When she saw Roscoe run to meet him and then dance in circles around him, she knew he was real.

He wore a sweater and jeans, and his hat, which she did not allow her gaze to light on. She noticed his easy stride, a saunter, really, which sparked her anger.

He said, of all things, "Hello, beautiful lady."

She tossed aside the empty bucket of grain and strode past him and straight for the house.

"Rainey? What'd I say?"

She did not answer, let the screen door bang, passed her father gaping at her and went on up to her bedroom, slamming the door behind her. Flopping down on the side of the bed, she stared at the rug. She had been rude. She was being ugly and crazy and petulant. But she was filled with emotions that she couldn't sort out.

She heard Harry's footsteps come up the stairs; she could tell them from her father's footsteps.

He knocked at the door. "Rainey?"

After a moment, she said, "I can't talk to you now."

He hovered outside the door. "Your dad told me about you going down to Houston. I'm sorry I wasn't there. Rainey, come out and let me talk to you."

"I can't."

She really couldn't. She wasn't certain she could move. She simply couldn't face him. She didn't want him to see her anger, which she knew was foolish. It wasn't anger at him. At herself, maybe. She was overwhelmed, overwrought, and plainly feeling as if she were out of control, and she didn't want him to see her like this.

She didn't think she could show him how much he meant to her. Thinking this, confused by it all, she could barely get her breath.

He didn't say anything else. After a few more long seconds, she listened to his footsteps as he went back down the hall and down the stairs. She listened until she could not hear any footsteps at all, nor any voices. As if the house had gone empty and silent around her.

Maybe Harry had left, she thought.

With this prospect, she jumped up, wildly flung open the door, raced down the stairs and through the rooms, looking for him. "Harry? Oh, Harry!"

Not finding him inside, she burst out the front door, thinking she might have to chase down his car as he drove away.

She stopped short, seeing him sitting with her father. Two men in the deepening shadows of the front porch.

He leaped to his feet and came directly to her and swept her into his arms, just as she had imagined.

"I was afraid you'd left," she mumbled into his chest.

"I'm not that easily put off," he said, with his warm, familiar chuckle.

"Oh, Harry."

In the privacy of the kitchen, Harry explained immediately about where he had been, as if he could not get the words out fast enough. "I was up at the University of Oklahoma, putting in an application and arranging for an interview next month for a psychiatry residency."

Rainey flicked the switch on the coffeemaker and then slid into the chair across the table from him, leaning forward and saying, "You'll be at OU?"

"Well, if I get accepted after the interview."

He told her then that he had written a letter to his father at last, pouring out his heart, and part of that was about Rainey. "I told him, 'Look, I'm in love with this Oklahoma girl, and I want to marry her, and to do that I've got to get up there with her, so I'm going to apply to the medical school up there for a psychiatry residency. They have a real good program, and if you can help get me in, I'd sure appreciate it.'"

"And he did?" she asked, breathless, already going on to imagine it, his burly father coming in his double-breasted suit and talking gruffly, hating every minute of it, but being overcome by his magnetic son.

Harry nodded. "He came to see me at the clinic, and he said, 'I guess if you're going to be stubborn about this, I might as well see what I can do to help you get the best training. Let's go.'

There's nothing my father likes better. Control is why he's the surgeon he is."

He told how he and his father had driven up to Oklahoma City Thursday morning. In addition to putting in his application and arranging for an interview, which wouldn't take place until January, his father had hauled him over to the VA hospital, where his father knew a bigwig and got Harry an interview on the spot. Harry would start a position there at the end of January. Doctors weren't exactly beating down the doors of VA hospitals, but it was a good place for Harry, as this was a place for old men in need of help.

"I guess I was hitting Oklahoma City about the time you were heading for Houston," he said, reaching for her hand. "I didn't call and tell you about what I was doing because I wanted to come over here and surprise you with the news, if it looked like it was going to work out. And I didn't want to tell you, in case it didn't turn out."

She gazed at his hand holding hers. She felt awfully guilty for her angry and doubtful thoughts.

"I appreciate so much that you went down to see me," he said.

"I wanted to surprise you, too."

"Well, you sure did." He rose and pulled her up, cupped her face in his hands, gazed longingly into her eyes and then kissed her in such a way as to melt her entire body.

When he'd finished with that, he told her, "Rainey, I love you and I want you to marry me. All I want right now is to set a date. You can pick any day from now until June, right before I start my residency in July. That ought to give us plenty of time to work out any thorns in our relationship.

"Will you do that, Rainey? Will you say you'll marry me?"

Gazing into his beautiful brown eyes, she said, "Yes." Then she added, "I love you, Harry, with all my heart."

As they embraced, she thought that she would have to try very hard to give to Harry as much as he had already given to her. She thought of the verse: Perfect love casteth out fear. Her fear, she thought, as she brought them coffee and he pulled her into his lap and nuzzled her breast, was fading away, at last.

It wasn't, she thought in a moment of sheer clarity, that she believed they would never have problems. There would be plenty of adjustments and even hard times. But now she believed that she could handle whatever came her way.

Winston Valentine smiled as he gazed through the glowing window at his daughter in the young man's lap.

"Well, Mama, you got it done," he said, turning his eyes to his wife's shimmering ethereal image standing four feet away and looking into the house, too.

She smiled at him and nodded in that knowing way she had.

He had not told anyone—they would think he was fully gone loony—but he had been seeing her since he'd had his heart attack. He could converse with her, although he never heard her speak. It was as if what she had to say just popped into his mind. Once he'd tried to reach for her, but she had faded. There was no solidness to her, but she was there.

"How we ever stayed together, I don't know, Coweta, but we did okay, don't you think?"

She smiled in agreement, and he heard, *"Yes, my darlin'."*

"I would not trade those years with you, honey, for anything in this ol' world. I came to love you more than I love life. And you know what, it was because of the difficulties, not in spite of 'em."

"Yes...now you know this." Her look was a little sardonic.

He noticed her clothing then, silvery-white as always. "What are you got up for? You look like a Wild West gal."

She did a little spin, extending her arms and showing off her sparkling fringed shirt.

"Well, I'll be dogged. They got barrel racin' up in heaven?"

"It is heaven."

She threw back her head with a laugh in the way that had always so attracted him. And over her shoulder he thought he caught a glimpse of a silvery-white horse back in the darkness of the trees, as if it awaited her.

"Winston, who are you talkin' to out here?" It was Bill, shouting his question.

Annoyed, Winston said, "Don't come out here yellin', Bill." He felt a little guilty, as Bill could not help yelling. But he could help tagging after Winston all the time.

Coweta grinned, fading and blowing him a kiss as she went. Bill couldn't see her, of course. No one else had acted like they saw her, although she'd been around plenty when others were with him.

"Winston, you shouldn't be peekin' in the window at Rainey and her fella."

"I'm not peekin' at Rainey," Winston said, and then he saw Bill step closer to the window and stare in as hard as he could, his mouth falling open.

Winston saw then what his old friend was looking at. He took Bill firmly by the arm and jerked him away.

"Don't be indulgin' in voyeurism with my daughter," he said.

"What'd you say?"

"Shush!" He continued to pull Bill along, and at the corner of the house, he said, loudly, "Come on, we'll go see if Mildred will let us watch her cable television all night. I bet she'll be thrilled."

* * * * *

Turn the page for an excerpt of Curtiss Ann Matlock's next book, the heartwarming Christmas tale
MIRACLE ON I-40,
available in October 2005.

CHAPTER 1

A Crisp December Evening

It's the time of day when the coral sun gives way to a satin starry night. The huge letters of Gerald's Truck Stop have started to glow bright red in the darkening desert sky along Interstate 40, which cuts right through Albuquerque, New Mexico. The sign serves as a beacon for weary truckers trying to get in as many hauls as possible before Christmas Day, and for frazzled families making the long trek home to Grama's house, and for footsore mothers needing respite at the end of a long day of searching out the perfect gifts. Big eighteen-wheelers chug in and out of the wide fuel bays, while minivans and sedans stop at the gas station, and speakers above each reverberate with Christmas carols.

The fluorescent lights of the restaurant shine out from the wide windows, promising warmth. Steam rises from the coffeemaker, and the bubbling punch machines give off a rather cheery yellow-and-red glow. Lights twinkle on the small plastic green tree at the end of the counter, and brightly colored piñatas hanging from the ceiling sway a bit whenever the front doors are opened.

A short, thick man in a white apron and with sleeves rolled up to reveal blue tattoos comes through the swinging kitchen doors, bearing a tray of pie slices. This is Gerald, the owner and somewhat compulsive pie maker. He goes to the lighted glass dessert case and puts the slices inside, saving one slice, which he plunks in front of a rather forlorn man sitting at the counter puffing on a cigarette. The man looks startled. His wide eyes follow Gerald, who sweeps on back through the kitchen door without an explanation. The man looks down at the pie, up at the swinging doors and back at the pie again.

The hands of the Pepsi-Cola clock on the wall read five-twenty, and there's a bit of a lull before the supper rush. In addition to the man at the counter, three elegant elderly ladies chat and laugh in the big corner booth, four truckers sit at a table talking low, and several other men eat alone—one a man in a suit who reads a paper, the other two robust truckers thoroughly enjoying their meals in the complete comfort of men used to eating alone.

There is only one waitress in evidence. She lifts the full pot of hot coffee from the Bunn machine and, swirling the contents, passes by her customers to refill cups. She casts repeated glances out the window, in the manner of watching for someone.

This waitress is a young woman, but not as young as she once was. Her hair is thick and wavy and the color of honey, and her eyes that particular green color of cactus in the spring. She is a pretty woman, like a thousand other pretty women, until she smiles. She has a smile so brilliant and so genuine that it actually, for brief seconds, arrests the recipients and causes them to stare. She smiles a lot, having learned that her ability to smile, even through her tears, is her greatest strength, the thing that has enabled her to not only survive but to enjoy life.

Lacey is the name printed on the small white tag above her left breast, and this is the story of a special Christmas in her life. It is a Christmas when she makes a choice to face wounds from the past and to place hope in forgiveness. She doesn't know how much her choice, which seems comparatively small in the scheme of things, will affect those around her.

Right that minute, Lacey has paused at a table and is smiling at a big, rough-looking man wearing a Harley-Davidson ball cap and a bushy gray beard. In a voice that yet bears traces of down-home, she asks, "More coffee, Web?"

Web Connor, not a man given to much smiling, had to smile back at her, of course, although he shook his head. "No thanks. I gotta get goin' if I'm gonna make Okie City tonight," he drawled and began to slide his hefty frame from the red vinyl seat. "Gerald out-did himself on that dried- peach pie today."

"I'll tell him you enjoyed it." Lacey picked up the bills he left atop his check. "You have a safe trip, and I'll see you again soon," she called after him as he wound his way among the Formica-topped tables to the door. Then she realized he'd left way too much money. "Web! Wait! You left this extra twenty." She waved the bill in the air.

At the door the big man turned and called back gruffly, "You think I haven't noticed how you always get me the biggest slice of pie and make sure my steak's done just right?" He raised a hand. "Merry Christmas from me and Milly."

Lacey stood there and watched him push through the door and walk rapidly away toward his tractor-trailer rig he drove for Outtman Trucking. Turning slowly back to the table, she tucked the twenty-dollar bill into her apron pocket, where it seemed to burn a hole. She blinked back tears as she gathered the dirty dishes.

She paused and looked out the window, peering hard, but it was getting so dark now that she saw mostly her own reflection.

She breathed deeply and thought, Thank you, Lord, for people like Web. Thank you for Christmas. It's just a darn good idea.

Smiling to herself, she began to clear the dishes and to hum along with the jukebox. *I'll be home for Christmas…oh, yes, I will…if all goes well.*

As Lacey rounded the counter with her load of dishes, the swinging doors burst open and a middle-aged woman with a youthful air, curly blond hair, reindeer antlers on her head and the name *Jolene* embroidered in large letters above the chest pocket of her blouse came through the door. "Doin' okay out here?" she asked, turning to adjust her antlers in the mirror that lined the wall back of the counter.

"Doin' fine. Not a creature stirring," Lacey said, and glanced at the clock. Five thirty-three. She was to get off at six, having worked yet another ten-hour day in order to get all the tips possible—although it was beginning to look as if it might turn out to be a slow night. It was just as well. She was tired, and very thankful that this was her last day for two weeks. *If all went well.*

Every time thoughts rose of what could happen with her plans, she imagined a radio dial in her mind and switched herself to a different channel, one where only happy and hopeful thoughts played.

She looked back at Jolene. "Someday you'll have to teach me your trick for keeping all the customers away from your tables and sittin' at mine."

"It's a secret I shall never reveal," Jolene quipped. "I employ it only when I'm tired and feeling generous—you need the tips more than I do." Casting Lacey a saucy smile, she danced away to the jukebox.

Lacey idly watched the older woman and wondered what it might be like not to have to constantly worry about money. But Jolene had no children. Lacey wouldn't trade places with her, not for an instant. Well, maybe for an hour, in which time she would get a manicure and pedicure. Lacey had never in her life had either, and she thought about this as Glen Campbell's voice sang out from the jukebox about Santa coming to town, and Jolene wiggled her hands in the air, her Christmas-red fingernails catching the light.

Changing the channel on her thoughts, Lacey hummed along with the music and stacked dirty dishes in the pan to go back into the kitchen. She looked out the windows again and reached into her apron pocket to feel the folded wad of bills, letting anticipation steal over her.

"Does that guy always slide his cup back and forth like that?" Jolene asked when she had danced her way back behind the counter. She inclined her head toward where a lanky J. B. Hunt driver sat alone.

Lacey nodded and slipped the funnel from the coffee machine. "He has ever since he came in."

"Glad he's over there. If he was any closer, I think I'd scream at him." Jolene reached into the cabinet and plunked a box of coffee filters on the counter. "What is it? Your eyes are lit up like Christmas trees…like you have a secret."

Lacey couldn't help smiling broadly as she discarded the used filter. "I've made enough in tips to get Jon the remote-control car he wants for Christmas—the exact one. I've been putting off buyin' any other model, hopin' I could get the real thing."

"That's good, honey. And how are the kids? Are they getting excited about the trip?"

"Anna has a cold, and yes and no to excitement." Lacey rinsed the funnel. "I didn't bother with a tree this year, since we're not goin' to be home, and the kids were none too happy about that. Jon said he didn't want to go, if we couldn't have a tree at home. But on the whole, they both see the trip as an adventure. They've told everyone—and I mean everyone, including the UPS delivery man—that they'll be ridin' across country in a big eighteen-wheel truck. And they started askin' all kinds of questions about their grandparents and what things were like when I was a kid."

"Did you tell them about the problems between you and your parents?" Jolene asked.

"I tried," Lacey said, jamming the coffeemaker back together. "But every time I lost my nerve. I was afraid of prejudicing the kids against their grandparents or makin' them disappointed in me. They're both too young to understand it all, and I don't want Jon to think his grandparents didn't want him." She sighed.

"I ended up simply sayin' that Grandpa didn't know we were coming, and it was to be a surprise. If things don't go so well, then I can explain more. Maybe." She didn't really know how she would explain if her father rejected them.

"I guess it would be a pretty touchy subject," said Jolene, shaking her head. Then she added, "So, are you all set for the trip?"

At that moment the front double doors opened, and along with a whoosh of cold air came a family of four. With some disappointment Lacey watched them head directly to the restrooms.

"I have a few last-minute things to get tonight," Lacey said, remembering to switch on the coffeemaker. "There's Jon's car, and nose drops for Anna, and new underwear for me. Why is it that women's panties don't seem to survive more than five launderings these days?"

"You could go without," Jolene suggested, studying a broken fingernail.

Lacey glanced at the clock and felt her stomach tighten. "I sure wish Pate would show up, or call. He said he'd pick us up at the house at six in the morning, but I was expecting to hear from him today sometime, just to make sure."

"If Pate told you six tomorrow mornin', he'll be there at five to," Jolene assured her. "He's as punctual as the sunrise."

"I know."

Jolene regarded her thoughtfully. "Pate's a lot like my Frank. You could do worse."

"Oh, Jolene. It's not like that with us. Pate's more like a father to me."

"What do you think Frank is to me? Like a father and a lot more. Older men can give you what younger ones never can—in more ways than one, if you get my drift." Jolene gave her a knowing look. "It's a thought."

"No, it's not."

"Okay—don't get touchy. I'm just giving you the benefit of my own vast experience."

There could be no doubt in anyone's mind that Jolene had far vaster experience than Lacey, but Lacey refrained from speaking the comment. Jolene, and a few others, often said that Lacey didn't know the facts of life; Lacey thought that she knew them only too well, and managed to rise above them.

The man at the counter waved his check at them, and Lacey moved to the cash register.

"Uh…that cook gave me a piece of pie."

"No charge, then." She thought he was a very sad-faced man, and made the effort to give him a particularly warm smile.

The man gazed at her, as if he didn't comprehend.

"He does that—gives out free pie when he feels like it. You liked it, didn't you?"

"Uh…yes. It was very good." He came close to a full smile, unable to help himself.

"Now maybe you'll order one again."

"I don't think so. I'm on my way to Louisiana. I don't have plans to come back this way."

"That's okay. If you ever do, you'll order the pie, and you can tell your friends about it, too."

"Yes…thanks."

"God bless you for your trip home," Lacey said impulsively. He seemed to need it.

He looked a little startled, and then he smiled a small but true smile and turned toward the door, drawing his coat up around him. Lacey watched him for a long minute, then swept a gaze around the parking lot, bending to peer as far as she could in each direction.

People all coming and going, all with their own pocketful of hopes and dreams and needs, she thought.

The family of four emerged from the restrooms and chose a booth in Jolene's station. Their expressions had lightened, no doubt reflecting anticipation of delicious food. Jolene looked from them to Lacey, sighed deeply and got a tray to carry water glasses. Then she pointed discreetly at the door. "Mmm, he's a sight to warm a woman's heart...and he's comin' right to your counter, you lucky gal," she whispered as she took up the tray and started away.

Lacey saw the sight to warm a woman's heart was a customer they all knew as Cooper, pushing through one side of the glass doors. A tall, lean man, he came through the door without opening it all the way, his head tilted downward just enough to conceal his eyes with his cowboy hat.

Lacey reached for a menu, even though it was probably a waste of time. She had been serving the man for some years now, and he either ordered the Texas T-bone or the Piping Hot Chili, always topping off with a piece of pie and ice cream.

And thinking of this, she remembered that he always sat in a booth, usually a front corner one all by himself, with a good view of the truck parking lot. His coming to the counter was unusual.

"Good evenin','" she said in her friendly customer voice. She set the menu in front of him, then glanced up and found herself looking into his dark eyes. He had an odd expression. A hesitancy? A nervousness?

Cooper, who did actually feel nervous and was blaming his discomfort squarely on Lacey Bryant, extended the folded piece of paper and said, "From Pate." He figured the note would explain, so he didn't think he needed to say more at this point.

The gal's pale, slim feminine fingers seemed a stark contrast to his large, rough, dark ones as she slowly took the note. Confusion and apprehension clouded her eyes. Cooper noticed they were the color of spring grass, just before she lowered them to the paper.

He ran his gaze over her glossy hair and ivory cheeks, and for the hundredth time he asked himself how he'd gotten hooked into doing this.

Maybe he would escape his own foolishness. Maybe she would simply refuse to go.

Either she was a slow reader or she couldn't comprehend the note the first time, because it seemed to take her an inordinately long time to read the few words. Cooper knew what was in the note; he'd read it, unashamedly curious about the exact nature of his friend's relationship with this young woman.

Dear Lacey,
Cooper will explain about me. He will also take you to North Carolina right along with hauling my payload on up to D.C. Cooper is a good man. I trust him with my life. So I can trust him with yours, too. Have a good Christmas. Hope everything turns out the way you want.

Love,
Pate

Cooper felt a bit of embarrassment over the high praise. And he wondered about it. He didn't think anyone, even a friend like Pate, knew him well enough to form such an opinion.

After what seemed like a very long time, the gal raised her eyes to him. Her face was white, her green eyes filled with confusion. "What…" She stopped and waited.

Just as Cooper opened his mouth to explain about Pate, a tall, good-looking sort of guy in a nice suit appeared at the counter near the cash register.

"Excuse me," she said, and stepped over to take the man's payment.

Cooper, annoyed at the interruption, observed the two. The guy called her "honey" and attempted to chat in an overly familiar way. She smiled at him with the same friendliness she gave everyone.

She wasn't what could be called a flirting type. Cooper, running his eyes over her, tried to come up with what type she was, and couldn't.

He had been coming into Gerald's and sitting at her table for over two years, maybe even three, because she was a darned good waitress. And also because she was easy to look at, but kept things cool. He had a couple of times even considered asking her out, before coming to his senses. She was one of those women a man didn't want to fool with. He wondered again about the seriousness of her relationship with Pate. Maybe Pate was the reason she didn't flirt. He and Pate had never talked women; they each liked a lot of privacy. And he had always sort of figured neither of them had a lot to talk about where women were concerned.

Finished with the customer, she returned and gazed expectantly at Cooper. "What's this all about?"

"It iced up on us in Santa Fe yesterday evening. Pate slipped and fell down the front stair at his apartment." He watched distress replace the confusion in her eyes. "Broke his leg bad enough to require a hospital stay. I told him I'd haul his payload and take you on to this place in North Carolina."

"Pine Grove."

"Yeah. He said west side of Raleigh."

She nodded, frowning and searching his face. Maybe now she would say she wouldn't go. Cooper waited.

The next instant she turned right around from him and went to the back counter. He had a moment of confusion, wondering if he should call out to her to come settle the matter. He watched her get a mug and the coffeepot, and then she returned to thunk the mug on the counter in front of him, filling it with coffee as she said, "Pate's in the hospital, then?"

Cooper nodded. "Yep." He automatically reached for the sugar. "But he should be released day after tomorrow. His son and his son's family are flyin' out from Richmond to spend Christmas with him and take care of him." The sugar came out faster than he had anticipated. He spilled some on the counter.

"Oh." She was staring at him, but she didn't offer to wipe up the sugar, just stood there holding the coffeepot and looking at him.

He stirred his coffee, then said, "I'll have the chili dinner…and I'll sit over there." Slipping off the stool, he inclined his head toward the corner booth, then headed for it, wishing the gal would simply get to saying that she had changed her mind about the trip.

As he slid into the booth, he looked into the night-dark window glass and saw her reflection back at the counter, standing there gazing over at him.

Lacey lifted the tray of food, took a deep breath and pushed through the swinging doors.

As she walked toward Cooper in the booth, her heart thudded. He had to have heard her footsteps, but he didn't look up from the newspaper he was reading. Maybe he didn't hear her. She stood at his table a moment, looked at his thick hair. Goodness, it was glossy brown. His mustache was, too, and tinged with red, just like the hair on his head. And his eyes were brown as buckeye seeds.

She realized suddenly that he was looking up at her.

He folded the paper, wrinkling it in his haste, and she set the plates in front of him, saying the chili was a little on the spicy side today, chatting in her nervousness.

She stood there uncertain, rubbing her hands together. Then she slipped into the seat opposite him. His eyebrow came up. He gazed at her a moment, then looked at his bowl and sprinkled cheese over his chili.

"How did Pate seem when you left him?" she asked.

"He was wide awake and flirtin' with the nurse." He glanced at her, then stirred the chili, jabbing in the melting cheese.

"How long will he have a cast on?"

"Eight weeks at least, the doctor said." He took up the bottle of dried pepper and shook it liberally over the chili. Without first tasting it, Lacey noted with a small bit of alarm.

"I'll get you a glass of water," she said when she realized he didn't have one. She'd been negligent—they always brought the customer ice water first thing.

She hurried around the counter and got the water, and as she brought it back, the father of the family of four held up a finger and called, "Oh, miss…miss, we'd like to order pie to go, please."

She set the glass of water in front of Cooper, stepped away, only to stop and abruptly return to put a napkin under the glass to get the drips, then rushed to get pie for the family in a hurry to get on the road. After that she had to attend the register for a trucker and the elderly ladies, who wished her and everyone in the room a very merry Christmas, and get menus for two truckers who came in.

Jolene had apparently gotten very involved with her antlers. Surely Paloma, who was supposed to work the supper shift, would come in any minute, she thought, heading back to Cooper's table with the coffeepot.

"You goin' or not?"

Cooper's voice startled her, and she splashed the coffee out of his cup. "Oh…I'm sorry." She dabbed up the spill.

They gazed at each other.

Again she slipped into the seat opposite him. "I know we'll be a bit of an imposition, and I really hate to bother you, only…"

"Look," he said, holding his knife like a pointer, "I told Pate I'd take you. The deal is still on, just like before, and I'll probably get you there a bit faster than Pate would have. I don't make a lot of stops. It's not like it was with Pate—I ain't Pate—but it *is* a ride. Now, do you want to go?"

Lacey stared at those buckeye-brown eyes.

"I'd be very grateful for the ride," she said.

He nodded. "Okay." And he looked down at his chili and scooped a spoonful into his mouth, hot chili and hot pepper.

Lacey sat there, gazing at him.

After several long seconds he looked up at her with a raised eyebrow.

"Pate was going to pick me up at home at six o'clock tomorrow morning." *Why did this man have to be so purposely disagreeable?*

"You be here at the restaurant at five, and we'll head out." He returned his attention to his chili.

Lacey opened her mouth, then closed it. "Fine," she said at last.

Rising, she walked straight-backed across the room and through the swinging doors. *Oh, Lord, why did you let Pate break his leg?*